Red Cabbage Blue

A DR MIKE LEWIS STORY

ANNIE TRY

To Andrey
May you enjoy
this book!
Annie

instant
ap□stle

First published in Great Britain in 2019

Instant Apostle
The Barn
1 Watford House Lane
Watford
Herts
WD17 1BJ

actual persons, living or dead, or actual events is purely coincidental.

British Library Cataloguing-in-Publication Data

A catalogue record for this book is available from the British Library.

This book and all other Instant Apostle books are available from Instant Apostle:

Website: www.instantapostle.com

E-mail: info@instantapostle.com

ISBN 978-1-912726-11-0

Printed in Great Britain.

For my dear sisters and brothers,
Margaret, Pat, Jonathan and Martin

Red Cabbage Blue

Blue dye? Take a large red cabbage. Chop it up and boil it in water that covers it for ten to fifteen minutes. Strain out the cabbage (only eat it if you don't mind cabbage overcooked) and reduce the liquid by boiling it until it is thick and syrupy, by which time it is purple. Add a tiny amount of baking powder, gradually putting in more until the colour is right. This natural dye looks like a very small amount, but it is quite intense. Use carefully.

1

Around Christmas, the Psychology Department becomes empty and eerily unfamiliar; even the smell seems to revert to its former use as a psychiatric ward. I was the only one in on the Friday before Christmas – the 'skeleton cover' required by management over the holiday period. Appropriately named, as it happened.

I checked the waiting area at 10.20 am for my new client. She was already there, with an older woman. The young lady had brilliant blue hair framing her extremely thin, gaunt face.

'Adelle Merchant?'

The young lady turned from reading the noticeboard, swiftly looked me up and down and replied, 'Yes, I suppose.'

She had scarcely responded before the older woman butted in, 'I am Adelle's mother. You must be Dr Lewis, pleased to meet you.' She put out her hand but I proffered mine first to Adelle; after all she was my client. Adelle shook my hand gravely, looking me in the eye. I thought I knew what she was pleading with me to do, and obliged.

I turned to her mother and held out my hand to take hers, which she had stuffed back in her pocket. She looked away, avoiding my gaze.

'Thank you for accompanying your daughter to her appointment,' I said to her half-turned head; then, smiling at Adelle, I invited her into my room. Her mother picked up a green handbag and matching leather gloves, then stood up. I stepped between them, saying, 'Appointments usually last about an hour. Please feel free to use the little kitchen down this corridor, if you'd like to make a coffee while you wait. There's some fresh milk in the fridge.' I didn't pause to register her response.

Adelle headed towards the better of the two scruffy armchairs in my room. She folded her raincoat neatly to hang over the back. As I sat on the second armchair, she pulled a blue shawl from her bag and, in one swift movement, swept it over to cover the chair before she sat down. Her outfit was all varieties of the colour blue. Her cheekbones stood out from the hollow cavities of her cheeks, emphasising the shadows surrounding her startling blue eyes.

I had known to expect someone looking rather skinny through the information in the referral letter from the psychiatrist, but I hadn't imagined her looking as she did. I waited for her to settle in her seat, ready to begin my assessment, but even as she pulled her shawl around her body, she said, 'I'm going to tell you something I have told no one else, Dr Lewis. You'll think I'm mad.'

Not what I had planned – but I nodded, stroked my freshly cut beard and waited.

'I've had a very strange experience.' She was leaning forward staring at me, her eyes wide open. 'I think I nearly died. I passed out and a light was drawing me towards it, or something. I don't know.'

'What did you feel?'

She turned her head, gazing out of the window. There was a pause before she said, 'You'll think this odd, but I felt peaceful; it wasn't frightening.'

'Tell me as much as you remember.'

Her stare was now fixed on the ceiling. She was very still; her bony fists were clenched in her lap but her voice was calm, almost matter-of-fact. 'I seemed to come back from the light. I realised I was high up in the corner of the room – well, my mind was. I could see myself on the floor with people standing around me and my mother shouting at everyone to stand back.' She glanced at me. I nodded to show her I was following her story. 'Someone was on the ground by me – I felt confused about what was happening, but I was aware of breath filling my lungs as I came down from the corner of the room and sort of went back into my body.'

I had questions I wanted to ask but reckoned she needed space.

She slowly pulled her gaze away from the ceiling and turned towards me, speaking almost in a whisper. 'What was it, Dr Lewis? Am I insane?'

There was an urgency in her voice that made me reassure her: 'Such an experience does not mean you are out of your mind.'

'You've heard of it before, then?'

9

I replied slowly, being careful with my words, having no idea how this young lady would respond. 'What you have described is more commonly experienced by those who have been thought to be right at the edge of survival, perhaps on an operating table or after a serious accident.'

My client was breathing fast – I gave her some time to adjust, with the only sound in the room coming from the soothing tick of my wall clock. As gently as I could, I asked her, 'Would you like to tell me more? Or shall we come back to it another time?'

'I want to tell you.'

Despite her words, I had to wait while she sniffed loudly then pulled her shawl up around her shoulders, and took a few deep breaths. I could hear her mother talking to someone in the waiting area, but Adelle was focused, drawing her thoughts together. Her words spilled forth in a rush.

'I collapsed in the street. My mother has told everyone I fainted from lack of food. It was more than that. I was told afterwards that the man leaning over me was from St John Ambulance. He was running a display in the shopping centre and somebody dashed off and fetched him. He took my pulse and checked my breathing, then started CPR. My mother said he made too much fuss, but I think he saved me.'

Cocooned within her shawl, she rocked back and forth as she spoke.

'That must have been frightening. Have you talked about it with anyone before today?'

She shook her head. 'I haven't had a chance. Every other psychologist, psychiatrist and mental health person has let my mother barge in with me. You asked her to wait outside. She thinks I'm mad anyway, so I didn't want to add more fuel to her diagnosis.'

I was tempted to smile at this, but nodded instead. I glanced at her file.

'Thank you for telling me today. Do you mind if I make some notes, Adelle?'

'Call me Bluedelle, please, and as long as the notes are confidential, that's OK.'

'Fair enough.' I thought now was not the time to give her the exceptions to confidentiality.

Adelle surveyed my room while I looked back at the referral. She had neatly disrupted my plan for the session. She was here with a psychiatrist's diagnosis of obsessive-compulsive disorder. I could see why. She was in blue from head to toe, only contrasted by her sallow skin. Her high cheekbones and blue-black eye shadow emphasised her extraordinary thinness. The psychiatrist had also diagnosed a non-specific eating disorder.

Adelle's gaze was now focused on the photo on my desk. I had only brought it in that morning. It was a laughing Ella, swinging Jamie around in a blur. Taken more than five years ago, before Jamie's illness.

'Is that your family?' she asked.

'Yes.' I managed to smile and move to safer ground. 'You said your mother thought you collapsed from lack of eating. Was that part of the problem?'

'Probably. I'd been eating only blue food for a long time by then and missing out on protein. That was what made my mother persuade me to add blue cheese, blue tuna and nearly raw steak to my diet.'

11

'Did you manage to eat the protein?'

'More or less – it's easier some days than others. Mind you, before I agreed, I negotiated the refurbishment of the summerhouse in my parents' garden in order for me to move into it. The fear of losing it is what is keeping me going.'

'So you are living in a summerhouse?'

'Yes. It's been insulated and converted. I've decorated it and made it my own. It's like a gorgeous holiday chalet now.'

I detected a note of triumph in her voice. She carried on talking, scarcely pausing for breath, 'You see, I'm jobless and lost my place at college. I had to have somewhere to live so I was still in my old bedroom and my mother was driving me crazy. I was like, no, am still like, a project being taken from one psychiatrist or psychologist to another. Exhibit A, the strange drop-out who likes blue and doesn't eat. Although that might finally stop now I'm seeing you.'

'What will stop? Liking blue? Your eating habits? Or being Exhibit A? What would you like, Bluedelle?'

Solemnly staring at my face, she answered clearly, 'No longer being Exhibit A, for sure. We'll see about the rest.'

I knew then that despite her being quite positive, she was not ready to let go of blue. We were in for the long haul. Meanwhile, I needed to come back on track with the assessment. I referred to my notes, and tried to take the lead for the rest of the session.

After Adelle left the room, I quietly and reverently placed the photo in my desk drawer.

2

It was odd when I met Mike. I was so surprised when he kept my mother out of the consulting room that I just blurted out stuff as if I'd known him for years. It's not like he was anything special. A bit scruffy, in my opinion, and he had a strange habit of stroking his auburn beard.

But he listened. He let me tell him all about the time I collapsed. He didn't correct me when I said I felt like an exhibit and then he just asked me about ordinary stuff like what I was studying, my skills and my friends. Telling him about the interior design course felt as if I were letting him in on a secret that had been too uncomfortable to think about. Not that I told him everything; just how difficult it was to use clients' colours in a specification, rather than the full range of beautiful blues. Perhaps I'll tell him what happens in my mind another time.

When he asked me about how focusing on blue had begun, I didn't want to say. So I told him so and he said, 'Fair enough, it can wait until you're ready.' Not like all those other psychs who pushed me and made me cry. I respect him for that.

Finally we got to the bit that I always have to do, ie those mental health questionnaires. He knew I must've done them oodles of times before because he apologised and asked me if I'd like a coffee or something while I did it.

Then he realised what he'd said and said 'sorry' again, this time for having nothing blue to drink. He was OK. I think I'll be all right with him.

And – the best thing about the session was, he didn't give me homework. That may be because it's Christmas. But we'd talked a bit about colour charts of various blue hues and I offered to bring some in and show him the ranges. We both found it funny when I told him about some of the most ridiculous of the names, 'Stiffneck Blue' and 'Parson's Gate', and that my personal favourite was 'Chef's Blue'. I even told him how I liked the colour I used most because I could get it from boiling red cabbage and how I could find no name for the colour it produced because it changed depending on how I used it, so I called it 'Red Cabbage Blue'. He seemed really interested. But then I suppose that's his job.

We had a sticky moment when I finally left his room – my mother was right by the consulting room door, an imposing figure in her green coat, clutching her tote bag and her gloves and trying to step into the room as I came out. It was obvious she wanted a word with Mike. But Mike said, 'Thank you again for bringing your daughter today and I'm sorry we kept you waiting for so long. Have a lovely Christmas.' And he turned back into his room and shut the door.

My mother exclaimed 'How rude!' as she marched out of the department. I could hardly contain myself. I don't think I have ever felt so good after seeing a psychologist.

The mood stayed with me as we went home in the car. For most of the journey Mother hardly spoke. We were actually turning into our road when she said, 'I heard you laughing in there.'

I was going to tell her why, but I stopped myself. Instead I said, 'I think I shall get on well with Dr Mike Lewis. He's fairly easy to talk to.'

'I shan't be satisfied unless he sorts you out. No good just chatting and laughing through the sessions – we need to see some real change. I hope he gets you eating sensible stuff next time you see him or we will have to try somewhere else.'

Sometimes I feel wiser than my mother and this was one of those occasions. 'Mother, I have been like this for six years. No one can sort me out, as you put it, in two sessions. You are lucky I have agreed to go back to this one and that I shall be seeing him on the NHS.'

I didn't tell her that next time I would go on my own. There was no need for her to come with me. I am an adult, after all.

That night, just before Christmas, when I had closed my 'Littlehampton Blue' door behind me, I felt triumphant and even nearly content. I put my fairy lights on the small blue-green conifer I had bought for a Christmas tree and made myself a blueberry milkshake, which turned out a little redder than I wanted. Instead of pouring it down the sink like I usually do, I dropped a little essence of red cabbage into it and drank it. I sunk into my cobalt sofa and began glancing through the carefully filed pages of paint and material charts I had collected – all shades from 'Morning Light' to 'Midnight Blue'. I felt myself relax into their cool calm.

3

Before I saw Adelle Merchant, I had considered that I might assess her and pass her on to another member of the mental health team. I had only taken her case because of the long-term absence of Ralph, our consultant clinical psychologist who was head of department. We had heard that it was unlikely he would come back to work, so I was sorting out some of his longer-waiting referrals.

Adelle herself changed my course of action. A client so keen to tell me things she had not disclosed before was a rarity. I could work with that. It indicated that she was ready to learn and maybe change. How long it would take was another question. I had yet to ascertain why and how she had come to the difficult mental state we were now going to address.

I wondered who Mrs Merchant had been talking to in the waiting area. As far as I was aware, I had been the only one in the department. The doors had been newly fitted with safety features, including an intercom. The mystery was solved when I glanced through the departmental message book – there was a note for me from Anita, the art therapist.

'Happy Christmas to you and Ella! Thank you for all your help, you were great.' I had no idea why she'd needed to come in when she was on leave, but it was kind of her to write a note.

I left the empty department at 3.30 after letting the staff on the switchboard know they could direct calls to my personal number if I were needed over the next few days. I joined the Friday-before-Christmas rush of jolly and slightly drunk commuters. This year was the first year in five that the general sense of bonhomie had not created a completely overwhelming feeling of loss and desolation in me that would drown any joy out of the festivities.

Nothing could bring Jamie, my son, back. But today I was en route to my old home – our home – where Ella was waiting for me. I was walking into warmth, love and the smell of mince pies. And we would have Christmas Day to ourselves because her fostered adult, Shaun, would be with his family.

I had bought Ella an eternity ring. On Christmas Day I wanted to suggest that we renew our marriage vows in a proper church service. I felt as excited as I was when I first proposed to her.

We had a great weekend, making last-minute preparations. I sorted out the Christmas lights when they blew the fuse, put fresh candles into their holders and wrapped small extra presents for Ella. I think she sent me to the shops three times for things she had forgotten – I remembered how this used to irk me, but now it seemed an absolute joy to be running around for her.

Much of Christmas Eve was taken up with ferrying Shaun to his parents, dropping in on his friend with a present first. Once home, we prepared the vegetables for the Christmas meal together, and we ate our first mince pies as we listened to carols.

I had been childishly excited about Christmas Day with Ella. To start with it was all I could have hoped for. Waking in the morning, next to my wife and cuddling together as we wished each other 'Happy Christmas' was a beautiful beginning to the day. But despite the festive decorations and the wonderful dinner we cooked together, we both missed Jamie. We tried to remember without becoming upset – I managed this better than Ella.

After we had eaten our meal and looked at several photos, sharing memories, I thought it was time for my surprise. I had the box in my pocket and made a great show of going on one knee to present it to her.

'Ella, I feel like we need to mark the fresh beginning of our life together. I want us to be together for the rest of our lives, and to confirm that I have bought you this.' With a little bit of a flourish, I opened the box.

I wasn't prepared for her reaction.

Ella looked embarrassed. 'You shouldn't have done that.'

I thought she meant that I was too extravagant, so I charged ahead with taking it out of the box and waiting for her to extend her left hand. She didn't, but paused slightly before offering me her right hand.

I put the sapphire and diamond cluster onto her ring finger on her right hand. I felt disappointed. Ella noticed.

'What's the matter?' she said.

'I wasn't sure which finger you wanted it on. I hoped you would see it like a second engagement ring.'

'Why?'

'I would like us to renew our vows.'

Ella looked at me, her head on one side. 'Listen, Mike, this is a lovely ring and I really appreciate you buying it, but we are a long way from being ready to renew our vows. We have only been back together for such a short time, how do I know this will be forever?'

'I'm ready.'

'You think you are ready. We need to wait. See how you are when we've finished our couples therapy. Until then, think of this as a time when we are renewing our courtship.' She stroked my hand gently as she talked but I was bitterly disappointed and only half-listened. I began to doubt her feelings for me. I went and made us both a hot drink, heating up some mince pies to give myself time to work through my feelings.

I brought in the tea and offered her the products of her own baking. She glanced up at me and I realised she knew she had upset me. I had to say something.

'I didn't mean to rush you. I still have the flat, if you want me to leave.' I could scarcely say the words.

'I don't want you to leave. But in case you want to, I suggest you carry on renting the flat for now.'

I didn't want to argue with her. I thought she was wrong and we should renew our vows soon. To my relief, there was one small indication that she wanted to go forward in our relationship – she kept the ring on her finger. I noticed her glance at it every now and again, moving it to catch the light.

'If we are courting, where would you like to go on our dates?' I asked.

During the rest of the day we planned some outings together. I realised this approach made a lot of sense – it would be harder to have time on our own once Shaun was back in the house.

The day went quickly and Boxing Day disappeared in collecting Shaun from his parents' home. So on the day of Adelle's next appointment I was very much looking forward to meeting Ella for a long lunch at the end of my clinic. I had plenty of time to take in lieu, so we had planned to go to the cinema afterwards – with the work mobile in my pocket in case the on-call psychologist was needed.

4

Adelle arrived on her own, half an hour early. I couldn't quite keep up with that because I was on the phone when I heard her arrive, busy answering questions from a lawyer about another client, who was seeking asylum.

I finished the phone call and quickly hid my dirty cups in the filing cabinet. I removed a file I had been trying to sort out from one of the chairs and just stopped myself using the sleeve of my new pullover to wipe across the coffee table. I found some tissues instead. By the time I had read through the last session with Adelle, it was still ten minutes before her arranged appointment time. I invited her into my room. She was quite bouncy – a contrast to the anxious young lady I had met only a few days earlier.

'How are you today, Bluedelle?' I asked.

'Pleased Christmas is more or less over. Although I managed it fairly well with my parents. Better than I expected, anyway. What about you?'

I couldn't very well tell her that I'd had the best Christmas since my son died. It had been full of hope and closeness, despite my disappointment about a date for renewing our vows. It was the first Christmas when I could share memories of Jamie singing carols in the school play

21

and of his joy at opening his presents. There were homemade decorations on the Christmas tree that he had made with Ella. I was pleased she still hung them up. I missed Jamie's excitement, but with Ella around, I felt comforted.

'It was good, thank you. But now the festivities are over and you and I are on a journey to discover how to help you.'

Adelle squirmed in the tatty armchair, shooting her blue flowery handbag onto the floor. She left it there but I had lost eye contact with her.

'How would you like this session to go?' I asked her.

'Oh, I expect you'll ask me all about my childhood and why I started eating blue stuff – that's what didn't happen last week and usually does on the first appointment.'

'What would you like to tell me?' I was determined to give her choice – when she had been given free rein the previous week, she made good use of the session.

There was silence for a moment before she said, 'Well, I suppose it might help you if I tell you how all this came about.'

'Yes, it may be useful, thank you.'

'Well, it's like this,' she focused on the corner of my office ceiling and launched into her story, 'I was at school. A girl called Cecilia, Cessy, made a bet that no one could eat only blue food and nothing else for the next six weeks.'

She glanced my way. I nodded to encourage her.

'We told her it was impossible. At least, the others did. I felt quite excited as I thought about how I could do it. There was this big debate going on about whether blue cheese was OK, then I pitched in with the information that there was plenty of protein in octopus blood and that was blue. Everyone made sick noises at that.'

I laughed, then settled back in my chair, reckoning that this tale might take some time. It did.

'We all had ideas about what could count as blue and most of them were rubbished by the others. In the end Cessy raised herself up to her full height, towering over the rest of us and declared, "I will accept Parma violets and the blue-sugared Liquorice Allsorts and ..." she paused then for effect – she was into drama – "... damsons, you may eat damsons. The rest is at your own discretion." Everyone just looked at her but I said, "I'll do it, I will take up the challenge." So, because this was the first time ever that I'd agreed to join in, everyone was startled and shamed into thinking it must be easy. Before long there were thirteen of us involved.'

All this was told to me with a fair bit of action by Adelle. Up to that moment it had looked like a little dramatic retelling, but she paused, her head turned to me, eyes sparkling. 'And I was the best at it by far. Then...'

Her tale wasn't over. I stopped her with a question.

'So when did this happen, Bluedelle? How old were you?'

'I was sixteen. We were all studying for our exams and I think we were getting bored.'

Her voice had lost its excitement. I preferred the animated storyteller – I tried to bring her back.

'I presume you won the challenge?'

Adelle gave me a condescending smile. 'Of course. I might not have been as brainy as the rest of the girls, but I am persistent. I knew I could stick to a task if I needed to.'

I think she felt a moment of pride because her smile changed to something more natural, genuine even. I grinned back at her, wondering what she thought about me. Under her scrutiny, I felt self-conscious about my untidy office and the fact that my beard never stayed flat, even when it was recently trimmed, and I smoothed it down every now and again. Despite the overuse of one colour, Adelle looked impeccable. I made myself concentrate.

'So here you are, six and a half years later, still doing it.'

She nodded. 'It's my way of life now.'

I was back on track, wondering what function the colour fixation was fulfilling or had fulfilled. What was maintaining this unusual behaviour now? I probed.

'What has happened since the challenge, Bluedelle? How have your family and friends taken to your love of blue?'

'I didn't expect you to ask that.'

'Why not?'

Adelle paused for a moment, shrugged, and then appeared to make a decision to talk openly.

She sat up straight, turning her remarkable eyes steadily on to me.

'I have seen school counsellors, paediatricians, doctors, mental health nurses and a psychiatrist. Ever since I started wearing blue as well as eating one colour. Each professional, whether NHS or private, has told me off in some way. Maybe not immediately. And my mother – you did well to leave my mother in the waiting area – usually she has barged into the consulting room or whatever and told them how awful it is to live with me.'

Adelle paused for breath, her eyes still fixed on me.

'Is your mother very angry with you?' I probably sounded surprised because of her mother dressing so completely in green. Apart from her greying blonde hair, she had looked rather like a green version of her blue daughter.

'Yes, she was furious with me and still is, really. She paid for a good school and had plans for me – but, according to her, the only thing I seem to be really good at is being obsessed with blue stuff. And being a college drop-out.'

Adelle looked down at her lap. She sat quietly, lost in her own thoughts, eventually beginning to talk a little more slowly. 'She may have been worried as well as furious – I couldn't get enough fodder over the first winter and I had been unintentionally turning blue with the cold. I had to layer up to disguise the state I was in when my ribs began sticking out through my jumper.'

I nodded. I should think most mothers would have been very worried, but I could see the mother–daughter relationship might be rather rocky. I prompted about her friends.

'Yes, well, there's another problem. I've never ever had a really close friend. No, that's not quite true, I can remember playing and holding hands with a girl my size when I was very small. Perhaps two, or three. They are my earliest memories. Then she disappeared – I think her parents moved or something. I've had some friends since, but I've always had to make an effort to get along with them. That's how it is with a lot of people, isn't it?'

'I suppose it can be.' She nodded slowly and I asked her a question. 'Tell me more about some of these professional appointments, Bluedelle. Was there anything that helped you?'

'Well...' Adelle dragged the word out, 'paediatrician number one was a rather overweight woman who appeared to admire my resolve to eat nothing that wasn't blue. I took to her at first, because she showed a real interest in my "diet" as she called it. But then she suddenly changed and told me it was now time I stopped all that nonsense and began to eat sensibly. My mother was in the room and couldn't resist telling the paediatrician that it was exactly what she herself had been saying, over and over again. It was awful.'

'That does sound like a very difficult situation.'

'It was – and I didn't handle it well. I was absolutely furious! I flounced out of the room and left my mother and the doctor-with-the-real-eating-problem to tell each other they were right.'

I had been listening intently to her, jotting down the odd word in her psychology notes so that I could recall it all later. I knew from her medical file that from the first records, which began when she was five, her mother had a history of rushing Adelle into A&E at the first sign of anything that might, in her eyes, kill or harm her in even the smallest of ways. I wondered why her mother was so overprotective.

'How did that affect you, Bluedelle, when your mother and the paediatrician appeared to be saying the same thing?' I had just stopped myself from saying 'colluding'. I must keep aware of the already fragile relationship between mother and daughter.

'Seeing that woman made me more determined to keep to my plan. I was probably a bit too enthusiastic – finding stuff on the internet became my task when I was bored.'

I was leaning towards her, encouraging her to continue.

'Through doing a search on the computer I found I wasn't the only person who would only eat blue. All sorts of strange ideas were throwing themselves at me, from people with odd names like Cerulean or Electric or Indigo.'

'Such as?'

'Peculiar things. Some I rejected outright – extracting a blue tint for food colouring through boiling navy cotton garments left me wondering whether Indigo would ruin her digestive system. I sent her my concerns via Facebook.'

I nodded my approval. I noted that this young lady was able to be sensible, even when locked into this unusual pattern.

'Were you, are you, able to put together a balanced diet?'

'Probably. I've worked hard at trying to eat all the food groups. But I am killing myself, according to my mother.' Adelle crossed her arms and legs.

I shifted to a slightly safer topic.

'When did you start to only wear blue?'

'It grew from a preference to a challenge. I like it now that my entire wardrobe is one colour – it's easy to match clothes.' Adelle looked at me directly, as if ready to face a challenge. I moved on.

'What about everything else?'

She shrugged. 'I expect it's in my notes.'

I appreciated she felt like she had said enough. The referral letter told me that she had painted her room, against her mother's wishes.

'All I have in this file, Bluedelle, is the referral letter. But it does mention that you painted your bedroom blue.'

I was surprised by a snort of laughter before she answered, 'True – guilty as charged. My mother was more than furious. It was dreadful! She shouted at me – "That design cost £98 a roll, Adelle, why have you splashed royal blue paint all over it? Have you gone mental?"'

'When was that?'

'Um – I had just started college.'

'So you were about eighteen?' I couldn't believe it – surely eighteen-year-olds could paint their own rooms if they happened to be living at home?

'Nineteen, to be precise. But good came out of it because that's when they started talking about me moving into the summerhouse. I'd been asking for ages.'

I glanced at Adelle's expression, wondering briefly whether she had manipulated her parents. She certainly seemed quite triumphant when she described her mother's fury after the wall-painting incident. Maybe that signified a moment of her having more control over her life. It hadn't stopped her fixation, though.

'You've stuck to this task a long time,' I observed. 'Are you bored yet?'

'Well, no. It's a challenge admittedly, but I've found a new way of life. I've created a new image and a new name – everyone calls me "Bluedelle" these days.'

'You certainly seem to be good at turning blue,' I said. She grimaced. I don't think she realised I was half-joking.

'I manage it mostly.'

Adelle's long fingers were fiddling with the necklace she was wearing. She became aware that I was looking at this and let it drop back behind her blouse, and smoothed her hair instead. Her hair was long and a lovely shiny colour – not at all like the blue rinse I can remember the old lady next door having when I was a child. She had the front of her hair tied back in a blue and navy band.

'What about jewellery?' I asked.

I had noticed the necklace was a silver chain with a pendant, which appeared to be a single green stone surrounded by small diamonds.

'Oh this,' she said, touching the chain. 'It was left to me by my granny. Anyway, as I was saying earlier, during those six weeks I had great fun finding all the ways I could make the food blue.' She began listing them at length and I noted down that I must come back to the granny. She had clearly changed the subject when I tried to talk about the necklace.

'I boiled the red cabbage to make the blue dye. But I must have had it bubbling away rather fast because I realised, to my horror, that I had blue spots all up my mother's cream wall.'

I couldn't help smiling as I asked, 'What did she say?'

'Well, not much, really. She was out quite a lot visiting Granny and I said sorry about the wall and explained I was cooking cabbage. She didn't realise I was trying to distil the colour and said she was pleased I was taking care of myself.'

Adelle then continued telling me all about how the level of acid affects the red cabbage dye so isn't any good with

29

pancakes and cakes unless you don't use baking powder. I let her talk as she told me about pasta, sugar strands and how to dye ordinary sugar blue. I saw her relax as she shared some of her expertise.

I sat back and encouraged her to speak until I decided I must confront her with what I now saw to be true.

'Stop!' I said, rather more firmly than I intended. Adelle looked startled and reached for her coat. I added, 'Sorry to interrupt you.'

She looked a bit annoyed.

'I needed to say something because I realised you said earlier that your mother was often visiting your granny during the initial blue challenge – and your granny left you the necklace. Presumably the same granny?'

Adelle nodded, looking caught out. I was as gentle as I could be when I asked, 'Was the blue challenge around the time when she died?'

She cried. Not an average little sob that could be carefully mopped with the corner of a lace hanky, but a heaving, uncontrollable letting go of all her emotions. I passed her the tissue box, but she shook her head. I remembered there were some blue paper napkins in the kitchen and darted out to fetch them. As I came back to my room, I was spotted by Adelle's mother. I was surprised to see her, thinking Adelle had made her own way here. She may have heard her daughter's crying because she stood up, her brow furrowed. 'Dr Lewis...' I interrupted. 'It will be fine, don't worry. Bluedelle will be with you shortly.'

I came into the room – Adelle had her back to me and was sniffing loudly. I passed her a napkin. She took it and began to blow her nose and mop her eyes. But she was still sobbing. I sat down and waited. Gradually she took control of herself.

She cleared her throat and began to speak.

'If you must know, she was terminally ill. The whole reason I was so keen on the challenge was because I thought it would take my mind off her being in the hospice. I didn't want to think about her dying. As it was, I was wandering round the supermarket looking for something I would allow myself to eat, so I wasn't even there when she went.'

I passed her more napkins and she slowly unfolded another one and wiped her eyes again. She seemed sad, but no longer crying.

'I am sorry. May I ask you something?' I said softly.

She nodded slowly.

I continued, 'If it was a distraction, why didn't you stop once she died?'

'I don't know. I needed to be out of the house or it upset my mother that I didn't eat with them. I had no appetite anyway. It was nearly exam time so I was doing extra revision as well and my mind was going all over the place so it was better to work at school. I even asked to board for a bit. It was easier to carry on, I suppose.'

'Did you want to stop?'

'Not at first – we had extended the time beyond the six weeks because of the exams. I selfishly wanted – no, needed – to win. I probably had won anyway, because the others all dropped out. But I like to do things properly, so I didn't want to win by default.'

'Why had they dropped out?'

'They blamed me, saying it was because it had got out of hand and was damaging my health. I think it was an excuse because none of them had the stamina to stick to it. I was determined to complete the whole six weeks and more.'

'Did you try to give up?'

'Well, no. I wasn't ready. I suppose I did want to later. I tried to, after Granny's funeral. But I couldn't find any food I could stomach. Anyway, I discovered that our local café had a fantastic blue sauce for their ice cream so I could mix it in and, hey presto, I had blue ice cream, and the weather was very hot and I was fed up with the struggle to concentrate enough to revise. I felt enthusiastic for something again. Then finding new blue food became my mission.'

'What's your mission now, Bluedelle?'

'Now, there's a question,' she said. I waited. She screwed up her eyes and nose as if the action would give her an answer. In the end she shrugged and said, 'I don't know; the same, maybe.'

I smiled at her; she shrugged again. In that short pause, it occurred to me that I must not concur with her preference for blueness. Even calling her 'Bluedelle' was not a good idea.

'Let's book some more appointments and see if we can find you a new mission. What do you think, Delle?'

She recovered enough to say, 'That's fine with me. But if we have to fade out blue, can we do it gradually, maybe via some closely associated colours?'

'I prefer "crowd out" or "overshadow". But we'll take it at your pace, yes. What did you like before you had the blues?'

She looked at me. There was silence before she said quietly, 'No one has said that to me before. That's what it is, isn't it? I had the blues and then the challenge happened.'

I didn't need to say anything. She may have noticed my involuntary nod. She sat and thought for a bit before she answered my question.

'I always wanted a cat, or a dog. My mother didn't want me to have one. I enjoyed decorating, still do, and I loved my interior design course. Art was part of the course and I looked forward to working on my oil paintings and watercolours.'

I scribbled in my notes, wondering whether I should say something that might upset Adelle's mother. I did.

'If you still want one, I think a pet might be therapeutic for you. If you had a pet, what would it be?' Even as I asked this, I knew the answer.

'A cat,' she said. And we chorused together, 'A Persian Blue!' While she laughed, I wrote down her next appointment on a bit of blue card that I found in my drawer and I set her a home task.

'Your task, Delle, is to research the cost of buying and owning a Persian Blue and discussing it with your mother too. I'm only suggesting that because you are residing on her property, even though you are not in the house.'

'She won't mind, my place is quite separate. It's great in there – I have a living room with a kitchen area and a small bedroom with an en suite. It's perfectly suitable for a cat –

Mother wouldn't have any clearing up and it would be my furniture ruined, not hers. She really can't object.'

'I hope you're right,' I said, adding, 'but whatever happens I shall see you next week and will be ready with a fresh supply of blue napkins, just in case they're needed. I'm not sure I can paint any walls by then to make you feel more at home.'

When Adelle left my room laughing, her mother did not look at all pleased. She stood up and said, 'May I have a word with you, Dr Lewis?'

I was not going to undo all the good rapport I had built up with Adelle. 'I'm sorry, Mrs Merchant, that won't be possible. Not only do we not have enough time today, but I would have to gain your daughter's permission to speak to you as she's over eighteen. Perhaps another day, if she'd like me to talk to you? Although it is not usual to involve parents of an adult unless the client's life is at risk.'

Mrs Merchant stood with her mouth open. But Adelle said, 'After you, Mother,' and steered her out of the department, turning to give me a quick thumbs up as she followed her mother through the door.

I went back into my room and looked at the referral again, in the light of the appointment we had just finished. I realised I had failed to complete all the psychometrics required of me – the ratings of depression and anxiety formally completed by a client. There was one assessment outstanding. Never mind, if I had given this to her to complete, the whole appointment would have started off on the wrong foot, Adelle may have been less forthcoming and I may not have noticed the telltale fiddling with the necklace her granny had left her.

I filled in my scant notes, recording how Adelle looked and behaved when she had said the words I had seen fit to write down.

I noted down a tentative hypothesis: this was not obsessive-compulsive disorder, but an unusual grief reaction of a depressed teen leading to a chronic condition persisting into her adulthood. There was something else niggling in my mind as I made the notes. Ah, yes, the one and only best friend from her early childhood. I wonder what became of her?

I closed the file and turned to a management task. I had made the decision that I should be embracing my role as acting head of department and seeing if I could resolve some of the issues that were arising.

Nearly two hours later, after having put together a draft scheme for the whole team to tackle the enormously long waiting list, I set off to take Ella on our lunch date. On the way I realised that I had referred to my client as 'Bluedelle' when speaking to her mother. I hoped this hadn't caused a problem.

5

The visit to the psychologist had changed something in me. I recognised this blueness now. Mike Lewis had helped me to see it in its true colours. I don't mean as variations of blue – cloud blue, chalk blue, grey-blue, whatever the paint charts decided to name it. No, it was something else. Not just 'the blues', either. It had a name, an entity of sorts. I knew what that name was. 'Emptiness'.

Emptiness – blue – vacuousness – a blue-black hole – the hole in my heart. The longing for something or, in fact, someone I had lost.

At home, I paced up and down my small blue-shaded house, trying to shake off the feeling that was now invading my thoughts. The colour had been externally expressed in the skylight walls, the indigo rug, the soft blue-washed floorboards, the patchwork multi-blued quilt. Everything the same tint – it was now seeping into me, draining me of all I had been, all I had wanted to be. I realised it had done that already; demolishing my career prospects, sweeping away the choices in my life, sapping my strength, causing me to pour away my brightly coloured oil paints, dispose of any other coloured clothing and, along with that, any bright thought.

Why? I had imagined I was bringing in something – a new me, a fresh identity – but no, I was emptying my surroundings of colour. Now that was happening within my very being – blue was emptiness – blue was nothingness. Blue was what I had become. I could bear it no longer.

But nor could I change. Blue was now my safety net. I was known by it. Who was I without it?

Feeling trapped, I walked into my bedroom and pushed myself under the quilt. I closed my eyes from the blueness, the emptiness. I sobbed myself to sleep.

It was getting dark when I woke. I was hungry. I stuck a Salad Blue potato into the microwave. I ate it with nothing. I cooked another. It was dry and unappetising. But the emptiness did not go. It was all around me.

I turned my computer on and watched the circles on the blue screen page swirl in front of me. They seemed to spiral away in front of my eyes. What could I do to fill this lonely, empty, hollow inside me?

Opening a new Word document, I started to write notes from the morning session. It took a while to remember it – it had seemed so upbeat at the time, apart from when Mike talked about the death of Granny. Or did he? No, he just remarked that she had died during the blue challenge and that was enough. But I'd left in a good mood, hadn't I? What was that about, then?

I remembered the cat conversation. I tried to shake off my low mood, telling myself that if I was empty, I needed something in my life to fill the gap. I made myself a blueberry milkshake that went reddish purple, added some blue drops of red cabbage dye, and sipped the resulting drink while I went about the task of finding a cat.

I felt a bit better. I loved doing research – every project I had been set at school had totally absorbed me. I sat up at my breakfast bar with my shiny blue laptop on the counter and did a search or two, or three or more. The cats were astoundingly expensive and, I might be naïve, but I expected them to be somewhat bluer. They were a gentle sort of grey – well, some were cream and brown – so I had to imagine a lovely fluffy grey cat walking around the room with a big blue ribbon on his or her neck. I considered the various hues of blue. I had never gone far down the greyish-blue route, although I did have a favourite blouse that was bluey-grey. I tried pushing my screen slightly away from me to get a better idea of the cats' colour. When tilted at a greater angle they did look bluer.

I made myself a second drink and had some fudge. Not ordinary fudge: I made this myself with food colouring and blueberries in it. It had become my life-saver – maybe literally – because the amount of sugar in it acted like an immediate pick-me-up. I boiled the kettle again and filled my hot-water bottle. I went and sat on my sofa, taking the laptop with me. I had a lap tray and organised myself to keep warm while I continued the search. I was scribbling notes on pale blue paper. It was a mystery to me why anyone used black pen on white – it looked so harsh. Despite my revelation that blue equalled emptiness, I still loved it. The colour of periwinkles and Cornish sea, of summer days and forget-me-nots.

Although I was so thin, I soon warmed up. I did wonder what it would be like out here when it went below freezing. It was bad enough already and although the weather had been described as mild, I often shivered in the evening or went to bed with several hot-water bottles. The year before, all the insulation had not been finished so I ended up going back to my old bedroom on very cold nights. My father had brought over one small oil-filled electric radiator but it didn't make a lot of difference. He had taken it away again and put it back in his hidey-hole, the shed behind the garage. He did mumble that he'd find me something better, but I think he really needed to keep warm in his own shed. That has no insulation at all. At least Dad had ensured there was decent wadding behind the new plasterboard he put in the summerhouse ready for me to take up residence.

While I thought about all this, I had found online the most adorable kittens that were for sale. I was transfixed. There was a little video of them playing together and I watched it over and over again. I moved the laptop round the room, and right through the summerhouse. I was imagining them playing on the rug by the door, under the bed, in the wardrobe. They were the most gorgeous little animals, apart from one thing – they still weren't blue.

I had realised they were grey but was still hunting for a bluer grey – after all, they were described as Persian Blues. I searched again and eventually accepted the fact that if I wanted a cat – and I definitely, definitely did – I would have to settle for grey.

I turned my search to cat beds, litter trays and cat toys. They could all be exactly the right colour for my home. I wondered if I could find the right coloured cat litter – or blue cat food, for that matter. It would be a challenge.

There was a knock on the door and then it opened. It had taken me three months to train my mother to knock and it never occurred to me that I would have to train her to wait for me to say 'Come in' as well. She was wearing a particularly lurid green. I winced as she came in and sat on my beautiful peacock blue chair. She clashed, in every sense of the word. The look of the colours crashed loudly in my mind.

'Hello, Mother.'

'Hello, Adelle, I forgot to give you this postcard.'

I glanced at it – a brief message on the back from 'Jack'. I thought that might be Jackie but it didn't look like her writing. It was from Malta. I envied the writer – whoever wrote it was warmer than I was. I poked it into the nearest book, my mind imagining kittens romping in the sun. My mother asked a question.

'What have you eaten for your tea?'

My immediate reaction was to think that she was playing Food Police again.

'Mother, it is only 5.30 pm and I have already eaten two jacket potatoes. I had a sleep and woke up hungry. Why are you asking now? It's not even my usual teatime yet.'

'Well, someone's got to check up on you.'

'No one has to check up on me, I'm an adult.'

'You don't behave like one.'

'I've never been allowed to be one.'

Her clashing and crashing colours did not just upset the harmony of the room. We clashed, day in and day out.

We carried on quarrelling like this, in the same old groove, trying to get one up on each other. But we are old hands at this game and as good as each other at it. There was a time – pre the blue challenge – when I would just give in and get upset. I argued now. The Bluedelle approach. I don't know that my mother could understand it when I first started talking back. It wasn't exactly arguing then, more a little try-out at making myself and my opinion known. No, a precursor to that – I was showing her I was there. I had lived too long in the shadows, shy and oppressed.

The spat between us had carried on without either of us paying much attention until we ground to a halt. By then, neither of us could remember the last point we'd made.

'Fancy a cuppa, Mother?'

'Could do. What colour?'

Even as she asked this, it occurred to me how odd it would seem to others. In fact, it was a perfectly reasonable question. I drank blueberry or blue pea flower tea, naturally, or one that vaguely resembled it. My mother, on the other hand, had a penchant for green tea. On most occasions I considered this very appropriate because I approved of her drinking tea to match her clothing, if only in name.

'I think I can find you green tea.'

I found the green tea but it took a little while moving all my blue stuff around in the cupboard to discover the sugar. I used a teaspoon to crush the lumps in it.

I made the tea, humming a little blues song under my breath. I was pretty sure I knew why my mother was there. She had hardly spoken on the way home from me seeing Mike. She was really put out that he hadn't wanted her opinion. She shouldn't have been there at all, but for some reason she had an appointment in town and had to accompany me. I had made her promise to keep away from the Psychology Department – a promise she broke.

With green tea in front of the green person and blue for me, Mother, predictably, asked me about the session. I didn't hear her for a moment because I was busy thinking about green being naïve or untaught or something and how, in fact, these days it often felt like that. I remember feeling wiser than my mother. It was odd.

'Sorry, Mother, I was just thinking about something else. How terribly rude of me. What did you say?'

'First I asked you why the psychologist referred to you as "Bluedelle" and then asked what he said about your mental health. Does he agree that you have anorexia and schizophrenia?'

'He most certainly does not. Do you even know what schizophrenia is, Mother?'

'There is something gravely wrong with you, Adelle, you know that. It is serious.'

I wished she hadn't said 'gravely'. I hate that word. It reminds me that Granny has gone. I experimented with imagining she had said 'gravy'. She was still talking, but it felt much more fun to be thinking of gravy. Take out another letter and you have gray. OK, an American spelling, but from grey you come to the colour of a Persian Blue.

'I'm going to have a cat. Guess what type.'

'Adelle, have you been listening to me? Why, girl, do you never concentrate on what I am saying?'

'Did you hear what I said, Mother? I am about to buy a cat.'

My mother sighed, obviously giving up on what she was about to say, 'Why are you getting a cat, of all things?'

'It's something I always wanted and now I have my own place, I can do it.'

She turned to me – her voice rose. 'You do not have your own place – this is our garden and our summerhouse.'

I sighed. 'It is my own place, because I am renting it from you.'

'You call the pittance you pay us "rent"? It hardly covers costs.' I was thinking, 'Here we go again, here we go again.'

'Then you are better off because when I lived in the house, I paid nothing.'

We carried on for a bit like that, once more in the secure familiarity of the same old rut. I started to paint my nails. They were already a glittery sky blue but I decided the gentle colour didn't suit my mood so I was covering them with cobalt blue. I could do this argument at the same time as something else. My mother began washing the cups. I remembered I wanted to tell her about the cat.

'Mother, leave the dishes and come and talk. I want to tell you about the cat.'

'What cat? There is no cat. You can't even look after yourself, let alone a cat.'

I went and took the tea towel from her and hung it on the hook on the back of the door. It felt like the moment for a truce. I took her hand.

'Come on, Mother dear, I want to show you some pictures of really cute kittens.'

I made her sit down on the pale blue chair; it looked better with that disgusting colour she was wearing. Then I sat by her with my laptop.

'Here we go. Persian Blues.'

'They are rather sweet. But aren't they...?' My mother clamped her lips together.

'Yes, Mother, they are a watercolour wash of blue-black, that's grey to you. But I will get my kitten blue bows and she will at least tone in with the blue.' Then I had a sudden flash of inspiration, so added, 'Or I could give her a blue rinse.'

'You can't do that to the poor little thing – that would be terrible.'

'I wouldn't,' I said, although it had seemed a perfect solution.

My mother took the laptop away from me and peered at the screen. It sounded as if she were making purring noises.

'Which one do you want, dear? They all look so soft. Gorgeous, even.'

'I have to think about the distance, before I choose.'

'Why the distance?'

I carefully explained that some of these dear little bundles of fur lived rather a long way away. South London to Edinburgh would be a very long journey for me, let alone a little kitten.

'Where is the nearest?' she asked.

'This one, still about ninety miles away.'

'We could go in the BMW. Daddy will drive.'

'No, Mother, this is not a family outing to treat your dear daughter to her very first pet. This is me, Bluedelle, an adult, buying my own kitten.'

'Bluedelle? That's what that psychologist called you.' I thought I'd skirted away from talking about that and now I'd mentioned the name myself.

'Yes, Mother, I am known as Bluedelle among my friends and I rather like it.'

'Well, I don't.' I waited for the next line, which was just waiting to burst into the conversation. It came. 'I have a strong dislike of blue. You know that. Your friends have far too much influence over you. You wouldn't have had any problems like this blue business if it hadn't been for them.'

Together we rode the ups and downs of the merits and demerits of my friends. As usual, I called a halt at the stage when she started calling them my 'so-called friends' and asked me what they had done for me.

'I'm getting a bit tired here, Mother. I'm going to have some fudge. Do you want some?'

'I won't ask you what colour it is.'

'I'll offer you blue fudge. I'm hoping to make you some purple fudge for your birthday. What do you think?'

My mother sighed, her face relaxing. 'That would be nice, dear. Although I'd prefer green.'

I laughed. I suddenly saw all these patterns like a great big mess of hair in a hairbrush. The hairbrush making everything smooth every now and again but always at the expense of hair being tangled in the brush.

I gave my mother a rare hug and promised green fudge for her birthday. I could probably manage sea green.

6

Going back to Selsdon after a day's work still felt like a treat – something special. It took me longer going by Tube, train and bus than it did when I lived in Sydenham. I used to dread leaving the office to go back there. It wasn't home at all. Now I returned to my wife and, when he's around, to Shaun. There was laughter, love and a space to be sad in my home. Despite the awkward journey, I was so glad to be there at last.

The journeys during those few days after Christmas were taken in less-crowded trains. My mind was full of several new clients I had taken on because of the head of department's extended sick leave. I had taken two for assessment only, ready to pass on to other members of the mental health team. There were two more, one gentleman with a complicated history of depression and Adelle, the intriguing young lady who appeared to have an abnormal grief reaction.

It was the latter who occupied my mind two days after her last appointment. Earlier that day, there had been a message left on the secretaries' phone from Adelle, saying that she was about to buy a cat. I'd looked back over the notes, thinking there was some misunderstanding, but I was certain I had only suggested some research. I wondered whether the green-clothed mother had an opinion about this. If she did, it probably reflected back on me. I chastised myself for not recognising that Adelle was likely to rush ahead with an idea.

Thinking about Adelle had made me wonder about the friend in her early childhood who was so important to her. I had made a note in the file to encourage Adelle to talk to her parents about this and uncover the reason for the child disappearing from Adelle's life. Then there was the nature of the fixation on blue to consider. Was it in fact a condition rather than a preference or a symptom? When I considered how her life had changed, it became obvious to me that I would have to treat it as a 'symptom' for now and as a 'condition' if she could not budge it once we had progressed with some grief work.

I decided then and there that I would probably proceed more quickly if I used Adelle's art as part of her therapy. I resolved to contact our art therapist, Anita, as soon as she was back in the office. She had been so useful in a previous case that it seemed logical to enlist her help.

My train pulled into East Croydon station and I disembarked with the other people – all strangers to me at the moment. They looked weary and desolate, whereas I felt fired up and ready to meet my wife. I missed her when I went to work, and in this time of reconciliation it was, to me, a meeting of wonder and excitement. I hurried down the platform, delighted to see her – she was there to save me the twenty-five minutes on a bus – her beautiful eyes scanning the crowd, her face breaking into a smile as she spotted me.

7

It took some time for my mother to stop aahing over the kitten pictures I had left on my laptop. She mentioned again that she would 'love' to take me to fetch the sweetest little grey bundle, but I could not accept that offer. I had my pride, and her presence would be overwhelming.

Finally, Mother left my summerhouse, taking her terrible crash of green with her. I found a few spearmint sweets and a handful of blueberries to help tide me over until I felt ready to cook some pasta. I restarted my search for a Persian Blue in the hope that there would be cheaper ones nearer London. But no, the nearer the seller was to London, the higher the price. I did another search for pet carriers – the kind with a door like a little cage – but couldn't find any blue ones. I did, however find a blue bag to carry my designer cat in when I went out. I ordered it.

Now I was committed. I looked for cat litter online. None of the packets gave me any clue as to what colour they were inside but I did come across a blue litter tray with a lid. I was just about to pay for it when it occurred to me that an older kitten might not need one. I put it in the shopping basket anyway and added to it a blue cat bed, a blue pet blanket and some gorgeous striped blue pet dishes. I would leave them there and pay for the ones I needed when I knew I was definitely fetching my cat.

Feeling satisfied, I cooked some pasta, using a little of the dye from the red cabbage. From trial and error I had discovered the cabbage dye was not bad for this but not so good in cakes or bread because I needed to use a lot for the colour which could affect the taste.

I allowed myself to make a blue cheese sauce for the pasta. This was cheating, but was part of the bargain I struck when I wanted the summerhouse as my pad. Mother made me promise I would introduce three items to my regular diet that weren't blue coloured but were full of protein; this was difficult, so I had to include the blue cheese. Sometimes I added some blue colouring to the pasta sauce but it turned out a bit green. That day I mixed it through the pasta and made do with the resulting bluish mess. I knew that if I didn't look at it directly, I could manage to eat it.

I had no vegetables but figured the large quantity of blueberries I had snacked on earlier would cover that omission. I took my meal over to the sofa and put my TV on. I watched the news, imagining I had my new cat on my lap, purring gently while I stroked her thick, soft fur. I couldn't wait to have her. I knew that Dr Lewis only asked me to do research but he might be pleased if I reported that I had bought one. I wasn't doing anything behind his back – I had left a message for him. I still had some of Granny's legacy left and I was saving it for something blue.

That night, I fell asleep on the sofa and dreamed of crowds of grey kittens purring all around me. I had my first good night's sleep for many years.

8

It was over a week before I next saw Adelle. I knew I would have to spread the appointments out as January became busier with the usual clients. I had not responded to Adelle's phone message but would have to talk about it. She was early as usual and had no one with her.

She came into my room and after we had politely greeted each other, I asked her, 'What happened to your college course, Bluedelle?'

Her focus shifted from me to the corner of the room again – I was familiar with that avoidance of the issue. I waited as she seemed to consider what to say. When she spoke it was with a rush, as if trying to move distasteful information out of the way.

'As you know, I was doing interior design. I told myself I was taking a unique approach and that I wanted to be an interior designer who always stuck to shades of blue and avoided completely all the complementary colours.'

I nodded, urging her to tell me more.

'Sadly, my look did not suit many people. I failed three assignments and felt aggrieved because of the narrow vision of my tutors. When I was summoned to see my mentor, Dr Hastings, I thought it was my opportunity to complain about my treatment.

'I walked into her office, which was a riot of discordant colour from the huge abstract paintings that nearly covered each available space. I put on the blue-tinted sunglasses I usually had with me. The room became a little quieter. Dr Hastings smiled at me and said, "Sit down, Adelle. I have a problem that I wish to discuss with you."

'She was a cunning old bird – I decided my problems could wait, and relaxed, feeling honoured that she wanted to confide in me. I am so naïve. I nodded towards her, sitting down on what appeared to be a slightly blue chair.

'"My problem is this, Adelle."

'I leaned forward, trying to turn my face into a sympathetic "I'm listening" expression.

'She sighed. I waited for the big problem.

'"It is this, Adelle. I have one student who persistently defies me. I have pleaded with her to follow my advice and she does not, or maybe she cannot. This student has exceptional talent but without my guidance will never pass the course. What would you do in my shoes, Adelle?"

'I couldn't think who she meant.

'"Well, Dr Hastings, she is foolish not to take your advice. Perhaps you should talk to her and explain that the course might not be for her at this time."

'"Yes, Adelle, that is good advice."

'I actually smiled before she said, "Well, Adelle, I need to say to you that the course might not be right for you at this time. I don't understand why all your work has to be blue, but my suggestions to vary your palette have gone unheeded."

51

'I can remember staring at her, my mind in turmoil. I couldn't believe she had tricked me. Nor could I believe that my unique approach would lead to losing my place on the course. Then I regained my composure. I thanked her and stood up to go, but Dr Hastings hadn't finished.

'"Wait, Adelle. I meant what I said when I described you as having exceptional talent. That is, when you allow yourself to use a wide spectrum of colours. Your early work on the course was outstanding. When you are able to design properly again, I would love to see you back on the course."'

Adelle stopped talking and folded her arms, moving herself further back into the chair.

'So, at least you left that room with something,' I said.

Adelle shrugged and grimaced. I took the most positive slant on this anecdote that I could.

'So once we have worked on helping you overcome your problem with blue, you will be able to go back to college. That's good news!'

Adelle pulled her cardigan tight around her and avoided my gaze.

'Have you had work since then?' I asked gently.

Adelle took her time to answer, but just as I was about to let her off the hook and talk about something else, she spoke.

'I was employed by a department store. I got very tired – it was before I'd agreed to the protein in my food. I was in the needlecraft and textiles section. I really fought it, I did, but when a customer came in I nearly always directed them towards blue materials or threads or whatever it was.'

She glanced at me. I nodded.

'I was an excellent saleswoman but people wanting to repair red chairs went away with blue thread and those who wanted material for bridesmaids' dresses ended up changing the whole colour scheme for their wedding because I persuaded them that blue was better. I treated it like a challenge!' She smiled, remembering.

'My manager started snooping on me and eventually, inevitably, I got the push. It's a shame – I had applied there because of the lovely uniforms. A French navy skirt and a baby-blue blouse. I loved it.'

'I am sorry, I hope that didn't put you off finding a new job?'

'I tried other things, of course. My next uniform was green – which I hated totally. But in the garden centre it was easy to promote blue. There was plenty around. Petunias, irises, borage. Borage looks odd in that list, I know, but that's where I found out that borage has lovely blue flowers that can go in a salad. So do cornflowers – although to be honest they taste like grass. That's where I discovered Salad Blue potatoes too.'

'Did you grow blue potatoes?'

'Yes, I dug up a large area of mother's lawn behind the summerhouse and planted the tubers. Mother was furious, of course, but when I explained it was for potatoes, she was pleased I was diversifying my diet. I never have told her they are blue.'

I thanked Adelle for all the information and condensed it into a few lines in my notes.

When I glanced up, Adelle was sitting on the edge of her seat, waiting for me.

'Mike, did you get my message about the kitten?'

'I did, it was quite a surprise. Has anything happened since?'

'Well, I can't remember quite what I have already said to you in the message, but the excellent bit of news is that my mother is quite taken with the idea of me having a cat. She offered for Dad to drive me in the BMW to collect it. I don't want my parents to take me, though.'

'I'm glad your mother is positive. But are you sure? I only suggested you research the idea of pet ownership.'

'I did research it, but I was certain that's what I wanted. You have just encouraged me to go forward with my dream.'

'How far have you gone with taking things forward?' I was feeling rather responsible for this turn of events.

'I haven't found one yet. At least, probably not. I phoned three sets of owners and the kittens had all gone and I am waiting to hear from two more. They are all quite a long way away, though, because the few in London are a lot more expensive.'

'Perhaps it might not be such a good idea to spend a lot of money on a pedigree kitten. Have you looked at others?' Even as I said this, I was wondering what I was doing. This was turning into something other than a therapy session.

'I've thought about it. But I have enough money from my granny to buy exactly what I want.' Her hand shot up to the chain around her neck as she spoke, releasing the green pendant from its hiding place. A useful little movement to notice.

I nodded. Her money was none of my business and not relevant here, although Granny was.

'Did your granny have a cat?'

I had blue napkins ready, and she needed them. Between her tears she told me, 'Granny loved all animals. She was the kindest lady. She didn't have a cat as she grew older, but she more or less looked after her neighbour's. I don't want it to sound as if she was a bit daft, but she talked to the birds when she fed them, she bought dog food for a hedgehog that lived in her garden, she fed the ducks on the pond down the road and she stroked every dog she met on her daily walk.'

'Quite an animal lover, then.'

'Yes.' Adelle had stopped crying and began to tell me more about her grandmother. I noted that she called her 'Granny' whereas her own mother was always called 'Mother'. Not something to remark on, but probably an indication of the closeness of the relationships. I made a note to discover why.

9

Before Mike Lewis had started to talk about my granny, I had told him I didn't want my parents to take me to collect a kitten. That very evening I had emails back from two breeders near Manchester. They still had kittens to sell – I was ecstatic!

Now all I had to do was find someone to take me, but there was a problem with being 'Bluedelle' and that was friends. I did have friends, probably, but they were at uni. My other friends were more of the 'You're weird' type. They were fascinated by my blueness but a bit wary. So when I rang Sharon and asked her for a lift to Manchester, all she could say was, 'Look, Dreamy, I have absolutely no objection to going to the Cats' Rescue Agency in Bromley with you and finding a sweet little homeless cat or kitten for you to love, but I refuse to go all the way to Manchester for some special breed to satisfy your blue fixation. Anyway, Persian Blues are grey at best and some of them are cream.'

'I know, but they are very cute, you should see them. Go on, Sharon, we could make a day of it. And I would pay for petrol and buy lunch. It would be fun.'

'You don't eat lunch unless it's blue.'

'I could take lunch.'

'I don't eat lunch if it's blue.'

I tried to tempt and cajole her into taking me. In the end I agreed to go with her to the Cats' Rescue Agency and look. Then we'd go to the new tea shop that had millions of teas and I knew did blue macaroons. She could eat a proper lunch if she wanted.

All this delayed my cat ownership by a few days but I thought it might be a good investment. If Sharon saw lots of straggly, mean cats she would take pity on me and drive me to Manchester.

So there we were, two days later, looking at cats. At least, Sharon was. I was scanning them for colour. We saw the older cats first. I was surprised at how good they looked – well groomed and happy. Sharon stroked every single one and spoke in a silly little voice at them. We were looking at them for ages until one of the assistants came up and said to me, 'I think your friend will have problems deciding which to take. She seems to love them all.'

I told her I was the one who wanted a cat and I really fancied a Persian Blue. She looked quite cross but then said gruffly, 'We have a few grey kittens.'

I dragged Sharon away from a rather large tom she seemed to have fallen for. I know why; she was going out with a big, friendly chap who had a full head of auburn hair. And green eyes, exactly like that ginger cat.

We were taken to see the kittens. We washed our hands – or rather smeared them with something that smelled terrible – I can't think what the cats thought humans should smell like.

I will admit the kittens were cute. First up was a pair of black and white siblings, to be placed together. Sharon was enthralled. She took them both and plonked one into my arms.

'These are gorgeous, Dreamy, absolutely perfect for you.'

The one I held clambered free of my hands and climbed my jumper to nestle in my neck. It felt so sweet and cuddly; if I couldn't see it, I could love this one. I removed it from my neck before I was totally seduced, and replaced it in the cage. I was trying to stay true to who I was.

'May I see the grey ones, please?'

The assistant, whose badge proclaimed to the world that she was Margie, returned both the black and white kittens and came back with another cage. We were required to make our hands smell disgusting again. I was feeling quite excited. She hadn't exactly said they were Persian Blues but she definitely had said 'grey'.

She opened the lid and we peered in. My bubble of excitement deflated. All I could see were stripes. Quickly, the Margie lady passed me one of the kittens; it was soft, it was furry, it was quite grey – could I settle for second best?

'These two have only just come in; they haven't had much handling,' said Margie.

I didn't take much notice; I was in turmoil. I had set my heart on a Persian Blue but there was something quite lovely about this tiny, furry ball with one white paw and the other grey. I gently stroked the little creature. It felt so soft under my fingers. It was purring and I could feel the tremble through its fragile body. I touched its dear little white front paw. Without warning, it turned into an angry spitfire and clawed its way out of my clutch. The assistant caught it before it hit the ground. My hand was bleeding. I stood there looking at it while Margie put away the kittens. Then Sharon and Margie flustered around me with cotton wool and antiseptic wipes, cleaning the terrible scratch.

'Let's go,' I said to Sharon.

Sharon looked cross and embarrassed. We were led out of a side door – for some reason Margie didn't think it was a good idea to go out via reception.

Our visit to Hattie's, the new tea shop, was postponed. Sharon was 'not in the mood'. I decided not to ask her to take me to Manchester again. She hardly spoke all the way back home. She dropped me off outside my mother's house, refusing to come in for cake or fudge. I couldn't quite think what I had done – I was very gentle with the monster kitten. I didn't know it was going to morph into a mini tiger.

I moped around that evening. I so wanted a cat. Although my hand still hurt, being scratched had not put me off. I knew that if a lovely, blue-eyed, soft grey Persian Blue had scratched me, I would have overlooked it. Yes, I definitely wanted a beautiful Blue cat for preference.

Chewing a particularly sticky spearmint sweet, I went on the internet to see if there were any other Blue cats. I found the British Blues. There were some lovely pictures of rosette-winning cats but I wasn't sure about their less fluffy coats. Some of the adult ones looked like bouncers for a cat nightclub. Anyway, they were more expensive apart from one British Blue/Persian Blue cross. It looked adorable, but hey, it would be second best again.

The advert for the Persian Blue kitten was still online. The price was astronomical – £600. I looked again at the

Persian Blue cross – just as pretty and only £200. I phoned Sharon. I had to leave a message.

'Sharon, are you OK? I am so very sorry I upset you at the cat centre. Bye for now.' I stopped in confusion, unsure which of my names to use. She called me 'Dreamy' but I preferred 'Bluedelle'. I put the phone down when it occurred to me that she'd know who had rung by the mention of the cat rescue centre. That's when I realised that she was probably upset because she would have taken any of those cats home. She would love any of them to bits. In fact, she'd make a much better pet owner than I would.

I pondered over this thought while I cooked some blue tuna. It didn't look the same as usual, so I wondered whether Mother was sneaking in some other fish. I made a few blue chips to go with the fish and put it all on my pre-warmed plate. It looked terrible. I found some tartare sauce. I added a little blue colouring but, predictably, it went green. I chucked it away. I added a little olive spread to the fish and it went almost clear but left it glossy. I decided it was edible like that and moved over to the sofa by the television to eat it, distracting myself with the evening news.

The phone rang. It was Sharon.

'I was a bit fed up,' said Sharon, 'and embarrassed. That Margie was very apologetic and ran around cleaning that little scratch and sorting you out and you didn't say anything.'

'I'm sorry, I was disappointed. I quite liked the grey kitten and he attacked me!'

'No need to be so rude, though.'

'I thought you were going to walk off with that one that looks like your boyfriend!'

'Which one? Oh, the ginger tom! He does look like my ex, doesn't he? I haven't seen him for ages and it hadn't occurred to me!' She was chortling away and I was pleased I'd made her laugh.

'Where is he, then, if you haven't seen him?'

'I don't know, do I? He sort of lost interest in me and when I confronted him he said I'd been a substitute for someone else he wanted to be with. We parted on the spot.'

'Who's that, then – the person he wanted to be with?'

'Umm, he did tell me, but swore me to secrecy.'

I felt as if she had slapped me. I mentally went back to the Dreamy Delle days when all the other girls would be whispering together. I'd ask what was going on and they would all clam up. By the time I was Bluedelle I didn't care any more. I thought I was over it. I tried to regain control.

'You can tell me if you ever feel like it. You know I can keep quiet about things. It is a bit mean of him to dump you saying he's interested in someone else and then tell you to keep a secret about it.'

'Oh, I suppose so. But we always had a bit of an arm's length relationship. He will make someone else a wonderful other half, but not me. I liked him more as a friend before we went out together.'

I thought about the times I'd seen them together. Yes, they were more friends than boyfriend and girlfriend.

'So you didn't fall for the ginger tom, then? What about the black and white kittens?'

'I can't think that way, Dreamy. I can't have pets in my flat. I would dearly love a kitten, but I need a place to live.

It's practically impossible to find somewhere to rent where pets are allowed.'

'Oh, Sharon, that's so awful. I'm sorry, I didn't think. That was nasty of me to get you involved in a cat hunt.'

'Oh no. It was probably quite selfish of me to expect you to look at all those cats in the rescue centre. My chance of a free cuddle with them!'

I felt so sorry for her. My mind was buzzing. Was there something I could do? Could I have two cats – one of them being hers? Was that fair on her? She'd have to come over a lot to see it. Was I prepared to share my little sanctuary with her?

10

Wednesday 10th January

It was the day for therapy for me – an appointment with Henrietta – *our* appointment to be precise. Henry, as she liked to be called, had suggested this should be one with Ella, when we could face up to our differing ideas about the progress of our reunion. I was more anxious than I had expected. Perhaps this would act as a useful reminder of the anxiety my clients felt when they had a difficult issue to face in their appointment with me.

Having just started a locum teaching job, Ella had to arrange cover for her class for the first part of the morning, to be able to spend the full hour with Henry. I knew this annoyed her, so she was grumpy even before we set out together. This was our second couples appointment, and I thought the first one went well and that Ella had felt better after it. Therefore, I had high hopes, despite the niggling anxiety.

I knew better than to use the appointment to make Ella see that we could organise a day to renew our vows. I did not consider that she would ask me to leave the family home, despite her insistence that I should continue to rent the flat in Sydenham.

Henry invited us straight in as soon as we arrived. There were three chairs in a semicircle, otherwise her room was the same as usual, even down to the man-size tissues on the coffee table. I waited for both ladies to take their seats, which left me with the one nearest the door. I wondered whether Henry read anything into this, considering that I might if I were the therapist and not the client.

Henry asked us both how we were coping with being back together. Ella answered first, with a quick glance at me. I was surprised by what she said.

'It's fairly good, but I feel pressured by Mike. He seems to have forgotten that we were apart for five years.'

Before I could say anything, Henry turned to me.

'And what about you, Mike? Imagine Ella hasn't said anything yet.'

I couldn't. I was going to tell her that everything was good and we were working towards renewing our wedding vows, but if I said that now, then I would definitely be pressurising Ella.

'I thought things were going well,' I said, furious with myself that I could not think of anything better to say. I wanted to walk out of there, taking Ella with me, and get on with our lives. But I knew we had things to sort out.

Henry took our two differing views and helped us to carefully unpick them. Ella was able to explain how she had been used to spending more time preparing Shaun for his transition to independent living and had felt that since I had moved back, she had been failing as his support. I told Henry how it was great to be with Ella and how lonely I had been at the flat and how going back home and being wanted by Ella was a dream come true. Even as I said it, I knew that this was exactly the attitude that was making Ella crowded. I said so.

Henry didn't interrupt as Ella and I discussed all the areas where she felt crowded and I tried to put my point of view. I was eager to let her know that now she had said it, I could back off and perhaps be more like a lodger.

'What would that look like?' asked Henry.

'I haven't thought it through. Perhaps I could have a room I can use as a den? At the moment we share a room and so there is nowhere to go to give Ella space.'

This led Ella to say it was not physical space she needed but mental and emotional. I felt desolate.

Henry sensed I was upset. She leaned forward and, looking from one to the other of us, she said, 'I'm going to ask you both to spend a few minutes thinking about what that would look like in the context of you living under the same roof, and what it would look like if you were living separately.'

It was as if the word 'separately' was hanging in the air between us. I glanced at Ella but her head was turned slightly away from me. I closed my eyes, praying silently that I wouldn't have to go back to the flat. I couldn't bear that.

I tried to think what it would be like if we were in the same house. Did I plague her with questions? Was I always bothering her? What about those quiet contemplative moments we had together? Maybe they were too infrequent. Then I steeled myself to think about living apart again. Could I even do that now? I wouldn't be a burden on her, but would she need me? My mind was so full of questions that I didn't come up with answers.

Henry coughed politely. I looked up; both ladies seemed ready to go ahead.

'May we hear from you first, please, Mike?' asked Henry.

I outlined my questioning thoughts, trying to be as clear as I could. I finished by saying, 'I know it's not physical space Ella needs, but perhaps if I used the spare bedroom as a study when Shaun has no visitors, it would help Ella to feel she has time to think with me not drawing on her emotionally. Or I could even sleep in there sometimes, if that would help.'

Ella looked at Henry, who nodded, allowing her to speak.

'I don't think you understand, Mike. I have been an independent woman for five years, making my own decisions, doing my own things, thinking my own thoughts. I have tried to survive as a separated woman and I can't just switch back to being who I was before you left.'

I understood all that, so I nodded and half-smiled. She continued, 'I made friends with single people.' I probably looked horrified because she hastily added, 'No, not like that. But like you did with Anita. I know you became close because she called on you when she was in trouble and only you would do. You see her and others at work; I no longer see my friends.'

'I'm sorry.'

'Don't be sorry. It's thrown me; in the course of a few weeks I have had to switch back and I am different now. And you are putting pressure on me – think about the ring.'

'I know, that was bad timing.'

'Precisely, you are all ready to leap back into our marriage and I am, logically, but maybe less so emotionally?' This was phrased as a question aimed at Henry.

Henry told her quietly, 'You are the one who knows if emotionally you are not ready. It's good that you can say so.'

'I can wait,' I said, knowing almost at the same time that if she knew I was waiting then she would feel burdened. I added, 'I need to step back. Not into my flat, but I need to let you be your new you and discover you all over again.'

Ella laughed, 'You are sounding like the therapist, Mike.' The mood in the room had lifted.

'He can't help that,' said Henry, 'but it does show you he has insight. What do you think about living separately again?'

Ella and I looked at each other. I was frightened to say something first, but the silence was so long I felt I had to.

'If Ella definitely wants me to, I can move back to the flat. I don't want to and I think we will do better trying to negotiate our relationship while we are together.'

Ella nodded slowly. 'Let's try it together, but be prepared to look at other ways if we can't move forward.' I could not hide my smile of relief.

'I'll be happy to help if you need me,' said Henry.

As Ella and I parted at the door of the building housing Henry's office it was Ella who put her arms round me to say goodbye. We hugged each other carefully and I kissed the top of her head, before turning to go to the station.

It took the whole journey to my office in London to stop my emotional turmoil and turn my mind to the rest of the day ahead.

11

My next visit to the psychologist was very strange. It was almost as if he had forgotten our previous appointment altogether. He welcomed me into his room and I spread out my scarf and sat on the better of his two armchairs. So far, so good.

I was just about to launch into telling him all about the kittens, especially the monster grey, stripy one, when he pre-empted me by suggesting we go down to the art studio.

'Art studio? Do you have an art studio here?' It didn't seem to fit with a mental health department somehow.

'Yes, in the basement. I would like you to meet Anita Goodwin, our art therapist.'

'Aren't you going to be working with me any more, then?'

'Yes, I will. But even now I think we should be preparing you for your return to college, if that's what you want to do. Using the medium of art should help you to accept that the world need not remain blue.'

I nodded. My heart was pounding as I thought about all those colours. I was remembering a day at college. Nearly my last day, as it turned out. I had been in class, painting an abstract face of various blues, but the person next to me was using loud pinks, grating greens, and booming yellow, all with a purple background. I turned my easel away from her and all I could see on my other neighbour's easel was a cacophony of orange, yellow and red. I was beginning to feel sick and overwhelmed by colour. I picked up my easel, thinking I would move it to a less noisy area of the studio but the brightness was shouting at me in technicolour. I couldn't get away; it was like a nightmare.

While I was remembering all this, I was trying to calm myself down by taking long, slow breaths and blowing them out gently. We had gone down some stone stairs to a floor below the Psychology Department, which I hadn't known existed. We reached a door in the basement. I hung back as Mike opened it, but he ushered me through. I felt myself sway, my eyes half-shut against the expected pain of colours. We waited there by the door. A face swam in front of me. A friendly face, with an enquiring look. Curly brown hair.

I concentrated on the art therapist's face, trying to hear above the noise in my head. She was explaining to me the sort of work she did and how she could perhaps help me as I worked with Mike by gradually introducing more colours. I relaxed and took charge of my breathing again. There was something in the tone and lilt of her voice that was helping me to gradually calm down.

I dared to look around.

There was colour in the room, but only up on the shelves where art materials and coloured sugar paper were stacked. Some pale blue paper was out on the large pine table that was in the centre of the room. The floor and walls were a neutral colour – I could cope with the hum of that.

I saw a variety of blue pastels, water soluble pencils and poster paints arranged by the pale blue paper.

'Come and sit down,' said Anita Goodwin. I followed her to the pine table and took my place in front of the blue paper.

Having entrusted me to the art therapist, Mike took a seat near the door.

I tried to concentrate on what Mrs Goodwin – or was she Miss or Dr? – was saying. Something about it not being necessary to be a good artist to work in here and it was usually about working out feelings using art, or creating an understanding of one's life journey.

Then her face became even more questioning and I realised she had just asked me whether I wanted to draw anything at all. I obligingly took up a blue pastel. Then I stopped. This felt very, very strange.

'What have you done this week that you would like to draw?' asked Anita.

I found myself drawing cages – several of them, all in dark blue. Within them were eyes – cats' eyes. All blue, of course. I was having difficulties on the blue paper making the picture resemble what I had in my head, but nothing on earth would induce me to ask for other colours.

'That looks like caged cats – in the zoo perhaps, or an animal sanctuary?'

I found my voice, which seemed to have gone missing for a while, and began to tell her about our visit to the Cats' Rescue Agency. I finished with the dropped kitten and the scratched hand, wondering even then whether I had exaggerated the terribleness of the scratch. She laughed when I told her about being ushered out of the back door.

'Are you still going to get a cat?' she asked.

'I know I want one. So yes, definitely.' I glanced over at Mike. He nodded. I hoped that was in an approving way. 'But I'd like to talk to Mike about that,' I said. I had spotted a group of bright poster paints in their transparent bottles. My eyes kept being drawn to them and their blare was making me feel really uncomfortable. I wanted to turn down the noise in my head. I could feel my hands were sweaty.

'Are you coping in here?' asked Mike.

'I was,' I told him, 'but now I am having difficulty because of those loud paints in the corner.'

'No problem, try to slow your breathing and turn away from them to look at Anita.'

I had been hoping he would whisk me back upstairs to the sanctuary of his untidy room. But I did as I was told and felt better with my head turned towards her.

'Right, now tell me what's happening for you, Delle,' said Mike.

'I feel desperately that I want to look at the paints, but when I do it makes me feel dreadfully panicky.' Waves of nausea had begun to overtake me. I steeled myself to look towards Mike.

'Resist looking at them for today. That won't be a long-term solution for overcoming your problem, but we will be coming down here fairly regularly when it fits in with Anita's schedule, so we will build up to you being able to paint with all colours. Let's go back upstairs now.'

I heaved a sigh of relief and moved quickly towards the door.

12

I was pleased Adelle had managed the half-hour in Anita's studio, but once she was back in my room it became apparent that it had been quite an ordeal.

She plonked down in the usual chair, without even putting her shawl down on it first. I helped her slow down her breathing by counting her breaths with her, then we did a little progressive relaxation to help her relax.

Adelle started speaking. The words tumbled out of her as if a valve had been released.

'It was like being at college – I couldn't cope with all the colours – they kept crashing round me – they were making me feel faint; they were shapes, noises, pulling me towards them and pushing me away. I felt really sick.'

'Was that all the time, or near the end?'

'I had to fight my panic on the stairs and reason with myself. In the studio I was managing when I was concentrating on the quiet of the blue. So that was fine, but then I saw those colours. They were crashing around me, loud, chaotic.'

Her breathing was coming fast again, but she blew as she had on the stairs. I talked calmly to her and thanked her for telling me about the effect the colour had been having on her for so long. She still looked shaky, so I asked her a few questions about the rescue cats she had looked at with her friend. Gradually, her smile returned.

'I did my homework and had loads of stuff to tell you about the cat I want,' she said, pulling sheets of paper out of one of the folders she had left in my office when we went to the studio.

'You have worked really hard on this.' I glanced at my watch. 'Perhaps you could bring it back next week? Maybe that's the first thing we discuss.'

'OK – the first thing. But you never know, I may have a cat by then.'

'Do you need me to help make your decision?'

'Oh no. The decision is made. I will definitely have one.'

'I am impressed that you appear to have researched it thoroughly first. What's your next line of research, excluding blue food?'

'My future, I think. A job, or college. I'm not sure about art now, having been in an art studio again.'

'It wasn't meant to put you off, Delle. It was an introduction to help you progress.'

'I will wear some blue sunglasses from now on. I might manage with those.'

Time was up, so I let this go. Blue glass would only distort her experience of colours so may well defeat the object. But as a stepping stone it might be useful. Did I really need to demolish the symptom to help her overcome her grief? It was a difficult thing to decide because it would be quicker to acclimatise her to non-blue colours than to deal with her grief. Unusual grief needs a very individualised approach.

I showed Adelle into the waiting area, pleased to see that her mother wasn't there.

When Adelle left, I wondered whether I would see her again. Had I made a mistake in taking her to the studio? I hoped she trusted me enough to realise I would take it slowly. Meanwhile I needed to talk to Anita about synaesthesia – Adelle had definitely talked about the colours as if they were noises. I wondered whether this indicated that she experienced colours as sound. From my memory of the condition it was more usual to be the other way round – to experience sound, especially music, as colours.

I went to make some coffee and discovered Anita was there too. We both brought our drinks back into my office and pooled the little we each knew about synaesthesia, trying to unravel whether Adelle had panicked first and the heightened awareness had contributed to the abnormal effects of the colour, or whether the effects had come first, causing the panic. With such a chicken-and-egg conundrum unsolved, we decided to continue with a plan of very carefully reintroducing colour into Adelle's life.

13

My research into cats had reached stalemate. I dithered around, not sure what to do. If I found a cat and asked my parents to take me, would that be telling them I was still a child, when all I wanted to do was claim my rightful adult independence?

I made myself leave the summerhouse to meet Sharon in Hattie's teashop for the postponed post-cat-visit tea. I was there first and ordered what I wanted. Sharon arrived, looked at the small blue meringue on my plate and immediately took me to task: 'Really, Dreamy, isn't it time you gave up the blue thing? Can't you ask your psychologist to hypnotise you so that you can be normal again?'

'No, he can't. He doesn't work like that. I've got to learn how to gain control of my thoughts myself so that if the problem comes again, or if I get fixated on anything else, I can sort it out without anyone else's help.' I explained more, especially about cognitive behavioural therapy, while we waited for her order to arrive.

Sharon took a big bite out of her teacake and chewed, thoughtfully.

'Does that mean he's equipping you for anything that happens to you in your life?'

'Well, I don't know about anything, but he's working towards a long-term solution.'

Butter was running down Sharon's chin. I made a play of mopping my own chin, but she didn't take the hint. I watched it, wondering why she didn't feel it. 'You've got butter on your chin,' I whispered.

'What?'

I whispered it again, mopping my own chin again and she cottoned on before it dripped onto her lovely pale blue sweater. I wondered whether she had chosen the colour to please me.

'I like your sweater,' I said in a normal voice.

'Oh thanks. It's more your colour than mine, though. I was looking for my bright red one, but this looked so soft and warm I thought it would be better for today.'

I was disappointed. But then the thought came that if everyone wore blue all the time, I would probably be more inclined to favour red. Maybe that's how she felt around me. Maybe my blue affected her.

'Does it upset you? That I wear blue, I mean.'

'Not that you wear blue, although I think other colours suit you better. What does upset me is that you only eat blue. You look so thin.'

'I only lost an ounce last week.'

Sharon looked at me, her face depicting disbelief. When she regained her composure, she explained to me very carefully and thoroughly that no one, absolutely no one, measured their weight down to the last ounce. And that everyone's body weight fluctuated up and down a little every day.

'I'm buying you a second blue meringue and you are eating it all. It's not much, but maybe, just maybe, it will help you put an ounce on.'

I shrugged. I felt strangely affected by her attitude. Here was someone, other than my mother, who appeared genuinely concerned about me. I briefly wondered what it would be like to be Sharon, watching her friend lose weight.

I felt ashamed.

'I'm sorry, Sharon. I am really trying to sort it out now. But I am stuck. I'm not being obstinate, or difficult; I just have this terrible problem with other colours.'

'Why?'

'I don't know. It's something to do with the challenge being around the time when my gran died – at least, that's what Mike Lewis thinks.'

'Is Mike Lewis your psychologist?'

'Yes.'

'Well, I hope he sorts you out before you die of starvation.' Sharon returned to her teacake, taking a huge bite. I nibbled at the edge of the blue meringue, hoping she would forget to buy me another. They really were rather sweet.

'Can we talk about cats again?' I asked.

'I still don't want to drive you all the way to Manchester or Birmingham or somewhere else miles away. Sorry, Dreamy, if you want a designer cat, you'll have to find one nearer. Then I might take you. I'm not really into long-distance driving.'

Disappointed, I didn't know what to say. I shrugged and had another little nibble of the blue meringue, thinking of the beautiful Persian Blue kittens while I did so.

14

Thursday 18th January

As always, Adelle arrived early. She was sitting in the waiting area reading from an A4 lever arch file which bulged with paper. Her open rucksack revealed a second file. I hoped she wasn't expecting me to read it all. I called her name and she rose, grinned at me and gathered up her belongings to come into my office.

'That's my homework. You should have looked at it last week, I've found out loads more since then,' she said triumphantly, pointing at her rucksack. She spread her large shawl out on her usual chair and sat down. She showed no sign of acting discreetly this time – maybe as a result of having told me the effect bright colour was having on her, which had contributed to panic in the art room.

Pulling the second file out of her bag, she explained, 'This large one is mostly about cats. The other one has a section on food. It doesn't matter about the rest.'

I was intrigued by 'the rest'. What had she been looking up? Perhaps it was to do with her grief or being stuck with her blue fixation. It wouldn't matter – I wanted her to find her own way forward if possible, as that would be best for long-term success.

I sat down in the other chair, absentmindedly brushing off the crumbs from my lunch. I decided to mention the shawl.

'I thought you might not need to cover the chair today.'

'Oh, why?'

'You didn't use it when we came back from the art studio.'

She moved her shoulders in the familiar shrug. 'I can sit on other colours, but I feel squirmy and uncomfortable when I do.'

I nodded, and waited. She looked at me with a slightly puzzled expression. My space left for her to add to her statement became a little long for her. She filled the gap.

'Is this one of those sessions where you sit there for ages and expect me to say something and if neither of us speaks you say "your session is over" and if you were working privately you would charge £200?'

I laughed. 'No, I was waiting to see if you had more to say about sitting on other colours. Any strategies to cope, perhaps?'

'Well, I suppose I managed it the other day so I can tell myself I've done it before so I can do it again. But I thought you wanted to look at my home task?'

I smiled and waved at the lever arch file. 'When I asked you to find out about cats, I didn't expect a thesis.'

'You haven't got a thesis. I just looked stuff up and then ran it off.'

'Well, it looks impressive. Do you want to summarise your findings?'

So she did. She talked about the kittens and how blue equals grey in the kitten world in the same way as red equalling ginger. She described the differences between British Blue and Persian Blue and detailed the large amount of gear she had bought. I was quite surprised at this. When Ella and I were first married, a cat took up residence with us and, although we bought food and flea powder, we improvised for nearly everything else.

Finally, Adelle told me about the two possible kittens in the Manchester area.

'Are you happy that Persian Blues are grey?'

'I am now I've seen videos of them. I told my mother I would dye my kitten blue. She believed me for a minute.'

'Did you believe yourself?'

'No!' She startled me by shouting this out. We both knew that she half-believed it. 'It would look very pretty,' she told me, 'but it might not do the kitten's skin any good. I will make myself live with grey.'

She then told me about going to the Cats' Rescue Agency, Sharon's fascination with a large ginger tom that looked like her boyfriend (now ex), the two black and white kittens and the grey striped kitten that 'molested' her.

'So you were attacked by a cat and still want to own one?'

'Yes. I do. I'm ready for it to be unpredictable now.'

'Is your mother still fine about this?'

'Oh yes. She's offered again to take me to Manchester to look at the two I saw advertised.'

'Well, what do you think about that?'

She looked a bit nonplussed for the moment. 'I was expecting you to tell me if I should,' she said.

I inclined my head and waited for her to say more.

'I hate the thought but I might have to ask them to take me after all – Sharon won't and I'm a bit short of friends with cars.'

'Is it important you have the cat now?'

She thought about that for a moment.

'In some ways no, but to me it is, yes. I am terrible at waiting; once I have a plan I stick to it. I like to carry through my decisions quickly.'

'All decisions?'

'Well, not all. But big ones. Why did you ask?'

'Other nearer kittens might become available. Would that affect your decision?'

She tried to argue with me that there was no point in waiting because no other kitten might be available, at least not until next year. I don't argue with clients. I settled myself to listen as she took both sides of the discussion she was obviously having with herself. It was interesting to see how her thought processes worked when she was making a decision. She argued herself into a corner and dried up.

Then she surprised me with a completely off-topic question. 'My mother thinks I have schizophrenia and anorexia. Do I?'

'What do you think?'

'I was hoping you'd tell me.'

I was not going to tell her. I replied, 'I should think you know, Delle. You are great at research.'

Adelle thought for a moment, and then looked straight at me. 'I don't have either of those, do I?'

'No, you don't.'

'What do I have wrong with me, then?' Again she was questioning me. But despite her enquiring look with her head on one side, I batted the question back.

'I think you know.'

'But you're paid to tell me.'

'I think I am paid to help you understand yourself and move on. But I will help you out a little here. I think there is one thing wrong with you that you haven't acknowledged properly and another that is not as bad as you fear. So now you tell me what you think is the problem.'

'OK – I have OCD. Obsessive-compulsive disorder.'

'I thought you would say that. Some symptoms, certainly, although they are linked to the other problem, which is more relevant.'

She thought for a moment, probably going back over our previous conversations. I wondered whether she had taken on board my reference to 'the blues'. She spoke.

'I now think the colour blue represents emptiness, to me.'

'So why do you feel empty, Delle?' I stroked my beard, waiting for her answer.

'Grief,' she said quietly.

'Spot on. You'll be sitting in my chair one day.'

She smiled slowly. 'I am now.'

I laughed, noting that although she had managed to say 'grief', she hadn't burst into tears again. 'I think you know exactly what I mean.'

'What's next, then?'

'Now you are able to acknowledge the cause of the problem, we can work on that but at the same time chip away at the aftermath – the addiction to blue. Now then, how are you going to do that?'

Adelle pursed her lips and glared at me. Had I overstepped the mark? I persisted. I gave her time to think and saw her expression soften.

'I'm not sure what I do about the grief, but I have already started on blue.'

'Yes, you have, you are looking at a grey cat.'

'Oh yes.' She pondered on that thought for a moment but then added, 'More than that, I have promised to make my mother green fudge for her birthday. I am trying to experiment with different colours.'

'Your mother really likes green, does she?'

'She doesn't eat green food, but she does prefer green tea!'

I felt my mouth twitch at the corners but managed to control myself. I didn't say anything, but stood up and fetched a pile of coloured paper from my shelf. I passed her a pack of felt pens. Her reaction was rather over the top: 'I'm not a kid!'

'No, you are an interior designer. Please design a room for your mother. Is there a room she'd like changed?'

She nodded. 'She's always talked about a new kitchen. But she won't like it if I design something for her.'

But, nonetheless, she pulled out a pale blue sheet to work on. It was a big pack of pens and I had ensured there was a wide range of blues. She lifted up the brightest blue pen and hovered over the page. With a resigned sigh, she began to draw.

She quickly became engrossed in her task. I watched her draw cabinets and put blinds in a window. She spent time on the detail to the cabinet doors, adding some raised, carved trim. Then she drew a range-like oven and a dresser to match the kitchen cabinets.

It was all interesting, but not right. When she glanced up at me, I was shaking my head from side to side. She looked back at her drawing. I could see she realised it was totally wrong for her mother.

'I'm not sure I can do this; it's too blue for my mother.'

'There are other pens in the packet.'

She looked at me. I was absolutely serious – I needed to know what she could manage outside of the blue shades. She looked at the greens. One was nearly a turquoise. She shook herself and picked up the bluey-green. I wondered whether that little shake had indicated she had heard the colour, but resisted the urge to ask her. If she did have synaesthesia, it wasn't a mental health problem. I watched as Adelle used the new colour to outline the carving on the cabinet doors. It looked better, much better.

'That's much improved,' I said.

'It makes me shudder. Green grates on me. I can see it looks more like something my mother might want, but I want to screw it up and throw it away.'

I held out my hand to take it before she destroyed it. She reluctantly passed it to me. I quickly wrote the date on the back of the sketch and filed it in a transparent pocket. I was going to keep it for her but stopped myself. She was an adult and could do what she liked with her work. I gave it back to her and she clipped it into one of her lever arch files.

I said, 'Tell me more about the way green grates on you.'

'It's hard to describe. I suppose it makes a sort of out-of-tune sliding noise – up and down. It sets my teeth on edge.'

'I'm pleased you managed it when you were experiencing such an uncomfortable sensation. Apart from that, how do you think you coped overall?'

'It felt horrible.'

'No, I asked how you coped with the task, not how you felt.'

'I suppose I did as you asked.'

'Yes, you did. So you coped well. It might not be quite right for your mother's kitchen yet, but the cabinets are very good apart from the colours.'

'Perhaps one day I will be able to design a kitchen for her that she would like.'

'I'm sure you will. Meanwhile, may I ask you something that could upset you?'

She looked up at me. Her eyes looked into mine.

'If it will help, then, yes. I suppose it is to do with Granny?'

'Exactly. What would your granny say when she saw you were designing that new kitchen?'

'I'm trying to imagine Granny looking at the picture. She would study it carefully and I know exactly what she would say. It would be something like, "A beautiful kitchen, Adelle, but a trifle blue for your mother. She has always been so keen on green and cream in kitchens. Shall we try to humour her?"'

I smiled at the thought of an old lady saying that. 'What a lovely diplomatic lady your granny was. Did she often use the phrase "Shall we try to humour her"?'

'Yes, especially during my teenage years when I started calling my mother "Mother" as opposed to "Mummy". She realised I had problems relating to her even before I did. I seem to be stuck there, too. I haven't really moved on in my relationship with my mother since Gran...'

Her voice petered out, and I passed a blue napkin to her. She blew her nose loudly and regained her composure.

'I'm sorry.'

'Don't be sorry. Tears are natural and you did very well to tell me a little bit about your granny. And you are absolutely right about your relationship with your mother. What do you think about a joint meeting with her?'

'What? No, not yet. Maybe later on.'

'OK, next time we shall embark on some cognitive behavioural therapy to help you have the tools to control your mood.'

'I don't know about that, Mike. I've done it before and I am rather fed up with it.'

'Then humour me this time, Delle, and we will go through it enough to see how much you have actually applied it. I have noticed you still use some of the phrases that are typical of CBT.'

She nodded. 'But I always filled in the records I'm meant to do each day just before the sessions, so perhaps I'll try to do it properly this time.'

'Thank you,' I said. 'That would be very helpful for both of us. Would you be able to make a note of times when you felt anxious or upset, ready for us to use next session?'

'I'll do my best,' she said with a smile.

15

The last session with Adelle had set me thinking I would like to know more about the way she equated colours with sound. I had nothing in the office, but I remembered first reading about synaesthesia in a book on unusual reactions and nerve endings. That book was in my old flat.

I rang Ella and told her I would be going back via Sydenham and the reason why.

'We could both go to your flat. I should think it is rather dusty by now. I'll help you give it a good clean.'

'OK, I'll come home first, then.'

'No, you go direct and I'll drive there.'

When I put the phone down, I became worried. Why would she want to clean the flat if no one was living in it? Was this a gentle way of telling me that it was time to move back? She'd called it 'your flat', not 'the flat'. I tried to shake off the feeling that everything was coming to a crucial, unwelcome crisis. But I was remembering Henry questioning us about living separately.

So it was with some trepidation that I set off on the train from London Bridge to Sydenham. When I arrived at the flat, the whole house had a general air of neglect. It looked as if the flat below was empty. I climbed the stairs and opened the door.

Everything was more or less the same apart from dust, cobwebs and a horrible smell. I investigated the latter first and found a dead mouse, wriggling with maggots, under the kitchen sink. I removed it promptly and started to clean with an antiseptic cleaner. Soon it was smelling much better. I had not wanted Ella to walk in on that.

I cleaned the sink and wiped round the surfaces. Then I started to go through the packing cases for the book I wanted. Most of them had never been unpacked, but from when I was hunting for photos of Jamie, I had a fair idea of what each one contained.

I found the title in the second packing case. I was now surrounded by piles of books. I left them on the floor, thinking that if Ella did want me to move back, I would put them on the empty shelves.

I sat on the sofa and a puff of dust surrounded me, so I was actually beating the dust out when Ella arrived.

'Whatever are you doing?' she said as she walked into the room. 'How have you raised so much dust? I can hardly breathe.' I explained about beating the cushions on the sofa.

'Where's your vacuum cleaner, Mike?'

I showed her where it was and in a few minutes she was vacuuming the sofa, the floor and each separate cushion. She even vacuumed the piece of material I had put over another empty packing case so that I could use it as a coffee table.

I sat on the edge of the sofa and flicked through *Our Extraordinary Senses* until I found the chapter I needed. I tried to immerse myself in it, but the nagging thought that she was cleaning the flat so that I could come back to it would not go.

'Mike, give me a hand here. I don't want to clean all this on my own. You can read the book later.'

I closed the book, leaving it on the make-do coffee table, and started to help. We cleaned in silence, working around the pile of books on the floor.

'I brought some milk and coffee with me,' said Ella. 'Let's have a drink. Do you have any clean cups?'

I soon heard the kettle going as I polished the shelves. I put the books from the floor on the bottom shelf and emptied the rest out, ready to arrange them. She brought the coffee mugs through and pulled a packet of chocolate digestives out of her bag. We sat together on the sofa, looking out through the bay window.

'This flat has a lovely view across the park,' she said.

'Yes, I spent a lot of time looking over there.' I didn't tell her how upset I was when I saw the children playing and how, at first, every boy had looked like Jamie. We drank our coffee almost without talking, and she cleared the mugs away. It was then that she noticed the books on the newly polished shelf, and the pile of books on the floor.

'What are you doing, Mike?'

'What do you mean?'

'Why are you putting your books on the shelves and why are you unpacking?'

I realised what a fool I'd been.

'I thought you were cleaning because you wanted me to move back.'

Ella laughed her beautiful, ripply laugh.

'No, I'm not. Quite the opposite. When does your contract run out?'

'At the end of March.'

'And have I suggested you renew it?'

'Well, no. But you did say to Henry that you needed space – I know you said emotional space, but Henry asked us about living separately.'

Ella put her arms around me. She smelled of her shampoo and I kissed the top of her head. I returned her hug.

'I've decided I definitely don't want to live separately – cancel your contract. This place must be costing a fortune and it will deteriorate if it's left empty any longer. Ring your landlord.'

'Now?'

'Yes, now. And then we can go and eat out somewhere to celebrate that you are coming home permanently.'

'We're a bit dusty!'

'Don't worry, I'll take the vacuum cleaner to your jacket and we'll look fine!'

I didn't take my jacket off, nor did I stop smiling while she cleaned me down.

16

Although I found it very difficult to do, I was proud of myself for managing to try a non-blue colour in my session with Mike Lewis. I also felt enthused about working on an interior design again. But I had a worrying thought that my design might be rather impractical and would be very expensive. I searched on the internet.

Several kitchen installers' websites looked promising and I selected cabinets that were almost right for my mother. I then gritted my teeth and half-closed my eyes to use their paint palettes to make them green, then cream, then back to the safety of blue. It was no good – it was as if the colours were shouting at me and I felt very panicky imagining a pale green colourway – and scarcely any better with the cream one. I tried interspersing a blue kitchen with the other colours. Still my heart pounded with cream and green, only settling down when I focused on the blue kitchen. I tried this over and over again until I could bear it no longer. I felt exhausted.

But I remembered a phrase a previous psychologist had made me repeat like a mantra: 'I have done it once, so I can do it again.' I made a pact with myself to practise each day until I saw Mike again.

I ate blue stuff. It was more or less the same each day. I wondered whether there was any turquoise food I could add to my diet and if so, whether I would manage to eat it. Perhaps if I made my mother some fudge for her birthday, I would be able to eat one piece.

This thought led me into exploring websites all over again. I put in 'blue-green food' and came up with lots of cakes that used food colouring and not much else. The page had a link to an article 'Faddy feeders and how to make them change'. I clicked off my laptop in disgust.

I stood up and stretched. Despite my thick woolly and the throw over my knees, I was freezing. My back was aching from the cold and my shoulders felt stiff. I ran on the spot for a few minutes to try to warm up. For the first time it occurred to me that my father might have taken back the heater I used last year because my parents wanted me to give up living out here. For a moment I wondered whether to go and ask them – just to get warm in the kitchen, really – but I didn't want to take a backward step. This summerhouse was really good to keep independent from them until I could afford my own place.

I took my laptop and did the most sensible thing I could do – I ordered a small oil-filled radiator and a fan heater. My funds from my granny's legacy were dwindling terribly but these were necessities. Then I looked at job vacancies. It probably wouldn't be easy to find a job in January or February – it would be a quiet time for shops – but there must be something. If I applied now and it took several weeks to find some part-time work, then at least my kitten would be a little older to leave for a morning or afternoon.

Two hours later I gave up the job hunt. There was nothing unless I became a cleaner. I thought it unlikely that my mother would be pleased if I did that and anyway, I wasn't even qualified. Until I had my own place, I had scarcely cleaned anything. I was shivering. I felt so lonely and hopeless that I checked the kittens I liked had not yet been sold, then I gave up trying to be independent and went over the lawn to the warmth of my mother's kitchen.

I knocked, waited for a reply and then popped my head round the door. My parents had just finished a meal and the room smelled of roast beef. The kitchen was warm and, apart from the colours which rasped at my nerves, it was welcoming.

'Hello, dear,' said my father. 'What brings you all this way?'

'Just visiting,' I said, leaning against the Aga. The warmth on the back of my legs was glorious.

'You can put the kettle on, since you're here, Adelle, and make us a cup of tea and whatever you want.'

Whatever I wanted was usually nothing, but today I quickly dunked a teabag into the boiling water in my mug and surreptitiously took the blue colouring out of my mother's drawer and popped a few drops in. I'd chosen a mug with a blue inner, so the results were not too displeasing. Mother had her usual green tea and I made my father a small pot of English Breakfast.

'You haven't told me what you did with your psychologist today,' my mother said. There was a slight tone to the way she said 'psychologist' that made me cross.

'Dr Mike Lewis has told you that our sessions are confidential. There is a lot I would rather not tell you.'

My mother looked directly at me and I met her gaze. I think my father was startled too because he muttered, 'Gently does it, girls.'

Remembering the phrase from my teenage years when Mother and I could never see eye to eye, I felt slightly ashamed.

'I can tell you one thing that may please you.' Both faces relaxed as they looked up to me where I was standing near the Aga. 'He is encouraging me to design you a new kitchen.'

'A new kitchen, that's marvellous, I've always wanted one! But Adelle, please don't make it bl–'

I stopped her. 'Don't make it blue, I know. But my rough idea has been drawn in blue – that's all I can manage for now.'

'Have you drawn something already? Where is it, Adelle? Can I see?'

I ended up fetching the sketch I had done with Mike Lewis to show to my mother.

I carefully explained what I would do in which colours and she told me how she would love patterned curtains instead of the blinds I had sketched in.

'Look,' she said. 'Just see those delightful units. They will look wonderful in a sage green. Just imagine it!'

My mother began to work out the colour scheme. She has a fairly good idea about colour generally, but she overemphasised the green. It irked me – but it made me realise exactly how annoying my addiction to blue must be to them.

My father hadn't said much at all. I knew his problem – he hated spending money unless it was necessary, despite his successes on the stock market.

'Don't worry, Daddy. I'll keep the cost down as much as I can.'

Even as I said it, I realised I was committing myself to going through with this. Would I be able to manage it? I didn't know.

Despite the positive evening with my parents, I had a terribly troubled night. I often had times like this, and my mother put them down to not eating properly. She was probably right, but I would never tell her if she were. Nonetheless, by 4 am I was nibbling blueberries from the fridge and eating my fudge. I realised that I had forgotten to eat the night before. When I was young, I used to marvel at people who forgot meals, thinking they must be superhuman. Same with sleep – when I was told at school that Margaret Thatcher only slept four hours per night, I used to peer at her whenever she was on the television, looking for the bags under her eyes that my mother always told me I would get if I didn't settle down and go to sleep like a good girl. I was looking for the wrong sort of bags at the time – not just saggy bits of skin.

I snuggled back into bed at about six, too cold to stay up any longer, and promptly fell asleep.

17

After 6 am I slept soundly, not waking up until 8.30. I stumbled out of bed, determined to get up.

While I was in the shower, my mother knocked on the door and walked straight in.

'Excuse me!' I said, as I came through wrapped in a hurriedly grabbed towel. 'You must knock and wait, Mother, just as if you were visiting your friend Violet.'

'I never knock when I go to visit Violet. She would think I was being very snooty and stand-offish if I knocked. I have known her since I was fifteen when we both boarded.'

I was getting cold, so I nearly said, 'Oh, fair enough,' but I stopped myself. Instead I told her, 'Well, I have known you since I was born, but I would like you to knock and wait for me to invite you in when you come to my house.'

'It's not your house, it's mine.'

I carried on the usual argument while I went back into my tiny bedroom and struggled into my clothes in the small space by the door. She was still battling back when I started to dry my hair, by which time I couldn't hear what she was saying so I just shot out the odd phrase that always seemed to fit her arguments: 'But this is different, Mother.' 'Some people need their privacy more than others.' 'I would like to think that the reason I pay rent is to ensure I have my own place.' 'It may not be much but you never charged me for my bedroom.'

'Every adult is entitled to their own space!' I finally shouted, as I banged my elbow against a shelf while putting on my jumper.

When I came out, she was sitting on my blue sofa looking unhappy.

'What's the matter, Mother?'

'I only came round to talk to you about the kitchen and you've been shouting all that stuff at me.'

'I thought you were shouting the usual things at me?'

'I was, but I stopped.'

I sat on the sofa beside her. 'I'm sorry, Mother. It's like a habit now. I just expect you to say things and slot in the same retorts.'

'And I do, don't I? Always say the same things?'

'Well, yes. But so do I.' I thought of something. 'But at least we're talking to each other.'

I launched into a few tales of people who were no longer communicating at all. My mother sat and listened. I found myself winding down. I took her hand.

'Sorry, Mother. What did you want to see me for?'

My mother switched completely as she remembered why she came. 'I've spoken to your father and he is fine about the kitchen. He is very keen to have you do all the work or oversee it for people like carpenters and whatnot, and he wants you to design the curtains.'

Now I knew I had bitten off more than I could chew. I wondered briefly whether my mother had been talking to my psychologist. I didn't think so, because she would be totally unable to keep that to herself. No, it was all my fault; I shouldn't have shown her that drawing.

'Your father loved the way you had lifted the pattern on the units with some green outlining. I assume you'll be able to do cream on the pattern and a sage green base. He liked the enlarged window too.'

'No, Mother, it wasn't a scale drawing. The window will not need to be enlarged.'

'But he wants that! He said it will bring the garden into the kitchen.'

'You can do that by keeping your wellies on in the house.'

My mother gave me a withering look. It is not the same as other mothers' withering looks that they give their children. Hers is with her eyebrows lifted and her chin stuck out. I used to be able to spot that even when she stood at the back during school concerts and one of the violins played a wrong note. To be fair, it was once me, but from then on her attitude made everyone there think that I was the culprit – the child who destroyed the whole magical occasion in one toneless squeak.

'I will talk to Father. I don't promise I will do all that work. And I won't do anything until I have settled down my Persian Blue.'

'When are you getting that, dear?'

I didn't know. I was held up by not having a way to get to Manchester. I gave my mother a gift she dearly wanted – I became dependent.

'Any day soon that suits you, Mother. I would like you and Father to give me a lift after all, so that I can cuddle the kitten on the way home. But I am the person making the purchase and we will visit two places and I shall go in on my own.'

My mother responded as if in a Victorian novel, clapping her hands together and squealing with delight. 'I shall just go and tell your father. We could go tomorrow.'

She went, and I took stock. I had just agreed to talk, only talk, to my father about the kitchen, that was all. But I had said I couldn't start until I'd settled my kitten. If I went with them to fetch the cat, there would be no turning back. I would be designing and creating a new kitchen for my mother.

I wondered if that canny psychologist had foreseen this state of affairs.

I put on my coat to go to buy a pet carrier and soft blanket to go in it – the other stuff was due to arrive today and if it didn't turn up, I was sure I could improvise.

18

Next morning, my parents were so keen to be off that they were marching into my summerhouse before I was dressed. I had managed to contact both Manchester cat owners – one appointment was at 1 pm and the other at 4 pm. Of course, I might have to go back to the first if the second was no good.

I made my parents sit and write down addresses. My father was computer-savvy enough to be able to find out exactly where both places were – one out in the sticks somewhere, the other quite near central Manchester.

I gathered up all my bits and pieces for my new blue kitten. I wasn't terribly pleased with the pet carrier, because it had looked a deep blue under the glare of fluorescent lights in the shop, but in daylight it was more purple. My mother smiled when she saw it and muttered, 'Well done, darling, it's a lovely colour.'

I was going to snarl back, but stopped myself. After all, they were just about to take me to find my darling Blue.

The journey to Manchester was totally uneventful. The very lack of events made it quite an occasion. Whether it was because Daddy was present, or we were on a happy jaunt, I know not, but Mother and I did not fall into our usual pattern of disagreeing with each other all the time. It made quite a pleasant change, although it did make me feel a little uncomfortable.

My mother was delighted I was having a cat. She seemed to have forgotten her early idea that I couldn't look after myself, 'Let alone a cat!' In the car she produced a stick with a long piece of thread on it, at the end of which was a woolly ball. The kind of thing she taught me to make with two circles of cardboard when I was just a kid. The ball had felt eyes and a long piece of garden twine coming out of it. It was very obviously a toy mouse to be used to tease a cat. And, what's more, it was blue! A slightly greyish blue, but a definite blue.

I take it all back – the car journey was eventful, now I come to think about it.

We reached the first place with no problem. The road looked like a council estate with loads of houses the same – some super-neat, others rather overgrown and neglected. We drew up outside number 101 and for a moment I thought about the TV programme and ditching things down the chute of *Room 101*. I pulled my thoughts together and climbed out of the car. My mother opened her door.

'No, Mother, I'm going in on my own.'

'I thought you'd be pleased to have some company, now we are here.'

'No, Mother. I'm only looking, anyway – we have the other one to go to.'

My mother shrugged. She didn't look pleased. I didn't hesitate; I walked up to the front door and used the shiny brass knocker.

The door was answered by the lady I had spoken to on the phone, Mrs Weston. She was a neat woman in her fifties.

'Hello, you must be Bluedelle Merchant, please come in.' She looked round me. 'Are your friends coming in too?'

'Oh no, they just gave me a lift. They'll be fine in the car.'

'Well, we can always invite them in if we're a long time, can't we?'

The hall was shiny with many mirrors on the wall. There was a smell of polish and everything looked clean and fresh. It was a small house, but friendly.

I was shown through to the kitchen. There, stretched out by a wood burner on a multicoloured rug was a soft grey female cat suckling three kittens – two creams and one mostly grey, like her.

I took a breath in. 'They are so lovely,' I said.

I was asked to sit down and my hostess detached the sleepy grey kitten and brought it over to me. I was transfixed. 'She's gorgeous,' I said as I stroked her.

'I'm afraid she is a he.'

'Oh. I don't know why, but I had thought I would be more comfortable with a female.'

'If you would like a girl, then both the cream ones are girls. One of them is spoken for and another lady is coming to see the second one this evening, but I think she would be happy with the grey boy.'

I was still holding him and stroking him gently. I could feel a trembling purr. He had no sign of stripes, but one front paw was white and he had a white bib.

'He is very beautiful,' I said.

He was very much cheaper than the other kitten I had booked to see and so very soft and cuddly. I nearly succumbed but then I had that 'never settle for second best' feeling.

'I think I will go and see the other kitten that's for sale, if you don't mind. I might be back.'

'That's all right, love, it's a big decision. Would you like me to tell my next lady that he may be spoken for? Then if you don't come back, I can give her a ring if it's the boy she wants.'

'That's very nice of you, are you sure?'

'If you come back and do decide to have him, I will want to ask you a few questions to make sure you are a genuine pet buyer. You won't mind, will you?'

'What do you mean, a genuine pet buyer?'

'Not everyone buys with good intentions. Sometimes people sell them on, pretending they are something they are not. Or they have them to farm kittens, or be a stud. Then they don't have a very good life at all.'

'What do you mean?' I know I repeated myself, but I was astounded at what I heard.

'Millie here was rescued from one of those places. She was already pregnant with these kittens. She was kept in a cage. She was very, very thin. She has put a lot of weight on since being with us. She is quite healthy now.'

I took the little grey kitten over and put him down next to Millie. He snuggled in to her. She gave him a rough wash, to rid him of my germs, I suppose. I stroked her head gently. How could anyone keep such a lovely creature in a cage?

'My cat will be very much loved and may even be a little spoilt,' I said.

My mother was astonished when I reappeared without a kitten and with no sign of collecting the pet carrier.

'What was wrong, Adelle? Have they sold your cat?'

'No, but he's a boy.' My mother's well-groomed eyebrows shot up to her hairline.

'Don't you want a boy?'

'No, I don't think so.'

'Off we go, then,' said my father. 'Let's see if the next place can see us a bit earlier than 4 pm.'

I wasn't too sure about this, but there's no point in arguing with my father, so I let him drive north out of Manchester. Eventually we reached a remote farmhouse, with a long winding drive. The weather had turned nasty and I regretted wearing my kitten heels – I had thought them appropriate but it hadn't occurred to me that there would be so much mud. I felt very out of place and awkward about arriving early.

'Don't you think, Dad, that it would be better to turn round and come back at the right time?'

'Nonsense, girl. If they are selling a kitten at a great price, they'll be pleased to see you early.'

I climbed out, thinking that at least it had stopped raining. My parents both opened their respective doors of the car.

'What are you doing?' I asked.

'We thought we'd have a little walk while we waited for you this time.'

I looked uncertainly at the house.

'Well, OK, but don't go too far.'

I released the catch on the gate and walked across the farmyard to the nearest door. A furious barking started from inside the house as I approached.

It took some time knocking on the door before anyone heard me. Eventually it was opened and a small, wiry lady peered out at me – she held the collar of a sheepdog who was straining to reach me. I stepped back. I was very aware of my townie clothes, all blue of course, and my flimsy shoes.

'Yes, what do you want?'

'I've come to see your kittens. I rang yesterday. I know I'm a bit early.'

'Oh dear, I wasn't expecting you yet. You'll have to wait a bit. I'll give you a call when you can come in.'

The door was closed gently but firmly in my face. I walked out of the yard and went to lean on the car. My parents were nowhere to be seen. The dogs were still barking. I was feeling cold, so I stamped up and down on the spot. This wasn't what my day was meant to be like. I was really, really looking forward to getting my Persian Blue and here I was, standing in mud, in the middle of nowhere, leaning on my parents' car. After about ten minutes, I became angry.

I marched back to the farmhouse door and battered on it.

It was opened by the same woman, who was probably Geraldine Fendley, who I had spoken to over the phone.

'Look, I'm sorry, please may I come in? It's cold out here.'

The door was opened and I squeezed in. The hall was musty with a vague smell of cats.

'Wait here,' said the woman.

So I stood in the hall and waited, and waited. I was probably there for half an hour. I could hear footsteps going up some stairs somewhere and the creak of floorboards overhead. Finally, the door to a room was opened.

'You can come in now.'

I walked into the kitchen. The place was clean although the furniture looked old and battered. Two dogs were in their cage in a corner. They didn't seem happy. A large black one growled at me. There was no sign of any kittens.

While I was looking around a man ran in. 'Trespassers,' he shouted, 'on my land!'

He grabbed a rifle out of a wall cabinet and rushed out of the back door.

'Stop him,' I pleaded with Geraldine Fendley. 'My parents went for a walk; it might be them.'

'I won't catch up with him now,' she said. 'Anyway, I don't think he'll harm them; he usually shoots in the air.'

Now, I may not see eye to eye with my parents, but I didn't even want them to have sight of that gun. My mother might have a heart attack or something. I rushed out of the back door, losing my shoes along the way, and ran after the man. He turned round, with the gun raised.

He dropped it down by his side at the sight of me. 'What are you doing out here, lassie?'

'My parents,' I could hardly get my breath. 'Don't shoot my parents!'

He came back towards me. I walked backwards, away from him. I missed my footing, slipping slowly down into soft mud.

'Here, come on, lassie, up you get.'

The man was smiling as he reached out to me and pulled me up.

'Come on, let's get you back in the warm. Where are your shoes?'

I pointed to my little kitten heels stuck in the muddy path nearer the door. He fetched them, carrying them carefully, then came back to put his hand out to guide me round the worst of the mud. I followed him into the house. The dogs were still growling.

'Look who I found out there, Geraldine – have we got any warm clothes she can put on?'

I was horrified. 'No, no, I'm all right.'

Geraldine put a towel on a chair and told me to sit down.

'Do you want a cup of tea or anything, or shall I bring your kitten through?'

I had almost forgotten why I was there. I was shivering.

'I think I would just like to go home.' I turned to the man who had guided me back into the kitchen and warmth. 'Please would you find my parents?'

I felt about ten years old. I wanted a Persian Blue so badly and was just about to see one, but I couldn't concentrate. I was too frightened.

The farmer, who I assumed to be Mr Fendley, hung his rifle back up in the cabinet and locked it. Smiling, he set off to find Mother and Daddy. Geraldine came back with a second towel, which she wrapped around me. It was warm. My teeth stopped chattering. She produced a mug of tea and passed it to me. I didn't think I could drink it because it was brown, but I took it to warm up my hands.

After a while I sipped it anyway. It was sweet. I pretended it was blue and managed to drink about half the mugful. Geraldine kept apologising to me and asking if I had recovered from the shock. I nodded, at first to please her, but I did gradually warm up and feel more myself.

Mr Fendley appeared with my parents behind him. My mother rushed in. 'Whatever happened to you, Adelle?' I tried to explain. Mr Fendley told her all about picking up the gun because they had lost livestock last week and how I had run after him, telling him not to shoot my parents. He made it sound as if I were something of a heroine. I smiled gratefully at him over the rim of the mug.

My mother gave me a hug and then I gradually unpeeled the now-muddy towel.

'Oh, Adelle, you are in a mess,' said my mother. 'Did you see the kitten?'

'No, I didn't.'

'Shall I fetch her, now?' said Geraldine.

'Yes, do, please,' said my mother.

The kitten was obviously older than the boy I had just seen. She was a soft grey – not as blue as the other one – but very furry and sweet.

'Look,' said Geraldine. 'She's a bit older than we usually home them and she's the last one. And we gave you a fright – not intentionally – and I made you wait in the cold without meaning to. I thought you had driven here and would have the keys to your car. How about £400 instead of £600?'

My mother loves a bargain, but I remembered it was important to see the mother cat.

'She's lovely, but may I see her mother?'

'Yes, of course, and her father too if you like. But not in the same room. We think Blossom's breeding days are over so we are keeping them apart for now. That's why I was so long earlier – I was trying to check his whereabouts.'

She disappeared upstairs and brought down a very sleepy cat. The kitten greeted her noisily and the mother cat licked her all over her wriggling body. She batted the kitten away with her paws when she tried to feed. The kitten came and purred round my legs and I picked her up.

'Yes, please, I'd like her.'

'Well, let me just ask you one or two things first. Have you ever had a cat before?'

'No, but I've looked everything up on the internet.'

'She loves cats,' said my mother, 'and she has a place in our garden so I can help her.'

'A place in the garden?' Geraldine looked from me to my mother and back again.

I explained. 'It's a converted summerhouse with a sitting room and kitchen area and a bedroom with an en suite.'

'Well, that sounds lovely. Your mother says she'll help you with the cat. Is that something you'd be happy with?'

I nodded. I didn't tell Geraldine that my mother usually barged in without invitation, and checked up on me all the time. I was sure she would be even worse when there was a cat involved.

'Do you have the equipment you need, and do you know the cost of her keep?'

My mother started to answer for me.

'Let me speak, Mother. I have already bought a soft cat bed, the necessary bowls, towels, worming pills etc and a supply of cat food. I do need to know which food she prefers. Can you tell me about vaccinations, too?'

Geraldine smiled. 'I can see you have thought all this through. I'll get your papers.'

Eventually we left, with my little Bluey protesting greatly at being in the pet carrier. I was still muddy from top to toe, though, so we stopped at an out-of-town shopping centre to pick up some clothes for me. My mother shot into an outlet store and came back with a big blue jumper and some jeans, plus socks and a pair of flat shoes. The shoes weren't blue, but grey. I reluctantly left the kitten, now sleeping, in the care of my mother and went into the nearest café to change in the toilets.

I washed myself thoroughly in the small space in the ladies' toilets, drying myself with the paper towels provided. There was only one loo, so I was a bit worried that there would be a huge angry queue chanting 'why are we waiting?' by the time I came out. When I finally emerged there was just one lady who said 'That's all right, dear' when I mumbled an apology.

I felt together again. Clean and ready for anything.

'Could we make one more call before we head home?' I asked my father.

'Back to the first place, I suppose,' said my mother.

'Well, yes.'

'You'll have to have him neutered, you know. I knew you'd want him as well, as soon as Geraldine knocked the price down for Bluey.'

'Yes, I have exactly the right money for a second cat. If I have two, they'll be good company for each other when I'm back at college.'

My father turned the car round and headed back into Manchester. I could see his reflection in the driver's mirror. He was smiling.

Picking up my next kitten was easy and good fun. We all three appeared on the doorstep and Mrs Weston was delighted to see us. 'Oh, you've come back for Harry; I was hoping you would.'

I explained I had bought one kitten already but really wanted Harry as well.

'Come on into the house,' she said. This time we were shown into the small front room, where there was another wood burner, which looked as if she had just lit it. As soon as we sat down, she began to ask questions.

'Where did your first kitten come from? And what sex is it?'

I told her the address.

'I know them. Lovely couple. They had some bad luck last week; someone set fire to their pigsty. Are they all right?'

We all three nodded.

'They're very good breeders. Registered. Their kittens will have had the right injections and been wormed and everything.'

I confirmed they were and showed her the paperwork.

'That would make sense, but unless you want lots of mixed kittens, I would suggest you have Bluey spayed too.'

'I probably will, but she will have to be older, won't she?'

We talked for a bit about what I knew about cats and how I would cope. My mother came out with the extraordinary proposition that she could always have one of the cats if I couldn't manage them both. My father grunted and Mrs Weston and I exchanged a look. I think Mrs W understood that if my mother wanted to help out by having a cat then she would, whatever my father thought. I moved the conversation on.

'If I have Harry, will he be able to travel back in the same pet carrier?'

'Bring in your kitten, and we will see.'

Bluey, by then, had woken up and was trying her voice out in a caterwaul – I was pleased to bring her in. My parents had accepted an offer of a cup of tea and a scone. I declined both.

'I have some blueberry muffins, if you'd like one of those?' said Mrs Weston.

I looked at my mother. She knew what I was thinking, I'm sure. She shook her head. So she hadn't said anything, yet I was being offered blueberry muffins. Close enough to blue for this extraordinary day.

'Thank you – a blueberry muffin would be lovely, and maybe a drink of water?'

Bluey was being quiet, peering out through the panels of the pet carrier.

'Why not put the carrier down and open the door? Then when I bring Harry in we'll see what they do.'

We left the door open but Bluey stayed where she was. We had our drinks and I ate the blueberry muffin, looking ahead of me and at the blue lamp that Mrs W had in the corner. Finally, she fetched Harry from the kitchen.

Harry was smaller than Bluey and stared into the carrier cautiously. He backed off and looked in. Then he had a little wash. Meanwhile Bluey was beginning to venture out. She walked around him and then batted him. He turned and batted her back. Within a minute they were romping and rolling around on the carpet. There was a little hissing from Harry when Bluey fell on him, but otherwise all was fine.

'Let me pay for him,' said my mother. Tempting though it was, I declined the offer. I wanted both cats to be firmly mine.

My father took a second scone, obviously thinking he had better grab an opportunity before we sealed the deal. He needn't have worried – it took a little while to be given extra bowls because I now had two to feed and a spare bed 'just for now, until you buy him one', plus all the documents including vaccination history and a leaflet of instructions.

By the time we left, it felt as if I was taking this sweet lady's baby. Especially when she gave me a hug and her phone number for me to ring in a week to tell her how things were going.

As for Bluey and Harry, they settled down together and were asleep before we had travelled anywhere.

19

We reached the outskirts of London. That's when the kittens set up meows to wake the dead.

'They're hungry,' said my father. 'I can't bear that noise, we'll have to find somewhere to stop and feed them.'

This is not easy when you are on the M25 roaring around the outskirts of London. My dad kept saying he'd find somewhere to turn off, but somehow it didn't happen. I was feeling miserable. Two angry, hungry kittens both went for my fingers when I cautiously stuck them through the bars of the pet carrier. I sucked the blood out, trying to clean my hands. I needed to clean them with something antiseptic.

In the end I had to manage. I fed a few cat treats to the kittens just to get them home. It wasn't the best start to being a responsible pet owner, but they quietened down and we arrived back with no further incident.

By the time I had been home for fifteen minutes, both kittens had eaten their food beautifully, used two separate litter trays, then zonked together in the blue cat bed. I could hear them purring in unison. I gave my mother a cup of tea and she reluctantly left my summerhouse having remembered every kitten she had ever come across and so telling me what to expect.

I felt relieved when she left. I couldn't wait to contact Sharon and invite her round. I didn't want to gloat, but to share. They could both be mine, but Sharon would be welcome to pop in and see how they were doing.

I rang her home phone. I could hardly wait for her to answer.

Sharon answered, sounding sleepy. Her voice was all muffled.

'Hi, who is it? It's late.'

'Sorry – it's me, Bluedelle – Dreamy. I have good news.'

'Oh, hello. What is it?'

'I've collected two kittens, one male and the other female, and I want you to share them with me.'

'What? Whatever do you mean? How can I share your kittens? I'm not moving in with you.'

That knocked me for six. I had thought she would be pleased!

'I only meant, well, you know, you can't have one, I can, so you are welcome to come and see them any time.'

'And contribute to their care, I suppose? And pay for their food. Honestly, Dreamy, I never expected that from you!'

She put the phone down. I looked at my mobile, amazed. How could anyone turn down the offer of sharing a cat? And I wasn't expecting her to pay anything, although I would have let her if she'd asked.

I went over to my dear little kittens. Harry was lying underneath with hardly anything showing because of Bluey being the larger one. She was fluffier too – her fur was really soft to the touch. She woke up and stretched. Her little pink tongue was poking out. She stood up and I lifted her out for a cuddle. I took her over to the sofa with me. She promptly pulled away and ran around the room like a mad thing, leaping about on the surfaces, even running across the cooker. I was glad the hob wasn't hot. How was I going to cook? Without a separate kitchen I would have real problems, especially when both of them were charging about. I resolved to cook everything in the oven or microwave until they grew out of leaping around.

I did some microwave cooking straightaway. The only problem was that Bluey had now settled on my shoulder so I had to do it with her in tow. I only had fish so she mewed for it, but I managed to get it in the microwave before she reached it. I didn't think I'd be able to sort out a potato while I was carrying her so I cooked a little red cabbage in the microwave after the fish and that was my complete dinner. Bluey did have a little of my fish but promptly returned it on my brilliant petrol blue rug. I wasn't pleased. Then Harry started mewing. I gave them both some diluted milk, hoping that was OK, then put each of them on their litter trays, but Bluey decided she preferred the newspaper surrounding hers. I shut them in my bedroom while I ate my food. It was going to be quite a challenge looking after kittens.

I realised it was nearly midnight. I settled the kittens in the sitting room and put fresh newspaper over the floor in the kitchen with the litter tray in the middle of it. I checked they had water, then went to bed.

As I rolled under the covers onto the cold sheet the kittens began mewing. I could hear them taking it in turns. As one quietened the other started up. They were scratching on the door. I buried myself under the covers but could still hear them. I wondered what else they were scratching, if they were having a go at the bedroom door. I had forgotten to buy a scratching post. What would my sofa look like in the morning? And were the kittens crying because they were cold?

In the end, I gave up. I opened the door a chink and the kittens shot in, scrambling up the edge of the patchwork quilt and onto the bed. It was no warmer in the bedroom, but after a while I had two little balls of fluff that had crawled right under the duvet. I stayed awake for ages in case I rolled over them. Finally, I thought of propping myself on one side with the pillows. I managed it and closed the door to keep our heat in. It was a cold night indeed.

The next morning I woke up to the most terrible smell. There by my bedroom door were wet patches and little mounds of cat mess. I started to tell the kittens off until I realised they couldn't get out of the room. It was my fault, not theirs. I had a lot to learn.

20

The day before Adelle's next appointment, I had a phone call from her. I was in the office when it arrived on Rachel's phone so I stopped reading the message book and went into my office to take it. I then realised the file was in the office so hunted through my desk for some paper and rejected pink, finding a blue piece.

As I picked up the phone, I realised what I had done. Not a trap to fall into – she was the one with the blue fixation and I must be careful not to be drawn in.

'Dr Lewis, Mike, I have something to tell you.'

Adelle sounded excited as she told me all about her 'incredible kittens'. In the end, I interrupted her.

'They sound great, but couldn't you have told me about them during the appointment you have tomorrow?'

'Oh, I'm sorry. I rang to say I can't possibly leave them. They need looking after – I've only had them just over a week so they haven't really settled in. I'm sure that after a few weeks I could start keeping my appointments again.'

I thought this was outrageous. I hoped this didn't come over as I answered, 'Delle, it doesn't work like that. You have a block of my time apportioned to you and I cannot keep it reserved if you do not attend appointments. You will need to find a cat-sitter.'

There was silence on the other end of the phone. I could imagine her thinking that a private psychologist would have let her have appointments whenever she wanted.

'So do I have to come tomorrow?'

'If you want the best out of the sessions, it is imperative that you come regularly. I am delighted for you that you have your kittens, but do not let them stop you from having the treatment you need. I'm sure your mother would look after them.'

'But my mother has already done enough – she and father took me to collect them.'

I was insistent. 'I should think they enjoyed that. And I expect your mother will be over the moon if you ask her to look after them. You cannot shut down your sessions or other commitments because you have kittens. That would be a backward step.'

'OK, I will ask my mother.'

'Good decision. I'm sure she will be delighted. I shall look forward to seeing you tomorrow.'

I was relieved. With several new clients my time was fully booked. I had made an exception in seeing Adelle frequently to begin with, but it couldn't last. Now that everything had begun to get back to normal after Christmas, I found that as acting head of department I had more management meetings to book in than expected.

I hurried to prepare to meet my next client, forgetting that I hadn't finished reading the office message book.

It was with some relief that I found Adelle sitting in the waiting area the next morning when I arrived at the office.

'I'm pleased to see you, Delle. Do come through to my office.'

Adelle looked surprised.

'I said I would come. I'd have rung if I wasn't coming.'

She was a sincere young woman and I believed her. 'Yes, I'm sure you would, but not everyone does if I have had to persuade them to come.'

'I think that's extremely rude.'

I laughed, before saying, 'Tell me how your week has been.'

Adelle filled me in about her trip to Manchester. She described in some detail the two different places with kittens for sale and then said in a very matter-of-fact tone, 'I was really scared when the farmer grabbed his gun and ran out of the farm.'

I stopped her there.

'A gun? He had a gun? Where were your parents by then?'

'They'd gone for a walk, on his land, apparently. I thought he was going to shoot them!' Adelle burst into tears and I pulled out the blue napkins from my drawer. She blew her nose loudly.

Eventually, bar a few times when she stopped for another nose blow, she continued recalling the events of the Manchester day. When she reached the point of telling me that the kittens scratched at the door so ended up sleeping under her duvet, I felt it was time to change the subject.

'Well, what an eventful few days. Have you had time to complete your task from last week?'

She stared at me, a blank expression on her face.

'You can't remember the task, can you?'

She shook her head, looking despondent. I felt like a head teacher.

'You were going to jot down some times when you felt anxious or upset, for us to use in this session. Never mind. You've done new things this time and you are on the way to regaining control of your life.'

'But I have control already.'

'What would happen if I told you to stop wearing blue and eating blue food?'

'I could probably do it if I wanted to,' she replied defiantly.

'Why don't you want to?' I asked, in a calm manner.

'I don't need to.'

'I thought you were upset you couldn't finish your interior design course.'

'I was.' This was not going well – her answers were becoming shorter and shorter.

'How are you going to get them to accept you back?'

'Show them I can do it. I did draw that design for my mother – part of it was in green.'

'Yes, you did try to use a little green.'

'I have moved forward with that. I showed it to my mother. Unfortunately, I'm now really worried that I am committed to designing and overseeing a kitchen transformation that won't be blue. I don't know if I can do it.'

Gone was the excited young lady who had entered my room twenty minutes earlier. She looked defeated.

'Within a realistic time frame, I'm sure you will be able to manage. In fact, you are changing quickly. Think what's happened in one week.'

My client said nothing. I gave her a few minutes to think things through.

'I even mentioned to my parents that I would go back to college.' Her voice was flat, hopeless.

'You have had an incredible week and made real progress. Let's see if we can build on that and take it at a pace you can handle. You don't have to go back to college this year if you aren't ready – in fact, the college is unlikely to accept you if you can't prove you have changed.'

I was aware that I had moved away from CBT, but worked with Adelle for longer than her allotted hour, designing a hierarchy with her, which, if she were able to implement it, would gradually establish an acceptance of non-blue colours. She worked on the hierarchy but did not seem committed to it. She looked at our finished chart and sighed.

'I think I will have to try it,' she said, 'but I won't know who I am if I stop being Bluedelle.'

'OK, let's think about who you are,' I said. 'Tell me about your friends.'

'If I think far, far back, almost to no memory, I can remember holding a hand that was like mine. It was another child, someone like me. We were little, in matching dresses – blue ribbon in her hair, mine yellow. We ran around together holding hands. We sat side by side while someone put our shoes on.'

I sat silently waiting. With one giant sniff, Adelle regained control of herself.

'What happened, Delle? Can you talk about it?'

'I remember her, but I can't. It's strange. I don't think I've imagined her.'

'Maybe you should ask your mother? What about more recent friendships and relationships?'

She started to tell me about the girls, mostly, that she had contact with. Apart from those who thought she was weird, the only two that seemed to be a part of her life were friends she'd made at school, Sharon and, to some extent, Cessy. She seemed to lose confidence as she talked about them.

'Neither of them have been like that friend I had when I was little. There has never been a close relationship with anyone else quite like that.'

'Yet you weren't sure she was real?'

'She was and is real to me. I just don't know if she actually exists.'

I realised I was stroking my beard as I thought about this. 'Let's leave friendships to one side and talk about interests and anything you do well. You are not allowed to say blue.'

She tried. And she more or less managed to avoid the 'b' word, although she did include references to ink-like and indigo. She gave up almost mid-sentence to tell me again how she was feeling when she thought that farmer was going to shoot her parents.

I helped Adelle see that she had acted nobly and with extreme concern for her parents. She was heroic in her actions. I made a note in the file to look out for stress reactions.

The home task was to continue identifying interests and areas where she coped well. I suggested she used Sharon to help her with this. I figured asking her to record anxious times per se could wait until they naturally occurred through use of CBT forms. Adelle left the consulting room with a laugh and a smile, plus a promise to make every cabinet in the drawing of her mother's kitchen look a little more green by next time.

I realised we had gone through the whole appointment without her using a musical adjective to describe a colour, despite the frightening incident with the farmer. Her unusual panic disorder seemed to be confined to exposure to bright colours.

21

When I got home, after making my mother green tea, I sat with my computer and two purring kittens on my lap, and researched college courses. I loved interior design, but I loved writing projects and essays, too. I began to wonder whether I could do a fine art degree.

Then I looked up something that had been niggling away at me since I left Harry's owner for the first time to go and see the other kittens. Who were these people who abused their female cats, letting them get skinny and overbred?

My research shocked me. It wasn't just cats; it was dogs too.

I read with horror. There were pictures of sad, scrawny animals. The cruelty prevention organisations had raided puppy farms and rescued the bitches, which were thin, bedraggled and miserable looking. They must have been producing OK pups though, or they would have been thrown out. That's what seemed to happen when their breeding days were over. I wondered how the breeders got away with it – maybe they had started off with a beautiful creature and bred her once or twice, then became hungry for the money.

I clicked on links to find out more. There was a puppy farm that was raided in Yorkshire. They had eight bitches in old pigsties on the farm. There had been some effort, the newspaper reported, to use Perspex to provide some outdoor cover and there were heated blankets, which did not appear to work, under the straw. The bitches were cold and messy and although the pups thrived physically because they were fed extra nutrients, they were not at all housetrained when they left. That didn't just mean that they dirtied everywhere; they had hardly been handled. The puppies had been sold for upwards of £800 – their papers were forged.

My eyes were filling with tears as I read about the awfulness of these creatures' lives. Bluey stretched on my lap and I stroked her.

'It will never happen to you, my darling, you are safe with me.'

Harry nuzzled against my hand. I shut my laptop and concentrated on fussing my new pets. I tried to feel happy, but despite the soothing rhythm of their purrs, a great sense of sorrow was overwhelming me. When I felt like this I usually threw myself into finding something out about blue food, or choosing a blue item of clothing and ordering it on the internet. Instead, I tried to think about my granny and remember something about her. My tears were dripping on to the kittens. I wiped my face with my sleeve and reached over for the cat toy my mother had made. Granny would have loved watching these kittens as they leaped to catch the swinging ball. I think she had a cat when I was a young child – it was ginger and white. I tried to remember its name – I would have to ask my mother.

I chose a cruelty prevention charity and made a small donation. If I found a job, I'd be able to give more.

The rest of the week was fairly uneventful as I became used to the kittens. My days took on a new pattern, adapting to a cat-ordered routine. There was very little time to work on the design for my mother's kitchen, but nonetheless I pulled down most of my art materials from the loft area of the summerhouse. I had no oils, but I could manage without for interior design. I found myself thinking about what materials and books I would need for an art degree. I shook myself out of my daydream by remembering that I would need a great portfolio of my work before I could even be considered. With a new determination I began to draw again.

I spent a little time working on the curtain design, putting it away as soon as I found the colours too painfully discordant. I nearly put everything away, but I had the soft pencils to hand and found myself drawing the kittens, using a much bluer, greyer palette with which I could cope more easily.

I was trying a watercolour of the kittens when my mother walked in. Her style of entry had changed over the week resulting in a stealthy slide through the half-open door; kitten-conscious. She had stopped coming in when I was showering too – or maybe I was up earlier so avoided that particular invasion of my privacy. I was still working on teaching her to knock and wait.

I'd not slept well the night before. I had woken several times and lay in bed imagining, or maybe remembering, someone with whom I ran hand in hand into the woods. This was odd because my mother hates woods, so we couldn't have gone there when I was small. Perhaps my friend's mother took us.

I made my mother a green tea and went to sit by her.

'Do you remember when I was really small, Mother, and I had a yellow dress?'

My mother's reaction was startling.

'You know I hate talking about the past, Adelle.'

'No, I don't.'

'Well, I do. What's gone is gone and what we have, we have.'

I looked at my mother. Her face was flushed and she would not look me in the eye. I had obviously upset her. I was puzzled.

'I was only going to ask you if I had a special friend.'

There was silence. My mother was definitely avoiding looking at me. Then she seemed to recover a little and glanced my way.

'Mother?'

'I'm trying to think. Friend? Well, you had lots of friends. When you went to school everyone wanted to mother you, you were so little and sweet.'

This didn't sound like the girl I was imagining or remembering.

'Who came on outings with us?'

'Outings?' My mother looked as if I had punched her.

'Look, it doesn't matter, let's drop the subject. If she exists then maybe we can find her in your photo albums.'

My mother nodded and made some excuse about popping home to put the roast in the oven. I didn't remind her that she had nearly eight hours before their usual evening meal time.

I could not get my friend out of my mind. I saw to the kittens, cleaning out their trays to distract myself. But that smelly act took me outside to the compost heap and the trees in the garden reminded me of woods, which sparked thoughts of my childhood friend. I tried to shake away the memories, but even the kittens reminded me. Their togetherness had increased day by day as they began to copy each other's movements and as Harry grew more to Bluey's size.

I had the strong recollection of the hand in mine. She held my right hand and I held her left. This left us both free to use our other hands. I am left-handed – presumably she used her right. I could remember scooping up leaves in the autumn – still holding hands but laughing as we did it together. Throwing the leaves up in the air, we would briefly let go of each other to try to catch them as they floated down – then my hand reached for hers and we ran, scrunching through the autumnal ground cover. I remember reds, orange, dark brown and the smell of rotting in the woods. We did go to the woods – I began to remember more. I was sure my mother was there, looking after us. What made my mother hate the woodland now?

I gathered up the mostly blue-grey sketch of the pattern design for the curtains for my mother's new kitchen. It wasn't finished – or anywhere near it. I had added a little sage green but it needed other colours to make it brighter. I didn't really want to show her it, but I wanted something to edge into a conversation with my mother about my childhood friend. Maybe she would let me see the photos if she couldn't talk about her. There must be some, if any of my memories were correct. The more I recalled, the less convinced I was that I was remembering an imaginary friend. There was something else I was remembering now

– my big bed at my granny's house and Granny reading me stories. I wished Granny was still alive; she would tell me all about it – I was sure.

My mother wasn't in the kitchen. Nor the hall or the sitting room. I became worried as I walked through the house. It seemed very quiet and empty. I stood in the hall and listened – there was a noise. A sort of moan, coming from the attic. I galloped up the two flights of stairs and threw open the door leading to what was once my studio and my mother's craft room. I didn't think anyone used it these days.

My mother was sitting with photos on her lap. A pile of albums was beside her. She was visibly startled by my presence and began gathering things up.

'What is it?' I asked her, noticing she had pulled her hanky out of her pocket as she turned away from me.

'Nothing, nothing at all. Just a trip down memory lane.'

'You've got to tell me, Mother – not just pretend it didn't happen.'

'Pretend what didn't happen? What do you mean?' My mother's face was ashen.

'I don't know. I have no idea what it is, but something is there in the background that you won't talk about, I know it.'

My mother regained her composure and shrugged. She turned her back to me and as she stood up, I saw her nudge the usually locked drawer of the desk; it slid closed and she turned the key. She picked up the albums from the floor beside her.

'We'll have a chat over a cup of tea.' My mother couldn't quite disguise the fact that her voice was slightly wobbly. I felt sorry for her.

'I'll go and put the kettle on – can I help you with some of the albums?'

My mother passed me the bottom three and I went ahead of her down the stairs. I clutched the albums close to me. Somewhere in them, I was sure, was a clue to the friend I had lost. Why had I never seen these before?

I was eager to open the albums, but my mother reminded me to put the kettle on and set out two cups on their saucers. Then she made a pot of tea and poured some milk in a jug, and we took them over to the table. I took a small jug of hot water too. If I had to drink black tea, it needed to be extremely weak.

I sat down at the kitchen table and took an album at random. It was immediately taken away from me.

'Not that one. I want to show you pictures of you as a baby first.'

I'd seen some of them before, because framed copies were on the wall in the sitting room. But here in the album were some photos of me as a baby that I had never seen. The extraordinary thing was that they had been cut in half.

'What's happened here, Mother?'

My mother answered slowly, as if thinking carefully what she should say.

'You were born about the same time as your cousin. But we fell out, her mother and I, and then I found she had cut her child out of all the photos with you two together. It was very strange, but at least she left me the pictures of you.'

'What do you mean, you fell out? And who was the aunt – your sister, or Dad's? And why did I never know about this?'

'I wouldn't have told you now, but you were curious because you remembered,' she paused, 'you remembered...' There was a slight pause as if Mother didn't want to say more. She added quietly, 'Caroline.'

My friend. She was my cousin. Caroline. The name didn't strike a chord at all. But I felt excited.

'She was the same size as me. We wore dresses like each other's. We both had long hair.'

'Yes. She was very like you.' My mother sniffed. She had obviously been very fond of her niece.

'But what about Caroline's mother? Who was she? Can we get in touch with them now?'

'Um, on your father's side, Hilary. Actually, she was his cousin, so Caroline was your second cousin.'

This was getting confusing. Even my usually organised and precise mother was muddled.

'Can we find them?'

'Oh no. We tried, your father and I. We couldn't find her, I mean, we couldn't find them. Believe me, they can't be found.'

I looked at my mother. Her lips were pursed together, her eyes half-closed, her wrinkles emphasised. I dared not ask her more, she seemed so upset. But my mind was reeling. Why couldn't they be found? I remembered back as far as I could. So many fragments. Things didn't quite fit. So many unanswered questions.

Mother started to gather together the albums, her back to me. 'I think that's enough for today. We'll look at the rest another time.'

I picked up the open album with the mutilated photos. 'Please let me have this one to look at. I won't spoil it.'

There was a pause, then her voice sounded quiet, resigned. 'As you please,' she conceded, 'but don't let the kittens near it. I don't want them scratching at it.'

I drank my horrid black tea quickly – even with extra water it was too strong for me, but I told myself the sooner I got rid of it, the sooner I could go back to my summerhouse and discover what else the photos told me. As I walked back across the lawn, something dawned on me. It wasn't just a friend who I remembered, it was a relative – my second cousin, Caroline. Or was she really my cousin and my mother didn't want to let me know for some reason?

22

I was hungry. I ate blueish fudge and wished I had chocolate. I couldn't remember when I last had chocolate. Would I have eaten it if it were there? I didn't know. But what I did know was that I was strangely excited, and with the excitement was a hunger – not just for food but to know more.

I pored over photo after photo. There were gaps where other photos had been. I found myself counting them. Then I counted the photos of me on my own – thirty-one. And thirty missing photos. I bet they would have been photos of Caroline. Maybe Caroline on her own, or with her mum.

Where were the men in all this? I hunted through the album again and found my father in the background of two of the pictures. I suspected that he had usually been the one behind the camera. I wondered about Caroline's mother and father. Were they together? If Caroline's mother had been really angry, she would have removed all the photos of them both. But then I realised – she probably wouldn't have had the access to the albums. The owner of the photos would have been the one to cut them in half. My mother.

I stopped myself from running across the lawn to question her. That could wait. What I really wanted to do was find my cousin. How would I do that?

I looked through the album several times, hoping to see some clue about my cousin. Nothing. I gave up. The kittens were clamouring for my attention and I was feeling the cold. I brought through my duvet and we snuggled under it, all three of us. Then I clicked on the TV. Warm at last, I began to relax as I watched *Felix's Finds*, the smooth voice of the presenter and the purr of the kittens lulling me into sleep.

I woke to the adverts. A smiling couple framed in a heart dominated the screen, the proud result of getting together through a dating agency. I yawned and stretched, remembering the photos and my cousin, or second cousin, whoever she may be. Then it came to me. If we looked so alike as small children, perhaps we would now. We needed a lookalike match.

Immediately I grabbed my laptop and started to search for something like that. All I could find were lookalike agencies that matched people to film stars. It was swamped with would be Elvises and Spice Girls. Not quite what I had in mind. But maybe there was a lost relatives' site? If there was, I would find it and if not, I would start one. I found a 'find your friend' site. I filled in all my details and reasons for trying to find my second cousin. Then they wanted details of Caroline. That's when I realised I didn't know Caroline's surname so I couldn't look her up. There was no way I would find her through this site. I would have to ask my mother – but I wasn't sure she would tell me. Anyway, I wanted to find out now.

I set up a website. I was doing it all night – at least, until about 4 am. The final version was very simple – I loaded my photo on and I asked for anyone to send their picture in if they looked like me. I had to buy a domain name and after a lot of trial and error, finding various names taken, I settled on 'RUmydouble.com'. Then I went on to my Facebook account to advertise my new website, inviting all my contacts to add their photo. I thought it would work. I suggested people looked at the photos and if they thought they were like that person, they uploaded their own photo beside it, saying 'Am I your doppelgänger?' Finally, I could have some sleep.

I woke around 7 am. It was still dark. When I stumbled through to the kitchen area, I could see frost patterns across the window. Harry shot out of his bed and into my bedroom, closely followed by Bluey. It was funny how soon he had become the top cat, despite the still obvious size difference. I gathered up my laptop and took myself back to bed, keeping my dressing gown on and grabbing my thick blue cardigan to go round my shoulders. I wondered whether to find my fingerless gloves, but nestled into the warm area under the duvet instead. Both kittens had beaten me to it, but in a few minutes they were snuggled up against me. I propped myself against the pillows and had a look at my website – not one single extra photo or any response to my photo. To be fair, it was not my most flattering – my blue hair looked flat and uninteresting and I looked very thin and gaunt. My skin looked terrible. People might not confess if they looked like me.

I didn't bother looking on Facebook – I felt too despondent. I lay down and stroked Bluey, who had crept onto my chest. Eventually, I got out of bed, wrapped in my fluffy dressing gown with a throw over the top of it. I ate some dyed cereal for breakfast, with milk that had a dash of blue food dye, and a few blueberries. I fed the kittens and cleaned up after them. Then I just sat with them, feeling cold and very miserable. I didn't even want to get dressed. I felt friendless. I thought about Sharon – she might be home on a Saturday.

She was, although I think she may have been having a lie-in. When I rang she sounded cross.

'Oh, it's you, Dreamy. What do you want?'

'Sorry, is it too early for you? Shall I ring back later?'

'No, it's OK – I need to be up anyway.'

There was a pause. I imagined her yawning. There were scuffling sounds, which I interpreted as her getting out of bed. Then a clattering sound, followed by, 'Are you still there, Dreamy? I dropped my phone.'

'Yes – I just wanted a chat, really, and to see how you are.'

'In which case, can I ring you back in a minute, Dreamy? I need to go to the bathroom.'

'Sure, we'll talk later.'

My phone went dead. I put it down and went to make a hot drink. I remembered I had ordered heaters so, as I drank my strange tea, I tracked them. I was pleased to see one would be delivered that day. I would have to tell my parents because things were rarely delivered to the summerhouse, even though I called it 'The Summerhouse' before putting their address. I had labelled the door to the garden as well.

So I had an excuse to talk to my mother, but first I would need to work out what I could ask her about my second cousin and the photos. There was her surname, of course.

And I needed to know who took the pictures. I suspected it was my father, but I wasn't sure. I couldn't think what else but, first things first, I needed to have a shower and get dressed.

I put my two sleeping kittens back in their bed and tried to tell them that they could fill the gaps in my life, and perhaps I should let the past alone.

But my loneliness told me otherwise. I had to find my cousin.

23

Thursday 22nd February

As I was preparing for Adelle's next appointment, I looked back through the notes from our previous sessions. I realised I was short of pages for her file notes, so went to fetch some from the office. I saw she was already in the waiting area. She was wearing a knitted blue scarf that was trimmed with multicoloured tassels. While I was in the office, I glanced in the message book to see that I needed to talk to someone in Human Resources. I decided that could wait and found the relevant blank pages. I returned to my room, inviting Adelle in on the way. I decided not to mention the scarf until she did.

I welcomed her to the appointment and asked her how she managed her home task.

'I managed it, but I found it difficult. I had to ask Sharon what I was good at, and my mother. I thought of more interests.'

She passed me her list, which was on an A4 sheet, divided into three columns. The first was titled, 'My own thoughts', then we had 'According to Sharon', then 'According to Mother'.

Her own thoughts were mostly about things she enjoyed. She had highlighted 'Gardening', 'Sketching',

'Painting', 'Biology', 'Physics' and 'Ecology' and added such things as her music and film preferences.

Sharon's list included 'A good friend' and 'Loves animals', while her mother had been very specific: 'Keeps things tidy now', 'Enjoys digging up lawns', 'Lovely with her kittens'. I wished she hadn't spoken to her mother, but Adelle seemed pleased to have some positive remarks from her and had taken them at face value.

However, the first two comments looked cynical to me. I made a note that we needed to discuss her mother, but used the most positive comment to keep to task.

'Your mother says you are lovely with your kittens. Do you see yourself as gentle with animals?'

'I usually am. I disgraced myself in the cat rescue centre, though, didn't I?'

'Not for me to know. I wasn't there. But Sharon says you love animals. Is she a good judge of character?'

Adelle was thinking. 'She is, I suppose. Although I'm not too fond of snakes,' she said slowly, 'or most reptiles.'

'So you can own that as part of your identity?'

There was the merest of nods from Adelle. I waited, expecting her to respond. Instead she looked up at me, lips pursed, eyes angry.

'Delle, is something the matter?' I asked gently.

'I know you are trying to get me to see myself positively, but – I. Am. Rubbish.' The last few words were left ringing around the room while I caught up with this turn of events.

'We are all rubbish if we only look at the darkness in our souls.'

Adelle looked at me. There was disdain in her voice when she spoke. 'Who said that? I presume it's some fancy quote?'

'I don't think it's a quote. I just came out with it. But it is something we may consider.'

As she looked at me, I detected her anger subsiding. She asked, 'Do you think we have souls?'

Fearing we may be entering a spiritual conversation, which was not what I was paid for, I turned the question round.

'What do you think, Delle?'

'I have that darkness in me. I always feel guilty, as if I should have done something. But I don't know what. Maybe it's because I felt so helpless that I couldn't do anything for Granny.'

'Your grandmother would have died whether or not you were there. All that would have been different would have been that your memories of her would be tarnished, not only by her illness, but by seeing her die.'

'I know. With my head, I know, but it doesn't stop me feeling guilty about it. And there's something else, something I can't remember. Do you think I've done something awful and I block it out?'

It wouldn't be fair to turn that conversation back to her. I gave her some rope.

'That's unlikely. Somehow you would have found out about it. It is more likely that you think something is your fault but it isn't.'

Adelle stretched her arms out in front of her. She rolled up her sleeve to expose her right wrist. 'I have scars from when I was self-harming.' I leaned forward – they were old marks, white lines that didn't match the rest of her skin.

'Both arms?' I asked. She rolled up the other sleeve. I looked at the less deep lines. I remembered she was left-handed.

'I don't want you to show me, Delle, but have you cut yourself anywhere else?'

'I did, on my stomach. My mother found me in the bathroom and took me to the doctor. Although it had bled a lot, it wasn't very deep so the doctor stuck it together. I had to go back and be examined every three days for a few weeks. My mother wouldn't leave me alone for months.'

'Were the arm cuts around the same time?'

'No, they were more before and after. It took a lot of willpower not to cut my stomach again, but I kept thinking of the fear shown by my mother and how scared she was to leave me. I brought this to mind every time I wanted to do it.'

'So when did you last cut yourself?'

'About eighteen months ago. But I was nearly found out. Mother used to come into the summerhouse without knocking and I was stuck in the shower with my arm bleeding. The plasters were in the drawer in the kitchen. I had to pretend I had cut my leg while I was shaving and get her to bring me the box of plasters.'

'Did she see your cuts?'

'No, just blood on the towel. When I came through to the living room, I had a long-sleeved top on. Plus an unnecessary plaster on my leg, of course.'

I made a cryptic note in her file to write to her GP and ask if there was more I should know. There had been nothing in the referral letter about self-harm. I wondered whether she had told anyone about it, and whether her mother had wanted to tell me at the first appointment. The fading marks showed the cuts were old and not deep in the first place. I scribbled 'obs' in my notes to remind me to watch out for signs she was cutting again, but meanwhile she needed assurance.

'You've worked hard to overcome this, Delle. The strength of your willpower will be an enormous asset in our quest to move forwards.' She glanced up at me briefly before surveying the carpet again, saying, 'How are we going to do that?'

'Let's work towards a more realistic view of yourself, particularly helping you to challenge your negative thoughts. They are a major factor in your depressed mood.'

She nodded.

We spent the rest of the session looking at what she knew about CBT and I made the decision to start her a third of the way through the course. As she was familiar with the course materials, we worked out some usual situations straightaway. I was glad she had already spoken to Sharon, who clearly saw Adelle in a positive light. She would think about Sharon when she had to consider what an independent observer would say. I don't let clients use me as the outsider as I consider that creates a dependency, which ties a person to more therapeutic sessions.

Adelle left the room, smiling and ready to cooperate. I wondered how long she had struggled with this most enormous thought of being rubbish. Maybe the doctor would know. I composed a letter for her GP and attached the handwritten draft to her psychology file.

When I took it through to the secretaries' office, I was surprised to see eight large boxes in the middle of the room. I edged round them to pass the file to Rachel, who was on the phone. She pointed at her in tray. I picked up a pen from her desk and wrote URGENT on my draft.

I turned my attention to the message book and was busy crossing off the messages I had dealt with and noting those still to be done when she finished her call.

'What are the boxes?' I asked her.

'Everyone's computers. Ralph had an email to say they would be here this month, just before he went off sick. Sorry, I should have told you as acting head of department.'

The long-awaited computers. People had been asking where they were. We seem to have been the last department to be equipped with a personal computer for each practitioner. I could see no advantage in having them at all, apart from an occasional email to someone, but the secretaries had been doing that.

'One of the Trust's IT people will be over for two days next week – the first to set them up and the second to go round and show you how to use them. Most of the others will know.' Rachel was moving her papers around, tidying her desk, dropping her pens into an old mug and slamming her drawers shut. I knew what the problem was. When we were originally told we would be getting computers, we had been informed proudly by the manager that fewer secretaries would be needed.

'I'm sorry, Rachel. We can't stop this happening. Will one of you have to leave?'

'We don't know. We have contacted HR to see if we could both cut down on our hours. But we'll both need other part-time work somewhere. I don't know how you will all manage. Especially when our hours change before you are used to your computers. And who will do the receptionist bit?'

I talked unions and rates of pay, then who I could approach. Rachel produced a list of duties, which included some time typing letters and documents, plus the unpaid overtime hours they had worked over the last three months.

'Documents?' I said. 'They will be expecting us to type those long assessments and court reports? It would take all my clinic time. My two-finger typing speed is about ten words a minute. What a waste of expertise not to use a trained secretary!'

I went back to my office. Ignoring my pile of client admin, I began a fight to keep both secretaries on their present hours. I might not be successful, but I would try.

24

I felt so much better when I came out of the session with Mike Lewis. I still didn't know who I would be when I stopped being Bluedelle, but at least there seemed to be hope on the horizon.

I had that phrase going round my mind: 'We are all rubbish if we only look at the darkness in our souls.' I wish I'd asked him how we could look at the light in our souls. But I should think that was more or less what cognitive behavioural therapy did. It helped us to think positively. But was that our minds, or our souls?

I think we were right on the edge of talking about spiritual matters in that session. I wouldn't have minded but perhaps he's not allowed to. I didn't have anyone I could talk to about things like that. Not even about philosophical things, although to be fair, I'd never tried.

He was the only person I had talked to about the cutting and he didn't make any fuss at all. He congratulated me on stopping – I think he understands. I wished I could understand myself.

Although she'd forgotten to ring me back on Saturday, I phoned Sharon.

'Hi, Sharon. This sounds stupid, I know, but what do you believe?'

'About what?'

'Oh, I don't know. Life, the universe, religion?'

'What's brought this on?'

'I told my psychologist I was rubbish and he said something really strange.'

'Which was?'

'We are all rubbish if we only look at the darkness in our souls.'

'He's right, isn't he? We've got to let go of things. You're not rubbish, Dreamy. We've all done bad things and you haven't done anything awful. I think he means we drag ourselves into despair if we only concentrate on the rubbish.'

'Yes, I know he meant that sort of thing. But using the word "souls" sounded spiritual, if you know what I mean.'

I felt a bit uncomfortable – maybe Sharon wasn't the one to talk to about this. But she said, 'It does sound like one of those wise things you see posted on Facebook. Maybe he's just a wise man! How are your kittens?'

'Harry is fast asleep on my lap and Bluey is chasing imaginary flies. If I put the phone close you might be able to hear Harry purring in his sleep.'

I put the phone to his gently vibrating body.

'Can you hear that?'

'No, Dreamy, I can't. Can I come and see them?'

I was so thrilled she wanted to come round that I forgot all about my identity and spirituality and invited her round as soon as she could come.

'OK, I could come tomorrow, ten-ish? It's my college day but the first lecture is cancelled.'

'I'll bake you some flapjack to go with your coffee!'

'Dreamy, please don't make it blue!'

'I won't, I promise.'

When I put down the phone, I wondered what I had done. Not inviting her around – that was brilliant – but it was a long, long time since I had made flapjack. And I might struggle not to put any colour in at all.

I hiked across the lawn to go and borrow a recipe and get some tips from my mother. I thought about her and the time when I cut my stomach. No wonder she was so protective of me. She was a darling really. If only she didn't get on my nerves and make me so angry. I knocked on the kitchen door; there was no response, so I stepped in and called up the stairs. This felt like déjà vu – the last time she wasn't around when I called, she was in the attic.

I realised I had forgotten to tell Mike about the photos cut in half.

As I began to go upstairs, I heard my mother calling, 'Adelle, is that you? I'm on my way down.'

I walked back into the kitchen and sat on one of the chairs. I looked at the cabinets and imagined my design superimposed on them. Maybe, maybe I could do it.

While my mother hunted for a flapjack recipe I wondered whether she ever had one, or whether her cooking was such an expression of herself that it all just happened without any guidance, like my artwork used to. No, like my artwork, full stop.

My mother turned round, giving up her hunt.

'I'll just fetch my glasses, Adelle, and then I'll be able to write a recipe out for you. You might need to borrow the cup I use for measuring ingredients, though – I don't know how much the oats would weigh.'

Yes, her cooking was an expression of herself, even down to the chipped, bright green, fluted china cup she used to measure the oats.

I managed it! I nearly didn't because I absentmindedly dropped a few drops of blue food colouring into the mixture – but then scooped it out again. At that point I did halve the mixture to have some blue and some golden-brown flapjack. Not that the blue was really blue – more sort of unbrown.

I put the trayful of golden flapjack on my work surface to cool. Bad mistake – I had to pull Bluey off it. Luckily, she had only reached the edge, which I cut off and promptly dumped in the bin. I moved my stool further from the surface, then put the flapjack on the top of the microwave as well. She was getting too good at jumping.

I remembered that a friend of mine had told me (some time ago) that when she had a kitten, her aunt appeared at her front door with a puppy. The kitten shot straight up the nearest wall and balanced on the picture rail. I hadn't thought that was possible. Now I had my own kittens charging around, I believed her.

I saw Sharon walking across the lawn and I sorted out Harry and Bluey while she politely knocked. Sorting them out involved untangling them from a ball of wool I had forgotten was in a basket under my bed. It was left over from trying to learn to crochet.

I was 'wearing' a kitten on each shoulder when I opened the door to Sharon. Not for long, though – Bluey scrambled down me and nearly out of the door and Harry was gently lifted off by Sharon who looked like she was swooning all over him.

'This must be the little boy. He is adorable. Oh, just look at his whiskers – they look too big for him.' Harry was purring and gazing into her eyes. I left them to it.

'Tea? Coffee? Soft drink?' I purposely didn't offer her anything remotely blue.

'Coffee, please, Dreamy.'

'Milk and sugar?' As my sugar was blue I was quite relieved when she only asked for milk. I was trying very hard to be 'normal'. I wanted her to properly forgive me for the rescue centre incident.

We sat down with our coffees on the small table, together with the flapjack. 'You'll have to keep an eye on them,' I said.

Bluey leaped onto the table and I scooped her off. Harry had nestled into Sharon and looked as if he'd settle there.

'Would you like to hold Bluey?' Sharon shook her head. 'Maybe later, this little darling is going to sleep.'

I felt sorry for Bluey, so I took her on my own lap to stroke her. She wasn't having any of it and leaped onto the coffee table again. I had to go and put her in the bedroom.

'Have some flapjack, Sharon. I made it this morning, specially.'

'Thank you, I don't usually eat it, but I'll have a little piece.' She took it and nibbled at it. It put me off, so I went and found a blue piece. I kept my hand round it while I ate it. I hoped she didn't see.

'You know what you said about sharing the kittens?'

I nodded.

'Well, I'd love to. Maybe I can kitten-sit when you go out sometime?'

I didn't like to tell her I never went out. Well, only to see my psychologist, when Sharon would be at work, and if I needed to pop to the corner shop. 'That's good to remember. Thank you, Sharon. But you'd have to come here.'

'Why?'

'You aren't allowed pets at your place, are you?'

'I can't keep pets, but I'm sure I could look after them sometimes.'

I found I was feeling very protective about my kittens. I wanted to share, to be generous, but I didn't want her to take them away. Anyway, she hadn't even touched Bluey yet.

'Well, we'll see. I don't go out much, anyway.'

Sharon shot me a quick glance. 'Don't worry, Dreamy, I will only be their minder, not their owner. You do need to get out more, you know. And find yourself a real place.'

'What do you mean, a real place?'

'With all respect, Dreamy, this is only a shed in your parents' garden.'

I felt my voice rise as I responded, 'It's more than that. It's a self-contained residence.'

'Well, if you think so. Where do you keep all your clothes?'

'In my wardrobe, in my bedroom.'

'I've seen the size of your wardrobe, Dreamy. You don't keep all your clothes in there.'

'Well, my summer ones are packed away.'

'Where?' she said, looking around at what was feeling increasingly like a small shed.

'In my old bedroom – all right, I see what you're getting at.'

'And probably most of the stuff you need less frequently is in the house somewhere. And last year, when your water froze, where did you go?'

'OK, I know, back into the house.'

'You are twenty-two, Dreamy – you need to become more independent. My mother pushed me out as soon as I left school.'

'Your mother wanted you to go to uni.'

'Yes, and she was quite right. I should have gone then and I wouldn't be trying to juggle work and learning now. But that's not the point – I reached the age when I should be independent and if I wasn't going to do that at uni, I needed to do it some other way.'

'This is my other way.'

Sharon sighed.

'This is your sheltered way. It's like you are an old person living on a scheme with a warden next door. I'm glad you've got this place because otherwise you'd be sleeping in the bedroom you had as a child. At least you've made a small step. But your parents know who is visiting you, when you go out and come in. Gracious, Dreamy, what happens when your boyfriend wants to stay over?'

'I don't have a boyfriend.' All my pleasure at seeing her was evaporating. I felt like a small child.

'But you could have. You will have. I know there have been people interested in you. But this situation,' she waved her hand around to include my entire lovely home, from my sky-coloured mugs to my indigo bedstead, 'it just shouts that you don't want to grow up. And so does the blue phase that's gone on forever.'

Harry had woken up and was stretching on her lap. As he stood up, I took him and carried him through to be with Bluey.

When I came back, I didn't sit down.

'Sharon, my life is as it is because I have a problem. I appreciate you are only trying to help me, I think, but I do not need you telling me my home is no good and I should be more independent. As soon as I have completed therapy and gone back to college, I shall be hoping to live in halls.'

I turned my head away from her. I didn't want her to see me crying.

I felt her hand on my back. 'I'm sorry, Dreamy. It just grieves me to see you so dependent on your parents.' She put her arm round my shoulders. 'Is there anything I can do to help you get back to college?'

I shook my head. I sat down beside her and reached for a blue tissue. I didn't want to lose Sharon – she was the only person who had consistently stuck by me during all those years.

'You said someone had been interested in me. A boy.'

'I can't say who, Dreamy, I promised.'

'It's your ex, isn't it? The lovely one who I remembered when you were stroking that ginger tom.'

'Even if it is Jack, I don't know where he is now.'

I went all tingly. I hadn't known his name was Jack; I'm sure she had introduced him as Spence. But I could remember one party when she came with him and he was really friendly. He was such a gentleman, but Sharon spent most of the evening chatting to her other friends. I had gone to the party with Peter, who I had known from school, but he wasn't really interested in me. We only went together because everyone else was in pairs. Sharon's boyfriend and I had fallen into conversation for a while, until Peter, rather drunk, barged in, breathing all over me and lolloping on top of me. I pushed him away and he ambled off.

'I won't be getting in his car to go home,' I said to Spence. 'I think I'll go now.'

'Would you like a lift?' he asked.

'No, that's fine. Sharon doesn't look ready to leave. I foresaw this and primed my father to be ready to pick me up if necessary.'

But that was ages ago, and now I knew Jack must have liked me.

'You all right, Dreamy?' I was more than all right, I was excited.

'I know how to contact him,' I said.

'How do you know that?'

I said nothing but went and fetched the postcard I had been using as a bookmark. I showed it to Sharon. 'This came about two months ago; I didn't know who sent it – I thought it was some sort of joke. I didn't recognise the name because you called him Spence.'

All it said was 'Thinking of you, Jack'. There was a mobile number underneath. It was addressed to me at my parents' home.

'It's him, Dreamy. Jack Spencer. I recognise his writing.'

We looked at each other. Sharon's wide grin spread across her face.

'Are you going to ring him?' she asked.

'I can't – look at me!' I was thin, too thin. I knew it. He might not like blue hair, my navy jumper looked tatty and my jeans were unfashionable. I was wearing my normal multi-blue scarf – it was beautiful, but now, with the eyes of a prospective boyfriend, I realised some of the stitching was coming apart down one side and the fabric was snagged. I looked a mess.

'You could phone him – he won't be able to see you. Anyway, you smarten up really well even if you are rather monotone. I've never seen you untidy when you are out. Didn't you have blue hair when he last saw you?'

She was right, I did.

'I'll phone him later.'

'Promise?'

I took a deep breath as I thought about this. I let out my breath slowly, calming myself before I took a risk. 'Yes, I will.'

Sharon smiled. 'Well, at least I've achieved some small step towards normality for you. Mind you, I think Jack does like people to be a bit different. Why did you think that ginger tom was like him?'

'I don't know. The eyes maybe. Jack has green eyes and spiky hair.'

Sharon started laughing.

'What's funny?' I said.

'You are – I reckon you fell for him at that party!'

'No, I didn't – well, only a bit. I didn't know him. He was your boyfriend – he was out of bounds.'

She didn't stop laughing. Her laugh was infectious and we were soon sparking memories off each other. I even began to recall good and funny things from those days when we had just left school. We were laughing so much that the kittens started to mew so we let them come through and leap all over us. A little curl of happiness was weaving its way through me and I wanted it to unfurl and blot out my blues forever.

Sharon had to rush away at 12.30 to get to college. By then I had given up trying to think of anything I had that wasn't blue because she needed some lunch. She quite liked the blue potato I offered her but had to eat it with butter because she can't stand blue cheese. I had an onion, some blue carrots and red cabbage so I got out my food processor and made a quick coleslaw to go with it – I used mayonnaise with hers but added blue dressing to mine.

'Dreamy, you're going to so much bother. I could have had that other dressing.'

'I try to please my guests.' I didn't tell her that my dressing tasted pretty bad.

'Do you ever wear those blue glasses you had at college?'

I remembered a phase when I could only cope with life if I wore those sunglasses. I had used them in the principal's office that day when she suggested I should leave. When I got home I had stamped on them, blaming them for all my problems. I hadn't bought a new pair – just everything else in my life became bluer in itself.

'I haven't got them any more. But I was thinking I might try with some again now.'

'I'll get you a new pair. I said I wanted to help.'

I was touched by her generosity. By the time she left, after a good cuddle with Bluey, I felt so much better.

Her parting shot made me think. As I took Bluey from her she said, 'You'll have to give her a proper name, Dreamy. If you continue to call her "Bluey" and are trying to get rid of the blue problem, it might conflict.' She was right – I needed a name for her. I remembered thinking that blue signified emptiness. I couldn't call this beautiful bundle of fluff 'Emptiness'.

25

Thursday 1st March

The morning of Adelle's next appointment had been bright and clear. Not bad for St David's Day. I had enjoyed the bus ride to East Croydon, managed to get a seat on the train to London Bridge and when I eventually arrived in the office, I still felt ready for anything.

I had prepared in advance – I wasn't quite sure why because even when I had been well prepared for her previous appointments they had dived off into completely different directions.

As a client, she was doing well. She was engaged in therapy, doing most of the home tasks and sometimes going beyond what was expected. The sessions had become a little eclectic, especially since I had never known about the self-harming, and her previous therapy using CBT made it more difficult to follow the usual programme. But I felt committed to continue along this path, with her decision to 'do it properly this time'. I would try to keep her to that.

I had mentioned her case in our full allocation meeting on the Monday. There were all eight of us crammed into the family room. The room was large enough, but someone seemed to have donated a toddlers' slide and a whole play kitchen, which took up a great deal of space. I didn't know where these things came from and as acting head of department, I thought I should. I made a note to ask the secretaries.

Talking about Adelle led to a discussion around the foolishness of trying to stick with one approach. All of the psychologists had used several approaches with clients with complicated or unclear diagnoses.

'I only use CBT. The statistics show a very successful outcome for nearly all of my cases, and CBT was recommended by the National Institute for Clinical Excellence,' said our specially trained CBT counsellor, Rowena.

'Yes, but an assessment has been carried out by one of the team and the client has only come to you if we are sure they would benefit from straight CBT,' said our second-year research trainee, Helen. It was her first week of researching the effectiveness of CBT across all client groups. As Rowena started to bristle at Helen's remark, Anita saved the day by saying how wonderful it was when the best therapy for a client could be ascertained and someone like Rowena could work her magic. I breathed a sigh of relief, pleased that Anita was so diplomatic.

I remembered to tell everyone about the new computers and told them to sign up for a slot for training. I closed the meeting, conscious that Adelle often turned up early.

When I walked back through the waiting area to my room, I saw she wasn't there. That was very unusual for her. I checked in the office – there was no message either. I wondered whether I had been ditched in favour of kittens, but then she turned up twenty minutes past the arranged time.

I showed her straight into my room. She was trembling. She sat down in her blue coat without even putting her scarf across the chair.

'I'm sorry, so sorry.'

'Don't worry, you're here now.'

Adelle closed her eyes. She pulled her coat around her.

'Are you all right? What has happened?'

'It's nothing really. I was on my way to the Tube and some young kids, four of them aged about fourteen, surrounded me, joking and calling me names. They didn't threaten me physically, but I was scared. I don't know what would have happened if a chap who looked like a heavyweight boxer hadn't told them to get lost.'

'I am sorry. I'll ask Rachel to bring you a drink. Hot water, I presume?' She nodded.

I phoned through to Rachel and asked her to put two spoonfuls of sugar in the hot water. Adelle was recovering, but she had certainly been shocked.

'Take it easy, Delle. Carry on slowing down your breathing. That's right.'

Rachel knocked on the door. I took the drink from her mouthing a thank you.

I passed it to Adelle and she sipped it, making a face. I knew she didn't usually take sugar.

'I'm surprised you managed to get here at all.'

Adelle had her hands cupped around the mug. She looked at me over its brim. 'The chap, Ben, he walked with me to the Tube. He was my protector.'

I thought about the risk Adelle had taken to allow him to walk to the Tube with her. I decided not to mention it.

'It's good that there is still some kindness that can be shown to us by a stranger.'

Adelle sipped her sweet water thoughtfully.

'I had loads of things to ask you today, but they've all just gone now.'

'Never mind. When you feel ready, let's start with nice, safe, familiar CBT and see how we go.'

'I did my task. It's here.'

Adelle handed over a folder. It contained pages and pages of instances where she had recorded her feelings, all suitably challenged. I started to read through then realised she had highlighted some.

'Are these the ones that need discussing?' I asked.

'Yes – it's not exactly that I was stuck, but nothing I thought would help me reduce how I felt about the incident.'

We spent the next twenty minutes going through some of the difficult ones and comparing those that had excellent outcomes. It was obvious that Adelle had been working on difficult situations and had sought positive ways to think about them.

'Did anything else happen to lift your mood during the past week?' I asked. This gave Adelle the opportunity to talk about her friend Sharon who had visited. Overall the visit had been a success, although Sharon did make a big thing out of Adelle's lack of independence, as she saw it.

'What did you think about Sharon's comments?'

'I was upset – sorry, you didn't ask me how I felt. I suppose I partly agreed with her. But she doesn't know the full picture. She has no idea I'd been self-harming, for example, or that I was still grieving Granny after all this time.'

'And possibly grieving a lost friend.'

Adelle became visibly excited. She put the sweet water down and sat up straight. She became animated as she told me all about the photos her mother had with people cut out of them. She had gone back to her mother with loads of questions and found out some interesting information.

'You'll never believe it,' she said.

'Tell me.'

'My mother and my father's cousin used to be really close and my second cousin was born around the same time as I was. We were very alike and we more or less did everything together. Mother and Dad's cousin babysat for each other. Apparently we were the greatest of friends even as toddlers.'

'So is your second cousin the person you remembered from when you were small?'

'Yes. There was some sort of upset between them and the cousin cut all the photos in half to take away the pictures of my second cousin. Although I'm not sure about that bit; maybe my mother did and she doesn't want to tell me.'

'Do you know where your second cousin is now?'

She shook her head. 'No, I don't and nor does my mother.'

'Did you ask your father?'

Adelle shook her head again. 'I haven't, yet. It feels like checking up on Mother.'

'That sounds as if you don't quite believe her.'

'Oh, I do, I think. There'd be no reason for her to lie, would there? It's just that one thing worries me,' she paused. I waited. 'It's her name. It's really odd – I expected that when Mother said her name I would remember her even better.'

'And what was her name?'

'Mother said it was Caroline. But I was only about three when we stopped seeing them. Maybe I am just expecting too much.'

I jotted a few notes in her file, more to gain time than anything else. There was something odd about the whole incident of the quarrel. Adelle's mother hadn't told her why they split up, nor how her husband's cousin had managed to get hold of the photos and cut them up. Wouldn't an angry person just chop them into little pieces, rather than neatly cut their child out of them? And the cousin, didn't she have a name?

'What was the name of your father's cousin?'

'My mother said she was Hilary. But it's really odd because Dad's cousin, who I called Uncle Frank, was a bachelor. I wondered whether he and Hilary lived together and weren't married at all. Uncle Frank died a long time ago, when I was very young, so I can't ask him.'

I was thinking that there must have been another cousin for any of this to make sense. But to say so to Adelle was not appropriate. What was my business, was to support Adelle through the discoveries she was making.

'You need to sit your mother down with a nice cup of tea and see if she remembers anything else.'

'If so, it'll be green tea for her and blue for me!'

We both laughed.

Then Adelle started talking about her kittens and how they were getting on.

'Sharon thinks I should give Bluey a different name as I am in therapy to get rid of my blue fixation.'

'You are in therapy for an abnormal grief reaction. You are making progress on the blue yourself. You wore a scarf with multicoloured tassels on it the other day.'

'I did, didn't I? And you'll be pleased to know my granny knitted that scarf and that was the first time I had worn it since she died.'

'I must note that down,' I said, making a show of doing so. 'Now what about that name? Do you agree with Sharon?'

'Yes, I do. But I haven't really had any other inspiration unless I call her "Baby Blue" and drop "Blue" when I am through my therapy. But it seems a bit wet to be calling a cat "Baby".'

'Are there other names for blue that would do the same thing?'

Adelle thought for a bit. 'I know, "Sky Blue". Perhaps I'll make it "Skye" with an "e". That would work.'

Adelle left the session with more CBT tasks to do, but she also set tasks for herself.

'I have lots of things Granny made for me. I had put them all away because they upset me so much. But now I have coped with wearing the scarf, I think I will try to get one item out per day and if it makes me cry, I won't worry, but I will keep it out of the box even if I don't take it over to the summerhouse.'

'I shall be very pleased if you only manage one more item this week. See how it goes, but I would rather you conquered small goals successfully than stumbled because they are too big.'

'OK, I will acclimatise myself to each item and feel good about it before I take the next one out. Nothing is awful in there, it is all trinkets, really, and accessories she made for me.'

As she was leaving the room she turned and said, 'I really want to find my second cousin. I have started a lookalikes website. I am using baby photos and up-to-date ones. Do you think that's a good idea?'

'Shall we discuss that first, next time?'

'Oh, yes, I suppose so. I've had no replies yet, although other people have started looking at the site.'

With a smile, she was gone. I hoped those kids were nowhere near when she left the Tube station the other end of her journey. She was so distinctive with her blue hair that they would surely recognise her.

26

I was relieved to get home safely after my brush with some teenagers on the way. I told myself I should look more like Sharon, who always carried an air of confidence with her wherever she went and whatever circumstance she was in. I did feel more ready for anything as I made my way back.

I carried on practising walking tall when I had let myself into the summerhouse. I made myself a hot drink with my back straight, but my efforts at transforming myself fell rather flat as Harry and Bluey tried to climb up my dungarees.

I gathered up my kittens, one under each arm, and went to look in the mirror. I wouldn't pass for twenty-two, however I walked. I put the kittens down on the bed and pulled my hair back; no, that was worse. It showed up my skinny face. There were dark rings around my eyes, too.

I thought back to my conversation with Sharon about Jack. I hadn't told Mike about that. He might be shocked. Actually, probably not. I didn't know. I thought he would be pleased for me if it meant I would change for the better. But Jack liked people who were different, Sharon said. No wonder it hadn't worked for her with him. She was lovely, but fairly conventional. It occurred to me that Sharon said she wanted me to be more independent but was encouraging me to find a boyfriend. I wasn't sure the two things were compatible.

Imagining I was getting ready to meet Jack, I pulled off my dungarees and found a skirt from my little wardrobe. This wasn't fashionable either, but was long and warm, which I needed today, despite the very efficient oil-filled radiator. It was still freezing in the bedroom unless I left the door open all evening, then it didn't warm up enough in the living area.

I found my thickest jumper and a pair of long socks and my bootee slippers then gathered up a throw to wrap up in while I made a telephone call to fulfil my promise to Sharon.

I started to ring three times. The first time Harry tumbled off my lap and I had to make sure he wasn't hurt. The second time I lost my nerve and the third time I waited with my heart pounding while I rang. Eventually there was an answer. 'Hello, I am sorry I am unable to take your call at the moment, please leave a message.' By now I was in such a state that I wouldn't have known what to say.

I made myself a hot drink and moved a chair right next to my heater. With my knees against it, I rang again. It was the answering machine once more, but this time I knew what to say.

'Hi, Jack, it's Adelle here, also known as Bluedelle. You sent me a card a couple of months ago with this number. I'd have rung earlier, but I've only just found out your name. Here's my mobile number.' I said it slowly and as clearly as I could, then I added, 'Bye for now, speak to you soon.' As soon as I put it down I looked at the card and realised what I'd said. He would think I was stupid saying

I'd only just found out his name. It was on the postcard. It wasn't what I meant at all.

I couldn't concentrate on anything. I wanted to go on my computer and see if I had matches on my lookalike site, but I couldn't put my mind to it. Sharon must have been right – I did rather like him when I met him at that party, but I was right too – it would have been totally wrong of me to think there was any future for us. But I knew I would love to meet him again.

I hadn't had any lunch and couldn't face cooking a potato, even if they did take hardly any time. I made a sandwich filled with the last of the blue dressing. There wasn't much, so I used a bit of the leftover regular coleslaw as well. I had to eat. The thin face and darkly lined eyes looked terrible.

I managed the sandwich by thinking about the flavour, not the colour. Even that little bit of mayonnaise had improved the taste. I made myself eat two pieces of flapjack, one piece a little bluer than the other. Then I ate some blue popcorn. I felt more full than I had been for months.

It didn't take my mind off Jack, not at all. I was remembering his spiky hair and his eyebrows being darker than his hair. His open friendliness. In the party I had worried that he wasn't more concerned about being with his Sharon, but now I knew more about their relationship, I understood. I became conscious that I was imagining different scenarios, all of them with the two of us together in a lovely place. On the beach, in a field of wildflowers, at the theatre. I imagined him in this place, my little shed in my parents' garden. He might like it. It wasn't too girly –

but it was too blue and plain. I made myself stop thinking about it.

I was glad I had the kittens to distract me. I tried calling Bluey 'Sky Blue' – she seemed to respond in the same way as she had to 'Bluey', which was to ignore me until I found a small cat treat. From now on, I would try to call her Skye. I nearly reached for my mobile to tell Sharon but couldn't bear to miss a phone call from Jack. I waited all afternoon.

I forced myself to eat again at 7.30 pm. Rare steak and jacket potato. I'd used all but one blue carrot the day before, so I munched on the remaining one while I cooked the steak. I checked my mobile before I ate. I didn't put the TV on in case I didn't hear the mobile.

I ate. Then I waited. I ate some vanilla ice cream, which I mixed with blue sauce. I waited.

I fed the kittens and sorted out their dirt trays. Then I snuggled up under the throw with the cats and tried to read.

The phone rang while I was getting ready for bed.

'Hello, Bluedelle, Jack here.'

'Hello, Jack, sorry, I did know your first name, but not until Sharon came round yesterday. I thought you were Spence.'

There was a chuckle before he said, 'Sorry, I thought you knew I was Jack.'

'No, I hadn't seen Sharon for months and she just said she'd be at Peter's friend's party with her boyfriend, Spence. Then when you and I were both abandoned, we chatted. After that I was ill for a bit and lost touch with Sharon.'

I was breathless with the explanation and embarrassed that I now sounded really strange.

'What did you think when I sent you that card?'

'I was mystified. I thought it was a joke. I couldn't think of any Jack I knew.'

'Oh, sorry,' he said again.

'No, it doesn't matter. You couldn't have known. Luckily I used the card as a bookmark or your phone number might have gone forever.'

'I was very pleased you rang.'

I didn't know what to say, so I felt very foolish when I said, 'Oh, that's all right.'

'Shall we have a coffee sometime?'

By the time we'd finished talking an hour later we had arranged not only to have coffee, but to visit Hampton Court. It was too late to ring Sharon; I would tell her my news in the morning.

After all my excitement, I couldn't sleep at all. I got up at six-ish in the end, having barely slept all night. I felt like a zombie, but stumbled through to the living area and put the heater on, then the kettle. I took my cup of blue tea back to the sofa and covered myself with my throw. Two kittens leaped up to greet me, wide awake, obviously interpreting my activity as a signal it was morning.

I reached for my laptop and tried to make a space among cats to use it. The first thing I did was check my bank balance. Being on Jobseeker's Allowance was no fun, especially now I had two cats to feed. My savings account contained a paltry £41. I went on eBay and hunted for some second-hand curtains for the French doors into my summerhouse. The blinds were totally inadequate. I found some the right size, but they had a burgundy-coloured border. I nearly moved to look at others, but there was a cold draught coming from the offending doors, which made me hesitate. By now the kittens were mewing for their food, and they were right; I had wasted an hour and a half looking for curtains.

My kittens looked pleadingly up at me, then Harry jumped onto my lap and snuggled past my laptop, right up under my chin. I let him purr round me, feeling his vibrations through his body. Then I put him on the floor with Skye. I watched them as they tumbled together; grey fur, one darker than the other, not blue but totally adorable. I told myself that my need for warmth, along with theirs, was greater than my need for blue. Anyway, blue equalled emptiness. I took no risks but paid the 'buy now' price of £35 plus postage and sent for those lovely lined velvet curtains. I had introduced burgundy into my blueness. I wondered whether my mother would notice. I realised I would have to ask her whether she had spare curtain rings and those hooky bits. Dad had put up the rail when he did the internal panelling.

I was hungry. I remembered Granny saying, 'Don't get dressed, we'll have breakfast in our PJs; I'll cook some eggs for an egg butty.' I had eggs – my mother had left me some, which I'd found on my doorstep the night before, with a little note telling me to eat them because Betty had laid them specially. I knew the hens shouldn't be laying at this time of the year. I suspected they were free range from the supermarket.

Trying not to focus on their yellowness, I fried two. I cut two slices of bread and warmed them slightly in the microwave to take the edge off their staleness. The resulting egg butty was filling and delicious. When the yellow oozed out, I mopped it with more bread. 'I can do this in memory of Granny – she would have loved you,' I told my kittens. I cried a bit at the loss of her, but even the tears felt comforting.

At last it was time to ring Sharon and catch her before she went to work.

'Oh, hi, Dreamy, I'm in a rush, I haven't showered yet and I'm late.'

'I just wanted to tell you I phoned Jack and we are going to Hampton Court on Saturday.'

'Brill! Talk to you later, must rush. Bye.'

I felt totally deflated. I reasoned with myself and filled in a few CBT forms rationalising my emotions of yesterday afternoon, last night and this morning so far. Then I rewrote this morning's and put the day before's away separately. I wasn't ready to share with Mike that I might have a boyfriend. I would see how Saturday went.

I went to shower and wash my hair. My roots looked terribly brown against the blue dye, but there was no way I could get an appointment to do the roots before Saturday.

The day dragged on, long and eventless. I was worried about meeting Jack, about my hair and the state of my clothes. It was around 4 pm when I decided to go out to try to buy some blue hair glitter to put through my hair and hopefully disguise the join between blue and brown. But I knew there was nowhere near that would do it, so I would have to find some in the big chemist's somewhere, or perhaps in one of the hairdressers. I needed new jeans too.

I looked into my purse – £12.47. I gave up the idea of a shopping trip.

I paced up and down my small living area, feeling cross with myself for ordering the curtains; now I had very little of my own money for Saturday. I couldn't borrow from my mother because I did not want her to know about Jack. I would have to break my pledge to myself not to use my credit card. I had been trying so hard not to use it since my father bailed me out when I left my second job and it all went out of control. I was again in a similar position to how I was then – I needed a job. But how would that work out when I had kittens to look after and psychology appointments to go to?

I was about to phone Jack when Sharon called.

'Hi, there, Dreamy, how are you feeling?'

'Awful, I'm terrified.'

Sharon talked me down. She said Jack liked my quirky mind and she was sure he wouldn't mind a few brown roots.

'And haven't you got loads of clothes in the house? They might not be blue, but I'm sure you have something.'

She was full of tips and suggestions, all given in a really excited voice. By the time she had finished she had resolved the problem of the roots, suggesting I merge them in with a bit of blue mascara – or wear a hat. She could remember me in a swirly blue and grey skirt, which I thought I still had somewhere, and persuaded me it would go with my long navy boots with a navy jumper.

'What about money, Sharon? I only have a few pounds cash and nothing much to draw on.'

'Jack is a gentleman – he won't let you pay for anything. But if you have enough, offer to get him a coffee in the tea shop. If he accepts, you will feel OK about doing your bit. And you can always say "my treat next time".'

I couldn't say that to him – I couldn't presume he wanted another date. 'I can take my credit card as a backup, but I have been trying not to use it.'

'There you are, then, you're all sorted. Do not postpone it, or you'll find an excuse next time and end up an old maid.'

I laughed. 'I won't be marrying him on Saturday!'

'I know, but if he has remembered you after all this time, it might be the start of something special.'

I stood there trying to imagine myself as a girlfriend of Jack. It felt nice. Then I thought about him coming to the summerhouse and that the curtains wouldn't be up.

'Sharon, do you think he'll want to bring me home? And come in the summerhouse?'

'Probably. But you can always tell him another time would be better. You're perfectly safe, if that's what you're worried about. He thinks sex is for after marriage.'

I was embarrassed – I tried to explain.

'It's not that, will he think I'm odd, living in such a blue place?'

'Dreamy, you are odd, living in such a blue place – but just remember, he likes you.'

Could someone as great as Jack really like me? Only a day to make myself more normal. Could I manage that? I wondered whether I had enough ingredients left to make some more flapjack.

I gave up worrying; I was too tired to think about it. I decided to ask my mother about curtain rings and to take a look in my old bedroom to see if I could find that skirt. I made sure the kittens were settled down and made my way through the dark across the lawn.

27

I could hear the television on before I reached the kitchen door. It was very loud and so was my father's voice as he shouted out answers to the quizmaster. I knocked but they didn't respond so I stepped in, kicked off my shoes and walked through the dark kitchen, calling to them. They still jumped when I opened the door. My mother looked particularly flustered and pushed her book down the side of the armchair. I wondered whether she was reading *Lady Chatterley's Lover* or something else I had been forbidden to read when I was young.

'Sorry to disturb you, I want to look in my room for a missing skirt. And borrow some curtain rings, but I'll tell you about that when I come down.'

My father turned his attention back to the television. My mother smiled and nodded, and I felt her eyes on me as I left the room. It was all very strange.

When I opened my bedroom door, it was like stepping back in time. Living in the summerhouse had given me space to do things my own way. This room was all my mother's choice. She had replaced the paper I had painted over with one very similar to the one I had obliterated. It looked quite good if you liked green flowers. The room was arranged with the bed made up and folded towels with a little guest soap. She had told me she was using it as a guest room, but I don't know if a guest had used it. I walked carefully across the new, fluffy beige carpet. When I opened the wardrobe door, my clothes had gone. I looked in the dressing table drawers; nothing except some new drawer liners to match the wallpaper.

There was a large wooden chest in the corner of the room. I opened it, expecting to find it full of blankets but, no, here were my possessions, washed, ironed and folded up. I looked through them, lifting out clear polythene bags, all clearly labelled and neatly stacked. At the bottom of the chest were four cushions, two green and two cream. I pulled out the cream ones, thinking I might try them in the summerhouse.

I found the skirt. I didn't know if it would fit, but thought I would prefer to try it on in my own place. There was a pale grey jumper, a lovely thick one – I wondered whether Granny had knitted the cable design. I put it with the skirt then added a pair of navy tights – I don't know how I had missed them when I last went through my clothes. I found a pair of mittens that matched my scarf with the rainbow tassels. There was a hat, too, knitted with rainbow wool with a blue pom-pom. I put that in my bag because Granny had knitted it to go with the scarf.

It was quite a load to carry by the time I finished. I looked under the bed and found a long-forgotten tote bag. Not blue, but serviceable enough to take everything.

I glanced round the room to see what else might be useful. Nothing on display was blue, but there was a cream-coloured porcelain figure with a baby in her arms, about twenty centimetres tall. I had loved this and pestered my mother to let me have it in my room. I picked it up, it felt familiar and I remembered how special it had been when Mother gave it to me.

I walked downstairs with all my finds. The quiz programme had finished and Father was watching the news. 'Your mother's in the kitchen,' he said. I gave him a quick peck on his bald patch and went through to find her.

'I've been through lots of stuff and filled a bag,' I told her.

'What on earth have you got in there? It's bulging. I thought you'd taken all your blue clothes ages ago.'

'I had, apart from a blue skirt.' I pulled it out. 'It has grey in it, but I am going to try it. Oh, and I have taken the cream cushions.'

'The cream cushions?' My mother's face said it all.

'Don't get excited, Mother – I'm just going to try them on my sofa. That's all. Burgundy would have been best, because I sent for some curtains from eBay.'

'Burgundy ones?' My mother looked as if her eyes would pop out of her head.

'No, French navy with burgundy edging.'

My mother recovered herself. 'I'm sure they will look lovely, dear, and your cream cushions will brighten up your sofa.'

I didn't remind her that the sofa was bright blue anyway, but I knew she meant to be positive.

'I'm not certain, but I'm going to try them,' I said. 'But I would have preferred pale blue.'

My mother sighed. 'I'll be glad when you give up blue.'

She looked weary. She lowered herself down to sit at the kitchen table. It felt like a deliberate act, an invitation. I sat opposite her.

'Please tell me why you don't like blue, Mother.'

She took a few minutes to decide to tell me.

'I never got over the loss of your cousin. And her mother, of course. Little Caroline always had a blue ribbon in her hair and she was often dressed in blue.'

'Oh, Mother, I am so sorry. I picked the wrong colour for my favourite, didn't I?'

'Maybe it made you feel better. You probably missed her too.'

I wanted to tell my mother about how difficult I had found it to make friends and how I longed to have a friend like that first friend. I wanted to cry with my mother because I realised how painful it was for her. But I couldn't, I dared not. All I did was nod.

'About the curtains,' I said. My mother sort of shook herself and looked across at me. 'I've got the rail up, of course, because Dad did that for me. But I haven't got any rings or hooks or whatever they will need. I'll want to get them up quickly because they are nice thick ones to stop the draught through the French doors.'

'When are they coming?'

'I don't know – I ordered them today.'

'I'll go through my curtain drawer and see what I can find. I can always get you some on Saturday, I'm going into town.'

I nearly told her about my plans for Saturday, but backed out. 'I'll tell her after I've had my first date with him,' I thought. I carried my trophy bag across the lawn, hugging my secret to myself.

28

Saturday! I woke at 6 am – I wasn't due to meet Jack until 11 am but I couldn't get back to sleep. Despite the freezing cold I got up and ironed my skirt. I had ironed it the day before, but it looked as if it had crumpled in the wardrobe. It would probably crumple as soon as I wore it anyway.

I put it on the back of the chair and two minutes later it was on the floor, doubtless pulled down by Skye, who was now sitting on the chair. I put it on a hanger and back in the wardrobe. Nothing was safe with the cats around and I was too cold to dress yet. I heated some milk, put down a little for the kittens and popped a drop of colouring in mine. With my dressing gown still on, I slid back into bed.

I thought about Jack, obviously, and tried to remember his features. I could recall quite clearly his eyes and the shape of his nose, but the rest seemed a little obscure. I reached for my little sketch pad I keep by my bed, rummaged in the drawer for a soft pencil and began to sketch what I remembered. Gradually his face came into view. I felt as if I were making an identikit for the police. I asked myself questions such as, 'What were his teeth like when he smiled?', 'Could you see the shape of his cheekbones?', 'Were his eyes more hooded than I have drawn them?'

I really liked the look of the person I had drawn, but somehow it wasn't him. At least, I didn't think so. I would have to wait and see. I flapped the pages shut over his possible image and went to have a shower and wash my hair.

This took ages as I washed my hair three times to try to get rid of some of the blue. I knew it was hopeless, but I still tried. My hairdresser had used a permanent dye of good quality, telling me that it would hold its colour for many weeks. She was right.

I dried it, encouraging my natural wave to take over. I knew that if it had a bit of natural flow, the roots looked less obvious. When I added blue mascara to the roots it did little except to make it obvious that I had added mascara to the roots! I tried a light dusting of eyeshadow, which was a little better. I hastily sprayed hairspray over it, very lightly, and the eyeshadow shone a little, which helped. The rest of my hair was bouncy and shiny, so I decided that would have to do.

The tights and skirt from my bedroom still fitted, with a belt through the loops of the skirt. I was glad it was a cold day, because I could build up the layers of clothes to make myself look a little less skinny.

I set to, making some porridge and toast. I fed Harry and Skye at the same time. For a full twenty seconds we were all three eating together then they were off, scrambling around, leaping about. I took myself and my smart clothes to the kitchen area and sat on the high stool, ignoring both kittens. I didn't want them to make me spill something down the skirt – it was easily the most suitable thing in my wardrobe and I was even getting used to the grey in it.

To cut a long story short, all my getting ready, including my make-up was over by 9.30. I felt foolish – I was ready more than an hour early. I was behaving like a young teen.

I phoned Sharon.

'Hi, Sharon.'

'Hi, Dreamy, today's the day. I bet you are totally ready.'

'I haven't got my coat on, nor even my scarf, in fact.'

'What did you ring for, then? I thought you'd be worrying about what you had on and asking me what to wear.'

'Oh no – I'm wearing the skirt you suggested.'

'Good. Mind you, I was going to ask you if I could have it if you didn't want it any more.'

'It might be a bit small.'

'Fear not, Dreamy. I am an ace on the sewing machine. My weight goes up and down like a yo-yo so I am always altering clothes.'

'I don't think I'm ready to part with it yet.'

'Don't worry – I'm not really after your clothes.'

There was a pause. I wondered why I had rung her.

'Are you feeling really nervous, Dreamy, is that why you rang?'

It probably was.

'I suppose I am nervous. I can't really remember what he looks like, apart from his eyes.'

'You'll be OK with him. If you feel uncomfortable, you can always get a bus home.'

'Um.' I was thinking about the meagre amount in my purse and how far that would go towards a taxi. I would hate to get lost in London and I definitely would not want my parents to have to come to fetch me.

'Tell you what, make sure you've got your mobile on. I'll ring you at about 12.30 and I'll ask you if I can come round. Then if you want out of the situation, you can always say to Jack that I'm expecting to see you at three, say, so you'd better go.'

'Don't worry. I wouldn't do that to him anyway. Although I suppose he might want to be rid of me.'

'He won't. He likes you. He'll want to spend the day with you anyway, even if nothing more comes of it. Trust me. Remember, I used to know him quite well.'

I tried a laugh. I knew it sounded fake, but at least she'd know I was trying to be upbeat.

'Thanks, Sharon. That's really cheered me up. I'd better let you get on with your day.'

I was meeting Jack in our local coffee shop. It wasn't that I didn't want him in my home, it was just that I didn't want my mother to see him. She knew I was meeting a friend and going to Hampton Court, but she didn't know it was a male friend. I'd see how it went. She was going to come over later and check on Harry and Skye. I hadn't told her about Skye's change of name, so wrote her a little note adding instructions about treats and feeds.

I quickly tidied round and changed the kittens' dirt boxes. I went back to my note to my mother and added about changing them again if they needed it. They were out of immediate sight, but I really didn't want any smell if we did end up coming back. My stomach went all wobbly at the thought.

I put on my long boots, checked my lipstick and hair, and went.

29

I thought I was really early getting to the coffee place, but when I walked in, I saw him immediately. He came bounding across, between the tables, and took my hand to lead me through the room to the softer seats. I extricated my hand and sat down opposite him. We hardly said 'Hello' before he was buying a weak black Earl Grey for me. I tried to watch him while he waited. He could hardly keep still. I'd forgotten he was so bouncy. 'Like my kittens,' I thought.

His hair was reddish blonde and as bouncy as him. It wasn't spiky any more, but longer and slightly curly. I could imagine sketching the waves. His eyes were a strange colour – not really green at all – more hazel. I thought that maybe the party lighting had distorted the colour.

Over our drinks, we talked and talked. I had not forgotten how easy he had been to talk to, but had wondered whether a different place and a different atmosphere would make him clam up. Soon we were laughing together. I had no problems looking him in the face, and forgot about the brown roots showing in my hair. I even told him about losing my place at college because of the blue. He became concerned for a while, then I took a risk and talked about Mike Lewis. I added, 'If I had met you a few weeks ago, I would only have been able to wear blue from head to foot. You may think that's what I'm doing now, but I have rainbow tassels on my scarf and grey in the skirt and I just drank black tea, which I rarely do.'

'What do you drink?

I realised I had said too much.

'Has Sharon said anything about me to you?' I asked.

'I haven't seen her for a year or so. She did say then that she was worried about you. Your eating, I think.'

'I'll tell you all about that later,' I said. 'Let's go and look at Hampton Court.'

He didn't press me. He let it go. I so, so wanted to be normal that when I went to the ladies before leaving the café, I threw away my two emergency slices of blue flapjack and all my spearmints. I determined I would try my best to eat whatever I was given.

I tried to pay for the drinks, but Jack stopped me. 'Today is my treat, every bit of it. It was my idea and I really want to pay for the day – please let me.'

We didn't see much of Hampton Court before Jack suggested we stop for lunch. 'I didn't eat much breakfast,' he explained. 'I was too nervous.'

'I forced myself to eat porridge. But I was nervous too!'

We stood by the boards displaying the food and I felt myself tremble. I wished I'd kept my flapjack.

'I think I'll have an all-day breakfast,' said Jack. 'Would you like one? Or any of the salads, or a main meal, anything?' He waved his arms expansively, nearly knocking orange juices off the tray of the lady behind us. She tutted and Jack apologised to her, then grimaced at me. 'You'll find out I'm a bit clumsy,' he said.

188

'That's OK, I can cope with that,' I said, wondering what he would think of me when I confessed fully about my blueness.

I pleaded still being a bit full from breakfast and chose a baked potato with just butter. When he insisted that wasn't enough, I added a blueberry-flavoured yoghurt to the tray. 'I might come back for a muffin. That's all I want for now.'

We sat down and waited for our food to come. Something seemed to have changed.

'I feel really bad,' he said. 'My plate will be laden with sausages, bacon, two eggs, mushrooms, tomatoes and all the other stuff I expect they'll bring, and you will have a measly jacket potato.'

'Don't worry, that's all I want. Anyway, I am having a dessert.'

'Only a small yoghurt.'

There was silence for a bit. Then he asked, 'Do you have anorexia, Dreamy?'

'No, not at all.' This was a day for taking risks, so I explained, 'I do have a problem, but...'

My phone was ringing. I realised it was time for Sharon to contact me. What was I going to say?

'Excuse me,' I said and looked at my phone. It was from home.

'Hello, Mother, what's the matter? Are the kittens all right?'

'Yes, yes. But it's your dad. He's had a fall – they think he's broken his hip. We've got to go in the ambulance up to St Thomas'.'

'Do you want me there?'

'No, I just thought you should know. You have the day with your friends. I put down extra food for the cats, they're OK.'

'All right, Mother, I'll be thinking of you. Give Dad a big hug from me. Love to you both.'

'Thank you, dear, bye for now.' I heard her sniff as she put down the phone.

I filled Jack in.

'I don't know what to do,' I said. 'I think I should be there.'

I took out a blue tissue and mopped my eyes. Our food arrived. Jack just looked at it.

'If you want to go, Dreamy, we can. Food doesn't matter.'

'No, let's eat this first and then, if you don't mind, I think I'll get across to St Thomas'.'

'He'll probably be fine; they can fix hips, do all sorts of clever things.'

I didn't tell Jack that Dad had already had a heart attack and had problems with his lungs. I started to eat my bare potato, pretending it was as blue as I was feeling.

Jack kept up a lively chatter while we ate. I rushed through a few mouthfuls of the potato and then ate the yoghurt, all the time trying to concentrate on what he was saying between his mouthfuls of breakfast.

'Come on, girl, I can see you're upset; let's go and get a taxi,' he said, before he had finished.

At that moment I realised I hadn't brought my credit card. 'I don't know if I have enough money for a taxi,' I confessed.

'Good job I have, then.'

I was in no position to argue.

The taxi seemed interminably slow to me. I was also worried about my mother meeting Jack; not my father, I knew he'd like him.

'I warn you, if you come in, then my mother will quiz you. She will know all about you in three minutes. Don't feel you have to become a part of our family trauma. I can ring you afterwards.'

'I'm happy to come in with you. This is our first date, remember? I don't really want it cut short and I don't mind about Hampton Court. We can go back another time.'

For a moment I was incredibly happy, despite having not fully revealed the extent of my fixation with blue. I didn't know whether I deserved someone like Jack. I tried to put these thoughts out of my mind and concentrate on the needs of my parents.

When we arrived, it was relatively easy to track down my father. He was in the X-ray department. My mother was sat on her own on a brown plastic chair, her face scrunched up into furrows of worry. I put my arms around her.

'Oh, Adelle, you came. I didn't want you to spoil your day with your friends.'

'It was one friend. Mother, meet Jack.'

My mother went into social mode and greeted him warmly, holding out her hand. 'I didn't know Adelle had a boyfriend.'

'It was a first day out, so he's not really a boyfriend.'

'Yet,' added Jack.

My mother looked perplexed.

'Well, it was kind of you to come with Adelle.'

'I met him years ago, Mother, at a party. You remember that postcard you brought over? Well, this is Jack who sent it. He's a friend of Sharon's.'

My mother wasn't listening. The door had opened from the X-ray room and my father was wheeled out on a stretcher. He was lying flat on his back, with a blue hospital blanket over him. His face looked so grey I gulped.

'Adelle is here, John,' my mother told him.

I leaned down to carefully give my father a quick hug. Two porters ambled over to us and with a cheery 'Back to A&E' they took the X-ray folder off my father's blanket and put it into the holder at the back. We followed them as they wheeled him out into the corridor towards the lift.

The time waiting in A&E was wearisome. I was sighing and so was my mother. Jack tried chatting to my father for a bit, then I took over with gentle, soothing statements, assuring him that all would be well. He closed his eyes and appeared to relax.

'Has he had anything for the pain?' I asked my mother.

'Morphine.'

Dad began to snore gently. With Dad asleep, I was able to focus on my mother. She told me about how he would insist on wearing his old slippers, even though they had gone all baggy, and he had slipped on the stairs. When it happened, he had screamed with the pain, but then he went quiet and she called for an ambulance.

'You did right, Mother; this was one time when you needed to call in the experts.'

She nodded. I put my arm round her and she leaned against me. 'Thank you for coming, dear.'

Jack had disappeared while I was concentrating on my father. I didn't know whether he was giving us family space or not. But he arrived with three cups of tea on a tray. The tray was wet with spilled pools of drink. He smiled at my mother. 'I couldn't find any blue or green tea, but I did find Earl Grey!' I wiped the bottom of each cup with a tissue as I passed them round.

'How did you know I preferred blue tea?' I asked.

'While you were looking after your father, I offered to fetch some drinks and your mother told me that she likes green tea and you make a blue tea.'

I relaxed. 'Thank you.' I sipped the tea. It was with milk but it tasted not unlike my pea flower tea. If I didn't look at it, I would manage.

We were at the hospital for another two and a half hours while my father's X-rays were looked at by the consultant and they found him a bed. He had a hairline crack and resignedly accepted the doctor telling him he would probably need an operation. My mother looked as if she was ageing by the minute. I left her by my father while Jack and I went off the ward and wandered around the corridors together.

'I'm sorry Jack – our first date, ruined.'

Jack held my hand and we carried on walking as he said, 'It's not your fault. And at least I met your parents.'

'That was a bit soon. We weren't really going out with each other.'

'I like the past tense. Does that mean we are now?'

'Jack, you don't know all about me and you may be upset when you do.'

'Dreamy, I don't mind. I can see there's a problem with blue and I should guess that probably goes deeper. I have my problems too. You already know I'm clumsy. I'm sorry I spilt the tea.'

I laughed. 'It doesn't matter. It was kind of you to fetch us all drinks.'

'I really would like us to be together. We can find out about each other as we go along.'

I gave his hand a gentle squeeze. 'That sounds like a plan to me. But until you know more about me, don't let's get too close or when we break up it will be really difficult for both of us.'

'What do you mean "when"? I should think we are very likely to make a go of it.'

I was less sure. But he was so lovely and had helped so much.

'Maybe. But I think you should go now, Jack. I'll stay with my mother and we'll get a taxi back home when she's ready. I don't know how long she'll need to be here. I'll pop in the shop and get Dad a few bits so that we don't have to come back until tomorrow.'

We had to return to the ward to fetch Jack's coat. He politely said goodbye to my mother and father – who was scarcely awake – and then we walked off the ward together. I went downstairs to the shop, which was by the main hospital doors, with him, and we kissed goodbye. Just a brief, friendly kiss.

'Let's meet tomorrow,' he said.

'I'll have to ring you because I'm going to be up and down here, I should think, for a bit. I'll try ringing late afternoon or early evening.'

'OK, then, Dreamy, over to you. By the way, Dreamy suits you better than Adelle. Girl of my dreams and all that!'

He moved away and waved as he stepped through the automatic doors, before I could tell him he was too soppy for words. But I felt slightly uncomfortable about him choosing what to call me. I preferred Bluedelle. I told myself not to be silly.

When I went up to the ward with as many necessities as I could buy with £12.47, my mother arranged them on the bedside cabinet. Then she looked helpless.

'I don't know what to do,' she said 'If he were awake we could say goodbye and go, or ask him if he wanted us to stay. It seems silly just sitting here.'

I think my mother was asking my opinion, which was a first. But I didn't have a chance to say anything because Dad croaked, 'No point in you two sitting here getting bored, I can do that on my own. Anyway, it's been a long day and I want to snooze.'

'Then I think we should leave, Mother, and I need to make sure you have something to eat. I bet you didn't have lunch.'

'She didn't, nor did I.'

'Would you like something, Dad? I can ask.'

'I wouldn't mind a cup of tea, but if I'm flat on my back I don't suppose I can have one.'

I found a nurse. She was very helpful, telling me where the nearest machine for tea was and the time of the next meal. I went back and told Dad I'd fetch him tea. 'That's if we've any money between us. I spent mine on your toothbrush and those other bits.'

That's when my father realised that the possibility of an operation meant he would be staying in hospital straightaway.

'Oh, good heavens,' he said. 'Just because I preferred my old slippers.' I saw my mother had firmly clamped her lips together – I admired her ability to hold back from saying, 'I told you so.'

We left the ward as soon as Dad finished drinking tea through a straw. He said he wanted another snooze before he ate anything. My mother looked relieved.

As we walked down the stairs, I put my arm through my mother's. 'He'll be fine, Mother, they do this operation all the time and we don't even know for certain if the consultant will agree he needs it.'

'I know, I know,' said my mother, her voice tailing away. I think she was too weary to even think.

30

When I finally arrived back at my summerhouse it was only 7.30 pm, but it felt like midnight. My mother hadn't wanted food, but I insisted on her eating a sandwich, and having a hot chocolate. I left her in front of the television with her knitting.

I had just picked up both my neglected kittens and made them purr when Sharon rang.

'Well, how was it? Sorry I didn't ring – I've had adventures of my own.'

'It's been a crazy day. But at least he's met my parents in hospital.'

This all took some unravelling, especially as I was so tired and the kittens were pestering me for attention.

'Phew, Dreamy, you've had a day of it. Are you seeing him again?'

'Yes. That's one good thing. I'm exhausted now; I'm going to ring him when we know what's happening.'

'You do sound whacked. I'll leave you to it.'

'No, wait. What was your adventure?'

'Nothing as chaotic as yours. But good news. I've had a big win on Premium Bonds. Well, my mum has had a big win; she won't say how much but she has promised me the deposit to buy a flat!'

'That's brilliant, Sharon. Does that mean you'll be able to have a cat?'

Sharon laughed. 'I really don't know. I haven't thought that far. I've been saving to buy my own flat for ages, so if she puts down the deposit I shall have enough for furniture. I've made an appointment with the bank to talk about mortgages.'

'Good.' I was yawning; I expect she could hear.

'You get some sleep. I'll speak to you tomorrow.'

'Bye, Sharon, and thank you for making me ring Jack.' I slept until 7.15 am.

The next morning, I had an early breakfast and sorted the kittens. I tried not to think about Jack – I had a father in hospital and a task to do – a cousin to find. I looked at several lookalike sites to see how mine compared.

An hour later I had worked out what else I needed to do to make mine look more professional. I hunted for a free image I could use. Nothing – loads of twins, but they were too alike – dressed the same, looking identical. I could do that easily enough with Photoshopping two photos of me, or maybe Sharon, as my hair colour might put people off. In the end, I found some fine drawing pens and tried sketching my own header. It was making me agitated drawing in black so I shaded it all in blue. That felt better.

I spent more time working on it, interrupted by my mother at about 10.30. She had phoned the hospital, who said they were keeping Dad comfortable; the consultant would make a decision about an operation and Dad was well sedated so there was no point rushing in. We had our cups of coloured tea together and she saw I was busy, so went away again. I gave her a hug as she went.

'Thank you, Adelle. I don't know what I would do without you.' She had another hug for that and when she left, I realised we hadn't criticised each other or had a cross word for the whole time she was there. I felt closer to her than I had for years.

For some reason, I hadn't explained the purpose of the website to her. I wish I had told her; it might have changed the way I went about it.

I had a name for it now: 'Dreaming of My Cousin'. It might not be the final name but I tried it under my header – it looked good. Perhaps it wouldn't say immediately what the website was about. I started to write an introduction and how to use the site. I said the first 200 registered customers would not be charged for using the site, but after that there would be a charge of £10. I figured it wouldn't be worth joining until we had a fair number of people registered. I changed the name to 'Hunting for My Cousin', then 'Searching for'. I tried it under my drawing of two similar girls stretching, reaching out for each other.

I was so absorbed in my task that I didn't notice the time. My mother appeared, all ready to leave for the hospital. While she put down some food for the kittens and fussed them for a bit, I grabbed my coat and threw some flapjack into a bag. I had a bottle of water in the fridge.

'Adelle, is that your lunch? I shall have to start checking up on you again. You aren't eating enough. Is your psychologist sure you don't have anorexia?'

'Yes, he is, Mother. And we'd better hurry, it's 1.30 and the taxi will be out at the front.'

My mother went running round to her front door and I put a few blueberries into a plastic box before I said goodbye to Harry and Skye, and locked up.

When we arrived on the ward, my father was no longer flat on his back. My mother was shocked and immediately took him to task.

'John, what are you doing? Why are you sitting up? Adelle, get the nurses to come and lie him down again. Honestly, I can't leave you for a minute.'

'Don't fuss so. I am allowed to be propped up. The consultant came and told me so.'

My mother plainly didn't believe him and hurried off to talk to the nurse. I was pleased to have my father seem so much better and glad Mother was having an animated conversation with the nurses, so that I had him alone for a little while. I sat on the chair next to his bed.

'Well, Daddy, tell me what the consultant said.'

'She'd looked at the X-rays and decided the fine crack is too insignificant to merit an operation.'

'That's excellent news. What is your treatment, then?'

'She has suggested that I stay in hospital for a few days to be under observation. I will need to continue with the painkillers. After that, I can rest up and she'll organise some physio input and advice from an occupational therapist.'

'I am so relieved. I was worried about you.' I gave my father a very gentle hug and he patted my back.

'Sorry to give you a fright, lassie. We old people can be a bit of a burden you know.'

'Daddy, you are not old; you are only in your fifties, and you are not a burden.' We sat there, smiling at each other –

with his head raised and pain reduced, my father was more like his usual self.

He noticed the chap in the next bed was watching us and called out to him, 'This is my lovely daughter, Adelle. As you can guess, she is an art student.' He was probably excusing my blue hair, but I didn't correct him; after all, I wanted to return to college on a different course. I wanted to paint freely, to have exhibitions, even to teach to earn my bread and butter, but I did not want to produce my art to order. My mother's kitchen was different – I would work towards doing that.

Mother came back and promptly told my father exactly what he had told me. He kept saying, 'Yes, dear, I know,' but she ploughed on regardless. When she paused for breath he said, 'Adelle, who was that young man you were with yesterday?'

Before I had a chance to say anything my mother was telling him all about my boyfriend. My father had been so full of painkillers the day before that I don't think he had registered the conversations going on around him. Today he was full of questions.

'What does he do for a living, Adelle?' he asked.

'Erm, I don't know,' I said. 'When he was at uni he was doing politics, I think. But our first date was a bit interrupted.'

My usually affable father didn't look impressed. 'Surely you knew all about him before you went out with him? How long have you been with him?'

'Yesterday was our first date. Although I'd met him several years ago – he's a friend of Sharon's.'

'Oh, good heavens. Your first date with him and you ended up bringing him here to see your old father at his worst.'

'He brought me. He paid the taxi fare. He was very...' I had to think for a moment, '... concerned, and could see I was worried about you.'

'Sorry,' he said.

I pecked him on the cheek.

'It's OK – I think I saw a really good side of him that I wouldn't have seen walking around Hampton Court.'

Dad turned to my mother. 'Rosemary, we must pay for them both to go again.'

'What a good idea,' said my mother. 'Perhaps we could go too; I haven't been to Hampton Court for years and years.'

My father shot me a despairing glance. 'No, Rosemary, we must let them have their first date. He sounds like a good chap. We mustn't crowd him out. I don't suppose Adelle would have introduced us to him yet if this hadn't happened.'

I grinned at my father. 'I certainly would not. Not until I knew he was going to be a long-term feature in my life.'

'That's exciting. Do you think he might be?' asked my mother, predictably. I felt uncomfortable – this was my business, not hers.

'Too early to say, Mother. I hardly know him, remember.'

I resisted saying that I wouldn't tell her even if I knew. Mother stared at me for a moment before muttering, 'Sorry.' I smiled, forgiving her in an instant.

All this talk of Jack had made me miss him terribly. I excused myself, saying I must go and ring him. My mother fished money out of her purse. 'On your way back, buy us a drink each, Adelle, and there's enough there for a sandwich and drink for you.' She turned to my father. 'She didn't eat any lunch, you know, got involved with something on the computer.'

'Easily done,' said my father, who hardly ever seemed to use his apart from emailing for catalogues, following stocks and shares and the odd search when he was stuck on a crossword.

I laughed. In that moment I felt extraordinarily happy and at ease with my parents. In fact, I felt at ease with the world. Maybe it was the sheer relief that my father didn't have to have an operation, my growing ability to cope with my mother, or thinking about Jack.

31

It was the day of Adelle's appointment, arranged for 11 am. I had arrived in work in good time for my session beforehand with the trainee, but we had just started when I was interrupted by Rachel.

'I have HR on the phone. They need an urgent meeting with you this morning. Can you go now?'

I went through to the secretaries' office to take the call. I argued that I had a full clinic that morning, but there was no way round it. I went back and finished talking about my trainee's most difficult client, then we curtailed our meeting and I asked Rachel to rearrange Adelle's appointment.

I made my way down to the small conference room next to Human Resources. I was surprised to find that no fewer than three of the managers were already there: one from HR, my immediate manager and the head of supporting services. The chief executive officer, who I had only ever met once, followed me in.

The CEO said, 'Ah, Dr Lewis, good of you to rearrange this morning to be here, do take a seat.'

I was mystified. For a moment I wondered whether I was about to get the sack. It was bad news, but not the kind

I expected. After looking at each other, the lady from HR spoke to me.

'I'm afraid we have to tell you that Dr Rollinson, your head of department, will not be returning to work. He has now gone into a hospice.' I knew his cancer had not been responding to treatment, so was not surprised, but the news still upset me. I expressed my concern for him and his family.

The CEO cleared his throat and began to speak.

'Dr Lewis, you have been acting head of department for how long?'

'Since Dr Rollinson first went on sick leave, so that would be nearly seven months.'

'How have you found that role?'

'In a way, I felt like I was just holding things together until Ralph, Dr Rollinson, returned. But recently, I have realised that this would be unlikely, so I have been trying to draw the team together and bring a new vision to the service.'

'We were impressed by your handling of a critical incident before Christmas. You went above and beyond the call of duty,' said the HR lady. She turned to the CEO and said, 'That was rather more than holding things together, wouldn't you say?'

There was a murmur of agreement from the group around the table.

I was dumbfounded. At the time I had acted on instinct, almost at great personal cost to myself. I thought Ralph might have handled things better. Before I could say this, the CEO spoke.

'You have certainly impressed us so far, Dr Lewis. But you say you have a vision for the service. Would you like to tell us about that?'

Relieved to be on safer ground, I told them about the last few months.

'Well, one way has been to tackle the waiting list through short exploratory appointments accompanied by the client's own assessment of their need and their present support or therapeutic input. We have just started this and it has helped us to prioritise the appointments and refer to outside resources if more appropriate.'

'Can you give an example?'

I was trying to think fast, with no idea where all this was leading. I decided to ask.

'I can, but I do have a full client list and a busy day. I would be delighted to come back at another time with a presentation on our new way of working and how we function as a team.'

There was a moment or two when the managers conferred.

The CEO turned to me. 'We have a problem here.' I must have looked startled because he said, 'No, not with you, Dr Lewis, definitely not with you. In fact, quite the contrary.'

I nodded, waiting.

'We are trying to ascertain whether you would be suitable to take over as head of department from Dr Rollinson. There are finances available, which will disappear at the end of March if not used. Before then we would like to have begun the process of appointing you as head of department, to ring-fence funding into the new financial year.'

'Does that mean I am being interviewed?'

There was general laughter, during which I said I wished I'd known, as I would have dug out my suit and a new shirt, which set them all laughing again. Then it hit me. I had not applied for this post, and I wasn't even sure whether I wanted it.

The HR lady said she would like to get back to talking about the waiting list initiative.

I gave them an example of someone with extreme back pain, who had been referred by her GP as he thought it was psychosomatic. Our short assessment appointment had identified that this was unlikely, despite her previous episode of extreme anxiety, and she had then privately paid for an osteopath and we found out that her back was better.

Two more examples were sought, and I was able to explain that we were now introducing information sheets on anxiety and depression for people to use while they waited for regular appointments, and in two or three cases this had led to such a change that the initial appointment had also been the final one.

'Your initiatives seem to be saving some NHS money,' said my immediate manager. 'I don't remember you telling me about this at our last meeting.' I reminded him that we were due our three-monthly meeting the next week and the short appointments had only been running since Christmas.

The CEO seemed impressed. 'So do you know how many appointments have been avoided and how much you have shortened the list?'

'No, but I can find out. It came out of the crisis of the long list from having had a psychologist short since Ralph went on sick leave. It will only improve the situation; we still need a new psychologist,' I added hastily. Our waiting lists were always long; the team were overworked.

I must have been in that room for around two hours. Partly it was my fault, because when they offered me the post I argued that there may be better people within the department. I was thinking of Anita at the time. They insisted it should be a psychologist, that I was the most senior and I had proved I was up to the job. I wondered whether I should tell them that two months before Christmas I was definitely not up to the job and that basically I'd been transformed by the hope and then reality of returning to my wife.

'Thank you very much,' I said eventually, 'but I will need to have time to think and talk to my wife about this. It will inevitably mean that I will be taking more on and so will affect both of us.'

'But you've been doing the job already,' said the CEO, somewhat abruptly.

'If I am to take the full role on properly, it will need some thought. Plus, correct me if I am wrong, but as this is now a vacancy, shouldn't it be advertised?'

Four pairs of eyes stared at me in astonishment. Then one of them laughed, as did the others.

'Wait a minute,' said the HR manager, and there followed another little sotto voce conference between them, from which I was excluded.

'We think that as you have been in an acting role for more than six months, that will not apply. We would like you to take the position.'

I thought of something important.

'If I do, I would like to keep on the secretaries we already have, despite the introduction of computers on everyone's desks. We need secretaries more than ever, because of the increased footfall of clients during the information surgeries and the number of leaflets we are producing.'

'We'll look into that,' said the HR lady.

So I was in a good mood when I went back to the department. I did not expect to be greeted with the information that Adelle had waited for me for more than forty minutes, because the message to her had gone astray. I was furious with myself for letting her down. I rang and left a message on her phone. I knew that wouldn't be enough, so wrote a note to myself to ring again and persevere until I could talk to her. I resolved to book all appointments on the mornings when Anita would normally be doing admin, so that any problematic sudden meetings in future would be covered by Anita.

Back at home that evening, I didn't mention the strange interview until we were drinking our coffee after we had eaten. I hoped to have a discussion with Ella about whether I should take the job, but it was difficult – she jumped straight in with her opinion.

'Of course you will take it, Mike. What an honour to be offered the post.'

'But I am worried that it will take more time when you and I are not fully settled back together yet.'

'You can't turn it down because of me, you would never forgive me.'

'But you turned down a post in Australia because I was back in your life.'

'No, not really. I wanted to get away and start again, but not necessarily go that far. I think you returned at exactly the right time to stop me making a great mistake.'

I put my arm round her and gave her a hug. 'I've got to make my own mind up about this, have I?'

'I think you are doing so much of the job already that it will not make an awful lot of difference. In fact, if you are able to recruit another psychologist to take your place it will lighten your load.'

'I can, but at a lower grade than I am at the moment. I suppose I shall go up a grade and become a consultant.'

Ella looked at me, shaking her head. 'Don't you know? Didn't you ask?'

'Well, no, I had no idea I was walking into an interview so was completely unprepared. But I did say I would only accept the job after I had talked to you and if I could keep both secretaries on at their present hours.'

'Oh Mike, you are a darling, fancy thinking of them.'

'I was rather dismayed to realise that I had let the situation go on for so long without having put up a fight earlier.'

'But that's settled, then. You have to take the position, or Patricia or Rachel will lose their job. I think being a consultant will suit you. I'm so proud of you. Congratulations!'

'They've only offered it to me, I haven't actually been given the post yet. But I'll ring or email Human Resources in the morning.'

'Don't forget!' said Ella, with a smile. She took our cups out to the kitchen and I could hear her humming as she put them in the dishwasher.

32

Dad was still in hospital on the Thursday after his accident. It was the day for my appointment with Mike.

I had neatly filled in CBT sheets – with hardly a mention of Jack. As requested by Mike I was bringing in photos of Granny and had also borrowed the album of me as a toddler – with all the missing halves of the photos. My mother let me bring some other albums saying, 'They'll all be yours one day anyway,' which made me acutely aware of the fact that one day my parents wouldn't be around. I became aware of the urgent need to sort out my relationship with my mother. They were only in their early fifties but my father's fall made them seem much older.

I went off to see Mike with mixed feelings. I sat in the Psychology Department waiting area, on my blue shawl, wondering how I could avoid telling him about Jack. I kept looking at my watch thinking he must be running late. After ten minutes, I asked the secretaries if he knew I was there.

The younger secretary looked flustered. 'I'm so sorry,' she said. 'I tried to ring you but then something came up and I forgot to ring you again. He will be a little longer; he had an urgent meeting with management that was only fixed up this morning.'

She looked upset, so I didn't say anything much but sat down again. It was a real nuisance because I wanted to get to see my father and I had told him when I would be there. I didn't want him worrying. I sat there feeling more and more anxious. By the time I had been there for forty minutes, I decided I had had enough. In fact, by then I had decided that Mike no longer wanted to see me and it was a ploy to finish the appointments. I was also disappointed that I had steeled myself to get there, knowing that Granny was to be the subject of the session, and now he wasn't even here. Surely he knew how important it was.

I went to talk to the secretaries again.

'I'm going to have to go – my father's in hospital and if I am late to see him, he will worry.'

'I can only apologise,' said the secretary. 'Can I organise another time for you to see Dr Lewis?'

I don't know why I didn't do the sensible thing and arrange something. Instead I said, 'No, don't worry. I'm sure he has more urgent things to do than see me.' The secretary looked appalled. I felt momentarily ashamed and then full of righteous anger.

I hurried out of the department hoping I didn't bump into Mike. I pushed through the double doors and let them bang behind me.

Only while on the Tube did I think back over what had been said and how I had behaved. Perhaps I had been a bit harsh. I didn't know now whether I would have any more appointments with Mike Lewis, which was a shame, because I knew he had helped me.

My father was propped up in bed with all his clothes in a hospital bag on top of him, apart from his coat, which was draped around his shoulders.

'I'm going home,' he said. 'I have to rest. I mustn't use the leg to load-bear at all. I have crutches and I think the occupational therapist is coming with a wheelchair with a doughnut thing on it to keep the weight off my bones. And I have a list of exercises. And another list of do's and don'ts. Plus I'm waiting for painkillers.'

I was horrified. How were we going to keep my father off his leg once he was home? I didn't want to question him, so I went to find the nurse in charge to find out what was happening.

She greeted me with, 'Isn't it lovely? Your father can go home!', which was not the point at which I wanted to start talking about it.

'I thought it might be dangerous for him to go home with a hairline fracture. How will we keep him from making it worse?'

'We aren't doing much for him here and he has been pleading to go home, saying you and your mother will look after him. Hasn't he told you that?'

'No, he hasn't. Does that mean he has discharged himself?'

'Not exactly. We have discussed his whole health with the team, including his consultant. If we keep him against his wishes we are likely to see a drop in mood. We have considered the small risk to his long-term healing of the hip against the possible long-term problems with his mental health.'

I could see the sense of that. But I wish they had involved us in the discussion. 'How much say do my mother and I have in this?'

'I'm afraid we have rather set it all in motion. Your mother did talk to staff yesterday, saying how much she wanted him home and how she could cope, with your help.'

'Thanks, Mother!' I thought, but said, 'Sounds like it's a fait accompli. What help will he have while at home? Will the occupational therapist be coming round?'

'I'll have a look. Normally the OT would have done a home visit before discharge, but this hasn't happened. I don't know if something is planned. Wait here.'

For the second time that day, I was left hanging around waiting. She was gone for some time. I could hear her voice from a small office, but not what she was saying. She seemed to ring several people. I wondered whether in fact I was being a terrible nuisance and should just gather up my father and take him home. Then I remembered how awful he'd looked the first time I saw him on the ward and decided I was doing the right thing. If he came home, he must be supported in some way.

It took time, but we got there. A home visit was arranged for the next morning, and an ambulance for transport. A wheelchair and crutches were to be borrowed. I had strict instructions that he was to sleep downstairs so I phoned my mother and told her to get our neighbours to help her to bring a bed down for him and set up the dining room as his bedroom. I had ignored my mother's exclamations of horror at 'turning the house upside down', as she put it, and been firm in telling her that if she wanted her husband at home, then these were the conditions.

Mother was desperate to come to the hospital, but I convinced her that her role was to get their home ready and I would travel back in the ambulance with him.

Dad, meanwhile, had been calling out to the other chaps on the ward that he was on his way home, and it wouldn't be long, he was just waiting for his drugs.

Two porters appeared on the ward while all this was going on. Dad became really excited, thinking they had come for him, but after talking to the nurses on the desk they went away again.

'False alarm,' I told him. 'Don't worry, it shouldn't be long.'

The nurse came over.

'I'm afraid your drugs still haven't come up. They should have been in the last batch. I'll just go and check down in the pharmacy.'

When the nurse came back, it was bad news.

'The pharmacy is waiting for one of your drugs. It is unlikely that you will be going home today, Mr Merchant. I will put you on the list for a meal.'

My father was visibly upset. I found his hanky and passed it to him. I settled him down then went up to the desk to try to sort it out. I should think those nurses were taught how to deal with disappointed relatives because they were very sympathetic, but assured me that there was absolutely nothing they could do.

I went out into the corridor and phoned my mother.

'I'm coming up there straightaway to sort them out,' she said.

'You can't do that, Mother – the pharmacy will be closed by the time you arrive. We will just have to put up with it. Look, I haven't been back all day; please can you just check on the kittens and give them some more food and some love? I'll ring again when I know what's happening. Take your mobile with you, with it switched on, while you see to the cats.'

My mother muttered about the NHS. I was inclined to agree with her after the day I'd had. But I kept calm and pleaded that it was time to get back to Dad. Before I did so, I sent a quick text to Jack. I really wanted to see him, but instead I just texted that I was tied up at the hospital waiting for drugs so that Dad could go home. I dithered over what to put at the bottom of the text, but in the end wrote 'Love Adelle'. As I sent it, I wondered whether it looked a little like a command.

I was about to put the phone in my pocket when I noticed I had a missed call and had been sent a message. It was Mike Lewis. He apologised at great length for missing our appointment, saying that he was very sorry that the secretaries had not told me in advance. He offered me a new time. I felt ashamed that I had been so rude earlier in the day and rang straight back, leaving a message accepting the new day and time.

I nipped down to the shop to buy myself a bottle of water and then went to sit with Dad. I had very little money again today, so I hoped I wouldn't be in the hospital for too long.

Dad was asking the nurse for some painkillers. I think being propped up for so long was taking its toll. But the trolley with the meal on was now in the ward, with patients being asked what they ordered. I told Dad to stay propped up for now and suggested we would get him lowered down after eating.

'If I lie down, they'll give up on trying to get me home tonight. Same with eating – perhaps I can refuse food, like a hunger strike, until I go home.'

I remonstrated with him and by the time the food trolley was at the end of the bed he had agreed to eat something. Although it might have been that he didn't want to offend the rather glamorous, cheery middle-aged blonde who was bringing round the food. He had focused on her while I was talking to him.

'It's Liz – I like her,' he whispered to me.

'What did you order, love?' asked Liz.

'Nothing,' said my dad. 'I'm meant to be home by now.'

'Well, if you're just going, we can miss you out then,' came the retort.

I intervened and told her that he might not go home so the nurses had ordered a meal for him. She relented and gave him his choice of cottage pie, without vegetables.

'And can I have two yoghurts for afters?' asked my dad. 'And a spare spoon?'

'I think your father's looking after you,' said Liz. 'Here you are, love.'

I was inwardly recoiling against the strawberry and raspberry yoghurts, but I took them from her with thanks.

'That was thoughtful, Dad,' I said.

'They were both for me and the extra spoon was for my gravy,' he said.

'Oh.' I put the yoghurts on his table.

'Just kidding, go on, choose your flavour. And if you go and get an extra plate, you can have a bit of this; it's too much for me.'

I looked at his plateful. I was in two minds whether to refuse, but my lack of food was making me feel dizzy.

The food trolley was just leaving the ward, so I scurried across and gained a plate plus a generous dollop of leftover potato from the cottage pie. 'I reckon you've been hanging around all day with nowt to eat, and look at you – thin as a rake,' said Liz.

I managed to eat that dollop of potato and a little of the meat from Dad's plate by concentrating on the blue curtains round someone's bed. I was pleased I was getting nearer to eating normally, but also began to feel a little better. Even the strawberry yoghurt went down all right while I imagined it bright blue, tinged with cobalt, sky blue and turquoise.

Two porters were back on the ward. They were by the nurses' desk again. One of the nurses spoke to the porters and came over to us brandishing a white paper bag.

'Look what I have,' she said, grinning triumphantly. 'They went to the wrong ward!' She talked my father and I through the medication routine and then called the porters.

It took hardly any time for my very happy father to be transferred to the stretcher and wheeled down the corridor. The porters were very jolly, joking with him and teasing him. I walked behind, feeling weary. Why is it that hospitals drain the visitors of all energy when they are trying to heal the patients?

The ambulance whisked us home without a hitch. The paramedics wheeled my father into the house.

My mother had done a good job. The bed was in the dining room and she had remembered to bring down the pillow support Dad always used. There was no sign of her.

I then remembered I hadn't rung. She was probably in the summerhouse.

By the time she puffed into the kitchen, she was quite angry with me, and the paramedics were just about to go.

'Wait a minute,' she said. 'I have questions.'

'It's all right, Mother, I have had full instructions from the nurse, and the occupational therapist is coming tomorrow.'

She ignored me and quizzed the poor paramedics, who knew very little about his care.

In the end one of them rang through to the ward on the house phone, leaving my mother to talk to the nurse in charge while they left.

It took a while to settle her and Dad into some sort of new way of being. She was now technically his carer/nurse, at least overnight. I finally managed to draw myself away to the sanctuary of the summerhouse.

Once there, I snuggled under the throw and let the kittens push their faces round my neck. It felt like midnight but was actually 8.45 pm. It was only then that I noticed my new curtains were up. My mother had opened my parcel! I was upset with her for only a few seconds as I realised she had hung them for me. 'Thank you, dear Mother,' I thought. I picked up my mobile to ring her, when I remembered I hadn't phoned Jack. I rang his number first.

'Hi Jack, I'm home.' I felt too weary to talk.

'Shall I pop and see you, then? I can't wait.'

I couldn't believe what I said next. 'No, not tonight. I'm exhausted from the day. I just need to have some sleep. I'll tell you all about it tomorrow evening, if you are free to come.'

He tried chatting to me. I just couldn't concentrate. In the end he said, 'Sweet dreams, dreamy one, I shall see you tomorrow evening – I'll be over around 7.30 – is that OK?'

'Yes, see you then, goodnight, Jack.' As I ended the call, I wondered why I was accepting him calling me 'dreamy one', when I had fought against it at school. The only person who was allowed to call me 'Dreamy' was Sharon.

I was too exhausted to work it out. I went to bed.

33

The next day, Mother spent much of the morning on the phone because there was no sign of the occupational therapist by 10 am, when the nurse's notes said the visit was arranged for 9 am. I had been dispatched to the chemist even before then for a urine bottle because Dad didn't seem to manage successfully with a pot. We had no idea whether he could be moved to use the commode, which I'd brought down from the attic and polished until its dusty wooden frame had revealed itself to be a beautiful example of reddish-brown mahogany.

My mother was becoming very agitated, so I suggested she phoned her GP. A sister from the surgery appeared within an hour. She efficiently showed my father how to use the crutches to weight-bear when he got out of bed to reach the commode. She rearranged his bed and pillows and I helped her turn the bed so that my father could see outside and the commode could be placed closer to him. She asked my mother to find a small table for all his bits and pieces so that he would be encouraged to stay and rest. I fetched him pen, paper, the newspaper, a puzzle book, a John Grisham novel he'd probably already read, the *Financial Times* and his mobile phone. Meanwhile, my mother fussed around, neatly folding an extra blanket over his feet and constantly asking him if he was comfortable.

The nurse removed the folded blanket and explained that Dad didn't need extra weight. Mother brought the towel rail into the room, poking it behind the commode and laying the blanket over it, 'Just in case you're cold, dear. You can reach it from there.'

'I think we're there,' the nurse announced, after about forty minutes when the room had been rearranged and all was shipshape. At that point, the doorbell rang. It was the occupational therapist.

My mother made them both a cup of tea and they sat in the kitchen discussing Dad's care. Then the OT came back to Dad and had a look at all the aids we'd accumulated, before fetching a walker from her car. She explained to me and my mother how we should manage Dad. I asked her to go over it again while I wrote it down, but she produced a list of her advice. My mother looked down at it, perhaps realising for the first time how much care she would have to give my father.

'How long will we have to look after him like this?' asked my mother.

'Probably six weeks,' the OT said cheerfully, 'then he will have an X-ray to check there's healing going on and he will either need bed rest for longer or can just be using his crutches for a while until he can cope with a walking stick.'

My father groaned, 'Six weeks? I've got to lie here for six weeks?' My mother shook her finger at him. 'It's all because you were a silly old man and didn't want to buy new slippers!'

Which led to the occupational therapist demanding to see the slippers, putting them in the kitchen bin, and showing me on her phone which ones I should buy for him, 'Pronto!'

Duly told off, we were quietened. Both the nurse and the OT left at the same time and I could see them stood by the front gate, nattering; no doubt talking about our collective incompetence.

I kissed my father on the top of his head and made my excuses. The beguiling blues of my summerhouse had never been so inviting.

I spent the afternoon completing my new website. I made up my face, curled my hair a bit to try to disguise the brown roots, and took a picture with my webcam, creating a fresh photo for the website. I filled in my own form, explaining I was looking for my cousin and she had been my best friend until I was about three years old, when they had moved away. I sent a text to Sharon suggesting she look at it, and asked her to upload her photo if she didn't mind. I asked her if she could possibly invite other friends to join. I wasn't sure whether I'd ask Jack.

My face looked a little less gaunt now that I'd curled my hair. I closed up my computer and began to think about when Jack was coming. I carried on with my heated hair tongs until my hairstyle looked really soft and natural, apart from the colour. It didn't seem quite so shiny but it made me feel a little different. I was pleased because otherwise I was Bluedelle and blue equalled emptiness. Something was changing – I was beginning to accept 'Delle' and even trying out 'Adelle'.

I told myself I had to eat. Even as I thought about this, I wondered whether I had inadvertently invited Jack for a meal. Despite the fact that I was trying to fight blue, it felt really good to think about eating some bluey-purple mash – much better than the goo they served up in hospital. But then, that might be due to the better-quality potatoes, not just the colour. I had two blue pieces of flapjack left. I ate one before making myself a sandwich and eating some vegetable crisps without putting any extra dressing on them.

I organised myself to bake shortbread and some flapjack, without colouring either of them blue. I had crisps and snacky things already, but I had no idea at all whether Jack would have wine in the evening or would prefer coffee and biscuits. He'd definitely have wine if we ate a meal. I had an unopened Merlot that Sharon had given me for Christmas. The summerhouse felt claustrophobic with the smell of baking. It was too cold to have the doors and windows open, so I tried to make it fresher with some room spray. It would have to do.

I tidied around a bit, doing the usual clearing up from the kittens. They were asleep, having eaten before I had. They looked very cute, cuddled together. The two cream cushions I had brought from my old bedroom looked OK on the sofa, although I wasn't used to the colour. I found a shawl, my only non-blue one. It was basically cream, with burgundy and blue checks through it. I folded it over the arm of my sofa and it looked remarkably good with the new-to-me velvet curtains. The summerhouse felt warm and looked comfortable.

I still didn't know what to do about a meal. I could cook some steak. I knew I didn't have many vegetables in stock. Just cabbage, two small carrots and one onion. This was awkward. I could go and get some ordinary orange carrots or something from my mother – but then she'd know he was coming.

I phoned Jack. 'Hi, Jack, will you have already eaten when you come? I was so sleepy last night I can't remember what you said.'

'I'd love to eat at yours, if you're offering.'

I wasn't, but I said, 'You'll have to take pot luck, then. I've been sorting out Dad, and haven't much in. Perhaps a small steak and some mashed potato?'

'That would be fantastic, Dreamy. I mostly want to be with you, not eating you out of house and home, though, so don't worry if you don't feel like cooking.'

'You do know you come through the little gate at the side of the house and walk across the lawn to the summerhouse, do you?'

'I thought I'd have to knock at your parents' door. I'm glad I haven't got to disturb them.'

I was too, but I didn't say so. 'I'll see you at 7.30, then, Jack. Bye for now.'

I felt strangely excited. I went through to have a shower and changed out of my jeans to put on a dress. I only had one that looked vaguely new and it was blue. I grabbed back the shawl over the sofa and put it round my shoulders. That looked a little less blue, but I wasn't sure about it. Now I needed something brighter on the sofa. The shawl went back folded over the arm, like a throw, and I fetched my normal soft angora, pale blue cardigan.

There was a knock on the door and my mother marched in carrying a box. 'This came for you and I forgot all about it, with Dad coming home. You look nice, dear, all smartened up. Who's coming round? Or are you going out?'

I had to confess. 'Jack's coming, Mother. He'll be popping round about 7.30.'

My mother looked momentarily shocked. I waited for some comment, but all she said was, 'Well, if you're going to cook for him in that dress, don't forget to wear an apron.' Then she nodded at the box. 'Are you going to open it then, or is that a surprise too?'

'It's a fan heater, Mother, for instant heat when it's freezing.'

'It's much warmer with those curtains and your other heater, though, isn't it?'

'I'm so sorry –I forgot to thank you for putting up my curtains. I meant to ring you last night but I was so tired I just tumbled into bed. It was so lovely to find them already up. If I owe you anything for the rings and hooks, please say.'

'No, don't worry about that, I had plenty of them in the drawer. I like the way you've used that throw to pick out the colour of the border and the cushions. It looks more homely.'

'Good, I'm trying to make it look snug.' I moved the box from where she had put it and said, 'I'll put this out of the way for now – I won't be using it this evening and I need to get the meal ready.'

She didn't take the hint. 'I really don't mind opening it for you, dear, while you get on with your cooking. And it would be nice to say hello to Jack again.'

'No, Mother, you go. When I know if we are going out properly, we will both come over and say hello. But that won't be tonight. You go and be with Daddy and I'll tell you if I splashed gravy down my dress tomorrow. And I'll try to find out what he does for a living so that Daddy feels better about him.' I took the heater into the bedroom and plonked it on the bed. I was in there a few minutes while I tidied round, remembering that if he wanted the loo he would have to walk through to the en suite.

My mother was still there, fondling both kittens, who were purring loudly.

'I really must be getting on, Mother,' I said firmly.

My mother harrumphed a bit, but after stroking each kitten as she put it down in an exaggerated way, she made her way to the door. I gave her a hug as she went and she mumbled, 'I was going to tell you something, but it can wait. Have a lovely evening.'

Which meant, of course, that as I peeled the potatoes and chopped onions, I was wondering what it was. I just hoped she wasn't pushed out by me just as she was about to reveal something extremely important.

By the time Jack knocked on the door, I had the potatoes in a pan, the steak duly pounded and the onions chopped and ready to go in with the steak, and had prepared the last three small blue carrots. I had a few frozen peas ready as well. I had some ice cream in my mini freezer if he wanted dessert, or we could go on to flapjack or shortcake with coffee.

I opened the door and he stepped in. Jack made my summerhouse seem incredibly small. I remembered what Sharon had said about it, but Jack's enthusiasm at my 'pad', as he called it, drowned out the negative thoughts.

'Wow, Dreamy, this is great. I love those curtains. It's warmer than I thought, too.' As he spoke, he took off his coat and I noticed he was wearing a really thick navy jumper. I wondered whether he had chosen the colour to please me.

He moved across the little room and I indicated for him to sit down. I couldn't speak. I didn't know what to say.

He put his hand out to me, suggesting I sit by him. I said, all in a rush, 'Would you like a coffee or a glass of wine? And would you like to eat fairly soon? If so, I'll put the potatoes on.'

'A coffee would be lovely. I don't mind when we eat. Would you like some help with the cooking?' There was a mew from the bedroom. 'Are those your cats? Can I see them?'

I opened the door and the kittens, released from their confinement, shot out into the room, charging everywhere.

Jack looked on. 'They're amazing. What are their names?' I told him all about them, which included everything that had happened with the farmer and his gun, while I made us both a hot drink.

I felt so much better – my earlier awkwardness had scattered.

The rest of the evening went brilliantly. I don't have a table, so we ate off trays. The steak worked out fine and the potato was a novelty. I was pleased I had introduced some peas because otherwise he may have cottoned on to my blue food obsession, or whatever you would call it. I was able to not serve myself peas ('they're not really my thing') but ate everything else, so that was fine.

We chatted all through the meal, so it took ages. The red wine was good with it and enjoyed by us both. When we had the coffee and I offered him flapjack or shortbread, both homemade, he was impressed.

'What are we going to do next, Dreamy? Shall we go to a show in London?'

'We could, only won't that be really expensive?'

'Don't worry – my treat. You've given me a lovely meal, so now it's my turn.'

I wanted to ask him if he was sure he wanted us to go on another date, but then I didn't need to because he pulled me towards him and I rested in his hug. When we kissed, I felt so sure of him. I had to remind myself that I didn't know much about him at all.

Whether he had the same thought, I don't know, but we pulled away from each other a little and just looked into each other's eyes. My hands were in his.

He said, 'Tell me, Dreamy, are you still at art college?'

I didn't know what to say – my mind was in turmoil. He wouldn't want a girlfriend with the problems I still had. I took my hands away from his and walked through to the kitchen area with our glasses.

'Would you like another glass of wine?'

'No, thank you, I'm driving. A coffee would be good, though.'

I made some coffee in the cafetière. I knew I had been rude, not answering his question. I also knew that he may well have asked Sharon that same question about whether I was still at art college. Sharon may not have answered either – it was better coming from me.

'I should be at art college, but I had to drop out. I hope to go back, but probably not on the interior design course.'

'Why's that?'

I swallowed hard and went for it. 'I was asked to leave, actually, by my tutor. I was stuck on blue interiors and for a while I couldn't do anything but design rooms all blue. I've been seeing a psychologist recently and it is probably a combination of a silly challenge I had with my friends from school, and grief. My grandmother died at that time. If it worries you, that's all right, I understand; you are free to go.'

He looked appalled. 'I'm not that shallow! If you have a problem, then let's talk about it. Don't send me away.'

My eyes filled with tears. I didn't want to talk about it, but I didn't want him to go. In just a few days he had become enormously important to me. Jack's response to my tears was to pass me my pack of blue tissues, stand up and put his arms round me. We stood there, as I cried against his navy jumper, the smell of him and his arms around me comforting me. He stroked my hair and murmured soothing noises. When I was calm enough to listen, he was saying, 'Don't cry, Dreamy, it's OK.'

He moved me across to the sofa and made me sit down. He fetched two mugs and some milk for him, then poured our coffee. He watched while I sipped mine. 'I feel better now,' I said. 'Thank you.'

'Listen, Dreamy. I knew about the blue thing a long time ago, through Sharon. I didn't worry about it then and I don't now. I liked you right back when we were at that party and our respective dates for the evening disappeared. You had blue hair then. You are so great to talk to and laugh with. I've never forgotten you.'

'From that one evening?'

'Yes, from that one evening. If you will allow us to be an item now, there's plenty of time for you to get the help you need to cope with your grief.'

'I will overcome it. I've started to allow more than blue into my life. And yes, I will allow us to be an item, as you call it.'

Whereupon Jack pulled me into his arms again and we sealed our item-ness with a kiss.

'I'm glad you've got your own pad, Dreamy. Do you think we would have had that conversation in a room in your parents' house?'

'No. Certainly not.' I looked round my summerhouse. 'It's more than a shed, isn't it?'

'I love it – it's quirky and interesting and it's where we have started our relationship.'

I laughed and felt that little curl of happiness again. I told myself it was too soon to rest in it, but I didn't squash it.

We talked for hours. The kittens settled on us, Skye on Jack and Harry on me. Despite the oil-filled radiator, we began to get cold, so together we opened up my new heater and both snuggled under one throw complaining about the new heater smell until the place was warm again. We drank more coffee, then hot chocolate for Jack and blue tea for me. Most of all we just relished each other's company. It was gone midnight when Jack went home, and after we kissed each other goodbye I felt that loss inside me so deeply it hurt, yet at the same time I felt excited. I made myself go to bed because it was late, but my mind was so full it was more than two hours before I dropped off.

34

After letting Adelle down by not making the last appointment, I was expecting a furious young lady. But she had slid into the nearest armchair without even putting her shawl down first, with her eyes half-closed and a dreamy smile on her face. It was obvious to me that today she felt very content. I asked an unnecessary question: 'How are you today, Delle?'

She shook herself gently out of her reverie, responding to me slowly. 'I'm much, much better than I was. I had someone round on Friday and we talked for hours and I cooked. We ate steak and blue potatoes and my ordinary flapjack, not blue.' She was only half-focused on me. I reckoned she was in love.

'Did your special visitor enjoy the meal?'

'Yes, he did. And he liked my summerhouse and the kittens, and we met up again yesterday. How did you know it was someone special?'

'Just a hunch. Or perhaps because I can see why your friend calls you Dreamy.'

She sat up straight, looking directly at me. 'Oh, I'm sorry, I'm a bit distracted. Jack calls me Dreamy, though, and I think I like it now, although I'm not sure.'

'You are a young woman of many names.'

'Only three that have stuck. I'm thinking of dropping "Bluedelle", though, because I am trying to let go of blue. I have successfully renamed my kitten Skye. It works well for her. What's on today's agenda?'

'We were going to spend some of today's session talking about your granny. Did you bring the photos?'

'I'm sorry – I brought them for the appointment you missed, and I filled in loads of CBT forms, but forgot all about the photo album.'

'That's fine; we'll concentrate on CBT today. Unless you want to talk about something else first?'

'I could tell you about Jack, but it feels too soon. Can I do that another week?'

I appreciated her caution – in fact, I was quite pleased to see it. She opened her folder, which she had clearly relabelled 'Adelle Merchant – CBT'.

I realised there was no need for her to tell me about Jack – her thoughts on the CBT forms contained a great deal of information about him. She had to fill me in on her notes – they were sketchy in parts. I gathered she had been on a date that had been disrupted by her father's fall, but her young man had gone with her to the hospital and stuck by her.

The circumstances she recorded were nearly all about having a boyfriend, including her worries that Jack would think the worse of her for living in a shed in her parents' garden.

'Don't you live in a converted summerhouse?' I asked, pointing at her entry on the CBT form.

She responded far more powerfully than she had on the CBT form when Sharon had first called it a shed. 'It's my home. It's a space for me where I can be myself without interference from my parents. That's why I am cross with my mother when she walks in without permission. And it's why I design the place as I want it – even if that is all blue. Well, nearly.'

'Only nearly?'

'Yes – I have introduced some thick French navy velvet curtains with burgundy borders, plus cream cushions and a shawl, which I have put over the sofa arm like a throw. It is checked in blue, cream and the same burgundy as the curtains.'

'I am impressed.' Adelle's smug smile told me she was impressed with herself.

'I am going to try to do two or three changes a week. But the cream and burgundy still bother me, so I shall wait until I can cope with those colours before bringing in another one. I shall look out for a matching cushion next – I might find one in a charity shop. I'm a bit short of cash.'

She stopped suddenly, looking caught out. She often acts like a little rich girl, so I had assumed that her mother and father were giving her a large allowance. But perhaps not, and it could be that money was tight for the whole family. Perhaps they were coming into hard times; after all, they had previously seen a private psychologist. I glanced back at her file as if referencing her CBT notes – yes, a few references to previous counsellors, all independent practitioners. I returned to the notes she had made ready for the session.

'I love the way you have equated blue with "emptiness", Delle. I see you have used this idea to help you move forward and challenge yourself each time you choose blue over other colours or want to dye food. Apart from your own flapjack, have you managed to eat any other non-blue food?'

'I cooked the steak more, so that it wasn't rare. And I ate some of my father's mashed potato in the hospital plus a little meat – I hadn't eaten all day – and a strawberry yoghurt. A few weeks ago I would have starved, but I managed by imagining them to be blue.'

'That sounds a good ploy for now. I notice from your CBT forms that you haven't given yourself any credit for coping with new situations. Perhaps we should introduce the mastery and pleasure forms?'

'Oh no, I've done those before and I hated them. I'll try to do better at remembering to consider how I coped with the tasks.'

I spent the next twenty minutes going back over her forms and trying to put the ones where she thought she'd failed into a mastery context, emphasising that although she may have not enjoyed the task, she had managed it. She easily found the positive responses and wrote them on the forms, promising again that she would try thinking in those terms.

One thing intrigued me – there were many references to the 'new website'. I asked about it and she filled me in on all that she had started to do to try to find her cousin.

'I expect it's hopeless, though. I ought to move on with my life.'

I nodded. Although I didn't say so, I thought that the website was an excellent idea – mainly because it would be something worthwhile that she could do while she was unemployed.

'What will happen if you don't look for her?'

'I shall always wish that I had tried.'

'What would your friends say?'

'That I will always carry the feeling that I've lost someone important and regret that I didn't look for her.'

'So do you have a decision about continuing?'

'Yes, I will look, but only for a year. I don't want to be one of those sorry people whose lives stop because of something or someone they can't find.'

'Why not write down your pros and cons, so that you can look back and see why you spent time on it? You can do it here and now, if you like.'

Adelle smiled and immediately drew up two columns on a random piece of paper I passed her. It was white, but she only raised her eyebrows slightly before writing on it in blue.

I should imagine that the debate about whether or not to find her cousin had gone on in her head for some days now and had already led her to proceed with the idea. But today her thoughts were elsewhere and there were several comments in the cons list like, 'Now I am with Jack, does it matter that I've lost my second cousin?'

I carefully challenged whether this was, in fact, the same issue. If it were linked, I suggested that was a new question that needed to be tackled with pros and cons. Then I asked her to imagine herself in the future looking back at the decision now.

I counted up her list of pros and cons and asked if she wanted to weight them. She didn't, so I declared that considering her list by numbers of answers alone, she did not want to find her second cousin.

'Oh no, that's not right – I do want to find her.' Adelle took the list from me – I had put a pencil line through duplicates and indeed the outcome was that she was not going to find her cousin. She looked at me, dismayed.

'Delle, remember this was a tool, and through doing it you have discovered that emotionally you do want to find your cousin, whatever the rational pros and cons may indicate. Perhaps you had better continue with your website.'

'Oh, thank goodness, I thought I had to stick to what it looked like I'd decided. Yes, I will carry on. It will give me something to do until I'm ready to go to college, if I can't find a job.'

'Are you looking for one?'

'I'm going to try again now. I think I could let people choose their own plants or flowers so I might go back to the garden centre and ask if I can come back to work. They were lovely there. If I still have trouble with the bright reds screaming at me, I could send people to look at those and not go with them. If I work part-time, I'm sure Mother would help me with the kittens.'

'Delle, you don't have to tell me if you don't want to, but I wondered why you call your father "Dad" or "Daddy" and your mother "Mother"?'

'Because I was always angry with her when I was a teen – she suffocated me, always wanting to know what I was doing. It's still the same, although not so bad. Also, I was about fourteen when I decided "Mummy" sounded childish, so when she told me off for calling her "Mum" I used "Mother".'

'Have you ever discussed it with her?'

'No – do you think I should?'

'It's not up to me, Delle, so it's something for you to ponder over.'

'I might talk to her. I think I could now we aren't always at war.'

'A lot has changed for you recently, Delle. I am pleased to see that you are coping with all these new things.'

'At least one of them is very special,' she said, as she once more seemed to focus somewhere else, a slow smile giving away the destination of her thoughts.

'Before you go, Delle, we need to sort your next run of appointments.'

I wrote them down for her – not bothering to find her any blue paper this time.

After Adelle left the room, I phoned Anita to tell her I wasn't sure that the art room would be needed for a while. Adelle had only made one remark indicating synaesthesia, too.

'What did she say?'

'She talked about bright red screaming at her – it was in the context of finding a job at the garden centre.'

'That's interesting. Did you ever find out more about the condition?'

'I found a chapter in a book, when Ella and I went to the flat. But it didn't tell me more than I remembered.'

'Are you still renting your flat?'

I realised I had said too much. I didn't really want to talk to Anita about my relationship with Ella. Things had been very precarious with Ella at one point, when people had thought Anita and I were in a relationship. I said, 'The contract runs out at the end of the month, so we're clearing it out.' Then I quickly returned to the subject. 'Do you think we need to pursue the idea of synaesthesia, as it's not a mental illness?'

'It's not. But I suppose it might help to understand Adelle more.' She started to talk about it being a special ability, similar to that experienced by some people with autism. I knew all that but from habit I jotted down the odd note. My pen ran out.

'Hang on,' I said. 'I need a fresh biro.' I opened my desk drawer to find a new one and turned over the picture of Jamie. I felt a sharp pang and reflected that I might have let Adelle off from talking about her grandmother's death simply because I was still struggling with my own son's. I took the photo, in its bright frame, and placed it back on my desk as a reminder that grief must be dealt with or it ruins everything. It had undermined my marriage to Ella for nearly six years. I was lucky to be back with her now.

Anita was saying, 'Mike, are you still there?'

'Yes, sorry, Anita. It's just struck me while I was speaking with you that I have dodged the grief part of working with Adelle, probably because of Jamie. I must rectify that.'

'Look after yourself as well, Mike. If you aren't ready for grief work, then get someone else to work with her.'

'No, I think I can do it. Now that Ella and I are back together I am feeling far more stable. Anyway, I am getting some grief counselling myself.'

'Are you still seeing Henrietta, then?'

'Yes, I promised Ella I would work with her and it is really helping. Although we don't always talk about Jamie, things have changed to include rebuilding my relationship with Ella. We've been for couples therapy.'

'Is that going well, Mike?'

'In a way, but we have both lived apart for so long that we are having to adjust. But what about you, Anita? How are you feeling?'

'I'm having trauma counselling after the assault in the department in December. And I'm doing well, really – it's not so bad in the studio now we have alarms everywhere and security numbers to get into the room. I'll be fine.'

I'd been so wrapped up in sorting out my own life and sorting my caseload, I had not really been aware that Anita was still finding things difficult. Why on earth did I think that she would be immune from post-traumatic stress? I realised she was rather better at looking after her colleagues than I was. In fact, I was a pretty useless acting head of department all round. Could I even consider the post of head that was being offered to me?

35

After the last appointment I had left Mike's office feeling greatly relieved. I had remembered that we were going to do grief work but I really hadn't wanted to at all. I could only think about Jack. I knew I was going off into some dreamworld for some of the session. But I managed to keep focused long enough to do some CBT. There's one thing about that approach – the only thing I like: it is quite structured.

Mike was crafty to suggest a pros and cons exercise on finding my second cousin. When I was devastated by the result, I realised I desperately wanted to find her.

But I knew I'd dodged the issue with my granny and he had let me. I wondered why he had done that. Just to keep me coming to sessions, probably.

I held back a bit when I told him how I felt about Jack. My mind was telling me it was early days and I mustn't get too excited. I didn't even tell Mike that Jack knew I was seeing a psychologist and he hadn't backed off. My problem was that I now definitely wanted to let go of blue and he liked me being different. Would I still be quirky if I didn't dye my hair blue and always, always wear blue clothes?

For the first time for ages, I allowed myself to think about colours. I remembered my granny's garden and the beautiful roses she grew. I loved the deep red ones – not too far off in colour from the burgundy edging to my new curtains. I remembered forget-me-nots and larkspur, daisies with their bright yellow centres, and pink foxgloves. She loved her cottage garden. The colours didn't upset me in those calm surroundings. If I could move away from blue, flowers like that would look lovely in front of my summerhouse. I'd have to make sure I had a little white fence around the outside because otherwise my mother's formal garden would seem a bit strange with an odd bit of cottage garden area.

I imagined the garden most of the way home. It seemed so real and right for my little home that when I went through the side gate to my mother's back garden I was slightly shocked to see the my summerhouse looking very formal. Even my tubs either side of the French doors looked dull. I wondered whether I could trade helping with the new kitchen for having a picket fence and a few packets of seeds in a month or so. It was far too cold to plant anything now.

In the summerhouse I was met with a huge mess. The kittens had found a box of tissues and obviously enjoyed playing with it. There were little bits of torn blue tissue everywhere. I had to set to with the vacuum cleaner. It took ages because it kept clogging up, so I had to empty the bag several times. I was amazed by the mess that could be made from less than one box of tissues.

In the middle of trying to clear it all up, my mother knocked and sidled through the door without waiting for me to say 'come in'. She saw I was mid-task so she put the kettle on and made us both tea. 'You are practically out of your tea,' she called over the noise of the vacuum cleaner.

'I know, I'm trying not to order any more. Anyway, I haven't any money.'

My mother started looking in my fridge and my cupboards.

'Adelle, you are nearly out of food again.'

'I know, Mother, but I get my money tomorrow.'

She took the teas over to the coffee table and made me stop cleaning and sit down. I did, expecting a lecture for not eating. Instead she said, 'Your father and I have decided to give you an advance on doing the kitchen. It will help you get on with it.'

'Aren't you afraid I might take the money and not be able to do the job?'

'You've always been honest, Adelle, why do you say that?'

'Because I am still in the grip of this blue thing, so I sometimes can't get where I need to be, I'm just too anxious and stressed.'

'Your psychologist will help you, won't he?'

'Well, yes, that is helping. But some days are better than others.'

'You were all right when you were with Jack.'

'I was, but when I last saw him, I wasn't. I had to tell him about my problems and I was very distressed.'

'Oh dear, he was such a lovely young man, too. I thought you'd be able to cover it up and get to know him.'

'As you said just now, Mother, I am honest. Anyway, don't worry, he really likes me. And one of the reasons he likes me is because I am quirky.'

'Whatever does he mean by that?' My mother sounded offended.

'That's not exactly what he says, but he likes me because I am different. I don't think like other people. I daydream a lot. I wear blue all the time. I grow blue potatoes.'

'You don't have to do those things.'

'I can't stop daydreaming. And I like growing unusual things. I might be able to try for a different colour of something in the summer, if I carry on improving. Those strange gourds, perhaps.' I imagined them in all their weird and intriguing shapes. 'They're great to paint,' I said. 'All those twists and turns. Too orange and yellow, though.'

My conventional mother tutted and shook her head. 'What else does Jack like about you?'

'Oh, I don't know. Various stuff.' I was finding this embarrassing. I changed the subject. 'I've set up a lookalike site. I've called it "Searching for My Cousin". Do you want to see it?'

My mother looked shocked. I could hear a tremor in her voice when she said, 'I really don't think you should be doing that. People don't want their lives disturbed.'

Sometimes I cannot work out my mother. I didn't even want to try this time.

'We did a pros and cons during my psychology appointment and it came out that I shouldn't do it and I was upset, realising I'd make a mistake if I didn't look for her. We were little but must have been really close, Mother.'

246

'I'd better get back and see to your dad.' My mother stood up and straightened her skirt. Putting her cardigan round her shoulders, she went to the door.

'I'll be over later to see Dad,' I said.

My mother retorted, 'Oh, I shouldn't bother if I were you, he'll probably be asleep.'

She left without even a goodbye. I ran the conversation over in my mind a few times but still couldn't work out why she was so upset.

I gave up trying to understand her and went to fetch my laptop. I needed to see if anyone had responded yet.

No one had responded to me, but Sharon must have spread the word. I now had twenty-six people looking for someone like them. Two of them had replies already. One was Cessy – one of the original six in our blue challenge. She looked as if she had used a photo from back then in our schooldays, or maybe she hadn't changed one little bit. I was pleased she had joined in. I looked at the photo of her 'lookalike'. I could have sworn it was her, but then lookalikes would be very similar. The lookalike said she was from Scotland. The rest of the information was private between the two lookalikes. I was not sure about this because I wouldn't want anyone to misuse it. I decided I should change the settings.

I was just about to make everything public when I realised I had invited people to join and stated that their messages would be private. So instead I added a note saying, 'However, feel free to keep them public if you feel safer. As webmaster I will be able to access all conversations in order to prevent the site being taken over by anyone wanting to entice others to meet them in dubious circumstances.'

I then rewrote the rules to make it clearer that each individual could block those replying to them and I as webmaster would be able to block anyone misusing the site. I wasn't sure that this would be enough, but it may deter any predators.

The other lookalike seemed interesting. The person who had replied looked very like the original person, but his style of clothing was different, as was his hairstyle, and he had a small scar on his cheek. I was really pleased. I was delighted that the website already had 332 likes – one of them from Jack. When I saw his name a little frisson of excitement passed through me.

I wondered what my granny would think of Jack. Probably he'd have passed the relative test. Granny had always been my mentor and I wished she was around now to talk to. I thought about what she would think of me with my blue hair and clothes, but then, if she had still been living I would almost certainly not be wearing blue. 'Sorry, Granny,' I said out loud.

I went to find some food, fed the kittens and put my coat round my shoulders. I wanted to check up on my dad even if my mother didn't really want me to come.

I knocked on my mother's kitchen door – the light went on as she came to open it.

'Hello, Adelle. I told you there was no need to come.'

'It wouldn't be right not to see Dad while he's injured. If it were you, Mother, I would be looking in on you.'

I walked through to the dining room, now Dad's bedroom. Dad was sitting a little more upright and doing a crossword. His face became a beaming smile when he saw me. 'Adelle, where have you been? I thought you'd come to see me earlier. I'm really pleased to see you.'

I glanced quizzically at my mother before I pecked him on the cheek.

'I'll make you both a drink,' she said. I called out that weak Earl Grey would be fine for me. I knew she wouldn't have any blue pea flower tea.

'I've been bored silly,' said Dad. 'The painkillers make me sleep a bit, but when I'm awake I've got nothing I really want to do.'

'Have you got some books to read?'

'Well, I finished the one you put by my bed so your mother found a few off the shelf, but nothing really exciting. I think she thinks I ought to take the time to improve myself.'

I looked at the book pile beside him. *War and Peace* was there, along with a book entitled *A Passion for Perfect Russian* and another one – *The Elderly Husband*.

'I'll bring you a few crime novels, shall I?'

He took my hand and squeezed it gently. 'That would be excellent. Would you fetch more John Grishams? I can't remember which ones I've read, but I can always reread them.'

'We can choose a few from your own shelf, then, before I go. Meanwhile, I can help you with your crossword.' We spent a few minutes looking at it – I gave him the answer to one clue all about angled sides. 'Banks,' I said.

He laughed. 'I've been trying to do that for ages, thinking about isosceles triangles and right angles – that sort of thing.'

'Sometimes it helps to be hopeless at maths – you avoid thinking about it.' I passed him the pen and then waited while he finished off that corner really quickly. I loved watching him doing a crossword – he would think for a while, the pen in the corner of his mouth and then he would give the pen a triumphant flick in the air and mutter 'yes' before he filled it in.

He finished the whole crossword off, while I sat there waiting for a proffered clue.

When my mother appeared, he extolled my virtues as the only person who could have interpreted the clue that way. I protested, 'Of course I'm not, Dad, they wouldn't set a crossword that hard.'

He laughed. 'That means I'm hopeless at them now, then. The old grey cells are deteriorating; there's no hope for me.' His grin told me my father was back to his old self. I was glad he'd come back home – his mood may have been much less buoyant in hospital.

We drank our tea while he asked me about Jack. I filled him in with what I knew – especially his job as an articled clerk.

'A lawyer!' exclaimed my mother. 'Well, they are never without a penny or two.'

'Jack might be – he wants to concentrate on legal aid cases. Or go into politics. His degree was law and politics. The work he's doing now is quite a good foundation for that, I understand.'

My father looked pleased. He usually voices his opinions on politics quietly and wishes he could do something about the poor, or any injustice. But he is not a speaker so has never taken it further than putting a few leaflets through doors.

My mother shrugged but didn't say anything. She went off to another room; maybe she was secretly glad not to have to sit with Dad.

'What else was in the paper apart from crosswords, Dad?'

My father told me about the stock market and his shares. He was pleased with how they had performed. He was less pleased with all the other news. He despaired over hungry children on the other side of the world and atrocities far away and nearby. He was very upset over flooding in one place and drought in another. In fact, he was easily drifting into a rather gloomy mood. I changed the subject.

I told him all about the website I had set up. He asked me all sorts of questions, such as how I would get it out and about and whether I had used my real name. He gave some suggestions and offered to contribute to any advertising. I told him it had reached more than 300 people already and how there had been some hits, although not for me.

'I don't think you will have anyone respond who truly looks like you, and I think I know why that will be, Adelle. Would you be upset if I told you?'

I took the risk and said, 'No, tell me.'

'You don't really look like yourself – you are very thin and your hair is that bright blue colour. And I suspect in your photo you are wearing blue eyeshadow and matching lipstick. If there is someone out there who is your double, they may not immediately notice.'

'You mean I need to dye my hair back to its natural colour?'

Dad nodded.

'I'm not sure I can do that yet. It's part of my identity.'

'Then you may miss out on finding her, but I don't blame you for trying. I've tried through missing persons agencies on the internet, but I never thought of a website.'

'As soon as I knew about my cousin, I wanted to track her down.'

I was surprised when he said, 'Cousin?'

'Sorry, second cousin. Mother told me all about how she fell out with your cousin's wife, Hilary, and I never saw my second cousin again. She said Caroline and I were very alike. I'm hoping we both are now.'

My father didn't comment on that. It worried me that he seemed sad and I might have stirred up memories he would rather forget.

'Are you all right, Dad?'

'I'm a bit tired now, Adelle – it was all that thinking about the crossword. Maybe I need a rest.'

I picked up my now cold Earl Grey, pretended it was blue, and took a few gulps. Then I rearranged Dad's pillows, made sure he was comfortable and popped a kiss on the top of his head. Perhaps he *wasn't* back to his old self – his mood seemed to be all over the place.

'Have a lovely snooze, Dad, and I'll see you later.'

I fetched a pile of John Grishams and placed them by his bed. My mother was nowhere to be seen, so I wondered whether I was still in her bad books for something that I didn't know about.

I called up the stairs to her. She merely appeared on the landing, duster in hand, and shouted down a brief goodbye. I had wanted to tell her about my lookalike website. I hoped that my father would update her.

36

I had forgotten to take my mobile with me and there was a missed message from Jack. I turned up the heater and sat on the sofa with my throw over my knees, Skye snuggled underneath it and Harry settled in his usual place, under my chin. I rang Jack back.

'Sorry, Dreamy, I can't talk now. I rang you on my break. Are you in later?'

'Should be. I'm working on my website.'

'OK, good.'

I went back to my web page – more replies; none of them really looked very much like the people they were writing to. I looked up advertising costs on Facebook. I wrote them all down for my father to consider. I hoped the website would take off on its own. I had an idea that if it were successful then I would be asked to host adverts on it and be paid to do so. I didn't manage to find that information so gave up. I stretched, and with the room warmer, I came out from under the throw and went on a hunt for something to eat.

I found a few odd bits of my strange blue diet and still had a little ordinary flapjack. I wasn't sure I could cope with that – my father's suggestion that I dye my hair back had bothered me. I ate a little blue bread and some blueberries with the rest of the cheese. I had a drink of warm milk with only one drop of Red Cabbage Blue colouring in it.

I thought again, 'If I am not Bluedelle, then who am I?' I realised at that moment that no one in my everyday life was calling me 'Bluedelle'. Not even my psychologist. He had dropped the 'Blue' on the second appointment and I had let him get away with it. Both Sharon and Jack called me 'Dreamy', a name I had never chosen, and my parents still called me 'Adelle'. Even my names were confusing. I was trying to give up blue food and only had my appearance left.

Despite the panic that was rising, I went and looked in the mirror. Very carefully I removed my blue eyeshadow, eyeliner and lipstick. I slowed my breathing and made myself relax – well, tried to. I calmed myself with as many positive thoughts as I could manage to think up. I pretended the face in the mirror was not mine, but that of my doppelgänger.

I touched up my skin-matched foundation and put some lip salve on. This was blue, but colourless when on. I looked strange. I found my crocheted beanie hat and pulled it on. There was still some blue hair sticking out. Nevertheless, the resulting photo that I took on my phone was more of a natural look.

It took me a long time to upload it and remove my previous photo. There was no problem technically, but I had to calm myself several times. I still hadn't saved it as my new photo when Jack phoned.

'Hello, Dreamy, how are you today? What are you doing?'

I dodged the first question, as I was now in the throes of anxiety about changing a photo on the website – which I knew would sound ridiculous.

'I'm still working on the website. I've just removed all my blue make-up and hidden my hair a bit because my father said I should look more natural. I've taken a new photo and am deciding whether to put it on.'

'You should. It's a great idea. Or you could put a different one on each week – one all blue, then one all orange, or turquoise or something. I know, go through the colours of the rainbow.'

I realised he had no idea how fixated I was on blue.

'It would cost too much having my hair dyed; anyway, I prefer blue. If I do anything I shall go back to my natural colour.' There must have been something about the tone of my voice because Jack immediately tried to backtrack.

'Yes, sorry, I got carried away. I was thinking you could Photoshop it. I don't care what colour your hair is. I am just intensely flattered that you want to go out with me.' My heart melted. 'I wanted to ask you if you are free tonight, if your mother doesn't need you to help with your dad.'

'I'm sure I'm free. My mother doesn't seem to want my help, although my dad seemed really pleased to see me.'

'Well, I have a plan. Can I come to you straight from work and bring a takeaway? Then we can go and watch a film somewhere. Your choice.'

I froze. I couldn't think of a single takeaway I could manage, even with Jack there.

'Um, I'm not fond of takeaways and I've already had quite a heavy lunch today. You bring a takeaway for you and eat it here to save you going home. Otherwise it's a brilliant plan.'

'Oh, OK,' he said softly, 'but I found this place that does those blue potatoes you like, so I was going to surprise you and bring one.'

I was touched by his thoughtfulness. 'Well, that's different. Just one baked potato with nothing but butter would be fine. That's lovely of you to go to so much trouble.'

'I guessed you weren't a fish and chips person and wouldn't have brought curry without knowing if you'd eat it. But this place has a huge range of potatoes and fillings.'

He didn't have much time, so our conversation was quite brief. We arranged he would be over at 6 pm.

The rest of the afternoon was spent catching up with cleaning. I couldn't make more flapjack because I was out of some of the ingredients. We'd hardly touched the shortcake and I had some milk left over for his coffee. I hoped he would bring a big meal for himself as I had very little else.

With the summerhouse looking pristine, although probably not for long if the kittens found anything else to tear up, I went back to the website at about 4 pm. I bravely inserted the natural photo, remembering that Jack didn't care about the colour of my hair. Maybe I should try feeling like that too about my eyeshadow, my lips, my home and my food. If only it were that easy. I resisted reading the other matches that had been found. There were none for me. But I did notice that the website had been viewed more than 800 times. I wondered how many people needed to upload their details before someone had a really good match.

It was only a few days before my appointment with Dr Lewis. I would have a lot to report but on the other hand, I wasn't terribly sure I had done my homework. I wondered whether I could get away with another week of not talking about my granny.

I looked back at my week so far and began making notes for the next session, remembering that I must add some measure about how well I coped. I had done very well to minimise the blue for my photo and had put it on the site. I imagined Mike being pleased about that. This was the first time I had taken cognitive behavioural therapy seriously. It was working.

I glanced back at the notes I had made. Was there anything about my granny there? No. I wished again that Granny was here to see the website. Also to tell me about the bust-up between my mother and Dad's cousin. I sighed as I wrote it all down. I closed my eyes and used imagery relaxation – thinking of the soft waves of a lovely blue-green sea and letting my body relax. I felt better and went to eat a flapjack, with a sprinkle of blue sugar, then made myself ready for Jack to arrive.

By 6 pm, I was ready in my newest jeans and usual blue blouse and a jumper Jack hadn't seen because I hardly ever wore it. It had looked navy in the shop, but once under ordinary house lights it definitely was a dark purple. I'd pulled the collar of the blouse out round the neck, with the back of it raised, in the way Cessy always wore hers. I wasn't terribly sure this was completely me, so found my thick scarf with the rainbow tassels as well. I stroked it as I put it round my shoulders, thinking of Granny knitting it. I fussed the kittens as I waited for Jack.

He knocked on my door a little before 6.30 pm. He was laughing as he came but stumbled over the step into my little home, banging his knee on the kitchen units. I could see it hurt, but he grinned at me and said, 'Oops, sorry,' before giving me a hug.

My takeaway potato was rather purple, but since it matched my jumper, I didn't care. It was huge but I ate it all. Jack had the same type of potato, which rather clashed with his chicken tikka filling. When I commented on this, he said his stomach wouldn't notice. Being around Jack really lifted my spirits.

The film didn't start until eight. So even after coffee we had time to go over to Mother's to visit Dad. My mother seemed delighted to see us – well, Jack! She scurried ahead of us to check Dad was 'fit for visitors' before letting us into the temporary bedroom.

'Hello, Jack, how are you?' My father stretched out his hand in welcome.

He seemed to be sitting up even straighter than he had been in the morning and when I remarked on it my mother interjected, 'I spoke to the OT. It's all right as long as there's no weight on his hip.' I could see no way that there was no weight on his hip joint. I wasn't privy to the X-ray so I said nothing, thinking I would talk to my mother privately later.

We left at 7.30. Jack had his car so we drove to the cinema. I had left the choice of film to him. I wasn't disappointed he had chosen *Amazing Grace* – although the abolition of slavery felt rather heavy for a great night out.

We walked back to the car park, hand in hand. 'It was a good film, thank you,' I said.

'It was a bit full on, though, wasn't it?' said Jack.

'You mean the religious side?'

'I have no objection to faith, but I didn't know the film featured things done in the name of belief that are so wrong,' he replied.

He told me that his mother's church, which he sometimes went to, was more about showing the love of Christ to people. It sounded rather like something my granny would say. Whenever I had stayed with her over a weekend, I went to Sunday school and had fun drawing things and making models and learning the stories of the Bible. But that was the extent of my church experience.

'I'd like to go to church with you sometime but perhaps not your mother's yet. We almost talked about faith in my psychology session, but my psychologist veered away from it. He had just said that "we are all rubbish if we only look at the darkness in our souls".'

'That's a strange thing to say.'

'Well, I had just told him I thought I was rubbish. I think he was trying to get alongside me or something.'

'Why did you think you were rubbish? You certainly are not! My mother would probably say we are all good if only we have God in our souls.'

I laughed, but it made me feel warm inside.

But then I wondered why I said I'd go to church. I wasn't sure about walking into a church with my blue hair. Would people stare at me? I had no idea. We drove home in silence. Then as soon as we went into the summerhouse and I began to make more coffee, we talked about everything else: his job and hopes for the future, my hope of going back to college, my mother's kitchen, the kittens, and his parents. It was then that I found out that his father was killed in Afghanistan.

'I'm sorry, I didn't realise.'

'It was before you and I met. My mother remarried last year. Great chap, we get on really well.'

I took the drinks over to the coffee table with the remaining shortbreads. I hoped they weren't stale – it was quite a while since I had made them. I sat down next to him and snuggled up.

'I'd have liked to have met your father. Tell me about him.'

I leaned against his chest while he spoke, listening to the vibrations in his body. He told me about how good his father looked in his uniform and how proud he was to be representing his country. I heard about his childhood – days out when his dad was home on leave.

'It was always like a holiday when he was back,' he said. They would snatch a few days at the seaside; he and his dad would swim in the sea, his blonde mother sheltering under a sun canopy. He loved sitting between them, eating an ice cream, while they talked about their future, planning and dreaming of when Dad would next be home. They always played on the slot machines and played crazy golf.

'It was as if we had to cram in as many memories as possible. Mum would take photo after photo. It was as if she knew he would die. We went through them again and again after he died, so the memories are fresh in my mind. In some ways I still feel he is with me.'

'I feel like that about my granny – yet I get really upset that she is no longer around.'

'With my dad, it's sort of comforting to remember him now. It's taken time, though.'

'The psychologist wants me to take in pictures of my granny.'

'Well, you must. Do you have any I can see now?'

'I have one in a frame, and just two or three that I had with me to take in. The rest are in my old bedroom in the house.'

'Just show me the one you keep in the frame.'

I went and fetched it. She was bending down to me; I must have been about four. She was laughing, her nose almost touching mine.

Jack took it, holding it reverently. 'This is such a lovely photo. This must be you; what a gorgeous little girl you were. And what a sweet, shy smile. Can you remember that day?'

'I don't know if it was then, but I do remember Granny cheering me up after I had tipped water from the watering can all over my feet and into my shoes. I was distraught, but she helped me to see it was funny. We stomped all around the garden listening to my squelchiness before she took me in to find dry shoes and socks.'

Jack's arm stole round my shoulders. 'See, you can still remember all that. In that way she's still part of your life, your history, even though she's gone.'

I nodded and looked at him.

'I wish she'd been able to hang around to meet you,' I said. 'I think she would have liked you very much.'

'Even though I want to see legal aid cases or waste my life being a politician or trying to change the world some other way?'

'Well, she would not have thought that was a waste. Anyway, you've accepted me and I'm a college dropout, so she would probably have been grateful.'

'You know you are more than that. What will you do if you can't pick up your place in college?'

'I'm not sure. I'm sort of looking for a job now, but I do want to get some qualifications. I'd love to go back to college or I might do Open University, I suppose.'

'Unless someone sweeps you off your feet and marries you and you are busy with babies in a year or so.'

I must have looked horrified. 'Don't worry, only joking,' he said.

'Just as well – I want a child sometime, but I'm not ready yet. By the way, that reminds me, we've been invited to a wedding.'

It had come that morning – probably the smartest wedding invitation it's possible to get. From Cessy, of course. It actually said 'Dreamy and Jack' at the top. It seemed to presume an awful lot – the wedding wasn't for six months.

I fetched it from the bedroom and passed it to him. I watched his face as he opened it and fought through the layers of lace until he reached the embossed silver card. A slow grin gradually stole over his face.

'I remember Cessy. I met her a few times when Sharon and I were sort of going out together. This is our first invite as a couple, Dreamy. Aren't you excited?'

We grabbed each other and did a little impromptu dance around the room, with us both yelling whoopee and yahoo at various points. I seemed to have forgotten about being an adult, until we slowed down and he enfolded me in his arms. But something was bothering me. Seeing my nickname 'Dreamy' on a formal invitation was definitely wrong. It was time to insist on being called by my proper name.

37

Rachel called me into the office as I went past with my cup of black coffee.

'I have the father of Adelle Merchant on the phone.'

Intrigued, I mouthed, 'Put him through,' and went into my own room.

A gruff voice asked, 'Is that Dr Mike Lewis?'

'Yes, it is, how can I help you?'

We established that I was the person seeing his daughter and I told him that the contents of my appointments with her were confidential.

'Yes, I understand that and I am glad that is the case. It is as I would expect,' he replied.

'Well, can I ask the purpose of this call?'

'My wife and I feel we should find out whether she is of a strong enough mental disposition to take some news that might upset her.'

'What is that?' I asked, thinking she had already had news of her lost second cousin, which upset her.

'I'm sorry, but I can't really say. My wife is insistent that Adelle should know first. We were going to tell her after her GCSEs but my mother-in-law died around then and

Adelle was not in a fit state to cope, and you know the worries we've had about her since.'

'Perhaps you could give me an idea of the gravity of the news?'

'Well, it's about the person she is trying to find. We fear she may never find her, but we have information that will be very difficult for her to hear.'

'And you are not able to tell me what this is?'

'No.'

I was mystified. Was it possible that her cousin was dead? I couldn't reveal anything that Adelle had told me, yet I needed to know whether she would cope. While I was thinking, her father spoke to me again.

'She has told us that you think she is depressed because of the loss of her grandmother. Also that she probably has a deep unresolved loss. We think that is right. What we really need to know, Dr Lewis, is whether she is at risk of suicide.'

That I could answer in a way. 'A sudden shock can cause all sorts of reactions, but Adelle has coped well with finding out about her cousin.'

There was silence the other end before Mr Merchant spoke. 'I think it is time to fill her in about circumstances when she was a young child. May I ask you a favour?'

'You may ask, but I may not be able to grant it.'

'Please could you change the Wednesday appointment you have with Adelle to the afternoon? Then we can tell her in the morning and my wife can bring her to the appointment and she will be able to talk it through with you the same day.'

I glanced at my diary, checking I had no meeting with management that afternoon. The issue of my future role and of keeping both secretaries was still under negotiation. No, next week's management meeting was on Tuesday. I hated moving appointments. I hoped Mr Merchant didn't hear my involuntary sigh.

'Yes, I can swap appointments to do that at 2 pm. I suggest you talk to Adelle during the late morning and ask her if you have her permission to ring me to give me the information. She may consider it hers to give. And she may be angry that I have changed the appointment.'

'Should I tell her I have spoken to you?'

'You may tell her that you asked that I changed her appointment with me, because you had something to tell her. I will report to her the content of our conversation, if she would like to know. I want to reassure her that I betrayed no confidences.'

'Righto, then. It's over to my wife and me now. Thank you for your help, Dr Lewis.'

My next client was waiting, but I popped into the office to ask the secretaries to sort out the changes to appointments.

'Is everything all right with Adelle?' asked Rachel.

Surprised, I said, 'Why do you ask?'

Patricia answered, 'Well, we are sort of fond of her. She seems so young and so sad. At least, she did; you're doing a grand job.'

I smiled at the two secretaries, obviously harbouring a maternal instinct towards a client.

'I'm glad you're concerned about her, but I really can't tell you what's going on, even if I knew. Please just change the appointments.'

'It's OK,' said Patricia. 'We'll see what's up when we type up your letter to the GP!' I laughed and carefully did not comment that from the end of the month we might all be typing our own letters, if management decided that they would not appoint me. I had heard nothing since I sent an email last week with the terms clearly laid out that would have to be met for me to accept the post.

38

When I had a phone call from the secretary I was furious.

'Why does he want to change my appointment?' I asked. 'He said he would work hard to ensure I didn't hang around for a really late appointment again.' Even as I said that, I realised he was probably changing it because otherwise I would have to wait for him to come out of a meeting.

'I'm not sure,' said Rachel. 'But he is juggling lots of things around at the moment because he is acting head of department and we have a crisis affecting some of our jobs. It might be that. Or maybe he has had a request for an earlier appointment from another client. Do you want me to tell him you can't change?'

I calmed down. 'No, no. That's fine. At least he's let me know.' In some ways it was easier to have an afternoon appointment as long as it wasn't too late. I would have time in the morning, while the light was good, to look at my plan for my mother's kitchen and see if I could do any more. I wanted to talk to her about it before then, but she was being so off with me that I didn't like to approach her.

So I wasn't really annoyed – I just don't like other people changing things. Probably that's a control thing, like everything being blue. I went and wrote it all down on the CBT form.

I wanted to speak to Jack, but I managed to restrain myself. I knew he was busy tonight with his friends round for their usual Monday meet-up. I must give him space. I remembered Cessy crowding out a boyfriend once because she just wanted to be with him so much, it drove him mad. I hadn't had that experience myself because Jack was the first one I was always desperate to see.

So instead I went through my wardrobe and put in a pile for the charity shop all the items I was unlikely to grow back into because they were at least two sizes too large, and those that showed signs of wear. This was the start of my effort to wear something else less blue, other than my bravery in wearing the skirt that contained some grey and the scarf with the rainbow tassels.

At the bottom of the little wardrobe was a neatly folded dark red throw. I had hidden it in there over a year ago, when my mother gave it to me because the summerhouse was so cold. It wasn't quite as rich a red as the burgundy at the bottom of the curtains, but I took it into my living area anyway and put it on the chair that the cats usually claimed as their own. It didn't look too bad and would keep them warmer as it was quite soft. Of course, they didn't go anywhere near the chair once the strange covering was on it. But I left it there in the hope that they would get used to it. I ignored the clamour the colour was making in my mind. The burgundy in the curtains was affecting me less now, so I hoped I would adapt to this slightly brighter colour.

I played with the kittens, swinging their homemade toy and rolling a pine cone or two that I had picked up from Mother's garden earlier. They dashed around the room and Harry shot up the curtains. I took him down with a firm 'No', but then had to repeat it with Skye. After ten minutes I was bored with their game so put them on their bed in my bedroom. Before long they were crying to come out, and with their dirt trays in the kitchen, I decided I must let them. They settled down quietly as if they knew that they would be back in the bedroom if they climbed the curtains again.

There was nothing much on the television so I went and found the book I was reading. But I couldn't settle with that either. I looked at my website, but not much was happening there. I didn't like the fact that in my photo I was wearing a hat; no one else was so I looked a little frumpy. I left the site and looked up my old college. The degree courses looked fascinating. My interior design course had included a little fine art, but for a degree there were extra subjects to choose from: history of art, textile design, art and environment, and comic strips. All of the degress included three subjects in the first year then majoring on one or two of them. I had completed a first year of the diploma – finding out that I had passed it after I was asked to leave, ironically. If I were to aim for re-entry in the autumn, I would have to work really hard to produce an up-to-date portfolio to apply for a place soon.

This had taken me to nearly 8 pm. I ate some cereal with the usual coloured milk followed by blue jelly and blueberries. I hoped my mother wouldn't ask me what I had eaten today. It really didn't work to try to put on weight when you had no money for food.

I went into the bedroom to find my portfolio from when I first applied to college. I was nineteen years old then and now I was twenty-two. When I looked through my work I could see that the pages became gradually more blue as I progressed. Not as blue as my designs became during the first year, but I could see the change. I looked for the dates on the work – it had spanned six months. I wondered whether I could do the reverse for college now. Perhaps I wouldn't need to begin with a pure blue, though. I did have a sketchbook full of a variety of mostly blue foods. I could select some of that to give me a start and build from there. I now had a rough design for my mother's new kitchen, which included the colour green. I hoped that if I worked on that it could provide samples for the portfolio.

I thought about the fact that a mere two months ago I wouldn't have been able to think about going back to college, let alone creating a new portfolio with colours in it. Something was definitely changing. But I wished I didn't feel such a strong sense of loss. Was it losing a cousin? And why had my father acted so strangely when I tried to discuss what my mother had told me? Maybe it was because I said 'cousin' rather than 'second cousin' at first. It all seemed very confusing and I was fed up with thinking about it.

I washed up and tidied round my kitchen. I fed the cats and sorted them out. It was nine-ish now and I was cold and tired – definitely ready for bed.

But I could not sleep. In the end I recited to myself the colours in a box of pastels I had as a child. My first box, probably, with magical names. I would sing the names of the colours before bed. I could remember them all – I always put them back in their right places in the box, so that I could just reach for them without reading their names. Some of the colours remained my firm favourites for years, probably until the blue phase. Yellow ochre was the best of all; it spoke to me of a burning sun, a slightly damp beach and a pot my granny had brought back from Spain for my mother. It was the glorious colour of the ribbon in my hair when I had my school photo taken when I was eight.

I slept, dreaming of colours.

The next morning my mother knocked and sidled in while I was in the shower. I was disappointed. I called to her to make us both a cup of tea – she didn't ask what colour. I came out of my bedroom wearing all blue apart from that lovely scarf made by Granny. I didn't put any make-up on.

'Sorry I can't offer you a biscuit, Mother. Jack ate them all the other night and I couldn't shop until today for fresh ingredients.'

'Why couldn't you pop out yesterday? You needn't have come to see Dad if you needed to go shopping.'

'My money doesn't come in until today. Alternate Tuesdays are my shopping days.'

My mother looked at me sternly. 'Adelle, I have told you if you need money, you only have to ask.'

'I know that, Mother, but I want to fend for myself. I've got two little extra mouths with huge appetites to feed now.'

'Well, you are designing a kitchen for me. And supervising the buying of everything, and the installation. I told you we could pay you an advance. I'll get Dad to write you a cheque. How is the design for the curtains going?'

273

'I have worked out the repetition of the pattern, but not yet drawn up the design in colour.'

'But you will manage it, won't you? I would really love that material.'

I didn't remind her that no material existed at present.

'I'll work out the cost of printing on a good-quality fabric before I do more. I don't want to waste your money on something you might not like when it's done. What did you come over for anyway, Mother?'

'Oh, I nearly forgot. I have a dental appointment at 11.30. Would you sit with your father for me? He probably won't need you there all the time, but if you pop in every now and again, then I'll know he's safe. You can ring me, of course, if there's any problem.'

'Yes, I can do that. I wanted to talk to him about my cousin anyway.'

'No, don't you talk to him about her. He gets very upset, you know. Anyway, we thought we'd have a little chat tomorrow, if you can come over, the three of us. Then you can ask us anything you want to know.'

'That sounds good – but it will have to be in the morning. Mike Lewis has changed my appointment time.'

'Well, why don't you come for coffee around 11?'

'OK. But meanwhile you had better get a move on. I'll sort the kittens and be over as soon as I've had some cereal.'

My mother scurried away. I felt relieved that she was talking to me again today and prepared to talk about my cousin tomorrow. I saw to the kittens, ate cereal without any milk and picked up my laptop. I hadn't looked yet to see if I had any matches. I knew it was too soon to expect much, but I had to keep an eye on my website, I told myself. No one had responded to me. I quickly tidied my little home and crossed the lawn to look after my father.

In comparison to my mother, my father was in a reticent mood. He was fed up with sitting around. The occupational therapist had given him exercises to do. From her instructions they seemed very gentle, with absolutely no weight on his hip. I wondered how we were going to keep him off his hip for another few weeks.

I bullied Dad into agreeing to do them. I read out the exercises and watched him move gingerly. Mostly he had to wriggle his toes and push them away to keep the muscles in his ankles supple. For his legs he inwardly stretched his muscles. It looked remarkably like Pilates to me and the OT had written instructions like 'imagine you are pushing against a great stone. Do not move your leg away, but feel your muscles tighten'. I lay on the floor to try to demonstrate them to him, but he couldn't really see me so nearly fell off the bed looking. I fetched a footstool and did them again sitting on the chair with my feet up. I couldn't believe he had been out of hospital for so long and hadn't yet done these exercises he had been taught. I resolved to come over each day and make him do them and tell my mother off for not making him.

We then went on to crosswords and sudoku. The first crossword was a cryptic, so that took us ages. By 1.30 I had made my father and myself an omelette. I made a cup of tea and found some fruit cake for Dad. Still no sign of my mother.

We had begun a game of Scrabble when she turned up, laden with bags.

'Where have you been?' I asked unnecessarily.

'I had to do a bit of shopping for us, so I've bought a few things for you, too, since you are being so helpful with Dad.'

'How did you manage that?' She knew what I meant.

'It's not easy, is it, dear? I couldn't find those potatoes you like, so I just bought baking potatoes. Perhaps you can use some of your blue dye on them? I bought you two red cabbages. That's what you usually have, isn't it? And some blue iced biscuits, blueberries, grapes, the usual blue fish I buy you, steak – a bit extra in case your young man comes round again – and two different types of blue cheese. I couldn't find any of that blue bread you have; I looked everywhere.'

'I make it, Mother. I use a bread mix and add some colouring.'

'Oh, I didn't know that. I can find you a bread mix from my cupboard.'

I was overwhelmed. My mother had shopped for me and taken into account my peculiarities. I carried it all over to the summerhouse feeling loved, but worried that something wasn't quite right.

39

Wednesday was a lovely, bright, cold day. It was good not to wake up with frost on the windows. I dressed quickly, in my swirly patterned skirt plus a blouse that was dove grey. I had found that while in the house the day before. It was big on me, but only by about one size. I had also found a burgundy cardigan. This went on and off a few times before I threw on another, bulkier denim-blue cardigan.

When I had eaten my usual yoghurt I went over the lawn to my parents' house. My mother greeted me strangely.

'Lovely to see you, Adelle. We are meeting in your father's room.'

The cups rattled on the tray as my mother brought hot drinks into Dad's temporary bedroom. I wondered what she was nervous about.

She left me to pour tea from the best teapot while she went to 'fetch something'. Dad and I made polite conversation while we waited for her to come back. She bustled in with more photo albums under her arm.

'Dad has something to tell you,' she said.

I looked in horror, studying their faces. It was like a scene from a film where the heroine discloses she has cancer, or some other life-threatening disease, and has one day to live.

Dad cleared his throat. 'Your mother has been economical with the truth when she told you about your, er, cousin.'

'Second cousin,' I said.

'Well, whatever she explained to you. But I want to tell you the whole story.'

There was a pause. 'Go on, John,' said my mother.

Dad reached out for my hand. I was studying him urgently now, willing him to explain.

'When you were just coming up to three, you and the little girl you called your friend were very close. We had an outing to some woods near where we lived. Lovely place; there was a hill to climb where you could see for miles. I would lift each of you up and point in the direction...'

'Never mind all that,' said my mother. 'Get on with it.'

'It was a Saturday and it was busy. The warmest day of the year so far. Absolutely packed. We sat over near the woods and you two little girls played round a big tree. One or the other of you could be seen all the time.'

My mother was sniffing. My father's eyes were moist. 'Then you came round the big tree and you were crying "Amelie, Amelie, Amelie" over and over again. I shot into the woods and there was no sign of her anywhere. You were distraught.'

I was shaking with the half-memory of the occasion. My father stroked my hand. My mother came round to me. She was sobbing loudly now.

'I never saw my Amelie again,' she said.

My mind was fearfully frantic, rejecting the truth and then embracing it until I had clarity about Amelie's identity. I managed to croak, 'She was my twin, wasn't she?'

'Yes, darling, you are an identical twin. Your twin went missing in the woods and we have never seen her again.'

I couldn't speak. I was thinking of that little girl – no, two little girls – running together, playing together. Even looking in the mirror together – why had I forgotten that? I remembered Amelie's blue ribbon and my yellow one. Our dresses the same apart from the colour. I had no words to describe how awful I felt. I forgot about Dad's hip and lay my head on him – by now I was crying for my twin.

My mother fetched a sherry. That was odd, being offered sherry when you've just discovered you are a twin and your other half is lost. Had been lost for nineteen years. I could not sort out what I was feeling. Frightening colours were whirring round in my head. We hugged, the three of us. My mother cried as she stroked my hair. We calmed each other down. Then red anger charged through my feelings.

I shouted, 'Why didn't you tell me?'

My mother spoke softly. 'You had to go to Granny's. The police were sure we had done something awful to Amelie. We were constantly questioned and so very upset. It was a nightmare.'

My father added, 'You'd have come home earlier, but it was too much for your mother.'

'I had a nervous breakdown, he means. By the time you came home the following spring it was as if you had never had a twin. You asked to see your friend sometimes, but we said she didn't live with us any more. What else do you say to a child who is little more than a baby? We were afraid of traumatising you.'

'You kept asking to go to the woods, but we couldn't face taking you. We were terrified of losing you too,' said Daddy.

My mother started crying again. 'The story kept being run in the local paper. I lost all my friends. They didn't know what to say to us. They probably thought we'd hurt her.'

'I left my job in the City. The place was full of gossips,' said Dad.

My mother blurted out through her tears, 'I stopped going to church and the WI, and the only person I could talk to was your granny.'

'In the end we moved here, nearer Granny,' said Dad. 'I started up as an independent trader on the stock market. Mother needed treatment from a psychiatrist. It is an awful thing, losing a child.'

At that moment, all I could think about was how awful it was to lose a twin sister. I was struggling to control my anger. I could hear my voice cracking when I asked, 'Why did you cut her out of the photos?'

'Those were the albums for you, when you wanted to look at them. But you have seemed content to look at the ones in frames around the house until you started speaking to your new psychologist. I have copies here of you both together.'

I didn't want to look, but I did. There we were – a family of four, with two of them being me. I was holding hands with my twin. I felt weary with a fatigue I had never known before. I felt too exhausted to be angry now. I forced myself to ask the most dreadful questions I had ever spoken. 'Do you know what happened? Did they ever find Amelie's body?'

'No. And we didn't stop looking for her until you turned eighteen.'

I believed them and I knew they had no part in her disappearance. The fact that they didn't find any trace of her gave me hope.

'I wish I had grown up knowing,' I said. 'It would have helped me to understand myself and you two better.'

My mother was in no condition to answer. My father grunted, 'Sorry, Adelle, we could only do what we thought was best. There's no one who knows what to do in this situation.'

'We'll find her one day,' I said, for myself as much as my parents. If they'd looked for fifteen years, what chance did I have of finding her?

40

Wednesday 28th March

I had the expected phone call from Adelle's father.

'Adelle has had a shock. She's very shaky but her mother is on the way to bring her to the appointment.'

'Are you able to tell me what it's all about?'

'Adelle says I can tell you that she's not who she thought she was, but she wants to tell you herself.'

'Is she adopted?'

'No. She will tell you, I think, but if she doesn't, I will talk to you later.'

I didn't feel at all well equipped. Why did Adelle's father say she wasn't who she thought she was? I reckoned there must be only one explanation. I hoped for Adelle's sake that someone would tell her what happened to the missing child.

For the first time, Adelle wanted her mother in the room. I had foreseen this and rearranged my chairs, lowering my office chair and creating a slightly cramped circle, which would enable us all to be at the same sort of height.

Adelle went to her usual chair and slumped into it. She said nothing.

Her mother took the other armchair. She was shaking. I offered them both a hot drink and then went into the office to ask Rachel to make one very weak black tea and an ordinary tea with milk.

'Three sugars in each, please, Rachel. I think I am treating them for shock.'

I went back into my quiet office. Adelle's mother was trembling as she started to speak softly. 'It's our fault, Dr Lewis. We should have told her years ago.' She turned to her daughter. 'May I tell Dr Lewis what we told you this morning?'

Adelle had curled into the chair, her back half-turned towards me. She looked as if she could hardly lift her head, let alone speak. Somehow she muttered, 'OK.' Her mother told me briefly how Adelle was a twin and Amelie had disappeared in the woods with no trace. She had never been found.

I needed to be completely certain that what I suspected was right. 'There is no second cousin, then?'

'No, I'm sorry. She asked about the photos – I was caught on the hop.'

Adelle moved. From beneath her cardigan she pulled a brown photo album and silently passed it to me. It was warm – obviously having been hugged to her for some time. I felt I needed permission to look at it from one of them. Adelle had closed her eyes. I looked towards her mother, who said, 'I think Adelle would like you to see it.'

The first photo was of two identical babies, side by side in a cot. They were very small, but appeared to be looking at each other. As I turned the pages, I saw the girls as babies sitting up, then toddling together or towards each other, and several pages of them slightly older, running together or sitting, holding hands.

While I had been looking, Rachel had sidled in with the drinks and put them on the coffee table. Adelle pulled herself into a sitting position and her mother passed the drink to her, encouraging her to sip it.

Meanwhile I found some photos with both parents and others with just Mother or only the twins. Happy photos. Then there was a blank page – next to it was a photo of one child, Adelle, sullen and unsmiling, leaning against a lady I presumed was her grandmother. By the end of the album Adelle was the only child with her parents, still looking sad.

Adelle stretched out her hand to take back the album, which immediately disappeared under her cardigan. My emotions went crazy as I recalled looking at photos of Jamie over Christmas with Ella. My child had been lost, but mine was dead and I knew it. How did anyone live without knowing what had happened to their child? Or their twin?

'You have been through an awful experience,' I said to them both, thinking it sounded trite even as I said it. 'It must be almost impossible to grieve when you don't know what has happened to your child, or your twin, or even your friend as you knew her.'

'It's much worse than that,' said Adelle, her voice faltering. 'Everyone has lied to me, all my life, even Granny.'

I passed her the blue napkins, even as her mother produced a small packet of tissues. She took the napkins. Her mother spoke.

'Granny wouldn't lie to you. She agreed never to bring the subject up, at our request. She told us each time you mentioned Amelie and she always told you we were looking for her, which we were. It was such a long time before you came home that you had stopped talking about her.'

'I never forgot her.'

'We know that now. But Granny had taken you to Sunday school and you were friendly with a little girl there, who was a lot older than you and liked looking after you. Her name was Caroline, which is probably why I came up with that name when I told you that you had a cousin. You missed Caroline when you came home. I thought you had forgotten you had a twin. You were too young to understand.'

Adelle sat up straight and looked at her mother. 'I have never forgotten her. Never ever. No friend has come near to how close we were. It makes sense now. Maybe I stopped asking because I never got an answer.'

I didn't intervene – I didn't need to. Adelle's mother got out of her chair and crouched next to Adelle with her arm around her shoulder. 'I know, I know. I'm so sorry. I miss her too, but I had you.'

'I must look for her, Mother. I need to find her.'

Adelle's mother looked at me. I nodded; I didn't need to say anything.

'I understand. Daddy and I will help you. We love you and we still love her.'

I excused myself and went and made myself a coffee, which I drank in the secretaries' office.

'Is Adelle all right?' asked Patricia.

'She will be. She's had a terrible shock.'

'Can you tell us?'

'I'll ask you to type up a letter later today to her GP. She may need some tranquillisers.'

They both nodded. I was glad we had secretaries we could trust in the department.

I went back to Adelle and her mother, considering that the five minutes or so was probably enough for them to begin a new sort of bonding.

Adelle left the room for a little while to use the bathroom. I talked with a very subdued Mrs Merchant. When Adelle returned, no therapy was needed from me as I watched a mother tend to her adult child in a gentle, caring way.

They left together, early.

There was no hiding from working on my grief now. I was devastated by Adelle's story. I couldn't blame her parents for never telling her, but I genuinely believed that it must be worse to not know what happened. And when Adelle left the room, Rosemary Merchant told me why Adelle had been left so long with her grandmother. How must they have felt when they were questioned as suspects for the disappearance and possible murder of their own child? It is beyond thinking. No wonder Rosemary's mental health suffered.

Now they were gone, I needed to talk to someone. The only other person who had worked with Adelle was Anita. When I rang the studio, she was getting ready to leave the department.

'I'll pop up to see you on the way out,' she said. 'Perhaps I can be some help.'

I made us both a coffee – mine black, hers with milk.

While I waited, I wondered whether I had made something of a fuss. Adelle was the one in great distress, along with her parents. I was simply filled with the dread that I may not be able to help them because of my own unresolved grief.

Anita hurried in and we set to work. She has a good way of noticing details and asking questions I hadn't considered.

'How is Adelle coping with her parents not being who she thinks they are? Is she angry that she has been deceived? I would be!'

'She was still in shock. She did show some anger when she told her mother that she had never forgotten her twin. She had forgotten the missing girl was her twin, but it was the friend she had talked about with me before. She'd remembered throwing leaves up in the air together, running together hand in hand, that sort of thing.'

'There's likely to be more anger as she thinks about the extent of her parents' deceit. The father must have colluded as well.'

'Apparently it was John who insisted Adelle should be told now. Adelle had started a lookalike website to try to find her so-called cousin. The parents looked for about fifteen years.'

'I wonder whether they've used the internet.'

'They hadn't tried a lookalike site. Adelle has done a really good job to set that up.'

'What you must be aware of, Mike, is that this could become Adelle's life mission and she may therefore lose opportunities for other friends, relationships and her own family.'

'I know. She has a very new boyfriend. I don't know what he's like and whether they will be able to negotiate this new relationship, the twin, coming into their lives. Even if Adelle never finds her, she is there in her thoughts.'

We talked on for perhaps half an hour. This was certainly an unusual case. Anita knew there would be problems for me personally, too.

'I've been thinking,' said Anita. 'Is now the time for me to do some grief work with her, using art? She may need familiarising with the highly coloured studio first, unless I can create a blue setting for her each time.'

'Before this happened she was chipping away at the edges of her fixation with blue. Even today she was wearing a scarf with rainbow tassels.'

'That's good, but she has a long way to go.'

'If she can cope, it would help if she did some bereavement work with you. But which loss will we focus on? Her granny or the twin?'

'Both. And her identity, plus her ability to trust her parents.'

'There is so much here, isn't there? But thank you.' Anita stood up and glanced at her watch. 'I've got to go, Mike. I want to catch the earlier train. I haven't been able to get a seat on the later one.'

I left shortly after her. I needed to be home with Ella.

41

How I recovered after the devastating news I do not know. I felt traumatised. Maybe I was, because I must have been in danger too when my twin disappeared. I couldn't remember what had happened in any detail at all. I think my mother had hoped I would recall a person talking to us, or something else of importance, but I was too young.

I didn't want to talk to Jack or Sharon. I felt too numb. I could hardly respond to the kittens that just climbed on me and purred as if everything was fine. I ignored the phone when it rang a few times that evening, then I worried that Jack might think I had finished with him. He rang, just after 10 pm, and I answered.

'Hello, Jack.'

'Oh, thank goodness you answered. Are you OK? I've been trying to get hold of you all day. I began to think you were ill.'

'I've been out mostly. I was with my parents this morning and my psychology appointment was changed to this afternoon. I'm sorry, I must have had my phone off. I know you called earlier this evening. Sorry.'

'You don't sound like yourself, Dreamy. What's the matter?'

That made me burst into tears, but I managed to tell him that I'd had some bad news, didn't even know who I was any more, and I'd speak tomorrow. I needed time to sort myself out.

'Don't forget I'm here for you. Shall I come round tomorrow night?'

'Yes. Come then. I'm tired now. Bye, Jack.'

'Goodnight, Dreamy, sleep well.'

I felt none of the joy I had felt before when I talked to Jack. I felt completely drained. I threw myself into bed fully clothed and the kittens climbed in with me. I fell asleep crying for my twin.

I had a restless night. My dreams were full of tall trees and losing people. My mother was being dragged away from me and I was left holding a green ribbon. I woke early in the morning, my pillow sodden. I was cold and frightened.

I was in the shower at about 6 am when my mother knocked and sidled in through the door. The place was a mess – I hadn't sorted out anything the night before. Mother called out, 'It's only me, Adelle, take your time.' And then I heard her fussing the kittens and the chink of their cat bowls as she fed them. My shower water went cold and I guessed she was either filling the kettle or washing up. I did as I was told for a change, and took my time. I was reluctant to talk to my mother.

I eventually emerged feeling better and warmer, having spent longer in the shower once it was running hot again. I had no energy to tell her off for using the system while I was washing.

My mother looked after me and I let her. She put the television on for the news and cooked me breakfast. She brought a tray laden with an egg sandwiched between two pieces of my blue bread, with mushrooms, slightly bluish – she'd been cautious with the food dye – but it was acceptable. She had made a blue milkshake too. She sat opposite me with her egg and bacon and, between mouthfuls, she talked about Amelie. She described outings and how we two were inseparable. She told me about playhouses made out of blankets stretched between chairs, and Amelie bossing me around even in her baby language when we could both hardly sit up. Our milestones matched, our hair was always in the same style and our faces identical. Our clothes were mostly blue for her and yellow for me because no one could tell us apart and Mother wanted us to be treated as individuals.

I asked her what she thought had happened to Amelie.

'I think she was kidnapped; that's why we searched for so long. The police thought she was murdered, but they have never found any evidence to prove this.'

My mother put her arm round my shoulders. For some odd reason, I leaned against her.

'Do you think it is right for me to look for her now?'

'You have to do what's right for you. But don't let it consume you. I felt so guilty when I couldn't protect Amelie that I became a tense, overprotective mother. I think it has been bad for you and for me. Please forgive me for keeping you too close, Adelle. I couldn't do anything else. Still can't.' She was crying and I passed her a box of tissues.

I didn't know whether I could forgive her. But I said, 'I'll try to find her.'

'We will look again, too. And Daddy said I must remind you that if you need money to reach more people on the internet, he'll pay. We are right behind you.'

'Good,' I said. I didn't trust myself to speak. I wasn't really sure who my mother was any more, but somehow I understood her better than ever.

Mike phoned me that same day, the day after the 'final truth meeting', as I had begun to call it. His phone call came at a really difficult time – I was busy on the internet, my lookalike website having gone mad now it was going to so many people, with my father's financial help.

All sorts of followers were rejoicing at finding people who looked like them. I had opened it up expecting no responses to my post at all and found there were four. Two of them had photos of people who looked absolutely nothing like me. I sent them an immediate thank you and apologised to them that they were not my cousin. The other two looked hopeful, but one of those was in America. The British girl had picked up on all my similarities, but right at the end of her description of herself she revealed that she was three years older than me, so she definitely wasn't my twin.

Mike's phone call came just as I was about to respond to both girls, saying they were not my cousin. I closed my laptop as I answered my mobile. He had phoned to find out how I was and to talk to me about further appointments. I didn't really know how I was. In some ways I felt like a ghost of my former self. I was driving myself to find Amelie, yet thinking she was dead. But, at the same time, I had almost pretended that there was no problem at all and I would just look for a twin rather than a cousin.

I didn't confess to Mike how lonely I felt. I felt like a fraud and a criminal. I, at age nearly three, had been the one who survived, or stayed, at least. Why did they take my sister and not me? I was frightened too. Mostly frightened that I would never ever find her.

While I was thinking about all this, Mike was talking about Anita, the art therapist, helping with appointments because I would need more support following the revelations about my twin. Maybe he understood that I felt it was my fault. I tried to concentrate.

'I'm not sure I can cope with that studio yet.'

'We've discussed that. She has some screens which have been used before for display and dividing the room. She can create a blue area.'

'I've been wearing a skirt with grey in it, my cats are grey and I'm getting used to the burgundy and cream I've introduced.' I could not keep the flatness out of my voice.

'If you don't mind using those colours in your artwork, I'll tell her. Are you still designing the kitchen for your mother?'

'All I've done since we last met is search for my cousin, now my twin. I'm sorry.'

'Don't be sorry. You can bring your design so far to show Anita, if you like. But the main purpose of including her is to see if you would prefer to work on your grief through art, or through talking therapy, or both.'

At that moment, I couldn't care. 'OK, but no artwork of mine on the walls.'

'Don't worry, Delle, she will keep your work confidential. And I will still work with you as well.'

'I don't want to spend too much time on the appointments. I must find my sister; that's my main priority now.'

Mike assured me that he understood. I didn't know how he could; it just doesn't happen that people go missing suddenly like that. And for me, it felt as if she had very recently gone.

There was a knock on the door. Jack was waiting on the lawn holding a bunch of irises. I felt tears rise up in my eyes while I searched for my vase under my sink. I stood up and Jack passed me a tissue – I blew my nose and he gathered me up.

'You said you weren't who you thought you were. What does that mean, Dreamy?'

'I'm a twin,' was all I could say.

Jack made me some weak tea and himself a coffee. He found the shortbread I had made before I knew I was a twin. Somehow that seemed years away. We sat in silence on my sofa, each stroking a kitten. 'Tell me about it when you're ready,' he said.

So I did, starting with my memories, my love of Granny. It had all fallen into place now as I realised that I had bonded closer to her than I had to my mother. My nearly three-year-old self had been rejected; my mother had sent me away. Had I resented her ever since, or was it the loss that changed her?

Jack let me talk, with the odd word of encouragement. I was leaning against him, hiding my face in his jumper, so he sometimes asked me to repeat things. When I told him about my mother lying to me about my second cousin, I felt his body stiffen. I pulled away. The kittens leaped off the sofa and scurried behind the chair.

'Come back, Dreamy.'

'But you seem angry.'

'Not with you. I am angry with your parents for not telling you earlier, and your mother for covering up. I'm sorry, it's none of my business.'

'I'm angry and sad, really confused and yet relieved that I know. My mother came over and made me breakfast this morning and we talked properly, maybe better than ever.'

Jack said nothing and I stood up, ready to get us another drink. I remembered the steak my mother had bought.

'Do you want to cook something, Jack? I don't know if I have the energy. There's steak in the fridge and chips in the freezer.'

'Certainly, lead me to the food and I'll see what I can do.'

So, for the second time that day, someone else looked after me.

Seeing how tired I was, Jack left soon after he had eaten and I had nibbled at some of my steak. After he had gone, I resumed sending a regret message to the girls who had responded on the lookalike site. I hesitated over the American girl. Her birthday wasn't the same as mine; it was a few months later, but the likeness was so strong. I would keep the picture at least. But a bit of me didn't want to follow anyone up now. I needed space. I shut my laptop with an unintended bang, unplugged it and put it in my wardrobe.

The next few days were a muddle. I needed to be blue more than ever – yet my twin colour was yellow. My mother bought me a yellow cushion and I hid it under my bed.

Loads of colours seemed to be crashing around me. The yellow zinged at me and I couldn't look at the dark red throw that blared out. I put it in the washing basket. I could scarcely think about my twin without crying. I couldn't think what to do.

In the end, I phoned Jack to ask him whether he thought I should continue with the lookalike site. But that didn't help me – he told me to leave it alone for now and come back to it when I was ready. When I told him I might never be ready he went quiet. I finished the phone call without us agreeing to meet again. I felt desolate.

42

The next day I was feeling bruised – no, more than that – battered. The pounding in my head wouldn't stop. At one point in my life, that would have been when I began to cut myself. But this time my anger was not directed at myself but at my parents for the deceit woven around me. I had never known my true identity.

I shouted and raved at the unfairness of it all. My head was feeling even worse. I took a painkiller, my fingers hovering over the blister pack while I contemplated taking them all. I put them in the bin. I lay on my bed too upset to cry, my chest hurting. After a while, I became aware of Skye on the bed with me, softly mewing. I turned over and she snuggled up to me; the action of stroking her and her responding purr calmed me down. The pain in my head was receding, my thoughts becoming clearer.

I rolled off my bed and went through to my little bathroom. I washed my face and brushed my hair. I walked through and sat on my sofa, taking my laptop.

I made a list – I wrote down every way I felt I had been lied to and then another one of the consequences that the loss of Amelie had on my life. There were the obvious ones – the loneliness, the need for friends who were as close as a sister, the feeling of loss that I could not attribute to anyone or anything.

Then I wrote down the less immediate consequences – they were more subtle but standing out from it all was my mother's overprotective behaviour. The suffocating feeling of her presence when she invaded my space; the refusal to let me stay even one night with my friends during my teenage years; the missed school trips; her wish to know my every move; her general attitude towards me – still treating me as a child now I was in my twenties.

Although I still felt lost, I was beginning to find a way out of this tangled mess.

I realised all my notes revolved around my mother. I considered whether my mild father had contributed – yes, he had, in not telling me who I really was. But my relationship with him still felt pretty robust on the whole. The trust I had in him had been knocked back, but I knew he loved me and I felt we would come through.

But my mother had basically ruined my life. There were urgent changes I needed, starting with her respecting my privacy. It was a mistake to live in their summerhouse, but there was no changing that unless I suddenly acquired an excellent, well-paid job. Unlikely, especially as my desire to go back to college prevented that.

I cuddled my kittens, turned off my mobile phone to avoid being disturbed, and began another list.

Under the heading 'privacy' the first item was 'lockable doors'. There was a cost implication but I needed to establish some boundaries. Second on my list was the whole area of my eating – how many other twenty-two-year-olds were policed by their mother over what they ate? Then there was the issue of my friends – what right had Mother to call them my 'so-called friends'? With the exception of Jack, every one of my friends had been scrutinised by her. I hardly saw Cessy these days – I blamed my mother's disapproval.

I made myself a cup of tea, munched some fudge and considered the way forward. Was it fair to have all this out with my mother when my father was still incapacitated? I decided it had to happen while everything was still so raw and my emotions so high. Otherwise I would lose my nerve.

I practised what I would say to them both as I put down food for Harry and Skye. I nearly weakened as I thought how well my mother had cared for me the day before and how I needed her to look after the kittens sometimes. But the anger returned as I remembered my childhood – she had focused on me so much when I was growing up that I felt stupid; that is, until my teens, when I was labelled a rebellious teenager. In truth, I was trying to get away from being squashed. I decided the list was long enough to start change, so printed it.

It was time for action.

I marched across the lawn. I knocked at my parents' door politely, clutching the folded paper. They didn't hear. I hammered on it with all I had and my mother opened it a little, looking scared.

'Oh, it's you breaking the door down,' she said.

'Sorry, you didn't hear,' I said firmly as I marched in. 'I need to speak to you both, so shall we go into Dad's room?'

My mother nodded. She looked flustered but dried her hands on the kitchen towel and followed me.

My father was propped up in bed, looking miserable. I nearly weakened, but then my resolve returned and I disclosed the purpose of my visit.

'I've been thinking about the consequences of you hiding the truth from me for so long. They have affected my life greatly and it's time to put it all right.'

My father nodded; my mother slowly sat down.

'I have made a list of things I would like changed – I think you owe me that.'

'I'm not sure we owe you much,' said my mother, in a plaintive voice. 'We've given you all we could.'

'Except the truth, and that's affected both you and me, Mother. Yesterday you apologised to me about how you'd brought me up. It's time to put it right.'

I proceeded to read my list. I tried to sound conciliatory, but I knew it was coming over as harsh. It had to be. There was silence. I gave them space to think. The list was shaking in my hand so I folded it and stuffed it in the pocket of my jeans.

My father spoke first.

'I agree completely about the locks and will ring a locksmith immediately. If the present doors won't take a secure lock, I will get all the doors changed. I can also arrange to rig up a bell on the gate and make you a nameplate, if you like.'

'Thank you, Dad.'

'I'll try not to ask you all those things,' said Mother, 'but it's habit now.' I managed to keep calm.

'Then you'll need some therapy. You must break that habit.'

'But you won't eat unless I make you.'

'I will. You'll see.'

Softly, my mother continued her argument, 'But you need me.'

I resisted shouting at her. I could see quite clearly that she needed me to rely on her and I had to fight it, but my tone was as gentle as I could manage when I said, 'I am an adult and I must be more independent. I will help by arranging outings with my friends – maybe have a weekend or two away, or even go on holiday with them. Although I'm broke so that won't be yet.'

'I know you're trying to break away from us, Adelle, but how about an independence allowance to help you do that?' My father was really catching on.

'I'll have to think about that,' I said.

'If you were still at college we'd be paying for your course and if you were at university we'd be paying for your keep as well.' He'd made a good point, but I held back from saying that if I'd had a normal childhood I would have my degree by now.

'I'm not sure.'

'I have quite a few bonds in your name. They're legally yours. You could cash some in.'

I stared at him, trying to sort out what he had said. Then it twigged and I couldn't keep the anger out of my voice. 'You mean I am scrimping and saving, and I have money? Why didn't you tell me?'

'We didn't think it was the right time – we were waiting until you wanted to buy a house.'

I closed my eyes and shook my head. I was trying to take this in. How could it not be the right time when I was watching every penny?

The pause must have made my mother think we had finished talking.

'Shall we have a cup of tea?' she said too brightly. 'We've all got a lot to think about.'

My anger subsided, but my laugh was tinged with bitterness. My mother proffered strange peace offerings – a glass of sherry when I learned my twin was stolen and a cup of tea when I was told I had money after all. I felt like a puppet dangled on strings for their control and amusement. It was not funny.

I marched back across the lawn and made my own tea, in my own space.

43

Wednesday 4th April

I had wondered whether Adelle would come to her next appointment, but I hurried out of a meeting with Human Resources to find her waiting, alone. My mind was still full of the meeting and I needed to report to the secretaries, so I asked her if she could wait another five minutes. She shrugged, then nodded. She was early anyway.

I shot into the office with my news. Patricia was up a ladder reaching for archived files. I was impatient for her to come down.

'Come along, Patricia, I have a client waiting and I need to talk to you both first.'

Rachel immediately swivelled her chair to face me. Patricia descended the ladder with a sigh.

'Couldn't it have waited?' she asked in a flat voice.

'No. I wanted to tell you now.'

Here they were, the two loyal secretaries, both probably thinking they were about to lose their jobs.

'I have been appointed as head of department, and signed my new contract today.' Both ladies smiled and congratulated me – I stopped them and said, 'And I have something else to tell you.' They stopped smiling immediately. Patricia sat down. I continued, 'I have discussed your job descriptions fully with the management team. I have explained that valuable and expensive clinic time will be taken up if we have to begin typing up our own reports. I have talked about the quality of the department and your roles as receptionists, which are not outlined in your job descriptions.'

'And?' said Rachel.

'Despite the computers on everyone's desks, there will be no change of your roles in this department for the foreseeable future. In fact, your positions will not be reviewed for five years apart from the change we have made this morning, which is to add reception duties to your job descriptions.'

Conscious that Adelle might hear us from the waiting area, I had to quieten them down as they laughed and thanked me. They both gave me a quick hug, which I told them was unprofessional, before I made my excuses and picked up Adelle's file, retreating to my consulting room. I then needed a minute or two to adopt a more serious composure, before inviting Adelle into my room.

Adelle's mood was obvious from her all-blue clothing, the shawl covering the chair and her lowered head. Nonetheless, I asked her how she was after the last meeting we'd had.

'I don't know. I am confused. My parents want me to find my twin and I want to too, but I can't bear it. If she is alive, she has her own life now. And anyway, I no longer know who I am.' As she said this, her voice was going quieter and quieter.

'In some ways you are the same person you always were.' I knew she couldn't accept that, but I would have to drip-feed positive statements. Why hadn't her parents told her before? It made no sense.

'There's a girl in America who looks just like me. I can't make myself do anything. I haven't contacted her and I can't delete her picture. I feel frozen.'

'Maybe it's too soon, Delle. You've had a shock. It's time to reaffirm who you are, not wonder about who you would have been.'

She nodded but said, 'Did I ever know who I really was? Apart from knowing that I was obsessed with the colour blue.'

We talked about her identity, reviewing previous sessions and how she saw herself. None of that had changed. What had changed was the identity of her 'friend' when she was little.

But Adelle's understanding of herself had been knocked sideways. I began to talk about likes and dislikes, edging towards the boyfriend. We reached the point where she could talk about him.

'My life has been in turmoil one way or another ever since our first date, well halfway through our first date. I'm not sure if he'd still be interested in me if something wasn't constantly changing or happening. Now I feel so wretched, I expect he'll give up on our relationship anyway.'

'Why do you think that?'

'When I told him that I didn't know what to do about the lookalike site, he said I was to keep it until I was ready. I told him I may never be ready and he went quiet.'

'So why do you think he went quiet?'

'I expect he'd had enough of me.'

'Or?'

'I see what you're doing – this is when I should be using CBT techniques, isn't it?'

I nodded. She sat and thought for a moment.

'Oh, I can't do this today. Maybe he didn't know what to say. Will that do?'

'Of course it will. You've found another way of looking at it. I suggest you try to use the forms as you process everything that has happened during the last week.'

Adelle nodded. 'I'll try.'

'When you are ready, we can have your parents here to discuss things with them if you would like that.'

'I'm very angry with them. Not only for not telling me when I was younger, but because they have suffocated me by keeping me so safe.'

'Are you able to tell them so?'

For the first time during the session, Adelle sparked into life.

'I have done so. I drew up a list of changes I wanted and they have agreed. But my mother doesn't know how to approach me now – she has backed right off, but she seems rather lost.'

'Would you like them to come to one of your sessions?'

'Maybe, but I'm keeping my distance a little bit at the moment too. Is it awful that I can't feel sorry for them?'

'Is there a rule that says you have to?'

Adelle thought before replying. 'No. But I'd like to.'

'Then we can work towards that, very gradually.'

I told her that I thought she was doing as well as anybody could in the circumstances. After all, she had only known about her twin a week earlier. Adelle remained calm and thoughtful as we worked on how the knowledge of the loss of her twin would affect her life.

Right near the end of the appointment she told me about taking painkillers and how she had thought about taking the lot. I asked a few questions, assessing her informally for risk.

'I'm fine now,' she assured me. 'I became angry with my parents instead and that's when I sorted things out with them. I'm considering moving away, if I can. It's time for me to find somewhere more suitable than their back lawn.'

'On your own?'

'Maybe. Or with other students, perhaps. I'm determined to apply for college again.'

'Good. Anita will be pleased. She asked me to give you these appointments with her.' I handed the card to Adelle, saying, 'Would you like to concentrate on your work with her and then come back and tell me how it went? Or shall we pencil an appointment date in if you need it?'

Confounding my expectations, Adelle said, 'I expect you'll be talking to Anita about me, so if I need to see you she'll arrange it.'

'That sounds like a good plan.'

Adelle gathered up her belongings and I opened the door for her. She stopped in the doorway looking at my nameplate. Underneath there was now a second typed notice saying 'Consultant Clinical Psychologist, Head of Department'.

'I see you've been promoted,' she said. 'Congratulations!'

I was embarrassed but thanked her before turning into the office to tell the secretaries that it might have been better to let other members of the department know before putting a sign on my door.

'Don't worry,' said Patricia. 'I emailed everyone to tell them. You can't keep quiet about good news.'

I had the feeling that the secretaries ran the department in reality and I would be a mere figurehead.

44

It's strange – when I saw Mike Lewis a week after the final truth meeting, I felt as if I did not know who I was and thought all my dreams were totally smashed. But he helped me turn things around and my focus switched. But still I could not think about finding my twin nor talk to my parents about her. I turned all my energy to my art.

Despite this, I was dreading my first session with Anita Goodwin. It felt really strange when she came to fetch me from the usual waiting area and I was taken down those stone steps to the basement studio.

Mike was right – Anita had screened off a blue area for me. It felt odd. I had to resist peeping around the edge of the screen, knowing it would set my teeth on edge with the shock of the vibrant red and yellow poster paints that I knew would be ready to burst their rude noise over me.

I sat down by the table, trying to concentrate. Anita was talking to me but I could not listen. Gradually my mind settled and I began to hear what she was saying. She seemed to be telling me about a cabbage!

'Sorry,' I said. 'Can you say that again?'

'I was talking about the beauty all around us in everyday things, like a cabbage.'

My mind flipped to the red cabbages I boiled for my blue dye. She must have seen me drift off because when I pulled my thoughts back, she was waiting.

'OK?' she asked.

I nodded.

'If you can cope with faded colours, nothing bright, I would like to show you an old ornamental cabbage.'

This was even more peculiar than being in a partitioned area of her studio, but I nodded again, pushing red cabbages to the back of my mind.

Anita leaned down and opened a drawer behind her. Carefully, as if it were a baby, she lifted out a single stalk, with the large cabbage on the top. The veined leaves were beautiful – no shouting colours – just soft purples, yellows and greens as if life and colour were draining away, and there in the centre was a deeper, almost blue, purple. Somehow it reminded me of my granny with her papery veined hands and fading beauty.

I tried not to cry.

'Shall I put it away?' asked Anita.

'No, no, don't. It's beautiful. It just reminded me of…' I nearly didn't say what I was thinking, it seemed so bizarre.

'Reminded you of…?'

I told her. I described how Granny's complexion had drained, how her face looked yellow, how her hands looked streaked with blue as she lost weight and the veins became more prominent. I told her of my aching heart as I visited and watched her becoming weaker. I connected all my memories of that awful time together and talked about my granny's death in a way I had never spoken to anyone before, not even Mike.

Anita passed blue tissues when I needed to mop my eyes and finally, I was silent.

'Tell me about your granny when she was well.'

I pulled away from the rawness of Granny dying and talked about her hobbies. I recalled how she looked after her cottage garden so that it was a natural flow of colours through the spring to autumn, and even the foliage was pretty in the winter.

'Everything was very natural – there'd be no place for ornamental cabbages, although she did have a splendid vegetable patch where she grew red cabbage among other things.'

I was smiling now, remembering. I noticed the sketch pad and soft-coloured pencils on the table. Perhaps they'd been there all along.

'May I draw it?' I asked.

Anita smiled and nodded slowly, moving the pencils nearer to me. I took a blue one and began to sketch – I even filled in the purple in the middle, but left the outlines of the leaves empty, apart from drawing in the veins.

I stopped, feeling self-conscious. 'I need a photo of the cabbage so that I can try to draw some more at home. I can't do this here.'

'I'll take one,' said Anita and disappeared around the side of the screen, coming back quickly with a Polaroid camera. She took a photo of my work as well as of the cabbage. As we waited for them to develop, she talked about what we had covered during the session. I asked her to take more photos of the cabbage as the leaves continued to fade. I had an idea for my portfolio.

When I arrived home, I immediately found my water-soluble coloured pencils and pen and ink. I started again in my own sketchbook, carefully outlining the leaf shapes in ink. 'My first still life for a long time; let me have space to work on it,' I told Skye as she tried to scramble onto my lap. I finished the outline and looked at it. The stalk looked bare. I took a coloured pencil to carefully draw blue tears running down it from the leaves to create a pool at the bottom.

The life of the cabbage was draining away.

Seeing Anita for art therapy gave me a freedom I needed. I was painting thoughts and feelings in big expressive pieces that drew something out of me. My grief pictures began to absorb purple and eventually yellow. At home, I painted a series about my pets from kittens to cats – each including lifelike colours for Harry and Skye with coloured odd toys, cushions or furniture shooting out of the greyness. My father bought me a set of oils and a giant canvas, almost too large for my room. I don't think he approved of the resulting abstract, but I was so delighted that I had achieved an oil painting and used colours, albeit muted, without them screaming at me. I took photos for the portfolio.

As we came to the end of April, I rang my old tutor to arrange an interview date. She seemed pleased to talk to me and gave me a date in June, advising me how to put together the application forms and what work she would like to see. Inevitably, she stressed that she was expecting proof that I could now work in a variety of colours.

I did not tell my parents what I had done.

The day of the interview drew near. I had to stop myself from ringing to cancel it. Each time I worried about it, I used Mike's techniques to try to sort myself out.

I had prepared quite an impressive portfolio. The only interior design pieces I'd included were my mother's kitchen and the fabric design of her curtains. The rest were sketches and paintings, photos of work I could not take with me, and an occasional collage. I had not told Dr Hastings that I would like a change of course, although it was on my application form.

When I walked into Dr Hastings' room, she was the only one there to interview me. I began to shake, remembering last time we had met and feeling scared that this was not an interview to be accepted, but that she would be politely turning me down without even looking at my work. I didn't know what to do – I stood there, marooned in the middle of the bright room, holding my huge art case.

'Please sit down, Adelle, by the table.'

I walked over to a table that wasn't usually there and sat on the nearest chair. Dr Hastings took the other one beside me. I still hadn't said a word.

'Please put your portfolio on the table, Adelle; I'd be very interested to see it if you have brought it up to date.'

I managed to say, 'Thank you, yes, I have.'

I opened the portfolio and Dr Hastings began to look at the first pictures, all blue. There was a little frown that seemed to deepen as she studied them. She said nothing, but turned the page. There was my mother's mostly green kitchen. 'Well, this is interesting,' she said, smiling at me. There were more pages of gradually more colourful artwork before she reached my drawings of the ornamental cabbage.

She stopped and studied the page for a few minutes. I had drawn small pictures of cabbages up one side of the paper, across the top and down the other side. I had started with a fresh ornamental cabbage. The rest of the smaller sketches were of the same cabbage losing more and more colour. As they progressed, more blue drips, or tears, were running down the central stalk. In the gap in the middle was the large, final drawing where there was no blue at all in the cabbage – all the blue was freely running down the stalk and pooling at the bottom – a dropped leaf at the side.

I was glad she didn't ask me about it, because it had begun as grief work and evolved.

'Remarkable,' she said. 'Your use of colour is very subtle. Incredible.' I could say nothing; I was overwhelmed by how much she seemed to like it.

The next item in the portfolio was the curtain design.

'This is lovely, a gorgeous piece of work.' She read my notes detailing what it was. 'Has it been made up into a material?'

'No, not yet. And in fact I am working on another design as well, but it's not a complete design, so I didn't include it.'

'This one's very good – would you consider the textile option on your return to college?'

This was my chance, and I took it. I told her how much I loved research, how my renewed love of colours had made me think about a fine art with art history degree course.

'I had noticed the application was for a degree, but thought that you wanted to proceed to that when you had finished the interior design diploma.'

'I would prefer to move to a degree course now.'

Dr Hastings nodded. I couldn't tell whether she approved.

'What would you do with that when you leave?' she asked.

'I'm not sure, but probably teaching. Part-time, so that I can still be free to carry on with my own art.'

'You definitely have talent.' She turned to the curtain design again. 'I would recommend that if you are working for a degree, your third subject in the first year should be textile design.'

'I had hoped that would be possible. I love the intricacy of pattern.'

'Let's discuss this with the rest of the interview panel, shall we?' She left the room to invite other tutors in and I breathed a sigh of relief. I had been so sure she was going to let me down gently.

I enjoyed the interview. My nerves had gone completely and I was able to talk to the tutors about my art, my restricted access to materials at present and my influences. I was able to quote works of several artists and fill in the history of Manet and a little about the Impressionist Movement. There was a consensus of opinion that as I had passed the first year on the interior design course, it would more than count as an extra A level to qualify me for the degree course.

I was offered an unconditional place. I was so excited I felt like telling everyone in the street and on the Underground as I made my way home.

My parents hadn't known about the interview. Since the final truth meeting and my decision to make a definite effort to separate my life from theirs, I hardly kept them informed about any of my movements. But now I needed to tell them.

I took my portfolio into the summerhouse, then walked across the lawn and knocked on my mother's door. When she saw me I noticed her strained face before it relaxed into a smile.

'I have some news.' The reaction from her was so sudden and joyful that I quickly played down my success. 'Not about Amelie, about me.'

'Come in, I'll find your father.'

My father shuffled in, using his frame. His hip had not healed well and he was waiting for an appointment with the consultant. He seemed delighted I had come. I felt guilty and neglectful. I stood while they both sat down.

'I thought you'd like to know that I have an unconditional offer for a place in my old college to do an art degree.'

'How marvellous! Congratulations,' said my father, reaching up to give me a hug.

I looked at my mother. She was saying nothing. When she did speak it was not what I expected to hear.

'I thought you were doing an interior design diploma course?'

I sighed. 'I was, but I have had an interview and requested that I go on the degree course.'

'Does that mean you've dropped your present course?'

'I was already dropped and I'm not going back, but it has given me the qualifications to take the degree course which, if you remember, I couldn't do before because my A levels weren't good enough.'

'But it's not a university. Will it be a proper degree?'

I was getting angry now. 'Of course. We are affiliated to a university. It is a proper university degree, Mother.'

My father interrupted. 'Rosemary, your daughter is going to work for an art degree. She will have a BA. Stop asking questions and be proud of her! I am immensely proud.'

'Yes, I am proud. Of course I am. Well done, darling. Why didn't you tell us you were going for an interview?'

'Part of me being independent, Mother!'

I gave them both a hug and was about to go when Dad said, 'There's a bottle of champagne in my secret wine store. Bring your young man over tonight and we'll celebrate!'

I phoned Jack and warned him we were going to my parents' for a celebration. He was overjoyed, both that I had my 'well-deserved place' and that my parents were celebrating. He said he would 'dress appropriately', so I ironed a dress in honour of the occasion.

Jack knocked on my door at 7.15.

He enveloped me in a big hug before producing a small box. I was terrified he was going to propose, which I did not want just before going to college, but when I opened it I laughed with relief. It was a beautiful pendant, with a blue and green setting, in a semi-precious stone.

'Oh, Jack, thank you, it's lovely. Will I be able to wear Granny's necklace with it?'

'I know you never take that off, so I found one I thought would go with it.'

I put it on. Not only did it match my dress, but it made Granny's necklace look as if it belonged with it. I hugged him and it took us a few minutes to remember we were meant to be going across the lawn.

My parents were dressed up, too, so it felt like a real celebration. Mother had sorted out some fantastic nibbles for us to have with the champagne, and Dad made a speech. I was aware of my missing twin, but not so much that I couldn't enjoy the evening. I noticed that Jack was fidgeting a bit, walking around looking at the pictures on the wall and trying to make conversation about them. After he backed into a coffee table, which made my father's glass wobble before he caught it, it felt like time to go, but Mother was still talking about my degree.

'Just think of the celebrations when you are awarded your degree!' she said. 'We will have to hire somewhere and have a real party.'

'I expect she'll do that with her friends,' suggested my father.

'I'll do both,' I said, 'but we're going now. Jack and I have something to sort out.'

'Oh, what's that?' asked my mother, then she put her hand up to her mouth and said, 'Sorry, none of my business.'

I laughed. 'Will you ever be fully able to let me have secrets, Mummy dear?' I gave her a quick hug.

She beamed. I had used 'Mummy' in jest, and it still felt childish. But I resolved to try 'Mum' occasionally.

As we walked back across the lawn, Jack said, 'Am I allowed to know what we need to sort out?'

I laughed. 'Whether I should make you a sandwich or cook egg and chips. Lovely though they were, the nibbles my mother produced haven't amounted to a meal.'

'That's easily sorted – egg and chips, please.'

45

Sharon was having more spare time across the summer because she had no college days. I had two days' work at the garden centre. She still had work, but on our coinciding days off I went with her to look at flats. We were fed up with trooping up flights of stairs and seeing places that turned out to be bedsits, were smelly and crumbling, or had no balcony or garden for the cat she so desperately wanted.

She arrived at my little home one day in the second week of August with a pile of estate agent particulars. The top three had red stars in felt pen in the margins.

'I've had a talk with my mother and she can up the deposit a bit, and I'm now looking at two-beds and will take a lodger to help with the mortgage.'

The details looked good. Her top one was certainly the best. It was a ground-floor flat with three good-sized rooms, plus both a spacious bathroom and kitchen. It looked as if it needed redecorating but otherwise it was excellent.

'Where is this?' I asked.

'A little further out, but on the line to Victoria.'

'I love it.'

'And so do I, which is more to the point. It's too expensive, but let's look at it anyway.'

So while she phoned the agent, I made sure the cats had food and could get through the new cat flap and we went roaring off in her VW Golf – which was a gift from her newly rich mother.

Each of the other flats had made me pleased I wasn't flat-hunting but had my lovely converted summerhouse. But this one was different. The front garden was bedraggled and the path to the door broken, but when the agent said, 'It will need a bit of a tidy, that's the responsibility of the garden flat,' I was excited at the thought of helping Sharon choose plants and using my garden centre discount.

The rooms were spacious and full of light. The plaster was falling off the walls in most of the rooms but you could see what it could become. Sharon was saying 'I love it' in every room; even in the garden, where someone had half-built some decking that was painted purple, orange and pink, she wasn't put off. The garden wasn't large but the bushes were, so it was difficult to imagine the space.

I asked about parking. The estate agent took us round the front and showed us how others in the street had resolved this difficulty. Their front garden was converted to hardstanding for three cars.

'Oh no,' said Sharon, 'that will spoil the whole look of the place.'

'Do you both have a car?' asked the agent.

'I'm not buying,' I said, 'and Sharon can only drive one at a time.'

The estate agent looked at me as if I were completely deranged, but said, 'This being the end house, you could make a new entrance round the corner and park the car at the side of the house.'

'What about planning permission? Will I need it?' asked Sharon.

The estate agent raised his eyebrows, but said, 'Let's look at the other end of the row of houses and see what they've done.' So we took a walk down the road. Sure enough, the last house did have a car parked at the side, and a drive round the corner.

We had another look round the large flat. Sharon became more excited. I stopped her putting an offer in there and then. Eventually the agent managed to make her leave and we went off to find somewhere for a coffee.

I bought the coffees and then sat down with Sharon and made her work out if this was the flat for her. I suggested she found out about planning permission for parking, then look at the finances and consider what would happen if she couldn't find a lodger.

'I was wondering about a flat-share, actually, because a lodger might feel confined to their room.'

'The rooms are big.'

'Well, yes, but the person who I might invite to share with me is used to having her own place. Aren't you?'

'Pardon?'

'I'm asking if you'd flat-share with me.'

I felt flattered. I had spent my whole childhood feeling left out and now Sharon was talking about me living with her.

'It's tempting,' I said. 'I love my summerhouse but I must move on. I would never consider being a lodger now I've had my own little pad, but a flat-share is different. I and my cats would need the run of the place. It is in a good location for college. How much would the rent be?'

'I've no idea! Shall I look into it?'

'Well, you'll have to do that anyway, so yes. I'll have to handle it carefully, though, because officially I don't have access to the trust my father set up for me yet. So I'll be depending on his goodwill.'

That evening I told Jack about the flat and about Sharon's suggestion of a flat-share.

'You won't do that, will you?' said Jack. 'You've got a lovely little place here.'

'It's not really a house, is it? And the location is terrible.'

'Come on, Dreamy, appreciate what you have. It opens out on to a brilliant garden and it's been converted to meet your needs! I love it.'

'Yes, so do I, but I do need to move away from my parents.'

'But they are great people!'

For the first time, I felt as if Jack was more in love with the idea of me than with me, myself, as a person. I was angry.

'You will not dictate to me where I live.'

He was instantly repentant. 'I'm sorry – here you are independent, there you will be sharing. And we won't have privacy. That's all.'

He was right to a certain extent, of course. But I still felt squashed by him. I loved that flat and I needed to be out of my parents' immediate view.

46

It was near the end of August and I was looking forward to October when I would start my college art degree.

I was feeling ready by then, largely thanks to Mike Lewis and Anita Goodwin. Not only did Mike help me take control of my miserable thoughts, but both of them worked with me over my granny and over the strange loss of the twin I could hardly remember. I had fewer appointments with Mike, mostly being in the studio with Anita, and reporting how my paintings were changing over the weeks. When I talked the sequence through with Mike, his eyes moistened and he had to blow his nose.

Jack and I were still an item. We went carefully – he learned quickly not to keep reminding me about my double on the website. I needed to know what it was like to be boyfriend and girlfriend, not just co-researchers. And I needed to decide when to find out about the American girl.

Three weeks before the start of college, I looked again at the website, which I hadn't been able to open, apart from once, since the final truth meeting. I was frightened it would draw me into it at every moment and decided that I would try to look only twice a day, after the first day. I went back to the photo of the American girl. There she was, looking like a fuller-faced version of myself – healthy with rosy cheeks. I plugged in my laptop so that the battery wouldn't run down and left it open on the breakfast bar, with the full-screen photo on display.

'Hello, Amelie,' I said. 'Please be my twin.'

When Jack came round after work, the photo was still on display. I wanted him to see it.

He came in, sat down, and adjusted the cushions. 'Come and sit by me,' he said. I did and he pulled me towards him. I told myself to relax and managed to snuggle against him. We were quiet for a while, then he said, 'That's a lovely photo of you, Dreamy. When was it taken?'

'It's not me.'

The effect on Jack was tremendous. He grabbed me and danced around with me. 'You've found her – you've found her – you've found your twin!'

I stopped still. 'I don't know if it's her. We really can't go on a photo. Anyway, she's American.'

'Sorry, Dreamy, I just got excited by the picture. You're right to be cautious. May I see what she's written on your website?'

Reluctantly, I closed the photo down and found the post. It was from a girl called Lisa. Jack read out her details: '"I am twenty-two years old as you will have seen from my birthdate. I am 5'6" tall and my weight is around 8 stone 4. My birth certificate says I was born in Texas County. I know I was adopted when I was three."'

I took the laptop from him and scrolled back to the details under her photo.

'Look, Jack, her birthdate is not the same as mine. Anyway, she was born in Texas County. She's certainly my doppelgänger, but she can't be my twin.'

'Birth certificates can be forged,' he replied, 'and if she were kidnapped, it's likely she would be taken out of the country.'

I shrugged. I didn't know whether that was clutching at straws. Jack retrieved the laptop and continued to read what she had posted. I had nearly learned it by heart so I knew what he was reading.

'"I am answering this post because as you can see, I look exactly like you. But I don't want to get you excited. I don't think I can be your cousin, but who knows? I guess this might be my fantasy, but I don't know much about my adoption, and Mom is so ill now, I don't like to bother her without good reason. I did say something to Pops, when he lived with us, but he just shrugged. He's not with my mom now – I fly to New Orleans to see him about every three months. Do you ever come to the US? I sure would love to meet you."'

'She's not my twin – nor even my cousin. She says so.'

'But she also says she was adopted. You need to contact her.'

'I don't know, Jack. I have only recently come to terms with the fact that I'm a twin. And she was born in the States. That doesn't fit at all.'

I took the laptop from him and closed it down. I needed a hug. Jack noticed and we sat there embracing for a few minutes.

'Get your coat, Dreamy. Let's go and watch something in the cinema.'

I was in a strange state of wanting to believe Lisa was my twin, which made me feel excited, and not believing it at all. My mind was too muddled to think about watching a film, but I didn't want to disappoint Jack so I did as he suggested. I hadn't had any tea, but I put a large packet of blue macaroons in my bag and packets of spearmint sweets. I cannot for the life of me remember what we watched – my mind was buzzing all through the film and it wasn't just because of the sugar rush from the sweet stuff I ate throughout.

The more I tried not to think about Amelie, the more my brain told me I had to go and meet Lisa.

The minute Jack left that evening, I responded to Lisa and arranged a time when we could talk on Skype.

47

Thursday 30th August

It was nearly two months since I last saw Adelle, and I hoped we had reached the end of her therapy apart from a follow-up I had already arranged with her during the Christmas holidays, after the end of her first college term.

She was pacing up and down the waiting area when I opened my door, and she turned and rushed into the room.

'I have the best news for you, Mike. I am so excited.'

She was certainly right about being excited. I don't think I had ever seen anyone hop from foot to foot with excitement before – well, certainly not in my consulting room. I laughed with her.

'You'd better tell me, before you burst!'

'I've found her, I've found my twin. Well, maybe not, but she's very, very like me.'

She pulled her laptop out of her bag and flipped to the photos. The girl on the screen certainly looked like her, although with rather more weight.

'I hope you aren't jumping to conclusions,' I said, trying to be the voice of reason.

'I'm not. But my mother is – she is over the moon I have found her. In fact, she says someone must go and bring her back.'

'Bring her back? From where?'

'America. She lives in New York. She says she's adopted, but was born in Texas. I nearly deleted her, thinking that was too far away.'

'So why didn't you?'

'I don't know. The likeness, perhaps. It is uncanny how like me she is.'

'Who is going to bring her back?'

'Me, probably. Mother was terrified at the thought of me setting off for America, but Dad said I'd be fine with a friend if Mother didn't want to go. My mother has a phobia of flying. She's more or less accepted I'll go. I think her need to know if the girl is Amelie has partly overridden her fear of me going.'

'Are you sure you are ready?'

'I think I am now. I first saw her photo months ago. I've thought about her on and off, but I couldn't bear to be disappointed if following her up came to nothing. But this week felt different so I had a look at the photo on the website to see if the likeness was really there. Then I showed Jack and he became excited. My mother is convinced it is Amelie. She said it's up to me to prove if she is not.'

I was worried for my client. She had done so well, but now she was being carried along by other people's enthusiasm.

'Is there any way that this girl could be using your photo, slightly doctored, to fake a lookalike?'

'No, I've Skyped her. She's definitely real. She's really nice to talk to.'

'That doesn't make her your twin, you know.'

'I agree. But my mother doesn't – she and Dad are paying for me to go to America and visit her.'

'So who is going with you?'

'Dad's hip is not good and he is waiting to have an operation so my parents will pay for me to take whoever I want. It might be Sharon and it might be Jack. Jack has been to the States before, so he's the favourite.'

Even as she said this, Adelle blushed. I guessed he was very likely to have a free trip to America courtesy of his girlfriend's mother.

'Adelle, I need to suggest that you give yourself some time before jaunting round the world. It's understandable that you want to go and your mother wants to send you, but this is not just an adventure. This could be devastating for you and for the girl you are visiting.'

Adelle looked at me as if I had spoken out of turn. I had, she was right; I should have helped her to the point where she could see what a major step this would be, should she decide to go. I tried to retrieve the situation.

'This will be your decision – well, your family's decision – but why are you in such a hurry?'

'Her mother is very ill. It's terminal. We need to find out how Amelie ended up there.'

'You called her Amelie – is that the name she uses now?'

Adelle replied, slowly and with caution, 'No, it's Lisa. I should call her Lisa. But it's really hard because my mother is so sure. I wish I had never shown her the photo, but it's her daughter, or might be.'

'Let's try to think about this logically, Delle. How about a pros and cons for going to the States?'

'I've done it. Here it is.'

I should have drawn comfort from the fact that she was using this tool. She had made an effort to list all the problems associated with her trip. Her cons listed that it would be the first time she had flown any distance, her eating difficulties and the fear of absolute disappointment. The pros list was much longer, including that it would be an adventure, she would be forced to try new foods, she would be in good company, she would please her parents, and she would meet her lookalike. There was not a mention of the fact that she would find her twin, so perhaps she had more sense than she had shown during the session.

We spent the rest of her appointment time discussing how she would manage if her trip amounted to nothing, how she would keep safe, what she would need to cope with before she left and how soon she would be ready to go.

'You are aware that even in the unlikely circumstance that Lisa is your twin, she probably won't want to come back?'

'Yes, and I have explained that to my mother. She'll have her own life, her own friends and her own family. She's unlikely to want to give all that up.'

That was better – she was being a little realistic. I knew she would go and it would not be my place to stop her. I gave her a possible safety net.

'Let me know if you are definitely going. Don't forget to cancel your appointment with Anita and remember to take my phone number. If I'm busy, I will ring you back when I can.'

This was one young lady who had certainly changed considerably over the past few months. Her eyes were shining and her whole outlook had become one of hope. She left early and I rang Anita to update her. Anita listened carefully then pointed out that searching could be a necessary part of her grief reaction anyway. It could even be helpful for her. I wasn't so sure – I was concerned she was setting herself up for a massive disappointment.

Later that evening, Ella and I finished our meal and sat with our coffees, talking about losing Jamie and how we had coped with the different stages of grief. Without giving names, I filled her in a little on what was happening with my client.

'That poor girl,' said Ella. 'We must pray for her. There is so much that can crush her spirit here.'

'That's three things I love about you, Ella, you have empathy, wisdom and faith. I missed that so much when we were living apart.'

I don't know whether she was embarrassed, but she gave me a slight grin and turned her back on me as she gathered up the cups and went into the kitchen to start washing up. I gave her a few minutes then followed to pick up a tea towel.

48

It was little more than a week since I first replied to my doppelgänger's post. Despite my regrets about showing the photo to my mother, it looked more likely than ever that I would be going to find Lisa. I was excited.

Mother didn't even raise an eyebrow when I said I would go if Jack would come too.

'That's better than you going with Sharon. Jack is more responsible,' she said. I didn't know why she thought that when she didn't know Sharon, but I didn't argue.

'We'll pay for two single rooms in the hotel. Your dad's working it all out. You keep talking to Amelie, I mean, Lisa. You don't want to lose the link with her.'

'Mother, please, please don't be too disappointed when we find out she's not my twin. The chances of her being kidnapped to be adopted are all extremely small. I am going to meet with my doppelgänger. Nothing else. Don't get your hopes up.' I said this with great conviction, but in reality I hoped I was wrong.

It was stressful. I was struggling to maintain the new diet I had managed over the summer, but my anxiety was forcing me to revert to the safety of blue. I could manage chips – but mine were from the blue potatoes. I went back to mixing them with non-blue ones and eating them with my eyes shut with the barely cooked steak. I was getting there, but it made me so tense that I had dreadful indigestion.

Jack suggested I try eating while he had his arm around me. It was better, but wouldn't look good in the hotel.

'Dreamy, we will find you meals to eat. It will all feel different over there anyway. I was fifteen when I went with my family for a wedding. It was like walking into a completely new place. Probably no one will bat an eyelid if you only eat blue stuff.'

'Whose wedding?'

'Some relative of my father's. I don't think he lives in New York any more. He broke up with his wife. Shall I check with my mother?'

Jack phoned his mother then and there on his mobile. In that moment I realised that we had been going out for more than six months and he hadn't taken me to meet her yet. That was worrying – was he ashamed of me? I wondered whether I should be going to America with him if he didn't even want his mother to meet me. I began to sink into negativity before it occurred to me that his mother was simply treating Jack as the adult he was and hadn't asked about his love life. If it were the other way round, I might have kept Jack a secret – it was only Dad's fall that had meant they'd known about Jack from the start. Jack had a lot of explaining to do about going to America. I left him to it and went into my bedroom, closed the door and played with Harry and Skye. I felt in a real muddle. Too much was happening and now I might be staying with strange relatives of Jack's before I'd even met his mother. I felt pretty sure about Jack, but had been so busy sorting out my own problems that in some ways I still didn't know him that well.

I worked myself up into such a state of panic that when Jack shouted that he'd finished his phone call and I could come back, I nearly told him the whole trip was off. I felt awash with relief when he told me that his relative had moved out of New York.

I was going to say it was time to meet his mother, but somehow it felt too pushy.

The next two weeks were a real challenge for me. I definitely regressed. My pictures became blue again, my blue clothes came to the fore and I gave up trying not to eat food that wasn't blue because it was the only thing I had any control over – apart from giving progress reports to Lisa. I was scared.

I spent a morning with my father trying to organise when we could go. I insisted we were back for Cessy's wedding, which was the weekend before the start of college. My father set to making all the arrangements over the next few days, including paying for the plane tickets. There were visas to find, but he assured me he could do that in a short space of time for both me and Jack. He was on his computer organising my life with hardly any reference to me.

During those few days my mother came sidling into my home with the latest news.

'You travel on the 15th and return ten days later – Dad's booked the tickets.'

I felt cornered. I ate blue yoghurt, played with the cats and pushed the blue and grey skirt to the back of the wardrobe.

The next day she was over again, this time sidetracked by the cats, which she played with for about thirty minutes before she remembered she had a message from Dad.

'Dad wants to check out the hotel with you! He's found reasonable rooms next door to each other, but they have an interconnecting door. Is that all right?'

'No, it is not! I need my privacy.' I didn't want my mother prying into my sex life and this was not some romantic holiday – I would be on a mission. I marched across the lawn to sort it out.

Two days later, on my birthday, my father proclaimed that all the arrangements were made and we had three days to pack and go. I had known it would be soon, but felt totally unprepared. My mother gave me a map of New York and a beautiful new suitcase with my initials on it plus a luggage tag.

'I don't want you or your luggage getting lost,' she said with a smile. But there were tears in her eyes.

At my mother's expense and my father's suggestion, I spent an agonising three hours or so the next morning in the hairdressers having my hair stripped, dyed dark blonde, then having blue streaks put into it. Finally, it was layered, which took out all the dead ends. It certainly looked neater and well cut, but I felt so uncomfortable with my new look that I walked out of the hairdresser's, round the corner and stuffed my freshly coloured and shaped hair into my blue beanie. Fortunately, there was a blue streak near the front to pull out to hang over one eye.

My mother dragged me round the shops to try to force me to buy some new clothes, in various colours, but she had no chance. I did buy two pairs of new jeans, jumpers and a warmer coat. I was very worried about what I would eat in the US, so bought some more blue food dye. I didn't even know if it was allowed through Customs, but when we got back I put it in my now opened and waiting suitcase and hoped no one would find it. If it were removed, I could hopefully buy some in New York.

I was in a perpetual state of nervous ambivalence. I was scared about going, but worried about any possibility of not being able to go. Jack had organised time off work and I had cancelled my appointment with Anita – although she told me that Mike had already warned her I might be away. I rang Mike but had to leave a message about the certainty of my trip and that Jack would go with me.

I called Lisa via Skype two days before we left. She was excited and sad at the same time because her mother was getting weaker. I could hear her voice tremble as she told me, 'I'm not even sure she'll make it to next week. The nurse from the hospice is visiting three times a day now.'

'Would you like us to cancel the trip?'

'No, she wants to see you. Please come. That might be what's keeping her going.'

It seemed as if I had no choice.

Jack came over in the evening and we spent a lot of time talking about it and decided that if Lisa were my twin and her known mother was dying, then perhaps we'd be able to support Lisa in her time of loss. It all felt very strange, as if we were acting on a stage, with our lines not learned.

The day before departure was spent furiously trying to put together a ten-day wardrobe. Even with my new clothes, I wasn't sure I had enough to wear. In the end, I unpacked everything, putting the grey and blue skirt and burgundy jumper and scarf right at the bottom of the suitcase, and folded everything else back before I could change my mind.

Jack rang to tell me that his mother wanted to drive us to the airport and to ask whether my mother wanted to come as well. By then, I was so panicky I didn't really care.

'Yes, Jack, that's fine. I'll just go along with whatever you decide.' I knew my mother would be pleased; she had been worried about the drive to the airport but desperate to see us go.

49

Jack and his mother appeared at my little home at 5.30 in the morning, so met me as I was organising the cats' dirt boxes. They didn't really use them any more, but my mother would not be with Harry and Skye all the time. Neither of the cats liked the cat flap.

Jack's mother smiled at me as she came in. She waited while I washed my hands in the sink and said, 'I am really pleased to meet you at last, Adelle. Call me Ros, everyone calls me that. I'm Rosemary really.'

I scarcely had time to tell her that my mother's name was Rosemary too, when my mother came in. I shot across the lawn to wish Daddy goodbye and went back into the summerhouse to grab my case and rucksack. All the bustling around relieved my fears for a few moments, and I felt a little thrill of excitement. I remembered that both nerves and excitement have the same bodily sensations and decided I must enjoy the day.

The two Rosemarys seemed to hit it off well and nattered away in the front of the car, leaving Jack and me to ourselves in the back.

'You OK?' asked Jack.

'Yes, so far. Nervous, but I'm trying to enjoy myself. What about you?'

'I'm really excited – I'm off for a grand adventure with my girlfriend.'

'I'm sorry I'm not much of a girlfriend. I've been so anxious this last week that I've felt quite out of it.'

'There's never a quiet moment with my dreamy girlfriend,' he said as his hand clasped mine. 'It's what it's all about, Dreamy, being together through ups and downs. I'm sure I'll have some roller coaster experiences for you to support me with over the years.'

I nurtured the thought of 'over the years'; it gave me a warm feeling of safety and security, even when travelling to an airport to fly across the world to see an unknown girl. I would be all right.

At the airport, once we'd booked in, our mothers treated us to breakfast. Of course, my mother had the most difficult job, but she had brought some flapjack with her, which she offered around. It was not blue, but she had zigzagged it with streaks of blue icing. I was touched by her thoughtfulness and managed to eat it with a yoghurt and a cup of weak black tea. Before long it was time to go through Customs and I realised I had met Jack's mother and liked her. New experiences were stumbling all over me, but I was coping with them without having to work on it.

My mother clung to me and told me to be careful and to stay with Jack. Then she hugged me and 1 hugged her. There were tears in her eyes as she moved away from me. Jack's mother said, 'Bye, Son, hope you and Dreamy have a great trip,' and pecked him on the cheek. They both waved as we walked out of sight. Irrationally, I was irritated by her using the nickname 'Dreamy'.

Going through Customs was more or less uneventful. No one opened my suitcase to question me about my blue food dye. The flight was good; in fact, it was fun. Some of the time we watched a film, but mostly we just enjoyed being together. The food came in its strange little boxes and to my joy there was some blue jelly in it. I swapped most of my other food for Jack's jelly.

When we landed, Jack took my hand as soon as we were on land and kept holding it as we boarded the airport bus and went through JFK airport. I wondered whether my mother had told him not to lose her only remaining twin, and that's the point at which I realised what a massive thing it had been for her to let me come. Jack and I took a yellow cab to the hotel we had booked. I struggled to keep up with what the receptionist was saying when we booked into our rooms. I was feeling quite wobbly by then – probably it was emotional, but it might simply have been that I had never flown that far before. Maybe I was jet-lagged, or perhaps it was the strange feeling of sameness yet difference.

Jack's voice reached me despite my muddly head. 'Dreamy, do we want to book for dinner?'

'No, no, I'd rather not, thank you. I've been nibbling mints on the plane and I feel so tired, I just need to sleep. But you'll need something. You book a meal.'

I was too tired to notice that he didn't.

The hotel room was lovely – probably a fairly standard room, but I was focused on the large, soft bed waiting for me. I scarcely noticed the marble surround in the en suite and the plush carpet, nor the view of the city from the window. I walked into the room, dropped my bags and lay on the soft bed and dozed off. When there was a knock on the door, I woke with a start.

There was a knock again. 'It's me, Jack.'

I let him in and he gave me a hug. 'Are you OK? I've been out and brought food back. I'd rather eat with you, even if it's in one of our rooms.'

Feeling a little more refreshed, I felt selfish. In fact, I felt a real nuisance when he started to tell me how long it had taken him to find blue food for me. He produced a blue iced bun, cupcakes, blueberries plus yoghurt for me to add my dye to. There was all my usual food except the bread. He had even remembered to buy some milk.

'What about you?' I could smell something hot and spicy.

'I have a curry. I hope you can put up with the smell. And I asked at reception for some plates and cutlery – they're still in my room; I'll fetch them.'

The smell of the food had made me aware of how hungry I was. I looked around my room. There were two chairs and a desk, which I cleared for our meal. I put off the main light, putting the table lamp on. I moved my unpacked suitcase out of the way and brushed my hair. Then he was back for our impromptu meal.

'Your food smells delicious, Jack,' I said.

'It's chicken tikka masala. I have two forks here if you want to try a bit.' He was smiling at me with eyebrows raised, and a pleading look.

I wasn't at all sure, but with the subtle lighting I was able to eat a few mouthfuls, with my eyes shut pretending it was blue. To celebrate, we shared the iced bun afterwards.

It was 9 pm local time by then and I already felt tired. We watched some television, but I can't remember anything about the programme. I fell asleep in Jack's arms. I don't know what time it was when he woke me but he said, 'Find your nightwear, Dreamy, and get to bed. I'm going now; I'll see you in the morning.'

'Stop calling me "Dreamy", Jack,' I said wearily. '"Adelle", now, please. Lisa knows me as Adelle.'

'Don't be silly, Dreamy. You can be called by both names.'

I gave up. I was too exhausted to argue.

Jack's knock came at about 8.30 am. I was ready and just thinking of waking him. All my clothes were in the hotel wardrobe – closet – and I had on my best jeans and favourite top ready to meet my double, or possibly my twin. I didn't really want to have breakfast, but Jack insisted.

'I didn't come all this way with you just to have you fade into nothing before my very eyes. Come on, bring your food dye and we'll see what we can make blue!'

I expected the usual challenge, but I was wrong. On sight of us, the breakfast staff seemed to send a message round and a large tray was brought to our table laden with blue pancakes, blueberries and blackberry jam, plus marble fruit!

'You didn't tell them, Jack, did you?'

Jack nodded. 'I came down after I left you last night and had a drink at the bar. The bartender was making someone a blue cocktail and I said that my girlfriend's favourite colour was blue and she even liked blue food. It was his idea to tell the kitchen staff.'

343

'They will think I'm mad!'

'No, they won't. Apparently they do that sort of thing all the time. Purple is the most popular colour, followed by bright pink. For party conferences they make a feature of it with the party colours. They say it's all in a day's work for them.'

So I ate the beautiful pancakes and was relieved that I had listened to Jack and come down for breakfast. I was still on the edge of my seat, though, so waiting for him to finish his coffee was agonising.

'Can we go now? I need to go and see Lisa.'

Jack laughed, and called a member of staff over to organise a takeaway cup for some more coffee. At least that gave me a chance to thank them for the blue food.

Up in my room, the nerves really set in. Jack was ready and I was fiddling about doing my blue-streaked, dark blonde hair, and feeling very out of sorts.

'I'm nearly ready, I won't be long,' I kept saying to Jack. He realised how nervous I was even though no one could imagine what it would be like to meet a person who may or may not be your twin.

'Come on, Dreamy, you can do this. Have you rung her yet? You said you'd ring before we came.'

'Please call me "Adelle". And I will ring her. I just need to work out what to say.'

It took me some deep breaths and about ten minutes of speaking to myself to pluck up the courage I needed to ring her. But then the phone call was easy – she was thrilled to hear my voice.

'Adelle, I've been waiting for your call today. When are you coming over? How are you getting here? Do you have anyone with you?'

I answered her questions the best I could. I couldn't tell her whether Jack would come into the house. I might want him there.

When we had finished speaking, I put down the phone and I was so excited I grabbed Jack and said, 'Come on, we've got to jump in a yellow cab and go!'

50

When we arrived at the gates of the house, I didn't know what to do. There was an intercom on the gateposts. Everything seemed very forbidding. Jack told the cabbie to wait.

'Look, Adelle, you don't need me to come in. Tell Lisa you have arrived. Keep your phone with you and I will find a coffee shop and I'll wait to hear what you're doing. It looks as if you'll be safe here.'

It certainly wasn't a run-down house, so I knew what he meant. My hand shook as I pressed the intercom. 'Hi, it's Adelle here.'

'You're here already! Gee, that's great. I'll buzz you guys in and walk down the driveway toward you.'

'This is it,' said Jack. 'I'll wait and see if she looks like your twin before I go.'

'Do you think I'll be all right?'

'See what you think when you meet her. If you tell me "see you later", I'll go.'

Lisa came flying down the drive and before I could even say 'hello' she had thrown her arms around me.

'We are so alike, I can't believe it!' She totally ignored Jack – to be honest, I was ignoring him too because it was so eerie, looking at someone who resembled me so closely.

'Hi, Lisa,' said Jack.

'Jack meet Lisa, Lisa – Jack,' I managed to say.

There was a moment's silence while she and I looked at each other. Jack cleared his throat. I remembered our code.

'Don't worry, Jack, I'll see you later.'

Lisa had let go of me, so Jack gave me a quick hug and hurried back to the cab. Lisa and I walked up the drive – our paces matching, smiles wrinkling our faces in exactly the same way.

Once in the house, Lisa took me into a room with a large table. Without saying anything, we sat either side of it. For a while we said nothing, we were too busy examining each other's faces. The cameras on our computers had not lied.

Lisa spoke. 'When I was small, my mother said I had an imaginary friend like me.'

I swallowed. My mind tried to focus.

'That's a strange coincidence.'

She nodded. I wanted to know so much. How could my twin have ended up here, and with these parents? Could I ask this? In the end, I had to.

'When were you adopted, Lisa?'

'When I was three – there are no photos of me before I was about two and a half. I asked why not when I was about six.'

'Did your parents tell you then?'

'Not immediately. My father said the box with them in was lost when we moved.'

I tried to keep my excitement under control. Not wanting to tell her about the cut photos, I told her a half-truth.

'My parents only have a few of me. They are all in an album, with lots missing. My mother never told me until recently why they weren't all there.'

'And why weren't they?'

In a flash, I realised I had said too much. Where did I go from here? I could not tell this stranger, however familiar we looked, that my twin had been stolen. The implications for her could be horrendous. Thinking quickly, I used the lie my mother had first told me.

'My mother said there was a family dispute. My aunt fell out with my mother, so she got rid of some of the photos.'

The air became electric. Lisa looked at me across the table – my mind did funny things as I told myself there was no mirror in front of me. Her blue eyes met my own. I waited for her to realise we may be twins. Eventually she said, 'Adelle, could we be cousins?'

I shook my head. Then, realising what I'd done, I shrugged. 'Maybe, maybe not.'

'What do you mean? We are very alike – and if your mother destroyed all the photos with me and my mother in…' She stopped and tried to look me in the eyes. 'I was born in Texas,' she said. I was trembling. This had gone crazily out of hand. Lisa was breathing heavily.

'Have you told me the truth?' she asked.

I hesitated, remembering Mike's warning to me. I passed it on to her. 'The truth might devastate you.'

'It can't be worse than I'm thinking. I want to hear the truth.'

I shook my head. 'Lisa, I can't tell you what happened to you. I think you had better find out from your mother whether there is anything she hasn't told you.'

Lisa got up. She pushed open the door with her foot as she left the room. I could hear her banging things around in the kitchen. Then all went quiet. I had nowhere to go – I was her guest. What should I do? When I heard her crying, that made me decide. I walked into the kitchen. I put my arms around her. She turned and sobbed on my shoulder.

'I have hated being adopted and never belonging,' she told me, sniffing and wiping her eyes with the back of her hand. 'My brother, my parents and all my relatives have dark hair and I am at best a dark mousey colour. They're rather tall; I'm just short. Sorry, we're OK, but they're all lofties.' I nodded. Our heights matched perfectly.

'I have always felt lost,' I told her. 'I've wanted to find my childhood friend. We were the same size and played together all the time.'

'I think I had a friend like that when I was little, or it may have been my imaginary friend.'

I looked at her, searching her face. She stared at me. The air felt so laden I could hardly force the words out. 'This is getting really strange.' My voice was croaky, my heart was pounding so hard it hurt, and I was struggling against the tears.

'We are closer than cousins, aren't we?' said Lisa. 'Yet we can't be sisters. I am only five months younger than you.'

I couldn't hold back any longer. I blurted out the incredible truth: 'I don't care what your birth certificate says, I think you are my twin.' I was shaking.

Lisa folded her arms around me. We held each other so tightly I could feel her heartbeat. This was no dream of a reality show where long-lost relatives find each other under the glare of spotlights and the blank eye of the camera. This was reality itself – stronger than a dream – more real than my earlier lie.

'Where do we go from here, Lisa?' I asked my twin. 'Your mother won't be up to the shock.'

'My mother will know. I expect she wants me to know. Why do you think she encouraged me to answer you when your picture came up on the website? In fact, why did she ask me to look on lookalike websites in the first place?'

'It's time you found out the truth from her. In case she…' I couldn't finish the sentence.

'I don't know if we can be twins. Lots of things don't fit. Perhaps we should have some DNA testing before we say anything? But I will need to know what happened first. Do you know?'

How could I tell her? How could I even suggest that her mother, dying from cancer, could have stolen Lisa from me, from my mother, from my father – from her mother, her father and her twin? My mind was reeling.

'Not today. Let's just get on with being twins, whether we are or not.'

Lisa's face brightened. 'OK, twin – what's my real name, by the way? – let's go and do something and get lots of pictures of us together. You need to look a little less English, though. Come on, let's find a few things from my wardrobe – you're much skinnier than me, but I'm sure I can find something to fit.'

'Amelie. The name of my twin is Amelie.'

'Amelie and Adelle, Amelie and Adelle.'

As I looked at her, I remembered a blue ribbon in my friend's hair with a yellow one in mine.

If she were my twin, Mother would have her daughter back; I would have regained my sister. But could Lisa leave her adoptive mother, the one who probably stole Amelie from us?

I thought about the ill woman and hoped she hadn't stolen my sister all those years ago.

When Amelie opened her wardrobe, I was overawed. She had so many clothes. I had this strange idea in my mind that we should wear what we wore as small children – colour-wise, that is. She laughed when I tried to explain.

'Gee, that's some tall order. I'll have to think about that.'

In the end we settled on a nod to our former colours. I wore a sweatshirt of blue and yellow stripes, while she found one that was all blue. We both wore jeans – mine were my own blue ones while she wore some black ones.

'What about sneakers?' she said. There was a pair of baseball-style trainers which, with their laces pulled tight, were a good enough fit for me to wear. She found some similar sneakers, which were fairly new. We both had shoulder-length hair, which we put up in matching ponytails. The likeness between us sent shivers up my spine. Apart from my face being thinner, the only difference was a tiny mole in Lisa's hairline, on the left side of her head.

'If we had grown up together, it would seem very ordinary to see our faces side by side,' I said as we looked in the mirror.

'But then we would have missed all this excitement!' Lisa took my hand and swung it forwards and backwards. If there had been leaves in her bedroom, we would have been throwing them into the air.

We were laughing and crying at the same time when the door opened.

Lisa's mother stood in the doorway. She looked as if she could hardly stand; she leaned against the door frame. Tears were streaming down her face.

'Twins,' she said. 'You look like somebody's twins.'

Lisa caught her as she fell forward. She cradled her in her arms; the woman comforted by her daughter, my sister, my twin.

She guided her back into her bedroom and helped her lie down on the bed. I followed them. Only when she was sure her mother was comfortable did Lisa ask her, 'How did it happen, Mom?'

We both waited for her reply. The room rang with silence.

'Mom?' Lisa prompted. Her mother's hand moved out from the duvet, and she feebly beckoned for us both to come closer. Her voice was weak, her breathing rasping and heavy. We both leaned forward to hear.

'A woman came to clean. She had to bring her daughter because she couldn't afford the childcare.' There was a pause while Lisa's mother appeared to make a decision. 'She didn't take good care of you.' Lisa's mother gasped for breath as she spoke. 'You always came and cuddled me.' She was shuddering.

'So that's how I came to be adopted.' Lisa's voice was firm, matter-of-fact. Lisa's mother could scarcely nod.

Despite having tears in her eyes, Lisa adjusted her mother's pillow and her throw and wrapped her up carefully. Lisa's mother closed her eyes and I thought she had gone to sleep. Then, her eyes opened as, very quietly, she began to speak again.

'I'm sorry I didn't tell you when you were small. I was frightened you might feel more insecure.'

I searched my twin's face – not a trace of anger or hate. Just love for this woman who was so ill. She knelt down by her mother's side. I didn't know whether to go or stay, but settled for moving to sit on a basketwork chair, out of the way.

'Oh, Mom, I wouldn't love you any less. You reared me.'

'Your mom told me she would put you in an orphanage. I couldn't bear it.'

'Why would she do that?' I could hear the choking in Lisa's voice. Her pain pulled at my emotions and I found a blue tissue from my pocket to wipe my eyes.

'She couldn't manage financially and wanted to go back home. She said she hadn't told her family that she had a child and they would not accept her.'

We waited for anything else. Again Lisa's mother closed her eyes. When she opened them, she looked as if to far away.

Lisa's soft voice trembled as she started to speak. 'Did she give you any money for my keep?'

'She couldn't, she was destitute. We helped her out with the air ticket and a deposit for somewhere to live.'

I was desperate to tell her that the woman had stolen my twin and she should have reported her. But she was too

353

ill to take it and Lisa didn't yet know. Lisa said, 'So you and Pops adopted me?'

'Yes. Your brother was nineteen. You were three. Pops was all for it, he'd been so worried about you.' We waited as she struggled for words. 'He was sure you should come into our family.'

'Did I have a birth certificate?'

'Yes, you were born in Texas County...' Her voice tailed off'.

'Let's leave her to sleep,' I said. Lisa nodded, but her mother reached out her hand to stop her. 'Her lawyer came and we signed papers. He said nothing else was needed.'

'She brought her own lawyer to draw up the papers? Didn't you think that was odd?'

Somehow Lisa's mother managed to answer her, despite her gasping breaths. 'I think we both just loved you and wanted the best for you. It never occurred to me that she had another child.'

Lisa sat cradling her mother – her adoptive mother, who now lay in her daughter's arms like the child she had felt love for nearly twenty years earlier. I felt in the way, yet this was my story too. In confusion I stood up.

'Would you like to be alone?' I asked.

Lisa answered, 'No, please stay. I'm going to call the doctor. This is too much for her.'

I was in awe of Lisa's strength. She picked up the phone by the bedside and rang the doctor, calmly telling him that her mother was in some anxiety because of some shocking news. Then she took control.

'I'll make us all a hot drink. You stay with Mom, Adelle.' I felt totally inadequate as I sat there with myriads of questions whirring around in my head. Lisa's mother stretched out her hand from under the covers, towards me.

Between gasps, she said, 'I'm glad she's found you. I only thought she might be a twin when she showed me your website. I was hoping she'd find a sibling. Forgive me. I don't know why you weren't with your mother.'

I found myself stroking this fragile woman's hand – this must all be so confusing for her. I couldn't tell her she had never met my mother, and my twin had been kidnapped. Instead I said, 'I've found her now. That's what I wanted. We can't undo what's been done in the past.' She closed her eyes and the slightest of smiles quivered on her lips. I laid her hand on the top of the covers and moved away. I needed another tissue for my eyes.

There was no way I could tell her it wasn't her fault. I needed to know more. But what I did know was that she had taken my twin in, and she had loved her. And Lisa had given love in return.

And now I had found my twin. Or had I?

51

Lisa's mother appeared to be sleeping. Lisa and I sat on the high stools in the kitchen, talking. I didn't give her any more information and she didn't ask for any. I think she knew there was more to come but needed time to come to terms with what she had discovered so far. She checked her mother every fifteen minutes or so.

The intercom buzzed – the hospice nurse had arrived at the gate so Lisa let her in.

'I can take over now, Lisa. You go off with your sister, is it? You two are very alike.'

Lisa smiled and thanked her.

'Shall we go, Adelle? We'll have time to go to the mall.'

I felt we'd talked enough for a while, so agreed. To my surprise, Lisa took me down two flights of stairs to the basement. There was a garage with two cars in it – one a shiny red open-top. Lisa said, 'Meet my baby,' and climbed into the driver's seat. I hurried round to the right-hand-side passenger seat.

'I didn't know you could drive, Lisa.'

'I guess we have a lot to find out about each other.'

It didn't take us long to get to the mall and parking was quite difficult, so I think Lisa was showing off a little. I felt rather inadequate with not being able to drive yet, let alone have my own car. I told her so and she said, flatly, 'It's my father. He ran off and left my mom and he has overcompensated. He bought this for me and paid for lessons. I've been driving for a few years now.'

I could think of nothing to say. We were both silent for a while as we went up in the elevator in the mall. People were glancing at each of us and smiling. We were very obviously twins. Lisa tucked her arm into mine and we walked out among the crowds.

We didn't buy anything but we sat in a coffee lounge and talked. I told her all about Jack, my father's fractured hip, my college course and my difficulties with blue. She told me all about her college course, in music, and how she had flunked it too, when she couldn't cope with her mother having treatment for cancer. She had been working in a music shop until fairly recently when she left to mind her mother. I went into the washroom while she paid for our coffees. Someone said, 'Hi Lisa,' as I walked in. I smiled, not wanting to open my mouth and give away the fact that I wasn't her. I needn't have bothered; the same girl was talking to Lisa when I came out. I was introduced to the friend.

'Meet Adelle, my lookalike from England. She looks like my twin, doesn't she?'

I don't remember the girl's name, but when she said, 'I guess you two must have been separated at birth,' I was grinning from ear to ear and there was a tingle down my back.

When we returned to Lisa's house, the nurse was nearly ready to leave. Lisa's mother was quietly resting and the doctor had been to give her a sedative.

'It's time to ring Jack,' I said. 'He'll wonder what's happened to me.' He answered immediately and I told him I was ready. He must've been round the corner because even while I was gathering up my things, and saying goodbye to Lisa's mother, the intercom buzzer went.

'Tell him he can come in and we can eat if you like.'

I was feeling very washed out. 'Thank you, Lisa, but perhaps another day.'

'I shall see you and Jack tomorrow, then, both of you. And pick up some blue stuff for a meal before you come and I can cook it. I daren't leave Mom for long or I would show you New York.'

I gave my twin a hug and we walked down to the gate side by side, still dressed alike.

'OK, which one's my girlfriend?' said Jack, as he took my hand. Lisa and I went into fits of giggles.

I so loved having a sister. But would I lose her when she knew that she had been stolen? Would telling her this dreadful fact be accusing her mother of lying?

That evening, I decided I needed to talk to Mike Lewis urgently. It's a good job I had Jack with me because he patiently told me that I would get an empty office because all good people in the UK would be in bed. So I left Mike a message saying I needed to speak to him and that I would ring at 1 pm UK time. I hoped he stopped for lunch around that time, so set my alarm for 7.30, ready to ring at 8 am. At least I would still have a whole day to see my twin then.

52

When I arrived at work there was a message on the office answerphone to say that Adelle would be ringing at 1 pm. This would be really awkward for me because I had a 12.30 client – but there was nothing I could do about it.

'Shall I see if your 12.30 client can come an hour later?' asked Patricia. 'You'll have to lunch a little early and be quick about it, but that might work.'

Despite my horror of changing appointments this had to be done. I left it in Patricia's capable hands.

I finished seeing my 11.30 client and went through to the office to say I would pop out for a sandwich. I didn't need to. Patricia passed me a pack of two ham and cheese sandwiches with a till receipt.

'I knew you wouldn't have time,' she said. I felt smug that back in the spring I had managed to save both secretaries' jobs. What an investment that was in promoting the smooth running of our service.

I had just finished my sandwiches and black coffee when Adelle rang. The line was clear enough to catch her excitement as she told me all about her meeting with her twin, if that was who she was. I asked her a few questions and felt reasonably satisfied that she had some justification in thinking she may be her twin, although not everything matched up.

'Well, that all sounds very good. Did you want to keep me up to date or was there another purpose to this call?'

'Another purpose. I haven't actually told her that she, or rather, my twin, was kidnapped. I have listened to her mother's story about what happened, but it may be that Amelie was not stolen to order, or something went wrong. But Amelie's mother thinks that it was my mother who gave Amelie to her by adoption.'

'So I guess your problem is believing her mother.'

'Well, yes. But also, what will it feel like to know you were kidnapped? Will that be better than knowing you were abandoned by a mother who didn't want you, or worse? And if I say she was kidnapped, am I accusing her mother of lying?'

'I think, Delle, you have come across the universal problem of whether it is best for you to tell the truth as you understand it, or keep the truth to yourself to avoid hurting someone. If you don't tell the truth, you will have to pretend that you are living with the mother who abandoned Amelie. What do you think?'

'No, I couldn't do that. But Amelie's mother, adoptive mother, is extremely ill and needs her very much at present.'

'Did you say earlier that Amelie's adoptive mother encouraged her to go on the website?'

'She has been encouraging her to find people like her ever since she had her diagnosis.'

'Then she knew there was something odd about the adoption. And it sounds as if she has acknowledged that you must be twins.'

'I think she has. She said "somebody's twins" when she first saw us together.'

'Do you have a picture of your mother with you?' I thought she might have taken the family album she had clutched to herself at our appointment after her parents had told her she was a twin.

'Yes. I have an album of when we were little and an up-to-date picture of my mother and father on my laptop.'

'Obviously what you do is up to you. But you could see what happens when you show Lisa and her adoptive mother those photos. That might lead you into talking about Amelie's disappearance without accusing anyone of lying.'

All the time I was saying this, I was weighing up what was best in the situation. Adelle was going to their house as a guest and could be turned away at any time. The adoptive mother was seriously ill but seemed to know more than she was saying. Why was she encouraging Lisa to find someone resembling her? And was it possible that Adelle's mother was lying and had gone to America with one twin specifically to find an adoptive parent? I kept these thoughts to myself but said, 'Also, you may want to ask if she has some early photos of Lisa with the lady who gave her up for adoption.' I didn't suggest that it might have been Adelle's mother, but there was a gap after the child's disappearance when Adelle didn't live with her parents. 'And I want you to ring me, Delle, if you are upset in any way. In fact, because of the time difference, I will give you my personal mobile phone number and will try to remember to leave it switched on. Then you can leave a voicemail if I am at home or with a client with the ringer muted.'

'Thank you, Mike, I shall try not to use it. But it feels better that I can if I need to.'

I wished her all the best and came off the phone rather worried that I might be stirring something up that would be better left alone. But who knew in situations such as this? I hoped and prayed that the truth would come out without anyone being too devastated. Mental health is a very fragile commodity.

I was very glad that Adelle had taken Jack with her.

I spent a few minutes revising the file of the next client, and went out into the waiting area to invite him into my room.

53

My phone call to Mike Lewis was really useful. He had helped me think things through and given me some ideas. I had written a few notes while we spoke and felt much better about talking to Lisa. I may have tried to cover it up while I was talking to Mike, but I had become quite certain that there was a bond between Lisa and myself.

Jack had arrived during my phone call with Mike and I had let him into my room.

'Let's go to breakfast, Jack. I hope it's blue pancakes again.'

'Oh, I don't think it will be.' I couldn't tell whether Jack was joking, so I slipped the blue food dye into my pocket.

It was blue muffins and there were various blue cheeses on the side. I ate well, for me, and figured that I wouldn't need long here before I matched my doppelgänger's clothes size perfectly.

Between mouthfuls, I told Jack all about the phone call.

'Are we going over there every day?' he asked.

I really wanted to say 'Of course', but stopped myself. This was his trip too.

'We are both invited today, Jack. Will you come?'

'Will I be in the way? I don't want to hang around somewhere nearby all day. I was very bored.'

'The day revolves around when there is someone else with Lisa's mother, I'm afraid. We could do something in the morning and then go together at lunchtime.'

'You'll be like a cat on hot bricks, itching to go and see her. I'll tell you what, let's do it the other way round and tell her we will be there as soon as possible and leave at, say, one-ish; we can always change our minds about what we are doing.'

I felt relieved. I would have liked to spend every day with her, but she needed time with her mother at the moment. And I supposed I needed time with Jack.

'Sounds good. I bet you've looked up some places you want to go.'

'I have, but I haven't booked any tickets yet. Perhaps we can work out a schedule this afternoon and go to the tourist place to book a few things.'

I nodded. Perhaps we could. He didn't know how powerful the urge was to stay with Lisa. I hoped that she would still want to see me after I had shown her the album and the picture of my mother.

When we arrived at Lisa's home, she welcomed us both in and started asking Jack lots of things about his work and his aims in life etc. I was itching to get on with the purpose of the day, but Jack being there made it more awkward.

Eventually, I interrupted. 'Is your mother awake? May I go and see her?'

'Yes, she'd love to see you. I'll just make a drink and come too.'

She glanced at Jack, who immediately said, 'Don't worry about me; I have lots of brochures to look at and a book to read.'

'I'm sure my mother would like to meet you if she's well enough today.'

'No, don't worry about that. This is family stuff, or lookalike stuff at least.'

I went and sat by Lisa's mother's bed. 'Hello, it's Adelle here.'

She opened her eyes and smiled at me. 'In the third drawer down of that bureau there is an envelope for Lisa. Can you give it to her, please?' She closed her eyes again. I opened the drawer and deep down, under lots of correspondence, was a large brown envelope with Lisa's name on it. I sat with it on my lap, waiting for Lisa to come in.

Lisa noticed her mother had her eyes closed and crept across the room, putting her drink on the bedside table. I passed her the envelope, whispering, 'Your mother asked me to get this out of that drawer.' We both shrugged at each other. Lisa bent down by her mother and covered her arm over. 'She's asleep again. Let's look at this in the other room.'

She took me into a room I hadn't been in before. I nipped back and picked up my rucksack with the photo album in it. I was sure there must be photos in the brown envelope.

It was a photo that fell out of the envelope first, when Lisa shook it, upturned, over her lap. There was a tall woman with a small child stood sombrely by her. They weren't touching. On the back it said, 'Lisa's birth mother' and a date.

'I'm glad she kept a copy,' said Lisa. 'I had my own copy when I was younger but I didn't like having another mother so I cut it up.'

I was relieved the lady in the photo looked nothing like my mother. I nearly said something then, but remembered the tactic that Mike Lewis had suggested. Lisa was looking at the other contents of the envelope. There was a birth certificate, American-style with the Texas stamp, and an adoption certificate. There was a third certificate too – this one granting Lisa citizenship 'on account of her residency status'.

Lisa had examined each certificate and passed it to me. The citizenship one we looked at together.

'This is really strange,' said Lisa, speaking quietly. 'Why would I need residency if I was born in Texas and adopted in New York County?'

'I don't know. What else is in there?'

We found some court papers. We tried to sort out what the case was all about; it seemed to be linked to the residency. Lisa picked up the photo of her 'birth mother'.

'This must be your mother, too, then. I wonder why she didn't have you with her.'

'Let's look at my album,' I said.

Lisa was entranced. The two babies, so alike, looking at each other, and the final photos of us as toddlers, her in blue, me in yellow. Then one with my parents and us.

The penny dropped.

'This one here, labelled as my birth mother, wasn't my mother, was she?'

I looked at her, not knowing what to say next. Her eyes went from the photo of the four of us as a family, to the tall lady she had stood by.

'Do you know what happened, Adelle?'

'I know what my parents have recently told me, but it might really upset you.'

'Go on. I need to know.'

I told her as gently as I could about how we had been playing and she had disappeared. I told her about my parents being questioned and how no dead body had ever been found.

'So the woman my mother knew was probably a kidnapper.'

I struggled to understand that sentence for a moment, before I realised she meant her adoptive mother, lying in the next room.

'Probably. Yes.'

'My mother must have known.'

'Maybe it became apparent when she tried to get you a passport or something.'

There was a whimper from the next room. Lisa shot through to her mother. I wondered whether Jack was bored, so went and fetched him and began to show him what we had discovered. Lisa called me from her mother's room and I went, leaving the documents and my album spread out on the table.

'Have you both seen the documents?' said Lisa's mother, trying to turn over and grimacing with pain.

'Yes, but I don't understand it all,' said Lisa.

Lisa's mother appeared to be struggling for breath; she managed to say, 'There's another envelope. That's when I suspected.'

Lisa rummaged around in the drawer until she found a white envelope. She sat by her mother's bed and opened it. There was a newspaper cutting about a gang of child kidnappers. The photo had a circle in blue ink drawn around the woman. It was too blurry to see what she looked like. There was a question mark by it.

'Eight years ago I read this report. I was worried it might have been her. I went to a lawyer. He was sure it wasn't your mother.' She paused for breath. We were both waiting for her to be ready to talk again. 'In his opinion the birth certificate was not a forgery. But I wasn't sure about anything. I insisted he applied for citizenship for you in case.'

'Oh, Mom.'

I left my compassionate sister hugging her mother, and went back to Jack.

'She knows,' I said to him, my eyes filling up with tears. 'And she has proof about the kidnappers.'

Jack shook his head. 'Oh, Dreamy, I think you are wrong.'

'I can't be wrong.'

'Shh, we'll have to speak quietly to avoid disturbing them.' Jack nodded towards the bedroom. 'I've been looking at these documents and they don't match up.'

'But of course they don't. It was you who told me that birth certificates can be forged.' I was not accepting the fact that a legal person had verified it. If Lisa's mother didn't believe it, then nor did I.

'It's not the birth certificate, it's the photos.'

I took the photos from him. The top one was Lisa with her supposed mother.

'Turn it over,' said Jack. I did. 'Now just look at these dates.'

The date on the photo of Lisa with the lady who said she was her mother was nearly six months earlier than the date on the adoption certificate. I still didn't get it.

'How old were you when Amelie went missing?'

'Two years, nine months, three days.'

'How old were you in the last photo you have of you together?'

I took the photo out of the album and turned it over. I could read the date in my mother's unmistakable writing.

'We were just over two years, seven months.'

I looked again at the date on the photo of Lisa. The date was five months before Amelie was taken. The name of the photographer's studio was part of the date stamp. I went cold all over.

'Couldn't this be forged, or a mistake?' I said. 'Maybe because they forged the date on the adoption certificate, they changed this?'

'It would have made no difference. Nothing matches and the size of the child is wrong. She looks much younger on this than you both did in that photo of you taken two months before she went missing. I wouldn't mind betting that this is a genuine photographic studio with a very ordinary and correct date stamp. The address on it is New York, so perhaps we could find out. But it looks like proof that Lisa is not your twin.'

'That can't be true. It simply cannot be right.'

If we weren't both so aware of Lisa's mother in the nearby room, I would have been screaming at him by now.

'You need to accept it, Dreamy. However much she looks like you, she is not your twin.'

I felt awful. I did not want to hear what he was saying. Everything seemed to be crashing down around me. It was all a dreadful mistake. I hadn't found my twin at all. I was shaking and crying. In the other room a girl who had no link to me was tending her dying mother. What was I to do?

I calmed down a bit. Jack and I sat for about half an hour, scarcely speaking, with our arms wrapped around each other. I could hear Lisa's voice as she talked to her mother, but not what was said. It was a soft, loving sound. I wanted to go in and shout that it was all a mistake.

I remembered I hadn't spoken to my mother apart from letting her know we had arrived, two days earlier. I needed to speak to her. I missed her.

Lisa eventually emerged from her mother's room. She looked white and shaken.

'Shall I make you a drink?' I asked.

'Yes, thank you. Black coffee.'

I made us all a drink and we sat holding our mugs. I knew I had to say something, but couldn't. Jack came to the rescue.

'Lisa, I was looking at the photo of you with your birth mother.'

'Only she's not my birth mother, is she?'

'She may be. Look at the date on the photo.'

'Amelie disappeared when we were two years nine months. The photo was taken earlier,' I said.

Lisa looked at us, horror on her face. 'You mean, I am not your twin. You have come all this way to torment me with this while my mother is dying, and now you are saying I am not your twin?'

'It seemed like you were. Everything added up.'

'Not everything, apparently.'

'I'm sorry, Lisa. I thought you were Amelie.'

We were both crying. I couldn't see how this would work out. I didn't want to hug Lisa; I didn't want to do anything. I felt a new loss – the loss of a twin all over again.

'Well, who am I, then?'

I knew this feeling. The feeling I had when I found out I was a twin.

'You are still you, Lisa. And you are still my double. You are still twenty-two and you still drive a car. You are still caring towards your mother and you still have an older brother. You still have American citizenship.' I swallowed hard and tried to keep my voice from cracking as I added, 'You are adopted by a loving family and we have done you a great injustice thinking you were someone else.'

'What shall I say to my mother?'

I thought, 'What do I say to *my* mother?' but I said, 'Do you want me to come in with you and explain the date on the photos?'

'Yes, no, I don't know.'

We had another drink – we felt so close this morning but now we were strangers. Jack tidied up all the other documents, leaving the birth certificate, adoption certificate, my album and the two photos with Lisa and her birth mother. Lisa looked at the picture of her birth mother.

'This is the woman who rejected me because she wanted to go back to her parents.'

'She made sure you had a loving home.' My words sounded feeble. I wished I could take them back.

I felt wretched. Why had I set up that site? Why couldn't I have let things be? But I knew I couldn't. I tried to recapture that moment before her mother had said 'somebody's twins'. But it was as if it had never happened.

'You must be with your mom. You need to be with your family. Why not contact your brother, even your pops?'

Lisa didn't reply at first, then she said, 'I will talk to my mother on her own.'

Jack said, 'I think we should go now, Dreamy.' Then he turned to Lisa and said, 'Have you got Adelle's phone number? Or would you like us to ring you each day to see how things are?'

'I'll ring you if I want you.'

'Are you sure you want us to go now, Lisa?'

Lisa looked at me and nodded. Then we hugged each other almost at arm's length and Jack and I left the house. I didn't know if I'd see her again.

It was only when I was sitting crying on my bed in the hotel room that I remembered I had left my photo album there, and I was still wearing her blue and yellow sweatshirt.

I rang my mother – I explained that Lisa was not my twin but that we looked so alike that her friend had mistaken her for me. She was so upset that she wouldn't listen as I tried to explain how we knew. I was relieved when she called my father over to talk to me. He listened while I explained to him about the dates on the photos and that we had spent a whole day thinking we had found Amelie. I told him Lisa had a mole almost into her hairline and that yesterday I had been wondering why Mother had not told me about it.

'Amelie had no distinguishing marks,' he said. I knew in my heart that this would be the case, but it was the final piece of proof and I choked up as I said my goodbyes.

Our booked flights were seven days away. Jack and I tried to make the most of our time in New York, despite the fact that both of us felt like we were now in the wrong place. The days slipped by; we were both sad but making an effort for each other. Hand in hand we admired the view all around the Empire State building. We went round the Metropolitan Opera House and had a stroll in Central Park. We searched the shops for blue food and I had my first ever taste of blue corn. But everything was subdued. When Jack went back to his room, I was crying at night for the twin I thought I had found.

Lisa made no contact. I wasn't surprised; she probably thought we were fraudsters or something. As it came near to the day of our flight home, I decided I wouldn't collect the album. I had my mother; before long Lisa would have no mother. I didn't want to bother her at this time.

54

The phone call came the morning of our afternoon flight.

'It's Lisa here. Pops and my brother have come over. They are taking turns with me, sitting with Mom. Can I come and find you guys this morning?'

'Of course you can. Come straight to the hotel. I'll tell them you're on the way so that they can park your car for you.'

Jack and I finished packing our respective suitcases as fast as we could to give us as much time as possible with Lisa, if she wanted it. I was so pleased to see her that I rushed over to hug her.

'I can't stay long; Mom is very ill now. I need to be with her. But here's your album.'

'Can Jack take a photo of us together? You are my doppelgänger, after all.' She agreed with a little nod, and we stood in the hotel reception, smiling falsely into the camera. Then the receptionist came over and offered to take one of all three of us, saying to Jack, 'Which twin is yours?'

Jack retorted, 'Neither, both of these young ladies are their own people,' then he winked at me and smiled at the receptionist.

I desperately wanted to ask Lisa to come to London. But I couldn't – things were too up in the air for her. Instead I said, 'I've got your sweatshirt here. I'm sorry I couldn't wash it.'

'You keep it, Adelle. And when you wear it, think of me.'

We hugged for a long time. I said, 'I wish you were my twin. I shall always think of you, Lisa. And when you are ready, come and find me. And let us know what happens, please.'

'I will. I must get back. Sorry to rain on your parade, guys.'

We hugged again and I felt my heart beat with hers. 'Thank you for finding me today,' I said.

'I'm sorry I'm not who you thought I was.' Before I could answer, she turned and left us. I knew she was crying, as I was.

55

Friday 21st December

When Adelle came for her review appointment after her first term of her degree course, she was different. For a start it was the first time I had seen her with natural hair, even though she still had some blue streaks. She came into my room and sat on her usual seat, without the blue shawl. She was wearing a purple coat.

'How is your course, Delle?' I asked.

'It's wonderful. I am loving the art history and the opportunity to paint again.'

'I'm glad you settled down to it so quickly after your trip. Did you want to talk about that and the effect it's had on you?'

In a calm voice she filled me in on the details of the truth she had discovered, the last few days of the trip and the final short conversation. Before this, I had only known second-hand through Anita, who was still doing some grief work with her. I knew Lisa's mother had died soon after Adelle came home.

'And do you know how Lisa is now?'

'She's still in mourning. She is also trying to sort out the house because her father still owns half of it. He wants to sell up and let Lisa and her brother share their mother's half of the proceeds. Lisa's not sure what she'll do next.'

I nodded. Adelle continued, 'She asked me what I thought and I said she should stay near where she lived now and find an apartment. Then find a job or go back to college.'

'Is that what you'd like?'

'It's not really my business any more, is it? But I'd like to meet up with her again, at least for a holiday. She's so like me, it was fun to be together. But I can't face going back yet and anyway, I've got college. I think it's too early for Lisa to come here. At least we've started Skyping again.'

'How are you getting on with your mother?'

'We're getting there. I'm working on the new kitchen and she's really appreciating it. She's not crowding me any more. If she starts behaving as if I'm a child, my father sorts her out. Oh, I've got something to show you.'

She pulled a pad of paper out of her bag. She flicked through the pages and laid it open on the coffee table. On the squared paper was an exquisite floral design in blue, yellow and green with an outline of burgundy. The pattern curled the colours together and overlapped the edges of the main square, indicating repeats over, below and on each side. It reminded me of a William Morris material.

'That's lovely, Delle, is it your design?'

'Yes, for my mother's curtains. I've used blue – that's my Red Cabbage Blue dye – for Amelie, yellow for me, green for my mother and the dark red represents my father.' She seemed relaxed and enthusiastic. 'Drawing it made me realise that my mother wears green because of Amelie being blue and me being yellow.'

The pattern was beautiful. What it represented was clever and perceptive.

Adelle had shrugged off her purple coat while she was talking and I saw she was wearing a blue and yellow striped top. She probably noticed the expression on my face and said, 'It's Lisa's.'

'It's good that you can wear it when you were so disappointed she was not your twin.'

'I have a gift from my lookalike – that's how I see it now.'

I nodded – there wasn't much I could say about that.

'Now I am able to paint with other colours,' she said, 'I'm ready to abandon blue. I regressed in the couple of weeks before I went to America but I've made a new start.'

'How is that going?' I almost didn't ask, because I had already noticed red boots below her navy jeans, that her eyeshadow was purple and her shoulder bag was multicoloured.

'If you mean psychologically, then I am definitely improving. I haven't had any of those panic attacks when the colours seemed to be crashing around me. Not even one during this whole term.'

'That's excellent,' I said.

'And I'm facing up to my grief at the loss of Amelie and my granny. Mother has given me Granny's Bible and it had this in it.'

I looked at the bookmark she had passed to me – on it was a text, in bright yellow, obviously coloured in by a child, 'He knows what is in the darkness, And light dwells with Him.'

Adelle said, 'I gave that to Granny when I was five, apparently.'

I wasn't sure what to say, so responded with a nod.

'I think of it if I begin to feel like rubbish, to stop me looking at the darkness in my soul.'

I was surprised she had remembered what I had said all those months ago and pleased she had found a positive way of dealing with depressed mood.

'That's good,' I said.

'Yes, and I have begun to appreciate those I have in my life who care about me.'

'Does that include Jack?'

'Well, yes, he definitely cares for me. After we went to Cessy's wedding together, Jack said he wanted us to get engaged. I've told him we shall do no such thing until we've been together for a full year.'

I thought of my own position with Ella. She had been right to delay the renewing of our vows until we had sorted out any issues with the help of the counsellor. But now was the time for us and the service was booked for Sunday, the day before Christmas Eve, a few weeks over a year since we got back together. I forced myself to stop feeling excited and remain focused on the session.

'Is that something you want?'

'I am less sure now than I was back in September.'

I didn't say anything, but waited.

'I feel as if he is holding me back. Not intentionally, but I want to be more independent. Sharon is completing the purchase of a flat any day now. I'm going to flat-share with her, with my cats, of course.'

'That sounds like a bold new start.'

'I know, I can hardly believe it myself. My new bedroom is huge – almost as large as the summerhouse – so I will move a lot of my furniture in.'

I nearly asked her what her parents thought, but realised this was not the issue.

'So is Jack suggesting you don't move in with Sharon?'

'Not exactly. But he sees it as losing my independence – not gaining it. He doesn't live with his mother and although I don't quite, I am too close for comfort. My mother is furious and she says I am giving up my own place. Of course, this is ridiculous when she has previously reminded me, at every opportunity, that the summerhouse belongs to her.'

I noted down in her file that Adelle was standing up to her mother.

'Has your mother accepted that Lisa is not your twin?'

'I don't know. I have moved on and stopped dreaming. She keeps asking me when Lisa is coming to stay. She seems to think she won't know Lisa isn't my twin until she sees her.'

'I'm not sure that will work when *you* couldn't tell.'

'It's like being in love, isn't it? You see what you want to see. I couldn't see any difference between us because I didn't look. But now when we Skype I can see her hairline is a little different and while we were there I noticed a small mole in her hairline, and her fingers looked longer than mine even though I was skinnier. And her hair is thicker and fairer than mine.'

'How do you feel about the differences?'

'Fine – it would be very spooky if we were completely identical but not twins.'

I nodded, writing a note in the file.

We then turned our attention to the aim of our appointment, which was to review her progress and check there was nothing else major to work on. This scarcely needed doing, I had noted down so many positives already.

'Do you think we need any more appointments, Adelle?'

'No, I shall miss coming, but I am ready to go it alone, I think.'

'And that is what I think too. I shall be very happy to discharge you.'

'Thank you. And thanks for all your help. I have a follow-up with Anita before I go back to college – but then, for the first time for years, I shall be on no one's caseload!'

'And no longer Exhibit A!'

We both laughed. She picked up her coat and put it on with the blue scarf with multicoloured tassels. She pulled a multicoloured knitted hat from her bag. 'Did your granny make the hat too?' I asked.

'Yes – great, isn't it? I'm going to have different coloured streaks in my hair before I go back to college, to match it!'

'That will be,' I hunted for the words, 'interesting and colourful.'

'I'm really into bright colours at the moment. I so love my course and my art. It's brilliant.'

We said our goodbyes and she was leaving, when she stopped at the door and said, 'I forgot to say, I've given up the lookalike site but my father has taken it over. I am monitoring his progress to ensure he doesn't become fixated on finding Amelie. I'm letting him look only once a day. Happy Christmas!'

'Happy Christmas to you too,' I called. She turned to give me a cheeky grin and swung her bright bag over her shoulder as she pushed on the door to leave the department.

I smiled to myself as I locked her file away, tidied my desk a little and walked out of the silent department to go home to enjoy my Christmas with Ella.

Acknowledgements

I am privileged to have found a publishing house that runs like a family, supporting and encouraging its writers. I especially admire Sheila Jacobs for the hours she spent editing my manuscript, until it passed scrutiny – despite our computers refusing to cooperate. Those working on the cover design, layout, proofs, blurb and all those other vital elements have been an incredible team. But even before the script was submitted, wise ones read versions of this story and provided insightful comments. They deserve a mention too: Jane Clamp, Steph Richardson and Fiona Lloyd. Thank you all – *Red Cabbage Blue* would have remained in a dusty, discarded file without you.

If you've enjoyed *Red Cabbage Blue*, why not read the other titles in the Dr Mike Lewis series?

Jenny Drake's life has always been overshadowed by what she saw on a Devon beach as a small girl. Determined to be free, she forces herself to revisit the scene. Together with a local café owner Jim, she begins a journey to understand what happened all those years ago and why – a search that will soon put their own lives in danger.

Instant Apostle, 2017
ISBN 978-1-909728-61-5

Dr Mike Lewis is on the edge. Separated from his wife, Ella, and deeply wounded by the death of their child, the future is bleak. But when he is assigned the case of mute asylum seeker 'Johnny Two', things begin to change. Inspired by Johnny's response to therapy, Mike finds reasons to hope again – but then dramatic events overtake them all and force him to confront his past.

Will he find courage to face it? Do he and Ella have a future? And can the silence of grief be broken?

Instant Apostle, 2017
ISBN 978-1-909728-66-0